GOING UP AND GOING DOWN

Eva Bielby

To Dawon.

lots of love

Eva Bielby x

2014.

ACKNOWLEDGEMENTS

To my wonderful husband, Graham, my son,
Stuart and his wife, Kate, my daughter, Danielle,
and her fiancé, Jonny, for their love and support in
the last few months.
I would also like to take this opportunity to thank
my fabulous hawk-eyed proof-readers, Alec
James Hawkes and Georgina Ramsey,
my other special friends, J.A. Melville, Martin
Skate, Glenda Horsfall, June Starrs and many
other indie author friends, too numerous to list,
who have also supported me, offered advice and
kept me motivated. A tremendous big 'Thank
You' to each and every one of you.

DISCLAIMER

The characters and events in this book are totally fictitious. Any similarity to real persons, living or dead, is purely coincidental and not intended by the author. Just in case any of you were wondering, I would like to point out that I have never been a call girl and Helen's clients in this book are not real people!

TABLE OF CONTENTS

FOREWORD
A New Client

So there I was, sitting in a top notch executive hotel room in Paris with a guy I had only just met – my seventh client since starting out. Seventh client! I had hoped I would have started to get accustomed to the idea of having sex with total strangers after six clients, but I still couldn't shake off the apprehension. My stomach had been churning as I'd walked into the room, and I hoped the beads of perspiration on my forehead had gone unnoticed.

Two days before, when he had first called me, he had explained that Simon, my first client, had handed him my mobile number during a meeting they'd both attended some weeks ago. After introducing himself as David, he'd offered to pay for my return air fare from London Heathrow. I accepted the offer and agreed to the flight times he'd suggested. When I had collected my tickets at the airport I had been amazed to see the words 'business class' printed on my ticket. He was financially secure, obviously. I had prayed the husky warmth of his voice matched up to the image I had conjured up in my mind. When I'm being paid for sexual services it certainly helps the mood to find the client…at least a little attractive, particularly as my business arrangements were also a means of trying to fulfil my own sexual needs. Having been badly hurt twice in my past, I was adamant that my new career would totally eliminate the need to have boyfriends and emotional involvements in the future. I didn't need the hurt that always seemed to go hand in hand with love.

When he'd met me in the hotel lobby I wasn't disappointed. He wore an expensive suit and beautiful white shirt, his tie loose at his open collar. His eyes were a striking green and there were a few tinges of grey in his otherwise very dark hair. It was going to be both easier and harder this time. It would be easier because he was so sexually attractive, but also harder for the same reason. During my previous sexual encounters with clients I had been able to close my eyes to their imperfections (or vague attractiveness) and just fantasise. I remained emotionally detached and managed to thoroughly enjoy the physical waves of orgasm in the places where my wildest fantasies took me. I had no need to fantasise with this guy, but how could I close my eyes? How could I possibly avoid looking at him?

I felt quite heady, too hot – my instant infatuation with this guy the prime cause. I was trying not to be blatant but struggled to keep my eyes from drinking in his physique and his 'bedroom' designer stubble. He was a little too attractive for my liking. I needed to keep emotional distance from my clients and *too* attractive would mean too much temptation - temptation to look too deep into those eyes and search his very soul. I wondered if he could sense my eyes burning into him. He finished pouring the wine, turned around quickly and stared back at me, his eyes shining with desire and pleasure as they roved over every inch of my body. I was thrilled in one sense to be found so desirable by this perfect specimen of masculinity, but the excitement that I could barely contain, I perceived as an unwanted threat to my resolve. He came over and handed me a large glass of white and said,

"You're shaking and tense. Relax. I don't want anything perverted or anything that you're not willing to do. I want your warmth, your company, and your body, but later – much later. We'll spend a couple of hours just getting to know each other a little better. Is that okay with you?"

Was that okay with me? Phew! It certainly was – or was it? There was an element of doubt creeping in. I didn't really want to be in this situation – I didn't want or need to know anything about this man and yet I couldn't resist playing along with it all. Perhaps the alcohol was to blame for giving me that sense of bravado. I'd rather it was that, than any genuine eagerness on my part.

I heaved a huge sigh of relief hoping he didn't think I was reluctant. I was anything but reluctant, but not quite ready just yet. I wanted to wallow in the anticipation for a short while. Undress him in my mind…and get my head around what I wanted and needed. I needed to enjoy his body and show him the good time he was paying me for. My intent was to fuck him senseless and at the same time achieve my own selfish pleasures. The thing I really didn't want to do was to let this guy into my head, to mess with me!

"I suppose that would make sense." I uttered, barely audible.

"When did you last eat?" he asked, passing me the menu, "I'll order up some room service, just have a look and choose whatever you like."

I felt sick. I didn't think I would be able to eat and I told him so. Whilst I was struggling to understand what was wrong with me, I was vaguely aware that I had allowed him to coax me into ordering something light. He'd opted for something similar, placed the order over the phone and turned to me again,

"Right! Music or a film? I'll leave it up to you."

I could feel my eyes well up, touched by his kindness and consideration, as I smiled up at him, thinking I'd struck gold, but not in the financial sense. He'd paid for my airfare, was wining and dining me and allowing me to choose our evening's entertainment. I imagined that he would afford me that same consideration in the bedroom. In the short time I had been in his company, I was confident that selfishness would not be in his nature. Although I had usually managed to achieve orgasms during my assignations with previous clients, that was down to my own exuberance rather than any attempt by *them* to pleasure me.

Given my short experience, this was a very new approach from a client. I liked it. It was lovely to be treated in this way, as a person with real feelings, rather than as an object on which every orifice was to be used and abused. I had to keep reminding myself it was a business arrangement - he was paying for my time. Also at the back of my mind was the fact that he would be fucking me at some point, as had already been agreed, and I devoured that thought with relish, and that feeling was new to me. I felt a sensuous warmth and tingling course through my body, the wine glass trembling in my hand. It wasn't just the sex – I was beginning to really like this guy. The trouble was…I didn't want to like him. I wanted to feel indifference towards him and his…personality. I don't want emotional involvement with any man, I'm too insecure – the insecurity caused by two men, my two longest relationships. The unfaithfulness, the hurt – and how I feared having to ever deal with them both again. I don't think I could ever trust another man with my heart.

"Have you decided then…what is it to be?" "I f-feel like a t-teenager on her first d-date – being g-given a choice." I giggled nervously. He laughed. I don't know why I felt so uneasy, or perhaps it was because I could sense that I was being sucked in, against my will?

"Come on Helen, help me out here. You're my guest." He smirked as he threw out his arms in a gesture of mock helplessness.

My heart fluttered as he said my name for the first time, and slightly bemused by his insistence and his amateur dramatics, I considered the options – a film or some music? Was I actually interested in talking to the guy and getting to know him better? No, I certainly wasn't. It was a business transaction. So why did I find myself uttering,

"If we are meant to be getting to know each other, then a film wouldn't fit the bill, would it?"

"Good point. I'll find some music then pour us another glass of wine each." He held out his hand for my glass, so I finished what had remained and handed it over. I almost recoiled when our fingers touched briefly, not wanting to feel that connection – that chemistry. "We'll unwind and chat, yes?"

Taking the lead in our chat, I purposely kept the conversation general, skirting around any subject that may have led to questions about me and my life. He gazed intently at me and watched my every move. I could have sworn that in his mind he was already having sex with me and wasn't really listening, though he smiled often and asked or answered questions in the appropriate places. The conversation between us jumped from one subject to another and I marvelled at how amusing he was, how intelligent….and how …charming and sexy. There was a sudden lull in our tete a tete as he stood up and went to fill our glasses again.

Even though we had eaten nearly an hour before, the wine had taken affect and my nerves had settled down considerably when, unexpectedly, he slowly turned, head tilted to one side and asked, "Why are you doing this Helen? Why are you here in this hotel room with me, when you have evidently had so much? Tell me, why the sudden career change?"

He had such a puzzled look on his face…such a look of bewilderment, that I could barely contain my sudden urge to satisfy his curiosity. It was another first – a client who was interested in me enough to ask why. It filled me with warmth but rendered me speechless because

I knew that if I was to answer one or two of his questions, he would bombard me with even more. Maintain your silence, Helen, I silently reminded myself.

"You don't want to answer me." There was a genuine tinge of disappointment in his eyes as he spoke and he let his shoulders sag in an over exaggerated manner, but only momentarily. I was relieved to see his face break into a smile, and I smiled back, amused by his attempts at acting.

"Can I tell you what it is I can see about you? "I gave him my affirmation with a slight nod, lowering my eyes as I did so, not wanting to make eye contact as he told me what he saw. I wasn't even sure I wanted to hear his opinions.

"You have class. You are impressively intelligent. I'm guessing a private school?"

I glanced up at him for a moment, gave him a half smile and a nod before I looked down at my hands. I didn't really want to hear compliments from him - I was trying to keep an emotional distance, for fuck's sake!

"You are also well-spoken…beautiful…and you are fairly new to this…way of life. "I looked up then, straight into those amazing eyes, eyes that were trying to read me. I was overwhelmed by his compliments. My heart was racing, but this was in total conflict with my head. My thoughts told me to get out of that room and away from him and my feelings! I tried to steal my eyes away from him, afraid he was reading me too well.

I decided to play it down, so desperate to put emotional distance between us, I gave a pleasant sigh, curled my legs up beneath me on the settee to give him the impression I was relaxing in his company.

"We've only just met David. I know nothing about you - I don't want to, and you don't need to know about me. I take it you're not sorry that I am here?"

"Certainly not!" He laughed then, the puzzled expression gone. If he felt any disappointment at my reluctance to open up, he didn't show it. He joined me on the settee, leaning back with his hands behind his head and his legs stretched out in front of him, his eyes fixed firmly on mine.

Hoping to put the ball back in his court and get the conversation onto some safe subject, I asked,

"So what are you thinking now?"

"My thoughts?" Once more in his amateur dramatics mode, he placed the heel of his hand to his forehead and raised his eyes to the ceiling as if in deep thought. His mouth turned down then in mock disappointment.

"Well, as I'm not going to discover anything about you and your life – One - I can't wait to make love to you. Two - I'm going to have a bath and I want you to join me. Three - I want some more wine."

Make love? What the hell? A warning bell was ringing in my head. Only two men in my life had ever made love to me and they were not clients. He was paying me for sex, so why would he use that terminology? It slowly dawned on me. He was a gentle natured guy, and he was far too polite to say that he wanted to fuck me. He'd opted for a much nicer way to express it. I was pacified, I'd found my own answer to my question.

"Make love to me David?" I chuckled, shaking my head at him in disbelief. "Clients want to fuck me, do perverted things with me - not make love to me!"

He grinned at me saucily and chuckled. "Do they indeed?" He moved closer then, and put his arm around my shoulder. Leaning in even further he kissed me on the cheek and asked in a more serious tone,

"Does all that meet with your approval? Do you want to be made love to or do you want to be fucked, Helen? Either works for me."

Whilst the thought of being made love to excited me, I knew that I couldn't let that happen. I wanted this to be nothing more than a fuck. I leaned towards him playfully and returned the kiss on his cheek, ruffling his hair as I stood up.

"After the taxis and airports I could certainly use a soak in the bath, if it's big enough for the two of us. As for the sex, as long as it's good we can call it what we want, can't we? Let's see what category it falls under once we get started."

I was determined as ever that once we started, it was going to be one mammoth, dirty, fucking session, where the words 'love making' didn't exist. It would be sexual gratification without the heart strings. I was already feeling the warmth and dampness in my panties that accompanied the tendrils of a wanting ache that was spreading within the deepest parts of me.

I watched, fascinated, as he removed each item of his clothing to reveal a truly beautiful, tanned and toned body. I wanted to reach out and touch him, if only to confirm that I wasn't dreaming. His eyes roved up and down my body and I couldn't help but notice his delectable cock was stiffening even as he watched me. Conversation was minimal whilst we bathed. I sat imagining what it was going to feel like to be fucked by him and I relished the thought. I wanted to know what David was thinking, but with his demeanour and his eyes taking in every bit of my skin, it looked as though his thoughts were not far removed from my own. We playfully sponged each other down, but there was no awkwardness in our silence. I was comfortable with him and I knew he would treat me right. It was pleasant to relax and take in every detail of his body. Every last inch of him was perfection. I was finding it hard to breath and my body ached to have him inside me. We fondled tentatively for a short while before getting out of the bath. As he held the towel in his hands he had not started to dry himself. He was transfixed as I towelled myself dry.

"You…your body…is...so…sensual, Helen. It's beautiful." It pleased me to see the appreciation in his eyes and I beamed back at him.

"You've got a very sexy body yourself. I bet you work out at the gym a lot?" I asked.

"Not quite as much as I would like to. I enjoy a really good workout. It makes me feel good about myself. I think the best workout I'm likely to get this week is the one that I'm planning with you very shortly."

I was getting somewhat hot and bothered by this man, there was something really scorching hot about him, but I couldn't pinpoint why I should be so bothered. He had already told me that he wasn't in to perverted sex, so why was I worrying?

I checked my make-up (as always) before putting on a very short, lacy robe that I had packed. David just grabbed the bathrobe from the hook behind the bathroom door and I noticed he dabbed a little men's fragrance on himself before leaving and closing the door behind him.

When I went back into the bedroom, he had put some classical music on in my absence and he was laid on the bed with his head propped up on the pillows, hands behind his head. He looked, and smelled, amazing. I was looking forward to the sex, but I did have some reservations. Perhaps he was going to be a let-down in the sex department? You can never tell. Of the clients I'd had over the previous few weeks, I did tend to think it was the plainer looking guys that were the best lovers. They tried harder to turn me on. David wouldn't need to try. I was turned on already just seeing his body reclining on the bed.

"Come here, Helen. Come and lie down next to me. I've poured us another glass of wine."

Not wanting to appear too eager, I casually fiddled with a few of my cosmetics on the dressing table before clambering on to the bed. I noticed that his towelling robe was slightly apart and exposing the tops of his thighs with just a glimpse of his dick showing. I was flushed. I could feel the heat on my forehead and an excited tingle in my nether regions - I wanted him so bad. I wanted him to fuck me that very minute,

17

couldn't wait for him to touch me. It occurred to me that perhaps I should be paying him. I made myself comfortable next to him and leaning across towards me, he didn't open up my robe, but pulled the sides apart slightly to reveal some of my cleavage.

"You really are beautiful, do you know that? You are a truly lovely person. I was told that by the friend, well...acquaintance really, the one who gave me your number. If he hadn't told me, I could see it for myself in your eyes - the moment I met you tonight." His eyes locked on mine.

"It can't be easy, doing what you do." I didn't look away from his gaze - I couldn't, although I tried hard enough.

"It certainly makes my job easier – having a client like you. You are very hot, extremely good-looking - what more could a girl want?"

"Money, apparently." His comment stung and he must have seen it in my eyes.

"Touche!"

"I am sorry, Helen. I didn't mean it to come out as it did. I never meant to imply anything."

He looked mortified at the thought he'd offended me so I giggled, "I've had much worse things than that said to me over the years, before I was...before I made a career out of this."

He leaned further towards me as if to kiss me, and I kissed the side of his cheek and down towards his neck, though I so badly wanted his lips on mine. He caught on quickly.

"Ah. I see - that's fine."

I felt as if I had been scorched when his lips first touched my cheek in return and then copying my first move, he was kissing my neck ever so gently. I winced and he asked, "Are you OK?"

Rather than answer him I openly displayed my pleasure by gently nibbling his neck and moaning. He was setting me on fire so quickly I could feel the burning and wanton desire in the pit of my stomach and I tensed even further as he opened my robe and his lips traced a path down to my breasts, slowly tracing a circle around each of my nipples in turn, tormenting - and whilst his tongue had barely made contact, my nipples stood very proud and erect. He was breathing heavily and his hands were gently massaging my belly, first around the navel and edging each careful finger width towards my pubic hair. I was impatient. I was experiencing some awakening - something that had lain dormant for months. It was now re-emerging - an uninhibited desire to fuck and be fucked was taking over me. I was not going to wait - I was going to take the lead in this, such was my craving for him. I pushed him onto his back again and planted my lips firmly around his wonderful swollen piece of muscle.

He groaned out loud, "Wow! What a tigress, taking the lead. Do I turn you on, honey? Do you want it bad tonight? Do you want me to make you come?" I muttered a reply as well as I could manage, my lips caressing every inch of his dick. "You...are...turning...me on. I'm not...wanting *it*...bad, I want *you*...real bad. I want you…to fuck me…want to make…this…the best…fuck…you've ever...had in your life."

"I'm sure you will, but…hey, go steady there…don't make me come too soon. I'm finding this..." He broke off his words at that point and he was stroking my breasts again, tweaking and pulling at my nipples. I was feeling ready to explode and he wasn't even inside me yet.

"I'm going to fuck you now…wherever you'd like me to fuck you, let's do it…I want to shove my cock into you…feel you come all over me."

I reluctantly moved my mouth away from his cock and took his hand. I led him over to the dressing table and pushed aside all the bottles. I sat myself at the very edge. He bit into my neck again at the same time his hands eased that throbbing piece of delight inside me. He grabbed hold of my tits as I wrapped my legs around his bottom. I held him firm as he thrust at me and he reached all my nerves with one hard thrust - my g-spot, my clit and I held tight onto him. Every inch of him was inside of me. I tightened my inner muscles around him and could feel his nerves pounding. The power of his pounding was driving my desire to new heights and I didn't really want to come, I didn't want him to come, I wanted to stay locked like this, feeling the intensity of my emotions…and the anticipation. I don't know how I managed to hold it back for five to ten minutes but somehow I did. His movements back and forth were not long movements, his tool was only moving in and out maybe an inch, but the feeling was beyond ecstasy. His pubic bone was grinding against my clit.

"I…can't hold…much longer…can you…come quick, babe?" he gasped.

"Go for it David….just fuck me…but fuck me hard. When you come I'll explode, I know I will…just let me have it, let me have your spunk now."

His pace quickened and his thrusts were hard, much deeper, almost pulling out completely before thrusting in again, hard and deep, hard and deep, and it was breath-taking. My every nerve was at its pinnacle and the instant I knew he was coming, I finally let go. I was bathed in the flood of our warm fluids and struggling to catch my breath. My whole body shook from the orgasm that was slow to die away.

"That was…so good…beautiful" he breathlessly struggled to get the words out as he rested his chin on my shoulder "and I don't need to ask if it was good for you. I can see that you enjoy being fucked."

We stayed in our position at the dressing table for maybe five minutes and it felt so good to have his arms around me. I wanted to lay on the bed with him, be cuddled by him for the rest of the night. It had been good – too good. He cuddled up and we talked for a short while before drifting off to sleep. I could feel him kiss the back of my head just before I finally dozed.

When I woke up a few hours later he was stirring. Catching a glimpse of the clock I saw that it was 6.45am. I switched the kettle on, and using the complimentary coffee sachets I prepared the cups. With the noisy kettle coming to the boil he was soon awake. I went to freshen myself up and brush my teeth and he followed me into the bathroom to take a pee.

"Kettle's on…coffee? Or would you prefer tea?" I asked.

"Whatever you're having will be fine by me, babe."

"Coffee it is then. Get back into bed, and I'll bring it over." He kissed me on the cheek when I got back into bed, and asked if I had slept well. I assured him that I had.

After I had finished my coffee I went into the bathroom and got under the shower. I closed my eyes as I washed my hair, lost in my thoughts about this man. A shudder of excitement about him fucking me the previous night…not wanting to be overjoyed about it…worrying…about what?…frightening thoughts…So lost, deep in thought…until I felt his hands around my waist. I opened my eyes, blinking the lather of the shampoo from my eyelashes. He raised me up quickly and as I wrapped my legs around him he shoved his cock hard into me and my back slammed against the tiles. I was in heaven, his hard slamming sending me into a new dimension. His cock felt like a rod of iron. I rubbed my lathered hands all over his back with one hand as the other held tight around his neck trying to stop myself from sliding down his body. I didn't want to slide away from his rod, his throbbing was intense and my hole was on fire. After ten minutes his knees couldn't take any more and they started buckling…his cock slipped out of me and he moaned urgently in frustration, "Helen…get…on the…floor…quick!"

22

I half slipped in my rush to the floor…onto my knees…. eager to be fucked…for him to come inside me. I'd barely made contact with the floor when he rammed into my fanny again, so hard…so deep…and I was there…climaxing …I screamed out in pain and intense pleasure. As I screamed out for the second time, I felt his knob spurting, and with each spurt, I came again…and again. David groaned out loudly and bit into my neck. I threw my head back and closed my eyes, hardly able to cope with the intensity of my orgasm as I felt the last squirt of his juices inside me.

As my flight took off from Paris CDG five hours later I heaved a sigh of relief. I was finally away from him. Not being in his company strengthened my resolve. Much as I had enjoyed David's company *and* being fucked by him, it was a one off. I hoped he wouldn't be in touch with me again. I felt traumatised at the thought.

PART 1
Love.....and hurt

CHAPTER 1

As an only child I was lucky enough to have the most amazing parents in the world. They were unable to have any more children after I was born so I was lavished with all their love and affection and wanted for nothing. Yes, I was totally spoilt, but they were also sensible and down to earth enough not to let me become a brat, or a snob. Dad had inherited a nice sum from my grandparents when they died during my teenage years. He owned his own advertising agency, an apartment in central Paris and a villa in Marbella (for the golf, he told his friends). Our home, which they'd purchased when I was four years old, was a fairly modest four bedroom detached, and was situated in one of the most pleasant areas in Richmond. Mum was lucky in that since she had married Dad she had never needed to go out to work.

They paid for me to have the very best private education but only as a day pupil. I couldn't have coped with life as a boarder. I had it all – the ballet lessons, the ponies, the violin lessons, and as I approached my teens and throughout the teenage years, I always had the latest fashion in clothes, holidays abroad, almost everything a girl could ever want – except friends. I never had any friends. I was occasionally allowed to tag along with a small group of girls who tolerated me, but that was it. I was bullied constantly from first starting school and right through senior school years too. I never knew the reasons behind it all. They just tended to hit me (a lot) but nobody ever actually told me why. They called me Morticia, which I assume was because of my long dark hair. I had a few theories both then and since, but I suppose only the bullies themselves could give the real reason, although it is most unlikely that I will ever see them again to ask why.

My first theory was that they were all snobs, because despite my very privileged upbringing I was always down to earth and I never looked down on anybody as they did. I treated everybody exactly the same -wealthy or poor. My second thought was that their parents didn't appear to have as much money as mine. It was as if they were scrimping to give their kids a private education, but there was little left over for the holidays, ponies, and clothes - except for the parents with mounting credit card debts maybe. My final theory was that a whole gang of them caught me, aged eleven, and Alex Baker-Thompson (best looking lad in the school) behind the bike sheds. As a gang of the bullies approached from the playing field, Alex had his finger poking up the leg of my knickers. He'd been feeling around my newly acquired pubes trying to locate my fanny, and his hard little dick was poking out of his fly-hole for all to see.

It further didn't help matters that I was more sexually aware than they were. Without wanting to sound too cocky, the lads all seemed to fancy me (and some were so much better than Alex at finding and fingering my hole), and I was pretty much attracted to a lot of them, but mainly the older ones. Word also got around thanks to James Barton, that he had fucked me in the P.E. storeroom; one particular Friday lunchtime (it was true, he took my virginity and I was fourteen years old). That certainly didn't help my cause with the bullies! I tended to have a lot less bother with the bitches if I ignored the lads completely, so I tried hard to do so most of the time, at least when other girls were around.

Whatever the reasons for the bullying, I was well and truly alone at school. I never told Mum and Dad about any of it. I didn't want to be a cry baby, and most of all I didn't want to give the bullies the satisfaction of letting them know they'd got to me. I just took the slappings and never once ran away - I'm made of tougher stuff than that. Quite a few of the teachers were aware I was having a tough time and they would make sure the bullies noticed their presence when on duty on the school playing field. I always tried not to let it bother me, but sometimes I would silently cry myself to sleep and vow to keep in the background and unnoticed the next day at school. Surprisingly enough my lessons never suffered and I determined to get my revenge on the bullies by making sure my exam results were second to none. I left school with 3 'A' levels, all 'A' grades in Maths, English and Geography, meeting the entry requirements of the London School of Economics.

University was a whole new ball game. Although I felt quite shy and wary for the first month or two, I managed to make some genuine friends and one in particular, Roberta, known to her friends as Bobbie, became my first ever close friend. We worked hard, played hard, smoked some weed (nothing worse than that though) and life was good. Again I never had to go short of money and I didn't need any student loans - Dad paid for everything.

Bobbie was always so tired. She worked in a bar three or four nights a week to help pay her way through Uni. I was amazed at how she always managed to get to her lectures on time. Her Mum would come down every couple of months to visit, staying in a hotel just around the corner from Bobbie's student flat which she shared with two others. She (Bobbie) hadn't seen her Dad in eight years. Shame really, he would have been so proud of her. She was pretty, well-mannered, very amiable and extremely intelligent. Her degree was just a formality. Yes! I loved Bobbie to bits. She was the first female who had ever liked me and this was a big thrill for me – being liked instead of tolerated. We had so much in common - our love of music, men, visiting the City's art galleries, fashion and generally having good time.

It was during my second year at Uni that I met and fell in love. I wasn't out with Bobbie that particular night as she was working at the bar as usual. I was with some other friends who were taking the same degree course in Accountancy and Economics. We had decided to try out a new wine bar that had recently opened not too far from the main university building and the student flats. We had already downed a bottle of vodka between us before leaving my flat and were just getting our night into full swing when a gang of four or five dons walked in, ordered their drinks then came straight to our table and made themselves at home. Anna, Beth and Jennifer (my friends), mouths gaping in surprise at suddenly being surrounded by so much testosterone, were soon lapping up the attention of the guys. One guy, having made a beeline for the vacant seat beside me, was giving me his full attention and soon seemed oblivious to the fact that his friends and mine were still at the same table as us. Other than telling me his name was Gavin, he seemed more interested in finding out all there was to find out about me.

We chatted solidly for two hours, except for when he went to the bar to replenish our drinks. He was fair haired, had the deepest blue eyes and had a look of the fabulous rock legend, Mr Jon Bon Jovi. By 1am I was smitten. He was polite, well-mannered, interesting and more importantly – he was interested in me. Not my looks or my body, just me. In all this time I hadn't even noticed that all of the girls had partnered up with Gavin's mates and discreetly disappeared, I had been so wrapped up in my new drinking mate. He walked me the short distance to my flat at about 3am. We made a date for the following Saturday, he pecked me quickly on the lips and was gone. I was impressed - a man who wasn't out to get laid.

We met at 10.30am just outside the Natural History Museum that next week. We had both visited the Museum previously, but the date was more about us spending some time together, rather than further educating ourselves in historical knowledge. It was a very pleasant few hours, and spent in such awesome surroundings. We went on to Covent Garden to some quiet little restaurant where the prices were reasonable compared with many of the others in the vicinity.

We decided whilst eating that we would return to 'our' wine bar. What a perfect day it turned out to be. By midnight I was snuggling in my bed expecting to read, but finding myself thinking more and more about Gavin. He had walked me home and we had kissed very passionately for five or ten minutes, before he bade me goodnight and went on his way. He was the perfect gentleman.

Some two to three weeks later, and after more than a few boozy late nights with our friends, we decided it was time for a quiet night in. As I lived alone, my flat was the better option, whereas he would have had to bribe his lodgers to go out and even then it was not guaranteed. We had no booze, no weed, just a KFC bargain bucket, a bottle of diet coke and a DVD. We loaded the DVD but it ended up playing to itself as we chatted about our degree courses, our parents, our schools, and our tastes in music.

Taking his cue with the subject of music cropping up, Gavin switched off the TV and searched through my CD collection, choosing an Aerosmith album. We listened, snuggled up and we kissed (lots) and it was the most natural thing in the world when we slowly undressed each other and indulged in the most meaningful and deliciously exciting foreplay I had ever experienced. Each move on his part was tantalising, barely touching my skin, and his fingers were so gentle in their probing, his tongue teased my nipples until they stood aroused and hard. I shuddered excitedly in anticipation and my stomach ached for him. He drank in every minor detail of my body and whilst doing so he took my hand in his and guided it onto his impressive piece

30

of manhood. I gently rubbed it up and down, ever so slowly and he gasped in pleasure, savouring every moment until the time felt right. I massaged his cock and he fondled my clit and gently probed into my vagina, pushing further and further in. The moment arrived sooner rather than later as we moved together onto the floor, not wanting to lose our connection and with his hands cupping my face. His tool needed no further guidance and it was my turn to gasp as he eagerly shoved his cock inside me. It felt like heaven. His thrusts were gentle, slow and loving. He awakened all my senses, and that feeling of being aglow was amazing. I was holding myself back, not wanting to let go too soon. I wanted our first moment to last forever. He was so considerate in his moves, watching my face expectantly all the time – discovering what pleasured me the most and revelling in his discoveries. When he sensed that I could hold back no longer, his thrusting became faster, for minutes only, and we climaxed together, explosively - our juices fusing for the first time. Shuddering in each others arms with the intensity of the moment, I cried. I had just experienced what it was like to be made love to. I told Gavin I was in love with him and I was deliriously happy when he expressed his love for me also. We made love three times during the course of the night.

Time moved forward at a pace I struggled to keep up with - life was like a dream. We were out socialising quite a lot with our friends and Bobbie and her new boyfriend Phil were also included in that circle. I was quite surprised that I could ever get any work done – I was always tired and hung-over. I was also too wrapped up in Gavin and our love-making and our life together. I had friends, a best friend, and the best boyfriend I ever had, who I truly loved. He made love to me, and I loved being made love to. This was not the emotionless fucking or shagging I'd had experience of in my past. My heart melted each time I saw him, and I wanted to make love constantly. I even fell in love with saying the words 'making love.' I gave Gavin a key to my flat, and gradually he stayed more and more nights per week until he was living with me permanently.

During my third year, my bubble of happiness was popped one day when I received a very upsetting call from Mum - Dad had been rushed into hospital with a suspected heart attack. I left a message for Gavin back at the flat after leaving Uni and hurriedly threw a few clothes into an overnight bag. Shooting off in my car to see Dad in Intensive Care at their local hospital, my journey was filled with dread. I was afraid for him – and myself. How would I ever cope without my wonderful Dad, I loved him so much and he was far too young to die. I was also worried for Mum and wondered how she would cope without him if he died. The tears made it difficult for me to drive. I couldn't concentrate and I couldn't get there fast enough. My breakfast was threatening to make a re-appearance – I felt so physically sick. I was frightened in case I was too late.

By the time I reached the hospital the diagnosis had already been made. It had been confirmed that Dad had indeed suffered a minor heart attack but he was going to be okay. It hurt to see Mum so distraught, and wrapping my arms around her we comforted each other as we waited in the family room to be told when we could go in to see him. He looked reasonable (but otherwise very exhausted,) considering the ordeal he had been through, and he was still hooked to the ECG machine. He was pleased to see me there with Mum, and he even joked that he was pleased to *still* be seeing Mum as he had thought his time was well and truly up.

Bobbie called me later that evening to see if Dad was doing okay and asked how Mum and I were coping. I assured her that Mum and I were both doing alright and Dad was making good progress. She went on to tell me that she had parted from Phil, her latest in a long line of suitors, as well some other trivial bits of news from Uni. She didn't sound as if she needed any consoling about her break-up with Phil, so I said I would see her and Gavin maybe in a week's time and we said our goodbyes. Gavin rang me at bedtime to say he was missing me and I cried when I finally put the phone down. I ached to be with him but my parents were my priority –they had to be.

Three days later Dad was discharged from hospital care and told that he must take things a lot easier than he had been doing of late. It was nice to have him back at home and Mum fussed around him endlessly. I ended up staying with them for another five days and I continued to call Gavin each night, missing him more with each day that passed. Leaving Mum at home to look after Dad, I went out for a food shop for them, and stocked up with fresh supplies and enough freezer things to last for at least a month. Once I was happier to see Dad with much more colour back in his face and feeling so much better, I set off back to Gavin, my flat and Uni.

I scanned my key fob, struggled through the security door, and along the corridor with my own supermarket bags. As I turned the key in the lock, and was pushing the door open wider with my foot, I could hear the Aerosmith CD playing. That memory engulfed me – Gavin and I making love, and that was what I looking forward to in the next five minutes. I crept towards the lounge to surprise him. I knew it was unlikely that he would be expecting me so soon, or that he had heard the key in the lock with the volume of the music. The door to the lounge was just slightly ajar and I held the shopping bags out in front of me to push it open wider. I was frozen to the spot at the sight that greeted me - Bobbie was on her knees bent over the armchair and my Gavin was shagging her up the backside. Judging by his groans of ecstasy and her very vocal gasps, I guessed he had just ejaculated. I felt physically sick, numb and unable to move – I was rooted to the spot. So wrapped in themselves they weren't even aware of my presence. My so-called best friend and the man I loved – had been fucking – in my flat! I let the bags drop from my hands, and they both spun around quickly, guilty eyed and mouths gaping in surprise. Gavin pulled out of her muttering "Oh fuck! Oh fuck!" and made a rapid exit to the bedroom (our bedroom, *my* bedroom.) Bobbie stood up and grabbed at the nearest cushion in an attempt to cover her nakedness, as if it made a difference to me.

"Get your clothes on and get out of my flat. Get out of my life for fuck's sake, you bitch!" I screamed, my anger rising rapidly, "I loved you and trusted you, and you've abused it all. You come to my flat and screw my boyfriend - and whilst I have been helping my Mum care for my sick father! I never want to see you again! GET OUT!"

I was almost at boiling point and her lack of emotion was pushing me beyond that. I didn't trust myself to act. I feared I would go too far so I remained, trembling near the lounge door. Within two minutes, she was dressed, she walked past me and was gone without a solitary word to say – not even a sorry. Gavin shiftily slid back into the room when he heard the door slam shut after Bobbie. He had put on his dressing gown and from the look on his face, he thought we were going to sit and have some cosy little chat, in which he would try to talk his way round me.

"Babe…I…" he started. I hated him, couldn't bear to look at him, and I felt ready to lose control, I was shaking so much.

"Save your breath you bastard! Just get your clothes on, get all your things and fuck off! Don't you ever come near me again!"

The pained expression on his face served to anger me even more. "But where will I go, they've got somebody for my old room – I have nowhere to go!" he tried pleading.

No thought for the shock and pain he'd just caused me, he was thinking of himself only - it cut through to my core like a laser.

"That's *your* fucking problem, Gavin! Did you think I would still want *you* in here, in *my* flat, when you've just been found, up to your fucking nuts into *her*?" I screamed.

He fled.[Do all men look so stung and hurt when you kick them out for sticking their dick up another female? Like it's you that's the bad cruel bitch? Are they for real?]

It was fifteen minutes before he emerged from the bedroom with his black bin bags. His eyes were tear-stained, but I could not bear to look at his face for more than the fleeting glance. Was he genuinely sorry for hurting me or just sorry that he'd been caught? I didn't know and I didn't care. He came towards me, arms outstretched, until he saw me recoil.

"Babe…I…love you, since we met. Always!"

The bloody nerve of him!

"GET THE FUCK OUT MY FLAT – NOW!" I screamed at the top of my voice.

All I could find in the fridge was some dregs (maybe one glass, at a push) of Pinot. In my desperation to numb the pain I threw it down my neck then rummaged through the sideboard to see what spirits I could lay my hands on. Half a whiskey tumbler of Jack Daniels, his! What the fuck? URGGH…I knew there was a reason I'd never tried it before. I downed it anyway, and almost instantly brought it straight back up again – tasting worse on its way out than it did going in, if that's at all possible. I must have cried solidly for almost two hours. With insufficient booze to drink myself stupid I turned the music off and sat in silence, thinking things through. I thought of the plans we had made for our future how much I would miss him, how much I would miss our lovemaking. I was struck with a sudden desire to get out of the flat. The flat I had always loved, the flat I had shared with *him*, I now hated. I had to get out, I couldn't breathe. My toiletries were still in my overnighter. I grabbed the few bits of washing that were in the bag threw them into the washer and replaced them with some clean undies, denims and a T-shirt.

Within ninety minutes I'd settled into a room in a run-down hotel at Piccadilly Circus – the only one available that night. I made two resolutions during my waking hours. I would never get too close to a female again. Secondly, I vowed never to fall in love again – *ever*! Just for good measure I added a third one – never to cry again over any man.

On returning to the flat the next morning I called Uni, giving 'personal reasons' for my decision to quit. Secondly, I called the estate agent to terminate my tenancy agreement one month from that day. My third and final call was to Mum and Dad to inform them that their daughter was returning, full time. By late morning I had packed up all my clothes and personal things, loaded my car, and had cleaned throughout the flat.

CHAPTER 2

Seeing my car pulling into the drive, Mum and Dad came out to help me in with my bags. Mum and I took the cases and a few other items to the front door. Dad was still having to take things cautiously, so he came up and put his arms around me. I didn't cry. I rested my chin on his shoulder and took comfort from him, the one man in my life who I have always been able to rely on. He didn't say a word - he knew not to! He never asked me what had gone wrong. He wouldn't ever push me - I would talk when I was ready to talk and he respected that.

Mum had prepared my favourite meal, and we sat around the dining table enjoying a glass of wine and discussing Dad's progress. We were just covering the same ground as the previous day before I had left them to return to Gavin, my flat, and Uni. The events of the previous 24 hours seemed like it all happened a life-time ago. When we left the dining table to relax in the lounge, Mum brought through a second bottle of Chardonnay and the topic of conversation turned to current affairs, the weather, Uncle David's stocks and shares, in fact any subject that skirted around my problems. I knew they were sparing my feelings. They hadn't asked, but probably already suspected my reason for returning home. They knew I would reveal all in due course. I drank far more Chardonnay that night than the pair of them, relaxing more then turning maudlin as the night turned into the early hours. Dad needed his rest though, so not wanting them to feel obliged to sit with me all night, I made my way upstairs about 1am. I heard the door to their bedroom close shortly after. I wept (silently, I hoped) and much as I fought against it, I could not help relive the horrendous scenes of… was it just 36 hours ago? My mind flitted quickly back to school, and I compared this new type of hurt to the hurt I had experienced from being bullied. This new hurt was totally off the scale. Sometime around dawn, when the stress and exhaustion finally caught me in their grasp, I succumbed to sleep, restless though it was.

At about 11am, I heard Dad trying to open my bedroom door without making a sound. Thoughtful as ever, not wishing to disturb me in case I was sleeping, but nevertheless, he just had to check to see if I was OK. I waited until the door softly clicked shut then shouted after him,

"Dad, tell Mum to get the coffee on, I'll be down in ten minutes!"

He paused for a second outside my door before answering, "Okay, darling, when you're ready."

Until I had dragged my weary self into the en suite, I didn't realise just how exhausted I was. Splashing my face with cold water, I caught sight of my reflection in the mirror – very pale. Dark rings encircled my eyes, (in part, due to the mascara I had not troubled to remove before climbing into bed) and all I could think of to ask that reflection was, 'Why me?' The reflection had no answers – nothing to say!

I padded downstairs in my dressing gown and slippers. I hadn't even brushed my hair but just gathered it all up and clipped it in place for the time being. I could see Mum and Dad were sat in the conservatory as I approached the dining room. A fresh pot of coffee (and enough toast to stave off hunger for the rest of the day) sat on the coffee table.

"Hi, sweetheart," Mum greeted me as I sat down to join them, concern showing in her eyes despite the smile. "Don't try telling me that you slept, because I shall know that you're lying.

"I smiled weakly at her "I won't! Although I knew my parents wouldn't push me, I recognised that I was under close scrutiny.

"We thought that since it's such a lovely morning, it would be nice to have coffee in here for a change."

Yes! I had to give her that one – the sun was shining. A lovely morning – if you weren't hurting. If your boyfriend hadn't just fucked your best friend, it might be a nice morning.

"Well it's certainly brighter than my mood." I mumbled.

I realised I had to get it out there and then, make them understand how I was feeling. I couldn't just sit around depressing the hell out of them for days with my sad puppy eyes, could I?

"We are not expecting you to talk darling" said Dad "if it takes months until you are ready, we will respect that."

"Dad, I have to get it all out in the open now, a problem shared and all that. If not, it's going to eat me up inside, so when we've eaten, I'll get it off my chest, okay?"

The mountain of toast was wasted (they had already had breakfast earlier). I simply didn't feel like eating. I felt physically sickened but empty at the same time. I nibbled slowly on a couple of slices, just to keep Mum happy, or else I would get the lecture on how I must look after myself better. I was struggling to swallow even the smallest of nibbles so I discarded the toast and started talking. They hadn't needed me to tell them how happy I had been when I had first met and then fallen in love with Gavin – they'd seen the evidence of that for themselves over the last year. I told them about all the special times we had together, how much we had laughed together. The only details I omitted were about our raunchy sex life. I told them about all the places we had visited as a couple, the meals we went out for, the films we had watched together, how special he had been to me. I also revealed what our joint plans for the future had been – to go and live in New York. Devastated yet again at the thought that New York would not be happening, at least not with Gavin, the tears started rolling.

I stopped talking and poured myself another cup of coffee. I also took another piece of toast (that I didn't want) and by doing so I bought myself a little more time. It was going to hurt to have to speak about that scene, it hurt for me to relive it in my mind, and it was going to hurt to have to tell them.

"Darling, you are not ready – leave it for now." pleaded Dad.

"It is going to hurt, whether I do it now, or in ten years' time. So now it's got to be."

I left out all the vulgarity of the description of the scene that had greeted me when I'd arrived back at the flat. I had never heard either of my parents swear or use obscenities, so I described how I had found Bobbie, bent over the lounge chair, and how Gavin had been doing it to her, like a couple of dogs. The tears continued to flow. Mum kept handing me the tissue box, my voice seemed croaky and I couldn't stop shivering. Taking a few more minutes to collect myself, (it was out now) I vowed to keep calm long enough to finish my story. Describing Bobbie and Gavin's reactions on realising that I had seen it all, I felt the bitterness inside pouring out.

"That bitch, Mum! My so-called best friend moved in on the man I love whilst I was here. Dad was really ill. How could they do this to me? I would like to bet it wasn't the first time it happened."

"Sweetheart, whether it was once, twice or twenty times is irrelevant, it's all cheating." She hesitated for a few seconds before confessing "We haven't really been too keen on Bobbie since you first introduced us - there was *something* about her."

I was a bit shocked to hear her say that, they had always been pleasant to Bobbie when they'd seen her.

"Why didn't you tell me what you thought? I would have listened to you both - I've always trusted your judgement."

"Darling, we knew how happy and excited you were to have a best friend for the first time ever. How could we spoil that for you by expressing our doubts? We might have been totally wrong about her - it would have spoilt a good friendship for you." Dad explained.

"It might have spared me this heartache though." As soon as I'd said it I instantly regretted it. It sounded as if I was now laying the blame on my parents.

"Did you ask them how many times it happened?"

"I wanted to know - but I didn't want to know, so no, I didn't. I've already been punished, Mum, why add to the suffering? I really wish you had told me your doubts, it would have saved this heartache, but I understand why you kept your thoughts to yourselves. It's not your fault – they are the ones that have hurt me, not you two."

For the rest of the day, putting Gavin and Bobbie out of our minds, we talked about me possibly leaving London behind, but more so my decision to quit University. Mum and Dad made some suggestions, offered advice, and I listened to all of them. I did stress to them that I was incapable at that point of making any life changing decisions. I didn't know what I wanted (the clocks turned back, to before Dad's heart attack? No. That wouldn't have changed anything. I would still have rushed to be with Dad). When would I be over this waking nightmare? I didn't know anything anymore. I know they were upset about me quitting Uni but Dad assured me he wasn't too concerned about it. He knew that when I was ready, I would have a lot to offer future employers, whichever path I chose to follow.

For the next two weeks I hung around home most days, (except for five hours one day when Mum and I went out for a girly day. I read for much of the time and became engrossed in some of Mum's thrillers - an author I hadn't heard of before. He was an excellent writer and I became addicted to the stories, and fell in love with all the characters. My reading was frequently disturbed by my thoughts of Gavin. One question that kept plaguing me was if Bobbie had been out with us that first night, would Gavin have been attracted to her instead of me? Try as I did to put that question to the back of mind, the lack of an answer haunted me. Dad pottered around his garden (pottering was all he was capable of at the time) and he would sometimes creep in through the front door, tiptoe in his stocking feet into the conservatory and lean over the back of my chair, hug me then plant a kiss on the top of my head. He's always been like that. That's why I love him. I sometimes surprised him in a similar manner. Under normal circumstances we would laugh at these surprise hugs, so full of affection. This time though, that laughter wasn't appropriate - chiefly due to my dark moods.

If I wanted to be alone, I went up to my room. This was usually when I needed to think or feel sorry for myself, and I'd put on a DVD or a CD for a bit of background noise. Sometimes I didn't realise what disc I was loading (the first one I grabbed) and I got drawn into some of the films, usually my old favourite chick flicks, reaching out for the tissues before the end, which brought my own misery and worries back to haunt me again.

Every night after our evening meal we would sit at the dining table for hours, talking about anything but my troubles and enjoying a couple of bottles of wine between us. I was lucky to have such wonderful, caring parents who were so supportive to me as they always had been. They loved me and would do anything for me,

buy me anything I wanted - if there *was* anything
I wanted. I didn't want material things. I just
wanted to be there with them. They had never
done anything to hurt me, and never would. They
were the only ones who could get me through this.

Half way down our second bottle of wine
on one such night, Dad went into the kitchen and
returned with an armful of holiday brochures.

"Your Mum and I need a break, darling,
and so do you. We've all been through a tough
time lately, so no arguments. You choose. I'll go
anywhere you choose but preferably somewhere
we've not been before. Just bear in mind - no
sightseeing tours or traipsing around cities,
museums or temples. I'm going for a rest, so I
suggest sunshine and sun-loungers around a pool -
and doing absolutely nothing."

Whilst I was appreciative of their
generosity, the last thing I wanted was a holiday. I
wanted to stay at home and mope but I knew they
would only fret about me if they left me at home.
The last thing Dad needed was to spend a holiday
worrying, so for two days I concentrated on
browsing the internet, looking at the countries that
we were yet to visit. After some discussion with
Mum we both agreed on Cuba – a place we had
wanted to go in the past but still hadn't been.
After Dad visited his doctor and got the all clear
to fly we booked the holiday through an online
travel shop. The next six days were spent
frantically shopping for lotions, potions and new
bikinis for Mum and I. Dad paid a couple of visits
to his office for the first time since before his
episode as we now called it. He wanted to check
up on things and to see how his new recruit

Anthony, was settling in. Planning to return to work after our travels, he'd said his goodbyes and picked up the latest set of management accounts to peruse by the pool.

Although Cuba was still very much a poor country, we found everything about the place charming and quaint, if somewhat run down in places. Our holiday resort at Cayo Coco was reasonably new and had everything that we required. The food was good (although we did hear some very negative reports on the food served in hotels nearby), our rooms were immaculately clean, and the staff, excellent. We heeded advice not to leave towels, sandals and sun creams etc on the loungers overnight, otherwise they would disappear. I had never seen Dad look so well, considering what he had been through recently. He was fully relaxed, and was either sleeping or reading the days away, with a little gentle swimming and some short walks thrown in.

After three or four days of chilling out with Mum and Dad I decided I needed to give them some space, plus I needed some time alone. My darling parents, when we were together, talked incessantly. I knew that much of the time it was to keep me occupied. If they were getting my attention I didn't have time to brood. I needed some me time though, I wanted to brood, to get things straight in my mind. I needed to make sense of everything that had happened and start thinking of a way forward. Basically I wanted to put all the shit behind me. I went to see one of the tour reps and booked myself a day's sight-seeing in Havana, a salsa night on the beach and a dolphin experience. Swimming with dolphins, I was told, could be quite therapeutic – and I needed therapy. Dad looked at me, a question in his eyes when I told him about the three excursions I'd booked. I instinctively knew what he was thinking. He was wondering if I could cope on these tours when it was highly likely that I would be accompanied by couples. They understood me. They knew I was seeking time for myself as Mum did not offer to accompany me, although she would love to have come along too (well, perhaps not the salsa).

The sight-seeing tour of Havana was an education and I had never realised that Che Guevara was such a national treasure, (history had never really been my thing, even though I was fascinated with museums). I was enthralled by their old American cars and I just had to have a ride in one. Later in the day I found a tourist market and purchased one of the many oil paintings of those cars. Just as Mum and Dad predicted, the seats on the tour bus were predominantly occupied by couples, so the tour guide had paired me (for the short flight, coach journey, and for the included lunch) with Keith, a single Canadian guy (he never told me his age, but I suspected he was mid-thirties). He seemed like a nice guy but he reminded me of a puppy dog by hanging on my every word with his tongue practically lolling out. He fancied me and I would have been blind not to notice the fact. I enjoyed our conversations immensely; he was very intelligent, very amusing, and we shared similar tastes in music and film, but *I* was trying to recover from my broken heart and Keith was just not my type. We were back at the pick-up point

for the coach in plenty of time and I was looking
forward to relaxing for the evening. The busy
day's walking had left me feeling totally drained.
When we arrived at our hotel later in the day,
Keith gave me a peck on the cheek and made his
way to his room. At least I didn't have to put up
with him anymore – it had been a few hours too
many, he'd been in my face and had started to
bore me! During our later conversations, I had
deliberately avoided telling him of the plans I had
made for the remainder of my holiday.

I was in for a shock when the tour bus
arrived at the venue for the beach salsa three
nights later. Whilst gathering around for
instructions from the tour guide before our short
walk to the beach, I noticed Keith – the last
person to get off the bus. I had been one of the last
to board the bus back at the hotel and I'd failed to
notice that he had been at the very back. He came
over to me and putting his arm around my
shoulder, and said,

"Looks like we could be partnering each
other again, honey."

Oh crap! I felt so irritated and my
stomach sank. So much for my plans to find
someone interesting to spend the evening with!

We partnered for the salsa and as we
were learning we laughed at each other when we
got the steps totally wrong. After the salsa
finished, Keith entered the men's limbo
competition and he dared me to enter the one for
the ladies. He was an excellent limbo dancer and
managed close second to a very worthy winner. I
was eliminated about half way through my contest
when I leaned too far back and fell flat on my

back into the sand. To me, it was just an excellent night, good company and plenty of laughs. To Keith, it was many steps nearer to getting into my knickers.

After we left the bus back at the hotel, his arm went around my shoulder yet again, and he pushed me towards the wall at the back of the reception building as we were passing. Before I had chance to protest he planted his lips on mine and kissed me, hard and urgently. I struggled to get my head from between the wall and his lips but finally I edged free and pushed him away, seething.

"Stop it, Keith! You've spoilt what had up to now been an enjoyable evening!"

"Honey, don't worry, what happens in Cuba, stays in Cuba." he muttered, as he came towards me again.

"Look – I thought you were a nice guy, but I don't like you in that way. I don't want a relationship, sexual or otherwise with anybody right now. I haven't come on holiday for that!"

"Then why bother coming on holiday at all? You're the best chick there is around this resort, surely you realised that every man here would want to fuck you?"

Yes. Sure mate. And like all those men, like Gavin, *you'd* probably be another one that ended up fucking Bobbie. I didn't utter the words, but it was the first thought that crossed my mind.

"No, Keith, they don't. You're the only one who's tried – nobody else."

At that I turned my back on him and walked away, wondering if I'd ever rid myself of all the bitter thoughts. I just wanted the whole

49

episode behind me. I joined Mum and Dad the next morning and after breakfast we each gathered our books and towels, and claimed our loungers for the day. I was still furious about Keith spoiling my night out and I was having visions of him turning up on my dolphin day. I made a real effort to read but I was unable to get beyond the first few pages of my book.

"Are you alright, darling?" asked Dad. "I wouldn't ask but every time you've gone for a dip, I couldn't help noticing that your book has been open at the same page each time."

"I'm fine thanks. Just going over things in my mind, you know."

I needn't have worried too much. Keith was on the Dolphins tour but he had found another lady (or ladies), to work his charm on. I was already on speaking terms with them, having seen them in the swimming pool on a number of occasions. They were enjoying a girls' holiday, having left their husbands hard at work in the U.K. I didn't know whether they had made Keith aware that they were married but if so, it was not deterring him from giving it the full charm offensive. Good luck to him. I wasn't going to let him affect my mind enough to spoil another day.

The dolphins were marvellous, I swam with them and stroked them and attempted all the tricks. The day was therapeutic just as promised. I was in awe of those wonderful creatures - their intelligence, their intuition, and mostly of their interaction with humans. I had somehow managed to steer clear of Keith and his lady friends all day until it was time to return to the coach. He had his arm around the taller of the two women and I noticed the playful slap on her bottom as she boarded the bus just ahead of him. I saw both of the women the next day in the pool and we had stopped swimming to have our usual chat. I mentioned that I'd seen her with the Canadian guy and asked how she'd got along with him.

"Don't ask." she replied, "The story is - he was after a shag. I told him I was married and that I couldn't cheat on my husband but he didn't seem to care. He said 'honey, what happens in Cuba, stays in Cuba'."

I laughed at that and, seeing the quizzical way in which they looked at me I felt obliged to tell them of my own experience. They were disgusted, but relieved that I'd handled the situation fairly well. He had apparently turned rather nasty, when she (Dawn) had refused to give him a kiss but luckily two couples had been walking past at the time. The two guys had stepped in to help her and Keith had run off. Thankfully, none of us saw him again.

I was quite relieved when we were walking up the driveway, back home again. Unable to sleep on the plane (as usual) I couldn't wait to get a shower and go to bed. Despite being tired I was starting to feel much better. The holiday had been beneficial to me and Dad was looking fantastic again having been forced into relaxation with no gardening, no worrying about the business, and no worrying about me – because I had been where he had been able to keep his eye on me.

CHAPTER 3

We'd been back from Cuba two weeks. Dad had been going into his office two or three mornings a week and he was looking much better for his holiday. He had almost managed to convince Mum and I that he was feeling better than he had done in a long while. It didn't stop Mum worrying constantly for every minute that he was away from home. I managed to persuade her not to be calling the office or his mobile every five minutes to check up on him, even though I was sorely tempted to do it myself. With a little encouragement she busied herself with some of her voluntary work in the local 'Mind' shop. She also returned to the Ladies Circle and pottered about in the garden, though what Dad would think to her re-positioning of the pots of bedding plants and statues I hadn't a clue. It kept her busy, kept her off my case it and gave Dad a peaceful time while he was at the office, so I didn't think he would have too many objections.

Whilst I was feeling better after the recent events in my life I couldn't understand what was wrong with me since returning from Cuba. When Mum and Dad were out of the house (and unable to bear witness), my daily routine started to involve cleaning the house from top to bottom. If their activities kept them away from home for long enough I would start at the top and work my way down all over again. What the hell was I doing? Their house was always immaculate, due to the conscientiousness and thoroughness three times a week, of Anita their cleaner. I had never done this before and couldn't understand why I suddenly started being obsessive about cleanliness when I was a naturally untidy person? I was picking things up after myself, putting dirty laundry into the washing basket, scrubbing the bathroom and polishing the bath and sink until they shone. I plumped up the cushions, washed windows, changed bed linen every day and used antibacterial cleanser on every square inch of the kitchen. The bookshelves in Dad's den became an additional obsession. I sat for hours organising the books along the shelves. From the tallest books on the left I would arrange them in size order right along each shelf. I placed ornaments in perfect symmetry as well as the magazines on the coffee table. I couldn't stop myself. My other thing was my hands and arms, right up to my elbows – which I scrubbed with a nailbrush, twenty or thirty times a day.

The three of us had been out for a drive one Sunday. We'd stopped for a carvery lunch at a charming country inn and later had a pleasant walk around a local beauty spot. After walking for half an hour or so, we sat on a bench for Dad to take a breather and Mum edged closer to me.

"Sweetheart, we've been getting worried about you and your behaviour since our holiday. You have certainly not been yourself lately and we think you need some help."

She had certainly caught me off guard this time and my immediate reaction was to go on the defensive and I snapped at her, "To what behaviour are you referring exactly? The fact that I am trying to pick myself up after my boyfriend cheated on me?"

I saw the shock register on her face. I'd never spoken to her like that before and much as I didn't like to see it, it didn't stop me venting.

"That's not *behaviour*! It's something I will get over, in time. It doesn't happen overnight Mum! You've no idea what it's like!" Her face softened and she reached out.

"Look Helen, see these." She lifted my hands in hers and shook them gently. "I've seen them. Sweetheart, you've scrubbed them until they are almost bleeding. That's the behaviour I mean...and the rest!" she nodded knowingly.

I looked away, avoiding her gaze and Mum took that to be my acknowledgement of her stated facts. She put her arms around me, not saying another word, and I sighed heavily over her shoulder, my own acknowledgement of the truth. So they had known what was going on. I must have been crazy to think that they wouldn't. Dad had noticed his books and the meticulous placing of each and every one of them. Mum had noticed each time she went to bed that the sheets and duvets were fresh, the persistent smell of bleach in the bathroom - never there before, after Anita's days cleaning. Then there had been Anita herself, reporting back to them on my behaviour during their absences – telling them how tidy my room was these days, no CD's or DVD's to pick up anymore, no clothes to put to the wash or hang up, no bed to make. She had been creeping around the house watching me rearrange the books in Dad's study. Anita had also been the first to witness the obsessive scrubbing of my hands and arms.

First came the visit to our G.P. Dad accompanied me (which had been my idea), and he had to prompt me at times whilst I told the story of the last few months and the affect that those events were having on me and my life. Despite my resolution I cried. I tried holding back the tears I really did, but the doctor asked me such direct questions, I felt like I was backed into a corner. Two ways out of that corner – cry, or answer the questions. I did both. After listening for nearly twenty minutes (each appointment was ten minutes only and hadn't I grumbled many times before about people taking too long?)

Dr Jack opened his mouth to speak and Dad cut him off in an instant.

"I know what you're about to suggest, Richard, but forget it, she is not starting on anti-depressants - no way. I know people who have struggled to get off the bloody things…"

"But it doesn't have to be…" he tried to cut in.

"No! She needs some proper help, not medication. I want her to see a clinical psychologist or a counsellor. You can do that for her." Dad laid down the law and Dr Jack stared back at him, twiddling his pen around with his fingers, deep in thought.

"Okay, I will write a couple of letters - you should hear something over the next couple of weeks." He quickly asked how Dad was coping since he was back at work, and apparently satisfied, he saw us both back to reception where he shouted the name of his next patient.

Mum tried her hardest to organise the next couple of weeks for me. She cut down her charity shop hours to almost nothing, and the Ladies Circle was forgotten about yet again. She organised outings for the two of us – a spa day, trips out for lunch, shopping sprees and a couple of musicals in the West End. Dad did his little bit too by taking me to his golf club, telling me it would be good for me and it would give me something to focus on. He enrolled me, and afterwards stood grinning for half an hour whilst my feeble attempts to hit the ball managed to get worse with every passing moment. I know they were only trying to help. It was keeping me busy, entertained, and away from the house, bleach, vacuum cleaner *and* the soap, water and nailbrush. The spa day with Mum was excellent. In the morning we ate cream cakes by the swimming pool as we read our magazines - in the nude. A variety of beauty treatments and holistic therapies were on offer. I chose a non- surgical face-lift, a set of acrylic nails with a French manicure, and an hour of reflexology. Mum had an Indian Head Massage and Hot Stone Therapy and finished with a facial. It was a wonderful feeling to be utterly pampered and we giggled like a couple of school girls as we walked back down the street to the tube station. Dad surprised us both and prepared one of his special stir fries for when we got home - my favourite chicken and pineapple with some saffron rice and mixed salad leaves. We ate in the garden and sat out until dark. Mum and Dad drank a bottle of red whilst I consumed a considerable amount of water (being good for once) as recommended by the reflexologist. It helped to rid the body of toxins following my foot massage. With some beautiful classical music playing behind us in the conservatory, the birds twittering their good-night calls to each other at dusk, we whiled away the evening. Dad completed his Daily Telegraph crossword, Mum and I talked about our day at the spa. We all reminisced a little and I was feeling more relaxed that night than I had for such a long time, and without one mouthful of alcohol passing my lips.

It was nearly four weeks after my initial visit to Dr Jack at the surgery, before I received my appointment through the post to visit clinical psychologist, Mr Gillespie. The appointment was for a Friday - just over two weeks away. Mum and Dad were fairly chuffed the appointment had come through. They were thinking that their little girl was going to get some help with her problem, and that they would soon have her back to normal again. I didn't really see that I had a problem, not a psychological one anyway. What was so wrong about me wanting to be clean and tidy for once in my life (the tidiness, that is – I've always been clean)? The way I saw it, I was just helping around the house – something I had never done before I agree, but not before time. Mind you, there was still the obsessive hand washing and I suppose I had to admit to myself, that yes, *that* was a predicament. I was feeling more than a little apprehensive about the forthcoming appointment though and truly wondered if there was anything that could be done to help me. There was also another appointment I needed to make - and pretty soon.

CHAPTER 4

My other appointment came first – one that Mum and Dad didn't know about - and didn't need to know about. I was roughly eleven weeks pregnant and for the last six weeks I had been throwing up each morning. I had been on the pill since I was sixteen and I couldn't understand what the matter was when I had missed my first period. I *never* missed a pill – I made sure of that, they were always on the top of my bedside cabinet and I never failed to take one each night before going to sleep (even when I was drunk). Thinking back, the only possible explanation I could came up with was that I had been taking antibiotics for ten days, for a particularly bad chest infection, and they had counteracted the effects of the pill. Still, there was no time to be wasted, wondering how and why – the matter needed my urgent attention. I was too young, not too fond of children anyway, and I needed a career. A part of me wondered what it would be like to gaze down into a cot and see a little boy or girl with Gavin's eyes and nose. But I didn't let myself dwell on the thought for too long. For the most part I could only see the negative side - it would probably turn out to be a cheating, conniving, little bastard, - like its father. I wouldn't be responsible for bringing another of those into the world – there was more than enough already.

I told Mum and Dad I was going into the city for the day; a bit of shopping, some mooching around an art gallery, and maybe even a museum. Mum offered to come with me but I rapidly quashed that idea telling her I needed some time to think and plan for my future. I was so scared, I was actually tempted to tell her what I was about to do, to have her come along, hold my hand and let me cry on her shoulder after it was over. I got a shiver within the depths of my body. I hated having to lie to them but I was only doing it to protect them from the hurt and disappointment they would inevitably feel. "I'll be fine, Mum. Stop worrying. I'm having a day alone, that's all. I need to think."

Whether it was still the morning sickness or just pure nerves I didn't know but the nauseous feeling never left me during my journey on the tube. My appointment was for 10am in a private clinic not far from Harley Street. I had a ten minute wait after I'd checked in with the receptionist. I suppose like every other young woman who'd done this before me, I seriously considered walking out of there. I knew what I was about to do was morally wrong, but to have a child was not right for me. It was my fear that was making me want to run. Somebody came to take me into a little side office where I had some form filling to do and a quick consultation. By 5pm I was out of there - it was over and done with. It had been a strange feeling when I woke up - to know that the last little bit of Gavin which had been growing inside me, had gone. I felt a sense of relief. I had got rid of his foetus and I felt by having done so it would also help get him out of my mind – permanently. Like a type of exorcism. I caught a cab home just in case I started feeling queasy after my surgery. I had no desire to be passing out on the underground.

"So, darling, did you get any thinking done whilst you were out?" Dad asked as we settled down after our evening meal.

My guilt gnawed at my insides again and I hoped they wouldn't see the red flush on my face that must have appeared.

"Yes. I'm going to have my appointments with the clinical psychologist. After that I'm going to get a job - if I can," I told them, "in accountancy. That's always what my intention was. I'm just taking a different route."

"I may be able to help with that sweetheart" said Dad, "leave it with me for a few days."

My heart melted at his protectiveness of me and his offer of assistance, but it also made me feel small. I didn't want his help, I'd just robbed them of a grandchild I didn't deserve his help. I suppressed an urge to scream out about my shame. I needed to do something for myself for once. My parents had already done so much for me. They had given me a very privileged start in life. Now was the time for me to go it alone, without any strings being pulled by them on my behalf. Determined that I would sort out my own career, but wanting to show my appreciation for his support, I muttered,

"Thanks Dad."

My appointment with Mr Gillespie soon came around, and that first initial visit involved me telling him all about my life from my earliest memories and right through my school years, bullying included. It was hard work - there was no prompting from him whatsoever. He hardly said a word, he just nodded occasionally to acknowledge that he understood what was being said, his elbows on his desk, the fingers of each hand interlocked together. The half hour appointment dragged whilst I was in there and he told me to see the receptionist on my way out to book my appointment - he had suggested two weeks as an ideal gap.

The next two weeks passed by quickly but uneventfully. I continued with my daily cleaning routines to the house and unconsciously trying to remove the top layer of skin from my hands and arms through my constant scrubbing at them. Mum and Dad continued to watch over me whenever they were able. I really wished they would stop fretting. I wasn't about to do any serious harm to myself. I didn't have my finger poised over some self-destruct button. It was getting me through each day in the way I knew best. I didn't once have any guilty feelings about getting rid of Gavin's baby – I knew it had been the right thing to do – for me, at least. I think I would have resented the child – looking at his or her little face, seeing Gavin in every expression and every little mannerism. (Not once did I ever consider that it may have looked like *me*, and have *my* facial expressions, *my* temperament, maybe all *my* genes. I wouldn't let those thoughts even enter my head – I couldn't.) Any guilt I felt was for the loss my parents were unaware of.

At our next appointment Mr Gillespie got me started by asking about my life at University. He asked how I had coped with the coursework, what my plans had been for the future at that time – both before I had quit and after. I told him about the Uni social life, the constant partying, meeting

Gavin, and the events leading up to his betrayal – with my best friend. Whilst I was talking he sat, fingers yet again entwined, sometimes watching me, sometimes gazing out of the window – but listening intently, always. I hadn't failed to notice that there was very little note-taking involved. (Perhaps he wrote up his notes afterwards so as not to suddenly lose his patient's train of thought by hurriedly picking up his pen to start furiously writing lest he forget some minor detail, and leaving the patient wondering what he's writing about them, and does it involve the words total nutcase, loser, raving lunatic or recommend mental institution for the rest of his/her natural?) The appointment ended promptly when my thirty minutes were up. On leaving his room I called by the receptionist's desk to make my next appointment.

I'd already decided I wasn't going to waste that next fortnight waiting for session three with my shrink, as I now referred to him when speaking with Mum and Dad. Making a valiant effort not to clean and scrub as much, I sat in front of the computer composing an introduction/'enquiring if you have any vacancies' letter, that I planned to send out to all chartered accountant practices throughout the London region. I thought it through with the utmost care - the wording had to be spot on. I had to create an instant good impression and sell myself. My aim was to make them want to know more about me. I wanted interviews. It took me four hours in total. I edited, re-edited, made some additions, deleted a couple of words, and finally I was happy with it. One thing that worried me was the fact that I had quit Uni - would they consider me? I had stated in my letter, without going into detail, that my reasons for leaving University were personal. Would they just disregard me anyway, label me as a quitter to save themselves disappointment later in the day? Or would they give me a chance to explain those personal reasons in interview? I couldn't somehow see myself explaining to them 'well, I quit Uni because I caught my boyfriend fucking my best friend in my flat.'

I was in a rush to get all the letters sent out – I wanted to get something sorted before Dad could start speaking to some of his contacts and pull some strings. I wanted both him and Mum to be proud of me. My second reason for rushing to get a job was the shrink appointments – I wanted them over with. My way of thinking was if you get a job, something to occupy your mind, the O.C.D. will just automatically disappear. So the day after I'd done my letter I printed off fifty copies and used Google to search accountancy practices in London and the suburbs. I hoped fifty would be sufficient, but if I wasn't successful with those, there was plenty more I could try.

I had a pretty good feeling about the exercise and was quietly confident that I could land myself a position. I still had the quitting Uni thing niggling at the back of my mind, but I was sure that there was someone, somewhere, who would be willing to give me a chance by giving me the benefit of the doubt. I needed some interviews desperately, at least that would help restore some faith in myself.

A few days after I'd mailed all the letters, I paced around the lounge and hallway each morning waiting for the postman. The frustration when I shuffled through any mail to find they were all addressed to Mum or Dad was unbearable, but I am not the most patient person at the best of times. (Why do people take so long to reply to letters? I've never been able to understand that. To me, it's simple. You get a letter – you answer it. Just a straightforward 'yay' or 'nay' would do – why take days, weeks even?)

Two days before my next shrink appointment arrived, I opened my mail to find not one, but two letters from accountancy practices willing to offer me interviews and they had both given me a date and time. One was three weeks away, a Thursday at 4pm, and one on Wednesday, just a week away at 10.30am. I was thrilled. I had already received about ten rejection letters in the previous two or three days, some stating 'unfortunately, we do not have any vacancies at this current time' and the remainder saying 'sorry to inform you that your application has been unsuccessful.' I was overjoyed. I smirked as I thrust the interview letters into Dad's hands later that night,

"See? I can do it Dad." He grinned back and hugged me tightly, delighted to see me looking more positive.

"Well I always knew were capable, darling. I really hope you interview well - you will be an asset to any company, I'm sure." I hoped so too. I was desperate to do something that would make my parents proud of me. I needed to!

I went along to the next appointment with Mr Gillespie two days after receiving my interview letters. This time he wanted to know all about my obsessions. When exactly had it started, how often did I indulge in my obsessions? Was it every day? What did I feel I was achieving? How many times a day was I scrubbing my hands or showering? Did I think that this had all been triggered by Gavin having sex with Bobbie? (Of course I did.) Did I feel mentally contaminated because I couldn't rid myself of the vision of the two of them indulging in such a way? (What sort of question was that to ask? Wouldn't anybody feel the same way, having witnessed those two shagging like a couple of dogs?) Why was I arranging Dad's books in perfect symmetry? Was I trying to get my life back in order? (This is a total waste of my bloody time. I've come here to see this guy and he sits there telling me what is patently obvious.) He ended the day's session by confirming that I have Obsessive-Compulsive Disorder, and that as things had only recently started occurring, he was quite sure that with some additional help, Cognitive Behaviour Therapy, quite soon, it was possible that I could get past this stage in my life before it really took a hold. He would make the referral and the therapist would write to me offering an appointment. On the journey home I was feeling rather disgruntled and well – pissed off with things. I badly needed not to have to go through with the therapy.

I parked my car in the drive, ambled up the path and in through the door. Mum was in the kitchen preparing the vegetables for the evening meal, and asked me,

"How was today's session, darling?" and without pausing for another breath, or waiting for an answer "There's some more mail for you -

65

well, one letter – on the coffee table. The post arrived just after you left."

I left Mum alone in kitchen, muttering as she continued to attack the swede with a touch too much enthusiasm. As I ripped open the envelope and read the letter, I started to smile and couldn't stop myself from punching the air. I had been offered an interview, 10am Monday morning the following week.

By eleven am that following Monday morning I had been offered a position. No waiting whilst hundreds of other hopefuls had interviews, no hanging about waiting for the rejection (or in this case, acceptance) letter. He told me immediately that there was a position and possibly a future for me within the practice. I had liked the gentleman Mr Hopkins from my first impressions and it was all I could do to keep myself from flinging my arms around him and kissing him. He told me all the necessary information with regard to salary, holiday entitlement, sickness, and training. He would get the employment contract drawn up immediately and asked when it would be convenient for me to start. I left the office on cloud nine and with an overwhelming desire to punch the air again as I walked back to my car knowing I would be starting my new career the following Monday.

Mum and Dad were delighted for me and after some persuasion I think they both agreed that it would probably be more beneficial than seeing the therapist. They reminded the next morning that I should call the other accountancy firms and inform them I had been offered a position elsewhere which after careful consideration I had accepted. I made the calls to those companies and then wrote to Mr Gillespie telling him that I did not wish to carry on with our appointments or to pursue a meeting with the C.B.T.

CHAPTER 5

My life was quite dull for the next two years whilst I spent most of my spare time studying for my A.A.T. (Association of Accounting Technicians). I was enjoying working for the Hopkins Partnership and my first impression of Mr Hopkins had been right. He was an excellent accountant and had the utmost patience when dealing with trainees. He always explained things clearly and concisely and was willing to help with my studies if I ever found myself struggling to understand my assignments. Fortunately I never needed to ask for that help. Another thing I was fast learning is that there was nothing Mr Hopkins liked better than joining in with a bit of fun and gossip in the staff kitchen at lunchtimes. All the staff were extremely fond of him (as were his clients) and at practical jokes, he was master class.

My studies for A.A.T. were going to take about two years and if I managed to pass my exams I intended to do further studying and become a Chartered Accountant. Mr Hopkins gave me every encouragement, constantly reminding me that his offer of help was always there if I needed it.

I didn't much bother with a social life; I hardly ever went out other than the occasional hour or two in the pub with colleagues after work on a Friday. I had a decent holiday with my parents each year plus the odd visits to Dad's apartment in Paris. I occasionally went out on a date and I'd had a couple of steady boyfriends (nothing lasting more than two or three months) but they didn't work out from my point of view, and I tried to find the kindest way to end the relationships. One thing that was pleasing was that my O.C.D. very rarely surfaced. I was obsessive about having a tidy desk and bedroom and I still washed my hands more than anybody I knew, but the frantic cleaning of the house, and scrubbing my arms with the nail brush had stopped completely.

Some days at work ended up quite tiring where audits were concerned and I often had to travel, along with one or two of my colleagues, to various limited companies to carry out an annual audit after their financial year end. Some firms made us really welcome and went out of their way to clear spare desks for us and yet there were places that almost had us sitting in what could best be described as a store room where the radiator didn't work (if there was one) and our only work surface was a decorator's pasting table. Usually at these businesses we could go all day without even being offered a cup of tea or coffee.

On one of my audits during my second year of studying I was stunned to bump into Alex Baker-Thompson in the corridor on my way back from the loo (the boy from my schooldays, who was caught by the bullies fingering me behind the bike-sheds). We chatted in the corridor for quite some time and he told me he was employed as a draughtsman by the company we were auditing. He asked how Uni had gone for me. Not feeling the need to mention the Gavin situation I told him I had been really ill so was forced to quit. I saw him most days for the next fortnight until our audit was complete. On the last day Alex asked

69

me out - just as friends. I didn't think it could do any harm (he was still quite dishy). Maybe he would be able to tell me what had happened with some of the other people from school - where they were now, who was married, or any other gossip about them all, so I said yes. I didn't actually care about where my bullies were but I looked forward to having a proper catch up. We exchanged mobile numbers and he promised to get in touch over the following week or so.

We met outside King's Cross at early one Saturday evening later the same month and walked arm in arm around London for a couple of hours. We exchanged our family news, shared holiday experiences and things in general. I felt sorry for him when he told me about a girl he had been seeing for five months. Her father had taken some sudden dislike to Alex and told her in no uncertain terms to call it off. It was quite clear that Alex had really liked the girl and was still puzzling over what he had done to make her father turn against him. After a few minutes of searching we came across a cosy little restaurant and over our meal we discussed some of the kids from school. Alex hadn't been in touch with his school friends for quite some time and had very little gossip to report. However, he had read in one of the national newspapers that one of my bullies (Ann Stead) had died in a tragic car crash, about eighteen months previously.

We had a couple more casual dates before Alex asked if I would consider being his girlfriend. I wasn't sure - I was over Gavin, but I still hadn't been able to forget the hurt he'd caused me. I told him that I wasn't really looking for a relationship and that my studies consumed almost all of my spare time. I told him that I would like it if we could still continue to meet up as friends and though he looked disappointed he reluctantly agreed.

We continued to meet up each month for maybe three or four months and then one night (after we both had way too much to drink), he tried to stick his hand in my undies and I pushed him away. He was a bit taken aback and he responded aggressively,

"Come on, Helen, you didn't push me away behind the bike sheds. You were keen on getting poked and *plenty* of lads poked you." He made me sound like a slut and I didn't see it in the same way he did. We had been kids for heaven's sake, experimenting, doing what is natural – becoming sexually aware. I felt very hurt by what he was implying.

"Alex, I thought you were a nice guy, good-looking, funny, and I valued your friendship – but I'm sorry, you have ruined it. I was a young girl at that time, just finding out about sex and experimenting, maybe a little too much if I'm honest. You thought I would be cheap. A dead certainty you'd get laid! You've offended me!" I walked away, hailed a cab, and went home.

CHAPTER 6

I still wasn't going out much. I had no close friends, no boyfriend and to tell the truth I wasn't too bothered. Any social life (if you could call it such) was spent with Mum and Dad. I sometimes met up on a Saturday afternoon with the girls from work. We mooched around the shops and went to a pub for a few drinks. They went home to prepare for dates with their boyfriends - I went home to Mum and Dad - and my studying. Not wanting my co-workers to think I was totally dull, I invented a boyfriend, Justin. I had some exciting dates with him, got fed up with him and a few weeks later I was seeing John (my next creation). I wasn't proud of myself telling lies, but it was far easier than having to explain why I wasn't interested in men – why I preferred to study. What if I had told them the truth? I would probably have earned the label 'oddball,' started getting strange looks from them all and would never get invited to the Saturday shopping sessions ever again or anywhere else for that matter.

Dad tried getting me back to his golf club (where I was a fully paid up member), but that wasn't for me. He started dropping hints (in a bid to tempt me) that there were quite a few eligible bachelors with a really good handicap.

"You'd like Thomas, sweetheart, he's quite a dish. Well the ladies seem to like him anyway." I just laughed at him,

"You're not very subtle, Dad – stop trying to get me off your hands. Studying comes first; I'm still young, for heaven's sake."

72

There was cause for celebration later in the year when I achieved my A.A.T. qualification. My parents were thrilled and as I started making moves for further studies - towards getting my chartered recognition, Dad told me I needed a break from studying for a while. He had booked a cruise for the three of us, my first ever, during the Christmas and New Year period. I had to admit the weather in England had been abysmal and lazing about in the Caribbean sun relaxing on a lounger reading thrillers instead of accountancy, economics and contract law, or doing nothing else but daydream sounded excellent. The day we boarded I met people who were around my age group and we swam together, dined together and danced until the early hours. The weather was perfect and I thoroughly enjoyed everything about it. When the end of the holiday came we all swapped addresses, phone numbers and email addresses, swearing to keep in touch and true to form - we didn't.

Mr Hopkins was of the same opinion as Mum and Dad - thinking I needed a rest from studying. So whilst all three of them thought I was having a few months' break from studying, I was going to bed early but my bedtime reading was the text books that I had already purchased. I never left the books on my bedside cabinet for Mum and Dad to find; I kept them hidden in a drawer beneath all my undies. But what is it about parents - how do they always seem to know? I couldn't help but overhear a conversation between them one day – they both agreed they thought my studying had become an obsession and was perhaps another outlet for my O.C.D.

I made more of an effort to get out by joining a badminton class where some of my work colleagues were also members. I went to the cinema once a month with the same crowd. It surprised me to find how much I enjoyed the badminton - *after* the first four or five sessions at least. It had been exhausting, which was to be expected really as I hadn't done much in the way of physical exercise for so long. Once I'd learned more and was hitting great shots, winning some points and understanding the scoring system better, my competitive streak came to the fore and I was eager for Tuesday night to arrive each week. I was enjoying the Saturday shopping and drinking sessions more than ever, because I was able to join in with conversations about badminton and the latest films for the first time. I was fitting in at last and the people I had always referred to as colleagues were now my friends. We started to plan for a holiday together, the six of us that were unattached, which had to be taken between Christmas and New Year whilst the office was closed otherwise we wouldn't all be allowed to take annual leave at the same time.

We had a glorious week in Spain. It was the first time I had ever been on holiday with friends and it was also the cheapest holiday I had ever had; three star accommodation on a room only basis. The cleanliness left a bit to be desired and the beds were barely comfortable but I *didn't* feel the inclination to get the bleach out for once – I was too busy enjoying myself. We flirted, we were drunk almost 24-7, we sunbathed when we managed to drag ourselves out of bed in daylight hours, and we danced the nights away in the seedy little bars and discos. My new found friends would often cast me some looks of amazement – they were seeing me let my hair down for the first time. I shocked them even more so when I made the first move to chat up the odd guy who caught my eye. Not with the intention of getting laid or emotionally involved - I just wanted someone attractive to dance with, to laugh with and share a kiss at the end of the night. I was also trying to get my confidence back. We all had a fantastic time and I was quite sorry when the week came to an end. On arriving back at Gatwick on the 2nd of January we vowed to do it all again at the end of the year, somewhere different.

I continued my studies on a regular basis but didn't let it interfere with my social life anymore. I found it was quite beneficial to resume my studying after the odd nights and days off – I was more refreshed and was able to focus better. Mum and Dad went on holidays without me which was a good sign - they obviously didn't feel the need to watch my every move any longer. I went to Paris with them for the occasional long weekend but that was it.

Not long after our holiday in Spain, Cindy, the receptionist from work announced her marriage. She had first met Adam a couple of months before our holiday. Once she was back from Spain they became an item. He proposed on Valentine's Day and the wedding was planned for August. I felt quite honoured when she asked me to be a bridesmaid along with Gemma our office manager. We eagerly accepted and with only six months until the nuptials it was back and forth to the seamstress every two or three weeks, shopping for the right sandals and hair accessories and a trial run at the hairdressers. It was a busy time for us and Cindy's excitement was infectious. I felt quite envious at times. The wedding came and went. Cindy had looked so radiant, pretty and happy. I was pleased for her. Gemma and I didn't look too bad either. There was a weird moment when Cindy threw her bouquet into the eager crowd of waiting singles. I stood and watched, totally bemused, an innocent bystander, at all the young ladies and their eagerness for the exquisite, airborne blooms and berries, to fall into their grasp. When the flowers, which hit me on the forehead, landed in my arms and knocked off my headband in the process, there were howls of laughter along with some jealous mutterings from the wannabe brides.

As we all stood and watched the classic Rolls Royce, adorned with the old boots and tin cans as was tradition, pull away from the Majestic Hotel, Gemma whispered in my ear,

"That's one less for our holiday to Tenerife. We're down to five now. So don't you go off and fall in love will you?"

I widened my eyes in horror.

"I'm off men, Gemma, so that's not bloody likely to happen."

Christmas came around again along with the chaos that the British weather had been causing since early November. After a quiet but pleasant Christmas day with my parents Boxing Day morning soon arrived. The pre-booked mini-cab picked me up at 11am (after Gemma) then after collecting Nina, Gillian and Janet, our other friends, it was Gatwick here we come. We had yet another good holiday together doing exactly the same things that we did in Spain the previous year, along with two or three bits of excitement that we could have done without. Gillian left her handbag in a bar one night and on returning there to look for it, found that it was gone - nobody had handed it in. Her credit cards had been in there and she managed to call the card companies to get the cards cancelled and before her account had been used. Fortunately she hadn't taken too much cash out with her that night but obviously she was upset. Nina, despite protecting her very pale skin with a high factor protection *and* avoiding spending too long in the sun, still managed to get quite badly burned. We all attended the hospital emergency clinic with her and sat around for four hours before she was even attended to.

Then there was me. I was doing my forty lengths one morning while the pool was fairly quiet when some stupid kid, not looking where he was going, dive-bombed into the pool and straight onto my back. I seemed to be under the water for ages, panicking and gasping for breath, but I finally managed to surface. I was laid on the poolside in shock and in absolute agony with my back while a small crowd gathered around. The parents of the kid, sat on the opposite side of the pool, were glowering over at me with looks that implied, how dare I be in the pool when their little boy was having some fun, or stupid woman, it's her own fault. Serves her right for getting in the way! My back ached badly for a couple of days but thankfully there was no lasting damage.

We still managed to have plenty of fun and like all holidays it came to an end all too soon and we were back at Gatwick again. I wondered how many of us would be holidaying together the following December.

CHAPTER 7

I took a week's holiday from work just before I was about to sit my final exams. I knew I would have the house to myself during the day and it would be peaceful for my final round of studying. Dad was very busy at work and Mum was out most days doing more voluntary work than she could really cope with. I studied hard and for long hours. I concentrated mainly on the elements where I knew my weaknesses lay. I read, re-read, made a list of the key points and then focused on letting them sink in. By the Wednesday night I felt like my head was in overload and I was in need of some time out. I told my parents I would be taking some time off on the Thursday. My father asked if I would like to visit his office for a few hours to check out some new design software package that had recently been installed on all their computers. He was particularly excited about it and as I hadn't been to his office for years he thought it would make a pleasant change for me. I agreed to a visit just to keep him happy and told him I would be there for 11am.

As I'd pulled into the car park and parked my Mazda, I was aware that I was being watched and not just from one window. Dad had obviously made all his staff aware of my visit and they were all waiting to catch a glimpse of the boss's daughter - most of them for the first time. I was disappointed to find that only two of his original staff remained - Dorothy, his aging secretary and Graham, the financial controller who was also heading towards his sixties. To bring me up to speed Dad gave me a guided tour of the office. So much had changed since my last visit (which had been before I went off to Uni) and he introduced me to all the staff that I didn't know en route. Fifteen minutes later and once we had sat down in his office, Dorothy provided us with coffee and biscuits and Dad gave me a demo of the new software as promised – it was way over my head but I tried to show an interest. He was expecting Anthony, a staff member, back from a business meeting around 12.30pm, and as they would be going out for a spot of lunch Dad invited me to go along too, or I should really say he insisted.

Anthony had been a new recruit just before Dad had his heart attack and five years on he was the marketing director - and Dad's right hand man. It was 12.15pm when he knocked on the office door and stuck his head around realising that it wasn't closed properly,

"Is it okay for me to come in, Ken?" he spotted me sipping at my coffee and winked "I can come back if…" Ginger hair and green eyes. Definitely not my type!

"Come in, Tony, yes."

I did a quick appraisal as he came towards me to shake hands – smartly dressed, nothing spectacular but certainly not unattractive. I detected a hint of cockiness about him.

"Let me introduce you both – this is my daughter Helen…Helen, this is, Tony Pawson." He shook my hand firmly (too confidently in my opinion) and smiled.

"Pleased to meet you, Helen. I've heard so much…your father never stops…" he nodded as Dad cut in,

80

"Of course I don't stop, Tony. I'm a doting Dad." he chuckled as Tony still kept hold of my hand.

"Glad to meet you too Anthony," I uttered, easing my hand away, "though I can honestly say that Dad hasn't spoken of you much. Probably because Mum doesn't like him talking about work at home – she blames it for his heart attack." and I gave Dad a quick wink.

"Helen's joining us for lunch – shall we get going?" I had a feeling I was going to regret coming to Dad's office and joining them for lunch.

Thirty minutes later at their favourite gastro pub, with lunch ordered and a gin and tonic in hand, we sat down at a table situated in a large bay window. Whether he'd wanted to hear it or not, Dad gave Anthony a detailed biography of my life since birth. There were a few cringe-worthy moments for me but Anthony was clearly enthralled and smiled across at me from time to time when Dad paused in his story-telling for a few seconds.

Anthony had requested our first order of drinks be put on the bill so I wondered what on earth Dad was doing getting up to go to the bar for drinks when the waitress would soon be bringing the food – he could have ordered direct from her when the food was served. He wasn't being my idea of subtle! Even Anthony was amused as he made a comment,

"I think he's giving us some time together, Helen. Don't be surprised if when the barman has put the drinks on the bar, Ken will pay a visit to the toilet – to give us even more time alone."

It struck me how well he seemed to know my father. Either that or they'd gone through this before. Maybe Dad had tried fixing Anthony up before, in a similar way. It made my suspicious.

"Okay, I say let's play him at his own game. You start staring around in the opposite direction to me, I'll start searching through my handbag or sending a text - no talking, let's make it look awkward."

Sure enough, just as Anthony predicted, we watched as Dad made his way from the bar and over towards the corridor where the toilets were situated. We had a very brief conversation about how my studies were progressing and he asked if I had any long term plans for my future. He also enquired as to whether I intended to stay at the Hopkins Partnership or search for pastures new. That was where the conversation came to an abrupt end as Anthony, with a better view of the toilet door, mouthed

"He's on his way." I quickly grabbed my handbag and started shuffling through it, making a determined effort to look stony faced. I chanced a quick glance at Anthony, who was doing a sterling job of looking disinterested.

I couldn't resist commenting once Dad was back at our table,

"Dad, didn't you go to the bar to get drinks? You've come back without them."

"What? Oh…I'll go…."he stammered "I thought you two would be busy getting to know one another?"

Anthony's turn next, "Ken, we…um…well…I'm not sure that Helen's sufficiently enamoured with me. I seem to be…boring her."

It was hilarious - watching Dad's face as he stood open-mouthed, looking in disbelief first at Anthony, then back and forth between us both. A quick look at Anthony confirmed that he was struggling to stifle the laugh that was trying hard to fight its way out. Only seconds separated the guffaws that escaped from us both a minute later and Dad's expression remained one of disbelief, still open-mouthed trying to understand what the big joke was.

"What's…what is this? What's so hilarious?" he pleaded, trying to understand. The waitresses were approaching with our order.

"Sit down, Dad, we'll explain while we eat."

"We know what you're trying to do, Ken – to act like you're a dating agency. We might not like each other. Did you consider that?" asked Anthony. Dad emphatically denied the accusation and tried to convince us both, and perhaps himself, that his invitation for me to come to his office was strictly to offer a change of scenery and routine – a break from studying and home.

"So why the dinner invite?" I demanded "Surely after Anthony's business meeting this morning you have things to discuss. You didn't need to ask me to come along." His lips were moving, and I could tell that he was racking his brain for some excuse and he finally managed,

83

"How often do I get the chance to take my daughter for lunch? Tony and I can talk later - after you've gone home."

The lunch was excellent and I understand why they used the place whenever they entertained clients. I had to admit it to myself that it had been a pleasant change. I'd secretly enjoyed Anthony's attention and made a mental note to call into Dad's office a little more often in future.

As we drove back I told Dad that I would just get back in my car and drive home. I sensed a note of disappointment in his voice so I explained that I needed to make a few phone calls. Once we were back at the office car park, they walked me over to the car. After a few more pleasantries Anthony shook my hand, said it had been a pleasure, and as Dad had started to walk away he lowered his voice and asked me out to dinner that coming Saturday night. I hadn't envisaged being asked out that soon. I was delighted but I had to warn him,

"Do me a favour, don't tell Dad – don't give him the satisfaction please. I couldn't bear to see the smugger than smug look on his face for the whole of next week and beyond." He laughed

"Okay, you have my word, Helen." I joined in with his laughter and somehow we managed to arrange a time and place to meet, rather rapidly, so as not to give Dad any satisfaction (or hope) from any lengthy goodbyes on our part.

CHAPTER 8

I couldn't believe how fast the time was passing, probably due to all the studying I'd been doing. I had been dating Anthony for almost six months - *still* without my parents' knowledge. I was a certified chartered accountant at last and the news came as a bigger relief to my parents than to me. They were proud and loved boasting to family and friends. I got the impression that they saw my achievement as a sign of normality - like you have to be normal to pass exams?

My dates with Anthony had been *just* that, dates only – trips to the cinema, meals out, a drive out into the country, and 'Phantom of the Opera' at Her Majesty's. I had refused to get further involved. I had stressed to him that I didn't need any involvement whilst my final days of studying, and the exams, were first and foremost in my mind. No emotional issues, no sexual relationship or anything else that bore the potential to create complications.

With exams well and truly out of the way and qualifications under my belt, Anthony was pushing a little more each week to make our relationship public. More than anything I think he was desperate for my father to know, and to take it to the next level, which I understood to mean he wanted our relationship to become physical.

"So what are we going to do then," he asked, "about telling your parents? Do I casually mention at the office that we have been seeing each other? Or should we do it together - go back to your parents' house one night and just tell them?" I hadn't expected him to push the issue this soon, so I hadn't even considered the question of telling my parents. I supposed I would have to meet Anthony's parents as well at some stage.

"Let me give it some thought for a while, Anthony."

"Whatever you decide to do I am happy to go along with it, Helen. I just think it's time they knew."

He was right of course and I felt a little embarrassed at having been so secretive where parents were concerned. The conversation turned to other things as we dined that evening but by the time we left the restaurant I had made my decision.

"I'm telling my parents tonight when I get home. It will be better coming from me."

"Okay! What do you think your Dad will say?" he was eager to know.

"Not much! He was trying to get us together anyway so what could he possibly say?"

Two hours later I got my answer. My parents were happy, especially Dad. He hadn't even been that shocked to learn how long we had been seeing each other. He'd thought it was more than a coincidence that Anthony's mood around the office had changed dramatically since the day I had joined them both for lunch. He had also been further suspicious when people in the office kept asking Anthony why he was on a high and he'd been deliberately evasive and avoided any further questions.

"Things are good – that's it really." as he shrugged his shoulders dismissively.

"He's a good guy, darling. I'm really pleased. Excellent prospects - he's going to be running the business for me when I decide I'm ready for part retirement. I trust him with the business and I trust him to look after you."

It worried me, listening to him, and my tummy started churning. What he'd said about Anthony, it sounded like he was giving me the eligible bachelor talk, telling me what good prospects Anthony had. We'd spent such short periods of time together I didn't even know if we were sufficiently compatible.

"It's early days, Dad. We've only been dating up to now. I like him a lot and he's keen on me too but let's just wait and see."

Mum wanted to meet Anthony and she couldn't wait. She got a shopping list started – and invited him to a dinner party for just the four of us the following weekend. She was keen to make a good impression when he met her. I felt that Anthony might have preferred something a little less formal, like popping in to say hello for half an hour when he took me home one night but he seemed quite pleased that Mum was going to such trouble for him.

The evening arrived and the dinner party went very well. Anthony was his usual charming self. Mum went a little over the top trying to make him feel welcome and endlessly fussing. Dad talked business whenever he could manage to get a word in for Mum bombarding Anthony with her never ending questions about his family. He took me to meet his parents a couple of weeks later, we were in their house for just over an hour and other than nodding their heads at me and a grudgingly grunt of a greeting, I was ignored for the most part. I didn't take it too personally and told myself they were probably shy when it came to meeting people.

Meeting the parents was the proper start for our relationship – it was out in the open at last. Days later we slept together for the first time. We got engaged within six months and planned the wedding for eleven months later.

We both had fairly small families so the majority of the guests were my friends from work and Anthony's (and Dad's) friends from work. I invited some friends from badminton, and Anthony invited his friends from the golf club. Cindy and Gemma from the office were my bridesmaids, but as Cindy was six months pregnant the seamstress made a much looser version of the figure hugging navy dress that Gemma wore. They both looked stunningly beautiful as they watched me step into my bridal gown in our suite at the hotel. We had picked a top class licensed hotel as the venue for the civil ceremony, and we also had the wedding breakfast and evening reception there. We'd chosen the civil ceremony because we are both non-believers.

Dad was proud as he walked me down the aisle and I felt such love for Anthony as we said our vows. A love I had not expected to feel again for any man after Gavin. I was the epitome of the happy blushing bride. I had flushed with embarrassment at being the centre of attention, as Anthony, and then Dad, had made their very witty and lovely remarks. Dad had also used that well-worn expression about gaining a son, but I couldn't help but think when he said it that he had already regarded Anthony as a surrogate son before we had even been introduced. It was the perfect wedding day.

One small matter that bothered me was the distance that Anthony's parents seemed to be keeping. Not once throughout the whole day did they offer their congratulations to the pair of us, nor was there any polite chitchat or fun to be had with them as we posed for the group photos. It seemed like Eileen, his Mum, didn't care much for me and his Dad, John, wouldn't dare to like me.

On the Sunday morning we left for a honeymoon in Vegas -Anthony's choice. Dad drove us over to Gatwick and, as he left us at the drop off point with our luggage, he gave me a big bear hug.

"You looked beautiful yesterday, Helen. I was proud to be your father." His eyes filled with tears as he turned away and got back in the car.

I soon discovered why Anthony had been eager to honeymoon in Vegas – the casinos. He had never gambled before in his life, other than the occasional horse race like the Grand National and the Epsom Derby. Many of his friends who had holidayed in Vegas had been expressing their enthusiasm for the casinos - how it had been addictive for them, magical - the click of the chips, the constant supply of alcohol to those playing the machines, blackjack, other card games, and roulette wheels.

We fell into a daily routine. Anthony was exceptionally loving and attentive throughout the honeymoon. We made love every morning and explored the sights and attended some shows in the afternoons. We dined early each evening before visiting the casinos so that Anthony could indulge in his new found passion. I occasionally played a few of the machines but I was cautious, setting myself an affordable limit and once I reached it I gave up and was content to sit watching Anthony's game play.

He had also started off very cautiously, but having had some decent wins in the first few days he started getting reckless, gambling with higher stakes and not quitting while he was ahead. I panicked at times as I watched him use his winnings as his next stake.

Whilst I had no desire to spoil his fun, I was worried that he was gambling with our joint savings – savings which we had intended to keep for furnishing our new home in Windsor, which we had been able to afford only because of the sizeable deposit given to Anthony by his parents. As it turned out I needn't have worried – by the time the honeymoon was over, the balance of our savings account had increased by $14,500. Whilst it was nice to suddenly have a boost to our finances, I didn't take much comfort from it. He was already talking about visiting a casino in London, and having already seen the look on his face as he played, I was concerned that he had become addicted.

CHAPTER 9

Other than my concerns about Anthony's new found love of gambling, the first eight months of our marriage were almost perfect. Anthony continued to be loving and attentive and our new house had been beautifully furnished throughout that time. We laughed a lot. We went out two or three times a week together. I continued with the badminton and Anthony went to golf, sometimes with my Dad and other times with his friends. I started taking more of an interest in cooking and discovered that I quite enjoyed experimenting.

Anthony was always enthusiastic about the meals I prepared, so I bought more cookery books. Dad started a herb garden for me as Anthony was hopeless at anything that involved DIY or gardening. Once every two or three months we held small dinner parties. I quite enjoyed being hostess and considering that I had done very little cooking before getting married (university life had been mainly takeaways or nothing more adventurous than beans on toast and pot noodles) I was proud at some of the culinary delights that I managed to serve up.

The moment I had been dreading arrived soon enough. It was mid week and we had finished our evening meal. Anthony had just complimented me on one of my Indian concoctions. He had been too enthusiastic, too nice about a meal that I had thought to be mediocre and I sensed I was being softened up. First - the suggestion.

"Darling, should we have another dinner party on Saturday night?" he asked. I was surprised at his suggestion as we'd only had one recently. Much as I enjoyed them, it usually involved me spending the whole day in the kitchen. I found them quite wearing so I didn't relish the thought of another so soon.

"Oh, Anthony, do we have to? I've just recovered from the last one." His smile faded slightly, so I caved in a little.

"Who were you thinking of inviting?" I knew it was coming, it had to!

"My parents!" I felt my face drop...and he saw it.

"What's the matter, Helen? Darling, they haven't even seen our house yet. And you haven't seen them since the wedding – it's nearly eight months!"

I felt cross with him. It was like an accusation he'd thrown at me. I wanted to ask him what I'd done wrong to them. It wasn't my fault they hadn't been to visit, I'd asked them to. Didn't he understand that? He was waiting for me to say something...so I told him.

"Well...it's just that I have invited them to visit us on quite a few occasions now. When your Mum has rang you here...and you've not been in. I honestly don't think they'll come for dinner, Anthony. To be honest with you, I don't think they like me." His eyes widened in surprise...and then he looked stung. I instantly regretted my words.

"Don't be ridiculous, darling, of course they like you. You're imagining things. What on earth makes you think that? I'll call them tomorrow and ask."

I felt a sinking feeling in the pit of my stomach as I gave him a nod to say 'okay then.' Crap! Not only did his parents not like me, I didn't like them. I was going to be mortified if they accepted Anthony's invitation.

I had been home from work half an hour and had our evening meal well under way when I heard Anthony's car pull into the drive. I could see him from the kitchen window as he opened the rear passenger door to get his laptop. He turned around and waved, big smile on his face and I hoped the reason for that was that he'd had a good day at work.

"Sweetheart, you'd better get your menu sorted out, they're coming, Mum and Dad - I told you they would." he blurted as he came into the kitchen.

"Oh! Okay, that's not a problem." I managed, trying to put what I really wanted to say to the back of my mind…and wishing I was half way around the world. I finished preparing the vegetables but my enthusiasm for that evening's meal had gone. All I could think about was how much I was dreading seeing his parents again.

When we finally sat down to eat, Anthony had sensed my mood change,

"Darling, you've gone very quiet, what's bothering you? Don't you want to make an effort for my parents?" Me? Again! I was fighting to stay calm and wondering why he couldn't see what was staring him in the face and had been since he'd first introduced us.

"No, no, it's not that." I lied, "I just don't have a clue what sort of things your parents eat. You know - their likes and dislikes?"

"Right, well then, you should have said. Let's see – no fish, no pasta, nothing too spicy. You'll be fine. I'll trust your judgement on the food. I'll buy the wine tomorrow."

No getting out of this one then. My worst nightmare was about to happen. I felt as if I had been backed into a corner. I searched my mind for a way out and couldn't see one. Anthony was looking at me expectantly – for what? I didn't know!

"You had better cast your eyes over the menu when I get it planned then. I'd hate to serve up something that they don't like. Maybe there's something they dislike that you have forgotten to mention?" He appeared deep in thought, eyes looking to the ceiling for an answer, finally

"No, I don't think so."

I picked up a handful of recipe books and took them into the lounge so I could browse as I drank my glass of wine. It wasn't out of eagerness to plan the menu, but more an excuse to avoid speaking to Anthony, who was seemingly deliriously happy that his Mum and Dad were coming for dinner. I really didn't trust myself to speak lest I reveal my true feelings about his parents. Before we went up to bed I presented my proposed menu to him for his approval. Glamorgan sausages with red onion chutney and a small side salad for starters. For the main course I had selected lamb shanks, vegetables and potato gratin and dessert would be white chocolate cheesecake with fresh raspberries on the side. I also planned to serve a blackberry and elderflower sorbet to freshen the palate between each course.

"They've all been tried and tested at some of our other dinner parties, darling." I told Anthony "Do you think the menu's alright then? I don't want to try anything new in case I make a mess of things."

"This menu will be fine – trust me. They'll love it." I wasn't so bloody sure about that.

Anthony went out to welcome them as their car pulled into the drive. I tried to peer out of the kitchen window without being seen by them. (I had always been brought up to believe that it is good manners when you get invited out to dinner, to take a gift along – a bottle of wine, flowers or even some chocolates.) I noticed they were both empty-handed.

I walked over to the door to greet them as they entered the kitchen and held my hand out,

"Eileen, John, nice to see you again."

"Hello." she grunted, poker-faced as usual as she glanced at my proffered hand and walked straight past. John put his hand out, fleetingly touched mine and quickly let go again. Hell fire, did he think he was going to bloody catch something from me if he held on too long? I looked over at Anthony to see if he had noticed their reactions towards me – he had. He shrugged his shoulders at me and asked them both if they wanted a glass of wine. Eileen said she'd have a glass but quickly followed with,

"Your father won't want one, he's driving." (Like he had a choice in the matter!)

"Would you like a tour of the house, Eileen?" I offered politely.

"I can show myself around. You get back to heating the ready meal." She walked off leaving me totally flabbergasted. I heard her footsteps on the stairs seconds later. Again I looked at Anthony for support and mouthed the words at him 'get back to heating the meal up?' He mouthed back

'Shhh!' and shook his head. I gave him one of my looks and stomped back to the kitchen. So he was going to let his mother get away with everything. Maybe *he* would, but I was definitely not going to!

They took their seats in the dining room half an hour later and I served up the starter before sitting down myself. Eileen stared at her plate a few seconds too long, looked over at Anthony and asked,

"What on earth is *this*?" I just couldn't resist,

"Why don't you ask me, Eileen? Anthony doesn't really remember, and it was me who did the cooking." She didn't even look at me.

"They are called Glamorgan sausages (I pointed), and that is red onion chutney" I said (pointing again), indicating next the few lettuce leaves and cherry tomato, "and that's a bit of salad on the side."

I could feel Anthony's eyes burning into the side of my face and I didn't give a damn!

"Is it cheese?"

"Yes. Caerphilly."

"Cheese gives me a headache."

"Forgive me, Eileen." I said in my sickliest of voices, "I never realised." I caught a disapproving look in her direction from her husband. The main course also met with disapproval,

"I do think lamb is so terribly fatty. We hardly ever eat it."

I chose to ignore the comment, carried on eating, and listened to her continued, scathing remarks to Anthony about the décor in our bedroom, our choice of leather suite in the lounge, and how we rushed in to marriage far too soon. She pushed her food around the plate as she talked and I noticed the intent on her face. She had no desire to eat anything that I had cooked and furthermore, she was hell bent on insulting me at every given opportunity.

I could see that John was starting to feel very uncomfortable with her behaviour - and perhaps a little sorry for me. He ate everything on his plate and complimented me on the menu, despite the glower he got from Eileen. He was interested in, and asked me intelligent questions about my work and badminton, which he apparently, had been pretty good at in his younger days. The guy was actually quite good company, pleasant to talk to. I was a genius at being able to hold a conversation with one person and pick up on things being discussed in a second conversation, and sure enough, Eileen carried on her cynicism.

As I served up dessert and placed Eileen's in front of her I couldn't stop my sarcasm surfacing,

"Eileen, if the dessert is not to your liking I can get you some ice-cream from the freezer – something that *I've* not prepared." It was a waste of time, the woman was so thick-skinned. I was by that point avoiding all eye contact with Anthony, and John must have had some warning looks from Eileen while I had been in the kitchen as he became very quiet again. I ate my cheesecake and decided I had had enough tension for one night. Standing up, I announced,

"Do excuse me, folks, I have a headache and I'm going to bed. It has been nice to see you again, John."

"Too much *wine*, darling?" Anthony asked me sarcastically.

"No…it must be the cheese in the Glamorgan sausages. Good night!" and feigning calmness and serenity I walked out and left them.

I heard their car pull out of the drive fifteen minutes later, which was rapidly followed by Anthony's footsteps thundering up the stairs. He shoved the bedroom door wide open, hitting the chest of drawers behind it and pointed at me accusingly,

"YOU" he shouted loudly "have embarrassed me tonight, Helen. How dare you treat my mother in that manner?" I had calmed down and was ready for his onslaught.

"So it is just fine then – the way she has been trying to belittle me all evening? You did not find anything wrong with the things that she said to insult your wife, Anthony? That is acceptable is it – for her to speak to me the way that she did? Does my father talk down to you? Does he insult you at every given opportunity? He *never* would do that though, he has better manners, and at least he *likes* you. But if he didn't, I would still defend you, Anthony. That is what a husband and wife should do after all – support each other. *She* hates me! I think your dad likes me but he has to do *her* bidding. I feel sorry for him." I'd struck a nerve. The truth hurt! He was beyond furious. Unable to defend his mother further he shouted,

"Fuck you, Helen!" and with that, he slammed the bedroom door and was gone. For the first time since we married, I woke up alone the next morning. Anthony had slept in one of the guest bedrooms for the night.

CHAPTER 10

We soon got over the disastrous dinner party with Anthony's parents and I resolved that until Eileen started treating me with more respect there would be no more dinner invitations to our house. I genuinely tried to make more of an effort with them. I visited them in their home with Anthony a few times after that night but there was no imminent thaw about to occur in the foreseeable future - years with a bit of luck! Rather than insult me anymore she reverted back, as she had done before we got married, punishing me by totally ignoring me. She made no eye contact whatsoever or any attempt to include me in conversation. Why put myself through it, I thought. I gradually started building a wide selection of excuses to avoid the monthly visits.

Our life carried on in pretty much the same vein as it had before. We still laughed a lot and had fun but something *had* changed since that night – our love-making. I don't suppose it could be called love-making anymore. We were having *sex* instead. Fucking! Sex with a vulgarity, a particular crudeness to it – and strangely I loved it. We were both indulging in acts that were for our individual sexual gratification only - rather than one mutual act done in a loving, as one, sensual manner. It was as if we were taking out some mutual anger on each other – wild! But no less enjoyable!

We had never discussed having children. Anthony never gave the impression that he wanted to be a father, and to me it wasn't the be all and end all of a marriage. If it happened it happened, but if it didn't I was certainly not going to lose any sleep over it. Mum and Dad would have quite enjoyed playing the doting grandparents to, maybe a little boy, since they had not been blessed with a son. They never asked me if we had plans for a family and I didn't have the heart to tell them that it might never happen if they ever did drop some hints. I wasn't the maternal type. Other people's babies scared me…and the thought of the overwhelming responsibility for the upbringing of a child absolutely terrified me.

Within that first year, as a result of the honeymoon in Vegas, Anthony had visited casinos on three or four occasions with some friends of his and his luck had held up well. His risk-taking soon ventured down a different route however, when he started dabbling in the stock market. I was thankful that I had my own bank account, despite his pushing for a joint account, and that was the way it was going to stay. I didn't trust his luck to hold out, or, unlike my father, his judgement.

Over a four or five month period I also became suspicious about Anthony's drinking habits. He was arriving home from work at his usual time but when he walked in the house he occasionally seemed unsteady on his legs. I could often smell whisky on his breath even though he'd had to drive five miles home from the office. Whether he was leaving work early for a late afternoon session or secretly drinking in the office, I didn't have a clue and I didn't fancy a confrontation. I'd had enough of those already given the short length of time we had been married. It didn't even stop at the unknown amount of alcohol he'd consumed before coming home. He downed a bottle of wine each night with our evening meal and as a result he'd fall asleep on the settee and I would go up to bed alone. He very rarely joined me on those nights, remaining semi-comatose in the same position until morning came around again. I worried about him…and our marriage.

Our rude and crude sex sessions were happening less and less due to his drinking, our conversations with very brief - to the point and occurred at meal times only. Weekends were only slightly better. It was an advantage that he didn't work on Saturdays and Sundays, so at least it enabled me to try to talk and find out what was troubling him. He was evasive about what his problems were so I asked if it was to do with me. He insisted that our marriage wasn't causing him concern but refused to say what it was. He denied drinking too much and said there wasn't a problem at work. (I resolved to speak to Dad and ask if the business was doing alright.) He was adamant that I had done nothing to upset him. I just couldn't get to the bottom of things. All I knew was that our problems had started not long after the disastrous dinner party with his parents and things were just escalating. It was worrying me. I didn't feel loved by him anymore. I felt more like a possession than a wife and lover, and to me at least, it felt like our marriage was over.

CHAPTER 11

Ted Hopkins had arranged a meeting for me with a prospective new client, a limited company whose offices were about forty miles away. The structural steel firm had struggled to stay afloat during the early nineties recession that had seen so many casualties within the industry. The managing director had made redundancies, ran the place on a shoestring and kept the overheads to a minimum. He had priced jobs at break-even just to get the work and keep the place ticking over. Each month of every year since, had been a struggle. He had re-mortgaged his home and injected more cash to keep the business afloat – staying focused on his determination not to close the doors. His gamble had eventually paid off - for the last two years he had gradually needed to recruit more staff and had a forward order book worth more than six and a half million pounds.

I arrived at the office of Martin Farrer Structural Fabrications Limited with fifteen minutes to spare before our twelve o'clock meeting. His receptionist, Julia, provided me with a cappuccino and introduced me to the accounts office staff before taking me along to Martin's office and introducing us.

After a business lunch that lasted two hours, I made arrangements for the company's first audit before setting out again for the forty mile journey home. As the journey had taken me in the opposite direction to work Ted had told me not to bother returning to the office and to go straight home.

I was surprised to see Anthony's car in the drive when I pulled in. It was extremely rare for him to arrive home before me and it was only just past three o'clock. I wondered if he was ill. Quietly entering the house in case he was asleep, I dumped my handbag on the kitchen worktop and went through to the lounge.

I felt my body sag and the most unpleasant feeling of déjà vu at the scene in our lounge. My eyes and my head struggled to accept what was there before me. Anthony was reclining on the settee, trousers around his ankles. A young man was knelt on the floor fondling Anthony's balls and bent over giving him a very enthusiastic blow job. So engrossed he didn't realise I was there. Two pairs of denims and boxers had been thrown into the armchair. Anthony looked rat-arsed. I don't know where I summoned my self-control from. I could feel vomit rising into my throat and my hands were trembling but somehow I held it together. Without any screaming and shouting, or being predictable, I casually walked over to the settee, offered my hand to the lad and said,

"Pleased to meet you! I see you've met the prick." He jerked at hearing my voice and dropped my husband's scrotum as if he'd just been bitten. His mouth gaped and Anthony's cock went from seven inches to shrivelled-up slug in seconds as it fell from the lad's mouth.

"Helen…I…I…it's not…" stammered my twat of a husband.

"What it seems, Anthony?"

The kid was almost dressed and trying to get past me to make a quick exit through the kitchen. I felt sorry for him. He was barely in his early twenties. Anthony had brought him here so I didn't feel any malice towards him.

"Did he pay you, love?" I asked him "How much did he promise you?"

Staying in his way to block his escape I reached the kitchen before him and snatched my purse from the worktop. The lad could hardly get a word out,

"It's...it's ....okay. Sorry." I thrust five twenties at him. "I hope this covers a cab back to...Take it." He looked me in the eyes and after a few seconds hesitation he took the money from me. As the lad closed the back door Anthony came into the kitchen behind me,

"How...how much have you given him?" I was battling to stop the Gavin and Bobbie scene that had started replaying in my mind, wondering if there was ever to be an escape from it. And that's all Anthony could utter. I turned to face him.

"A hundred...you owe me a hundred pounds, you fucking arsehole!" I almost laughed at him. His eyes had all but popped from their sockets.

"Twenty is what I agreed with him. What the fuck do you think you're doing giving him a hundred fucking quid and expecting it back from me?"

"He deserves it for having to put up with all this...this...shambles! Call it embarrassment money - he's not much more than a kid! What are you playing at, Anthony? You were married for fuck's sake!"

My earlier calm was dissipating. My hands were starting to shake again – the shock kicking in! The shock hit Anthony like a sledgehammer as well – what I'd just said to him had hit home.

"Helen…were…? What…your Dad…? I…!"

"Don't worry about your precious position, Anthony!" I screamed, my anger building with each passing second "I'm not even going to waste my time telling Dad. He thinks the sun shines out of your every orifice – Mr Perfect!" then, "I…this is what I…we'll do…we carry on as normal. But from now on we lead separate lives, Anthony. My parents are not to know about this. Just don't you ever come near me!"

"Babe…Helen…I love you…!"

I felt hurt…again…always hurting. I wanted to cry. The tears were threatening and I spat my next words out with such venom,

"Love me? You have not loved me for ages, Anthony. I've never felt loved since your parents came for dinner. It's a marriage of convenience for you. It lets your parents think you're…. that you're...normal! You're anything but fucking normal! You couldn't even defend your wife against your mother! You fuck around with…rent boys…and expect me to believe you love me? You don't love me! You haven't made love to me in months….you've fucked me! Love?" He stood there, mouth wide open, looking…not sorry…but worried…and I could almost read his thoughts. What he was showing was not concern for me… he was worried for himself…and his position in my father's business.

"Helen…your Dad…I…" he stammered.

"I won't be telling him! And let's get one thing straight - I'm doing this for my father's benefit, Anthony, not yours!"

There was nothing I would have loved more than to be able to let my father know what an utter bastard Anthony had turned out to be, but over the past couple of months Dad had been very quiet again. He never complained or said he was feeling ill but there was something troubling him. He did worry about his health and fitness. I know Mum had asked him to cut back on the hours he was putting in at work, which he had done. I trusted that we would be seeing an improvement over the following weeks due to his part time hours and I didn't want anything to spoil that.

CHAPTER 12

The problems that Anthony and I were having in our marriage (if it could be deemed as such any more) prompted me to start getting out and about more with the girls from the office. I hadn't been to badminton for the last six months or so and it felt good to be playing again and get some physical activity back into my life. I joined Nina, Janet and Gillian on the Saturdays out again, but we tried to do something different this time. Once a month it was shopping, but on the others our outings could involve anything from a drive into the country for a walk, or a pub lunch, to a cinema trip and art galleries.

It made life interesting and was a vast improvement to the hanging around at home, watching Anthony recover from yet another hangover and having to listen to a thousand reasons why he should never have married me. Shit, I couldn't believe what I was having to listen to on a daily basis – I wasn't the one paying bloody rent boys, and gambling and drinking our life away! I had given in trying to converse with him, to find out why he had changed and was treating me in this way. I didn't want to know anymore. It had gone beyond that. Though as far as anyone else knew, things were still perfect between us. There was nothing to be gained from disclosing the harsh reality to my friends and colleagues, or my parents.

On one such Saturday (our monthly shopping trip) we stayed in the city much longer than normal and hailed a taxi to take us to Covent Garden where we sauntered around for half an hour trying to agree on a restaurant. It had been a fun filled afternoon (although we hadn't actually made any purchases other than a few bits and pieces like make-up and hair clips) and none of us were in any particular hurry to get home. Nina's husband was away on business and Gillian and Janet's boyfriends (who were friends) were both in Prague for a stag weekend. I told them that Anthony wouldn't mind me staying out. I went outside to call him (or so they thought). After we'd settled the bill for our meal we roamed around the area looking for a suitable pub (where we could rest our aching feet, park our posteriors and concentrate on getting smashed, for the first time in ages). By the time we reached the Lamb and Flag, we no longer cared,

"This will do, won't it? Nina urged "I need to pee, so it will have to do."

Inside, it was anything but quiet. The place was rapidly filling up and the atmosphere was almost party-like but we managed to find a table in a corner. Janet and I went to the bar to order the first round of drinks and we were immediately surrounded by a group of young men who had clearly been on the drink for a few hours.

"Why don't you young ladies come and join us at our table over there?" one of them asked us. Janet didn't waste any time trying to knock them back.

"Look guys, it's no use trying to hit on us. We're all in relationships, and in fact," she gestured towards me, "she's happily married, and so is Nina." She pointed to where Nina was sat, back to the window. If only she knew the truth.

"Okay then, that put us in our place. Look, come and join us anyway. We're only out to get pissed and have a laugh. Go on, you know you both want to. Go and ask your other two friends. We promise we'll try to keep our hands off you." Janet was looking dubious, and raised her eyebrows, but knowing what awaited me back home, I felt like having some fun.

"What harm can it do, Janet? I'll go and ask Nina and Gillian."

Five minutes later we were sat around the lads' table, all introductions made, and Ed (the gobby one amongst them) had gone to the bar for the next round.

"Come on, ladies, drink up, your second round is here!" he shouted as he approached the table with the tray of drinks for us girls perched precariously on one hand like a waiter. After slopping them down on the table in front of each of us (wrong drinks, order all mixed up), he set off back to the bar to collect the drinks for the six of them.

"Somebody go and help him," Nina suggested. "I don't fancy his chances with six pints." Two of his mates whose names I'd already forgotten went to his assistance.

They were such an assorted bunch (two mechanics, one builder, an IT manager and a plumber, the sixth one being unemployed), the conversation at times was nonsensical, but they were all flirty, fun and harmless. Even Janet, despite her earlier reservations, had managed to relax and enjoy their company. By 11.30pm we were all pissed and singing along with the songs playing on the jukebox. I had let my hair down and was enjoying myself for the first time in… it had been a long time. I can't even remember what time it had got to when Gillian said she had had far too much to drink and was ready to leave, so we made our excuses. The guys gave us all hugs and agreed on how much they had enjoyed our company. When Ed asked us if we had any plans to return there in the near future we broke into fits of laughter and joked on in a silly and flirtatious way, implying…nothing.

Much later, after I'd removed my sandals in the kitchen and as I climbed the stairs to bed, I realised exactly how drunk I was. I was making (what I thought to be) a conscious effort to keep quiet so I wouldn't disturb Anthony as I passed his room. It wouldn't do to wake him up. I couldn't cope with a full on confrontation, the state I was in. I stopped and listened (wobbling) outside his door - all was quiet. After I'd splashed some cold water on my face and brushed my teeth I just flopped onto the bed, unable to stand a moment longer lest I should fall. As my head hit the pillow I drifted off to sleep without even removing my clothes.

Totally unaware of how long I had been sleeping, I was horrified to be awakened by somebody roughly pulling my tights and panties off me in one swift move. How could somebody be in my room? I always bolt my bedroom door…don't I? It all came back to me in a rush, how pissed I had been, how pissed I was still feeling…and then…Anthony rammed his cock up me with the force of a madman and started nipping and squeezing my breasts so hard it was excruciating. I lashed out, laid into his chest with

111

my fists and then slapped at his head. He was causing me tremendous pain, both in my private parts and my belly. I realised I was hurting because I wasn't submissive…my inner muscles were tense and I was fighting his every powerful stab at me. He was dodging my blows, but not once did he stop ramming at me with his cock. I squirmed beneath him, trying to wriggle free…away from the violence of his selfish need. I was appalled at what he was doing to me…making me feel trashy, like scum. I was trying to scream out as he continued…to alert anybody who might hear me. Furious, he let go of one of my breasts and slapped his hand firmly across my mouth.

"Shut the fuck up, you stupid bitch…you're my wife!" he snarled. I continued my thrashing at his arms, chest, any part of him that I could reach as I tried to scream back at him.

"This…not…marriage…this…is rape…you bastard!" I managed to mumble to no avail, his hand blocking my words. I'd lost. I didn't have any fight left in me, due to my booze weakened body, and I was hurting - everywhere. He continued fucking me in his raging and violent manner as all I could physically do was lie there and take it and hope it ended soon. I cried, silently. It felt like it would never come to an end. One hand stayed firmly over my mouth. The fingernails of his other hand raked at and dug into my breasts. He threw his head back, fucked me hard and rough, and even harder as his intent to damage me drove him into some obscene pleasure and it brought about his climax. I couldn't bear to look at him and with one hand I pulled a pillow over my face and sobbed into it.

As I felt him pull out his disgusting, dripping cock he laughed,

"You always were a good fuck, Helen. I see that hasn't changed." From within my depths the rage I felt suddenly exploded from me in a final fit of energy and I threw the pillow from me.

"You bastard!" I screamed, and I kicked out at his back, a move I instantly regretted as he turned and slammed his fist into my eye. Once he'd left my room, I slowly made my way towards the door, bolting it this time – as I should have done those few hours earlier.

CHAPTER 13

Not surprisingly, I didn't sleep the rest of that night after Anthony had raped me. I showered, I scrubbed at my body and I sobbed. I lay on the bed breaking my heart and there was no one to care. The people who *would* care couldn't ever know about this. My plans of two years ago for my future were ruined, as they had been for a while. Even though the last few months had been hell for me, I was devastated, and shocked at what Anthony had become. My whole body pained me. I felt dirty in the most horrible way that a woman could – forever tainted…and cheap! I had no reason to feel cheap! I never heard another sound from him. I didn't know where he was, whether he had gone downstairs or back to his bed. I knew I wasn't leaving my room until I was absolutely certain that he had left the house.

Fortunately I didn't have to wait too long. I heard his car pull out of the drive about 9.15. I'd already been tiptoeing around the bedroom, packing a bag. I'd vomited – copiously for the last 2 hours. I was desperate for coffee - something to eat and drink, thinking it might settle my stomach, but I wanted to be out. Just in case he wasn't gone for long, and happened to return before I'd seized the chance to be gone. I grabbed my bag, ran down the stairs and within two minutes of him driving away, I was in my car and pulling out of the drive, screeching tyres as I sped down the street. I headed in the direction of home. Mum and Dad were away for their anniversary – cruising. They'd be somewhere in the middle of the Indian Ocean for three weeks. I wouldn't have

114

wanted to arrive at their house in my physical and emotional state if they had been at home. I would hopefully have plenty of time to sort myself out; they'd been gone only days.

When I arrived at their house and let myself in, I made coffee and some toast and took it upstairs to my old bedroom. I sat on the dressing table stool whilst I drank my coffee - just staring at myself in the mirror. The swelling around my eye and the upper part of my cheek looked angry. The blackness was coming out and I looked a mess. I wasn't only looking at my physical injury. I was inspecting myself, trying to delve deep under my skin. I was looking for a sign - any sign that gave me a reason as to why – why my husband would rape me, hit me, and leave me in this state. What had I ever done to warrant this kind of behaviour from him? Had I really deserved all that I'd got? I couldn't think of anything, but perhaps other people could see something in me that I wasn't able to!

After finishing with my breakfast I lay down on the bed and started thinking about what to do. I couldn't report it to the police. I couldn't put myself through that. Hell, I couldn't put my parents through it. What this could do to my father with his heart problems was not a thought I wanted to dwell on. The only thing I knew for certain was that I could not go in to work looking like this on Monday morning. First thing on the list to do Monday morning, I had to phone Ted.

I had drifted off to sleep at some point and when I woke up it was 4pm. For a few seconds I wondered what I was doing there. Smacked in the face again by reality when the memories returned, a fresh flow of tears rolled. I felt a sudden urge to shower again and I all but tore the clothes from by body. Once under the almost scalding water I frenziedly scrubbed at myself for ages until my skin was almost raw.

All the time I had been in my bedroom, the only item I had managed to get on my agenda was to phone Ted Hopkins the next morning. I was relieved that my parents had a well-stocked freezer. I had no desire to go out for shopping. I didn't want to see the stares and questioning glances from people if they caught a glimpse of my eye. I fixed something to eat and made a point of writing down the items I used from their freezer. I would replace everything like for like before they returned home. I didn't even want them to know I had been staying. Dad hadn't been too well before they'd gone away and I wasn't going to add to their worries.

I think work was behind it, but he always kept things like that from Mum and I. Anthony probably would have been the person to ask if everything was alright at the office, but at the minute I couldn't even contemplate asking him. I would have to go back to our marital home sooner or later but I wasn't relishing the thought. He had never hurt me when he'd been sober before and I'd seen him drunk on plenty of occasions and never been hurt by him, so why was last night any different? Could he have been cross because I had stayed out late and not let him know? I quickly talked myself out of that thought though. He didn't usually give a shit where I was. He didn't communicate with me if he decided he was staying out late and there were many times when he had stayed out all night. I never questioned him anymore, I didn't need to. We were not a couple – it didn't interest me where he was. He usually gave an explanation when I next saw him – like I cared! Since the day I found him with his rent boy in our house, I hadn't bothered. I always told myself that he was probably somewhere in a gay bar searching for his twenty pound blow job.

I tried shutting out my thoughts for the rest of the evening, by pouring myself a glass of wine and putting a film on TV, but whilst looking at the screen the film rolled on unwatched. All I could see was a rape scene repeatedly playing in front of me – with myself as the victim, time and again. I sat in silence, replenishing my glass periodically, carrying on drinking in an attempt to blot out the events of…was it really just hours ago, that same morning? Bleary eyed from drink and my tears, I pulled my legs up onto the settee…and slept.

Gillian answered the phone when I called the office and she wanted to chit chat about Saturday night. I snuffled and sniffled into the mouth piece,

"Listen, Gillian, can you please offer my apologies to Ted? I'm feeling rough. I think I'm getting the flu, I ache all over and I'm really not up to it."

"Gosh yes, you do sound a little snotty, Helen, I hope you feel loads better soon. Oh Hell, we were all out together on Saturday night. I hope you've kept it to yourself, honey, but I'll warn the girls. You get back to bed and stay warm. Dose yourself up." Her obvious concern for my welfare left me feeling guilty for lying, but how could I let them know the true reason for my absence?

"If anybody should want me urgently, Gillian, get them to ring my mobile please. I'm staying at Mum and Dad's, Anthony's away for a few days on business."

"You've done the right thing honey, getting the oldies to look after you - you'll soon be better. Keep us informed. Now, go to bed!" I'd mentioned a few weeks back that my parents were going on an anniversary holiday, but she'd assumed…I didn't correct her.

The only reason I sounded snotty was I was crying yet again. I hated lying to Gillian and the other girls. Well no, I wasn't really lying to them. I was being economical with the truth. They thought I was happily married and for the time being, there was no reason for them to know anything else. They would be horrified if they could see the state of me. I stayed off work for the full week and when Saturday morning came around, I thought I would pop back home to get some more of my make-up, and some clothes that would be more suitable for my return to work on Monday. Anthony would be at the golf course so I wouldn't have him to contend with. I wasn't too concerned about his car being in the drive when I pulled up. He was picked up by one of his friends every other week, and it was clearly not Anthony's week to drive. Letting myself in through the back door I could hear music, maybe from the television. I'd hoped he wasn't going to be in and my whole body stiffened. I was genuinely scared of coming face to face with him – my rapist.

It was like a scene I remembered from a movie I'd watched years ago. Three motionless figures - two were laid in uncomfortable looking positions on the lounge floor, one of them a man wearing nothing but a tee-shirt. Another was sprawled full length on the settee, his mouth wide open emitting gurgling noises in the back of his throat. As my eyes adjusted to the semi-darkness I could see that one of the people on the floor was female, bare-breasted, her skirt up around her waist and her genitals on display. I was livid. I stepped over them and flung the lounge curtains wide open, ignoring their reactions. Daylight streaming in, my eyes were drawn to the coffee table. There were some specks of white powder on the glass top which vaguely indicated where the cocaine had been in lines. A pack of drinking straws was opened, half a dozen of which were scattered, bent up on the floor. Three or four bottles of various spirits were half empty. Beer and lager cans were strewn around. A loud snore from him drew my eyes back to the guy on the settee. It was Anthony's friend Paul, a fellow golfer.

The moans and groans of his house guests didn't deter me from stomping up the stairs to see just how many had been partying last night. First port of call was my bedroom and I prayed that nobody had been screwing in, or been sick in it. A quick glance revealed it had been untouched since he'd raped me in there the previous week. I closed the door on it quickly, needing to focus on what I was doing next and to evade those memories that sought to engulf me once more. Opening the door of the spare next, again to semi-darkness, I could just make out two male and one female form spread-eagled across the double bed. All were in various stages of undress and seemingly dead to the world, either through drink, drugs or a combination of both. There was an open condom packet laid on the bedside cabinet, but the unused condom had fallen to the floor. Perhaps they'd all been incapable of unrolling it onto an erect penis, or maybe there hadn't been an erect penis….which wouldn't surprise judging by the amount of alcohol that had obviously been consumed by them, and that was without taking into account the drug usage.

I didn't bother them with a greeting. I doubted even one of them would have woken from their heavily intoxicated sleep. I slammed the door without a care as to whether I disturbed them or not. Crossing the landing towards Anthony's bedroom I realised that there was nothing that man could do now that would surprise me. When I flung open his door I wasn't even taken aback that he was in bed with two females, both naked and Anthony in the middle, also naked, mouth wide open and snoring loudly. The two girls stirred in their sleep and one of them, short blonde hair and I guess about twentyish, suddenly sat bolt upright.

"Who the hell are you?" she asked in a defensive tone.

"Me? Oh, don't worry about me. I'm only Anthony's wife. Not that it's any concern of yours. We live separate lives." I watched her face waiting for a reaction but there wasn't one. "I would say your biggest worry at the moment is: do you actually know where that dick has been?" I

120

paused a few seconds, giving her time to try and digest my question,

"Yes! That dick!" (I indicated my sleeping husband), "The one that was obviously stuck into the both of you last night?" She raised her eyebrows, starting to wake up a little faster than anyone normally would. I recognized the flash of panic in her eyes. "Shall I tell you where it's been?" I didn't wait for her affirmative before carrying on "Not so many weeks ago that dick was shagging a young man up the arse. Who knows what you might have… just…food for thought!" She leaned across Anthony and poked her friend, who had drifted back to sleep, in the ribs.

"Emma! Emma, come on! Let's get out of here, now! This guy apparently doesn't care…Emma, come on! This is his wife. We need to go, wake up!" Emma was fully alert in no time, panic showing in her eyes also. They both sat on the edge of the bed looking for their clothes in the half light. Anthony was still oblivious. I left them to it and returned to my bedroom. I threw a few clothes into my suit carrier, grabbed a few more toiletries out of the en-suite, and headed back down the stairs. The bodies in the lounge were still comatose, so I passed through to the kitchen, slamming doors behind me in my anger. I grabbed a few favourite tid-bits out of the kitchen cupboards and the fridge and quickly stuffed them in a carrier bag. Before I was finished, Emma and her friend (shagging partner for want of a better word) came tearing through the kitchen…obviously in a rush to get away. They cast me a quick glance before lowering their eyes.

They were going to leave without saying anything so I just couldn't resist.

"Think carefully about who you sleep with in the future girls. No condoms spells unwanted preg…" Emma's friend cut me off mid-sentence,

"We're both on the pill and..." I had to stop her right there, and I jumped in quick.

"Oh, I'm pleased to hear it, I'm sure. What about sexually transmitted diseases; AIDS…HIV? Have you considered those…little matters?" They exchanged stupefied looks and I eased up on them, knowing I had those same matters to attend to. I lowered my voice this time. "I'd get yourselves checked over if I were you. As I said…you don't know where that dick's been."

They cast me one final glance and were gone. I finished my grocery stealing and locked the door behind me. I passed the two girls hurrying further down the street, but I didn't feel it appropriate to offer them a lift anywhere. They'd got themselves into their own mess. Hopefully they would learn something from it.

There was only a slight yellow tinge to my eye by the time I woke up on Monday morning. After I'd applied my make-up nobody would ever know that I'd had a black eye. The staff showed such concern as I walked through reception, accounts and into my own office.

"Are you over the flu, Helen? Are you sure you're going to be okay?" "You should have taken a few days longer." and "You still look a bit peaky pale."

"I'm fine girls…still a little tired but I've been bored. There's only so many chick flicks you

122

can watch…It's been nice to stay there though, with Anthony being away." I had crossed my fingers behind my back as I continued playing along.

It was nice to be back to work. That much was true. I hadn't been bored because the O.C.D. was back again and I had cleaned my parents' house right the way through each day for the previous four days. Any more hurt in the future…the O.C.D…I knew it would keep coming back. I'd been raped, scrubbed myself red raw, and when there was next to no skin left to scrub I'd turned to the house. It was a good thing that I was back at work. I had friends in the office, I had my social life and I had clients to see. I made a promise to myself - no more cleaning! I made my excuses one lunchtime for not joining everybody in the staff canteen and I visited a private sexual health clinic not far away for an assortment of tests to be carried out. The wait for the results was going to be an extremely emotional ride.

CHAPTER 14

I moved back into home, if it could be called that anymore, three days before my parents were due back. Once I had made sure that Anthony wasn't there I called for a joiner to come out and fit a proper security lock to my bedroom door. I wanted to feel safe should he decide to come and help himself to my body again. I also needed to be in the house before he came home rather than have to walk in when he was already there.

I was making myself something to eat when I heard his car pull into the drive at seven o'clock. I hadn't announced my return to him and wondered what he would be thinking when he saw my car in the drive. I didn't dwell on the thought too long as I was already feeling nervous. Having just plated up my meal I hurried through into the lounge with my tray and sat down. I quickly switched on the television, made myself comfortable and started eating. I didn't want him to see that I felt intimidated by him.

Probably because he wasn't looking forward to facing me, he stayed in the kitchen pottering about making something to eat for himself. The microwave pinged after about fifteen minutes and I wondered if he would eat in the lounge but he must have thought it better to stay put. A bottle chinked against a glass so he was evidently getting himself a drink. He came sauntering through avoiding eye contact with me and plonked down into one of the armchairs. I was trying hard to stop myself from shaking. It wasn't easy, although looking down at my hands they didn't show a flicker of what I was feeling deep inside me.

His face and body were turned towards the television since he'd walked in the room and sat down. After a total silence between us for a few minutes or so he finally turned towards me.

"Helen, can we talk please?" his voice sounded strained.

Oh shit, did we really have to? My stomach started to churn and I could almost feel every beat of my heart. I hated him, how could I possibly talk to him? But somehow, after clearing my throat, trying to rid myself of what promised to come out as a nervous croak, the sarcasm came confidently spilling out.

"What would you like to talk about, Anthony? The weather? That's usually a good starting point. How about today's news' headlines?"

I stared directly at him, noticing his pleading eyes, the puppy dog…turned bastard.

"Come on, Helen, hear me out…please."

I didn't answer and continued with my cold stare. It seemed he took this as his cue to carry on talking.

"Helen, I am so sorry…really I am."

Somehow I found that hard to believe and I couldn't understand why he even had the gall to make an apology that he wouldn't genuinely feel the need to do.

"What are you sorry for then, Anthony? Sorry for raping me? Sorry that I caught you all after your little orgy two weeks back? Sorry for marrying me? Sorry for being a complete bastard? Go on, enlighten me!"

Proud at my venomous little outburst, I still stared at him intently, watching his body language and his facial expressions as he tried his hardest to convince me just how sorry he was. I wanted something to pick at while my brain was in an endless struggle to understand why.

"I…I…what I did to you, three weeks ago. There…I've said it. I don't know what came over me. It must have been the…the weed I'd smoked that night - it can't have agreed with me."

Weed? He expected me to believe that? He was avoiding my gaze, inspecting his fingernails. I was astounded but determined I wasn't going to start kicking off.

"You must think I'm stupid, Anthony. You've smoked weed before, I know you have. It's never made you like that. You *raped* me. You abused my body and you punched me in the eye. I had to stay off work for a week so nobody would know. Are you telling me you remember all of it? You remembered you'd raped me? Do you remember punching me in the eye, huh? If that's what coke's doing for you, those girls got away quite lightly didn't they? It's making you violent, Anthony. When will the next time be? Who will be your next victim?"

His eyes met mine and I could see that he was close to tears. I racked my brain to find some sort of emotion for him. I didn't feel sorry for him. Despite everything I didn't even hate him. I felt nothing whatsoever…indifference. It saddened me to realise that.

"I honestly can't remember hitting you, Helen. Truly I don't recall that. I am so sorry. You never deserved that."

126

"So I *deserved* to be raped then? Is that what you're saying?" I snarled.

"No! Helen, no! That's not what I meant and you know it! You didn't deserve any of it. You've done nothing wrong. It's me that's at fault here. Everything is my fault."

Yes. It was his fault. He'd raped me, there was nobody else to blame but him, but I was starting to get upset, I must be guilty too. I had done something wrong surely? He'd stopped loving me...months ago. I needed to know why.

"That can't be true. I must have done something to make you hate me, Anthony...there is something. I've tried to be a good wife to you...where did it all go so wrong?"

He got up and started pacing the lounge, his eyes staring down at the carpet. He appeared to be deep in thought and I didn't think he was going to answer my questions.

"It's work, Helen. I assure you that *you* have done *nothing* wrong at all. Just a few worries at work, and I haven't been coping with them. I know I've been drinking too much, the...drugs as well. I shouldn't have done any of it. I've let you down."

My first thought on hearing this was that he must have made some serious fuck ups at work in Dad's absence. I could feel my anger building again and snarled my next words at him.

"You sure have, and you've also let my father down. I hope there are no problems at the office for him to come back to. You know he hasn't been well lately."

"I *am* aware of that, Helen." he snapped back "The problems at work are things that I can

127

sort out without worrying your Dad. Are you planning on…telling him about…us…things?"

I was close to boiling point at his selfishness. The things he'd put me through, rape, his drunken orgy and drugs, and all he was concerned about was his position within my father's company. I managed to keep my voice a bit calmer as I answered him.

"Of course I'm not going to tell him. Tell him that I've married a total bastard, who hasn't treated his daughter right? That would be an understatement wouldn't it, Anthony? Dad's been close enough to another heart attack as it is, without me adding *you* to his problems, don't you think?"

He turned away from me, unable to meet my eyes any longer.

"Yes, I suppose you're right, Helen!"

"I know I'm right, Anthony!"

My heart was pounding, but I was struggling to breathe. I needed to calm myself. I had to lay down the ground rules if I was to continue to stay.

"I've moved back in here today. Mum and Dad are home in the next couple of days and I don't want to be at theirs….for obvious reasons. Let's get things straight. I don't want you bringing friends and…people over here. This is my house as well. I don't care what you do anymore, Anthony – but don't do it here. I don't want your bloody drugs in this house."

He nodded and gave a sigh, probably relieved that I still wanted my parents to have no knowledge of recent events.

"And now…I need your promise…that…that you won't ever…touch me…rape me…"

"Helen, never! I wouldn't…I promise."

A flash of understanding, he knew that I meant business. I decided not to mention to him the extra measures I'd taken for my personal security.

"Message understood."

I felt a sense of relief that it was out in the open. It was not going to be easy living under the same roof. We'd already been doing so for months, but things had changed. My thoughts turned to my parents and how long Anthony and I could keep up the façade.

He sat quietly contemplating for a while before asking if I minded him watching some documentary or other. I said I didn't have a problem with that and as I got up to go to the kitchen he told me there was a bottle of Vinho Verde in the fridge and I was quite welcome to pour myself a glass if I wished.

"Thank you. I assume you are telling me this because you would like one?"

That was the *only* reason he'd mentioned the wine to me.

"When have I ever refused?"

Precisely! He wasn't capable of refusing alcohol. It wasn't many months ago I would have been delighted to pour him a drink but we were no longer a couple. He was pushing my buttons.

We watched a nature documentary almost in silence whilst we drank a couple of glasses of wine. As the programme finished I

129

realised how exhausted I was feeling after our earlier talk. I stretched as I got up from the settee.

"I'm tired now. Goodnight!"

"Okay. Goodnight, Helen."

I cringed, irked by the way my Christian name still rolled off his tongue.

CHAPTER 15

I went to visit my parents on the Saturday morning and stayed the full day. They'd arrived back on the Friday afternoon, three days after I had left their house.

"What's Anthony doing today, darling?" Dad asked. "I thought he would have come along with you. I'm dying to ask him what's been happening in the office in my absence. Has he mentioned anything at all?"

"No. I never talk shop with him, Dad, you should know that. I think he's either gone into the city for the day or he's gone golfing, I'm not totally sure. He did tell me, but as usual I was not paying too much attention."

They told me all about the cruise and we spent the morning going through their holiday photos and I heard all about the tours they'd been on. Whilst we sat at the dining table after lunch, I asked Dad if he was feeling any better for his long rest from work. He was perhaps a little too quick to assure me that he was well rested. I followed this by asking if he was worried about anything at work.He was suddenly alert.

"What makes you ask that, Helen?"

"You were keen for Anthony to be here, so you could ask what's been happening while you've been away. All you had to do was answer 'yes something's worrying me' or 'no, of course not!'"

"There's nothing for you to trouble your little head with. I trust Anthony to sort out any little problems that crop up."

Hmm, that's what worried me and I wasn't impressed with Dad's lack of acting ability. He was skirting around the subject rather niftily. But instead of voicing my opinion we just moved on to the next topic of conversation. Mum as usual didn't have much to say, but I noticed she kept giving Dad a look of concern when she thought he wouldn't notice.

At 6pm I made my excuses and went off to meet the girls from the office for a few drinks. No late night planned - just a few drinks and hopefully a lot of unwinding. When I arrived home, Anthony was already tucked up in his bed, a peaceful night for him, which meant a perfect peaceful night for me too.

CHAPTER 16

Dad had returned to work and was managing to toe the line with his new part time hours. Things were ticking over in much the same fashion. Anthony and I were avoiding each other as much as possible when we were both home. I socialised with my friends and he with his. I knew the day was fast approaching when Mum would be inviting us around for Sunday dinner, and having already discussed this matter with Anthony, we had agreed that we would go for appearances sake. It should be quite easy really. If we turned up just before lunch was due to be served there would only be the meal to get through. Mum and I usually ended up in the conservatory and Dad and Anthony would either be in the lounge watching Sunday afternoon sport or else they would stay at the dining table and talk business.

Three weeks had passed since they had returned from holiday and we still hadn't been asked over for Sunday lunch. It suited me down to the ground. Anthony was also not relishing the inevitable.

We still met up in the lounge some nights and shared the odd bottle of wine but that is as cosy as it got. We discussed only what we needed to discuss - nothing more. I remained as pleasant as could be expected under the circumstances. Anthony seemed to find it quite hard to make eye contact with me. He was hopefully feeling ashamed…and guilty – as he should be!

To my knowledge, no friends of his had visited the house whilst I was out and that's the way that I wanted it to stay. I wasn't sure how long we could continue to co-habit without any more incidents or without my parents finding out. I hadn't asked if he had told his family about our relationship. I didn't really want to know. I had no doubt that if he had done, or when he eventually did, all the blame would rest firmly on my shoulders as far as they were concerned. Should there ever be any grief directed at me from his mother I would have no qualms about telling her that her son had raped me. I would happily reveal to her that he preferred the company of young men, enjoyed snorting cocaine and occasionally indulged in threesomes with young ladies. I could give her plenty to think about, although it would still be me that had led him astray and caused him to go off the rails, in her opinion.

I took the plunge one night and decided to ask Anthony how my father was coping at work and if he thought he still had health worries. He thought long and hard, continuously staring at the television for a few minutes before answering.

"I don't know, Helen. He spends most of the time in his office and doesn't have much to say unless it's about business. He looks well enough and is always pleasant to everybody in the office, the true gentleman as always." He then added, "If you're worried about him, why don't you ask your Mum?"

I didn't really know what to make of his answer and wondered if he would keep any worrying facts from me - not wanting me to fret more than was necessary.

"Well it was Mum who told me to ask you. She keeps asking him at home if he's feeling alright, and he assures her that he's fine."

He leaned forward in his chair and gave me a re-assuring smile (I wished he wouldn't). "If he's telling her he's fine I expect it's because he feels fine. I'm sure she's fretting about nothing - as you women always do."

He turned back towards the television and I pondered on his last words and shook my head, astounded by them. Being married to him I had plenty to fret about it was not…nothing.

During the next morning at work, I closed my office door around ten thirty and placed the call that I should have made nearly two weeks earlier but had been putting off time and again. I was delighted to hear from the clinic that the results of all the tests taken had come back negative. I cried with relief.

That same afternoon I had a meeting to attend in our office with some new clients. The two gentlemen had purchased a country pub a year ago and now had a development plan in mind for building some chalets around the pub's car park that could be rented on a short or long term basis. They required our assistance to produce some projected figures to show their bank. Ted and I would be joining them at their pub for lunch after the meeting to discuss matters further. With my home being mid way between the office and the pub Ted told me to follow him in my own car. It would save me driving all the way back to the office.

Leaving the men behind after our successful meeting and lunch it was three fifteen when I left the pub. Turning into our street half an hour later, I could see there was a car parked directly in front of our house, and as I drove another thirty feet past the large hedge that blocked the view of our drive, I noticed that Anthony's car was there. He was stood on the front doorstep and he was exchanging envelopes with a man with whom he was engaged in a deep conversation. My suspicions were instant. Anthony was never one for leaving work early (unless it involved alcohol). My last experience of him arriving home early had not been a particularly pleasant one. It didn't look as if there was a rent boy involved this time thank goodness, but the exchanging of envelopes was never a good sign.

Whether he had seen my car approaching and deliberately got rid of the guy before I pulled into the drive, I don't know, but the guy reached his driver's side door, got in and pulled the door shut just as I pulled into the drive. As I got out of the car, I watched him pull away, but the main reason I stared was to try and get a good look at his face. Anthony had already closed the front door before I arrived. No doubt he would try to deny seeing me driving down the street and whatever it was that the driver of the car had passed to him, would by now be stashed safely out of my way.

Rather than have Anthony insult my intelligence by telling me a pack of lies, I decided to play it cool and not ask too many questions. Using the back door as always, I walked into the kitchen just as he was filling the kettle.

"Tea or coffee, Helen? I haven't been in long, I'm having a tea!"

I was a little taken aback by his cheeriness but I answered him politely.

"Tea will be fine, thanks."

I couldn't appear too interested or he would be suspicious but my curiosity was getting the better of me. I was eager to watch his reactions so I chanced it.

"Who was the guy at the front door? I haven't seen him before," then I added "the one driving away as I pulled up?"

He was pouring the hot water into the cups so I couldn't see his face.

"Oh, him? He did some design work for us a few weeks ago, while Ken was on holiday. I promised to pay him in cash. He's just started up in business and has struggled along with his household bills in his first month. Just to tide him over until his cheques start to come in. I arranged it whilst your Dad was away, as I know he doesn't like making cash payments."

He must have rehearsed that one quickly, or he'd plucked it from thin air on the spur of the moment. I didn't believe a word of it. He would only have had maximum of three to four minutes from seeing my car until the minute I'd walked in the back door. I wanted to scream at him. To ask him exactly how naïve he thought I was. And ask about the envelope that had been handed to him!

I did some tidying up in the kitchen as I was drinking my tea, (puzzling all the while about what I'd seen) and he sat at the counter reading his newspaper. There was a long silence between us as I carried on with some little jobs and I saw him look up from his paper.

"You're home early today."

I didn't have to answer him, he was making a statement, but I felt that if I did it would keep things chatty and…casual.

"Well, we had a meeting with some new clients and went for lunch to the pub they own. They have plans to develop and build some chalets around the car park. It looks like it could be a money spinner for them. I left Ted there with them still discussing things. It made more sense than driving all the way back to the office."

I never took my eyes off him. Maybe I saw a flicker of something.Realisation that, whatever he was up to, he had come close to being caught. When I removed his empty cup from in front of him he stood up and announced,

"Just so that you know, I'm out tonight. I'm going to a casino with some friends. You'll have the house to yourself for most of the night." He grabbed the jacket of his suit from the back of the chair. "I'm going for a shower."

It was music to my ears to hear that he was going out. I loved having my own space but tonight I was going to have a private treasure hunt. Not wanting him to see me look so delighted, I scowled and delivered my perfect nagging tone.

"I'm warning you, Anthony. Don't you dare bring anybody back here. Or come into my room for that matter." I'd hit it perfectly. He went immediately on the defensive as he snapped back.

"I'll probably stay out all night. Don't worry. I told you I was sorry. That won't happen again."

"I know you did. I'm just reinforcing the message."

After he'd gone upstairs I heard the door close and the lock engage on his bathroom door. I quietly crept up after him, darting into his bedroom and swiftly checking his jacket and trouser pockets for the envelope he'd been handed by the mystery guy – nothing. I checked his drawers and under his mattress – again, no joy. I felt disappointed but if he wanted to hide something from me he wasn't going to make it easy for me to find.

Going back down the stairs as silently as I'd gone up I made a swift search under the cushions of the settee and chairs, in the drawers of the bureau and every possible hiding place I could see. No envelope! I remembered that he had been in the kitchen putting the kettle on as I walked through the door so having a re-think he would probably have thought the kitchen was his quickest option when he saw my car approaching. I expected him coming downstairs in the next minute or two so I didn't have time for a large scale search. I would have to stay in the kitchen until he went out. That way he wouldn't have any opportunity to retrieve what he'd hidden - if he *had* hidden it in there. My best option was to do some cooking - look busy.

Ten minutes later, he'd gone. He'd walked into the kitchen, shrugged his shoulders and, not in a caring manner, said "You should be relaxing, you've been at work."

139

But whilst I had been stood at the kitchen sink, and staring out of the window, it hit me like a sledgehammer - the greenhouse. It was situated just outside the doors that led onto our patio. The one place on our property where Anthony knew I never set foot. I sat at the kitchen table deep in thought for twenty minutes or so, giving him the chance to get some distance away. I paced it all out in my mind, and in practice, from Anthony closing the front door, a dash to the greenhouse and getting back into the kitchen again. He would have had a minute to spare. I was a little hesitant to carry out the actual search, scared of what I might find, but I knew it had to be done. I had to know.

I got my answer within twenty minutes. The envelope in question came to light inside the very bottom one, of a stack of unused plant pots. The envelope was unmarked, sealed and as I felt its weight and substance, it contained something like a powder. I returned it to its hiding place and left everything as I had found it. My worst fears confirmed. Drugs, it had to be!

CHAPTER 17

I kept a close watch on the greenhouse situation (and the envelope) at every opportunity over the next few days, and during Anthony's absences I checked on the envelope. I made a point of indulging in casual chit chat when he was home, to see if he would let slip what his plans were and where he was going each time he left the house. I realised that once I discovered the envelope missing, I would need to recall what his plans had been for the day to give me some idea of where the final destination was for the disgusting stuff! I couldn't decide whether Anthony was stupid enough to sell direct to the end users or whether he was just an insignificant courier in a large operation.

On the Friday night, of that same week he had been given the envelope, I intended being awake early the next morning and keeping myself busy in the kitchen. Anthony would be going out to play golf and it was his turn to pick up his partner. If there was any convenient time for him to remove the envelope, I thought that it would be the weekend. I had given no thought as to what I should do if I managed to see him retrieving the envelope. I hadn't given consideration as to whether I would involve the police, my parents, or even confronting Anthony. I'd not yet seen beyond my sole aim - proving something to myself. I just wanted confirmation that Anthony really was a bastard! Even though, deep down, I already knew!

I came to with a start - the slamming of a car door and an engine turning over being my rude awakening. It slowly dawned on me that it was Saturday morning and I sat up quickly, my eyes searching out the alarm clock. It was 9.30am. I shot out of bed and grabbed my dressing gown. It must have been Anthony's car that I'd heard. Without bothering to put anything on my feet, I put my gown on and ran down the stairs and through to the kitchen. I paused for a few seconds just outside the patio door. I chided myself at the breakneck speed with which I'd just descended the stairs. What I find or don't find in the greenhouse within the next two minutes, that situation would not be changing within the next few hours, so why the rush?

My forage into the plant pots revealed…the envelope was still there! I was surprised. I had genuinely thought he would have removed it that morning, his first real opportunity.

He stayed out all Saturday night and didn't return until the Sunday evening. I somehow doubted the envelope would be moved until the following weekend now (he wouldn't want to leave something like that in his car when he was at work), but I intended to check the greenhouse as often as I could.

An opportunity to leave work an hour early presented itself the following Tuesday. I hand delivered some audited accounts to a client on my way home but as her office closed at five o'clock I needed to be there sooner in case she wanted a few words. By twenty minutes to five I was out of her office and fifteen minutes later I was home, thirty five minutes earlier than usual. After I'd dumped my bags on the worktop, I opened the patio door and stepped outside. The sliding door to the greenhouse was not quite in position. I was stunned, and I desperately tried to remember whether I'd been in a rush the last time I'd checked. Perhaps it had been me who'd been careless – I had been trying to make a point of leaving it fully closed.

The envelope had gone. Somewhere between the hours of 8.15am and 4.55pm it had been removed and taken…who knew where? I made a mental note to speak to my father as soon as I could. I needed to know where Anthony had been, and without Dad suspecting anything.

CHAPTER 18

Not long after the envelope had gone missing from the greenhouse,I found out that Anthony *had* been out of the office for around four hours on that same Tuesday. I hadn't needed, after all, to wheedle any information from my father. He'd called me on the Thursday evening, to tell me he'd been for his check up at the hospital that morning and that the consultant had been thrilled with his progress. I could hear Mum's voice in the background, prompting him at times as we chattered on. I'd been on the verge of saying goodnight when he suddenly remembered something.

"By the way, Helen, I was so relieved when Anthony told me today that Eileen's feeling much better now. He was really worried when he dashed off to see her on Tuesday morning, even more so when he got back to work mid afternoon. All that time and her analgesia still wasn't working."

Our call had ended shortly after that ......my proof. I knew Anthony would have mentioned his wonderful mother being ill if there had been a grain of truth in it. He talked about her quite often, probably just to yank my chain. He knew there was no love lost between us. But thoughts of *them* drifted from my mind as my head was suddenly filled with visions of addicts waiting for a fix, young girls being given drugs and then forced into prostitution. The question came back to me - what role Anthony was actually playing in all of it and I was shaking with anger, and feeling sickened by my past

144

relationship with him…and that I bore his surname!

CHAPTER 19

I was finding it increasingly difficult, mentally, to cope with everything that had happened in the space of the last few months.Living under the same roof as Anthony was taking its toll. I was suspicious of every move he made and he sensed it. Whereas at the beginning of our estrangement, we'd tolerated each other and shared a forced politeness, we'd now reached a stage where we bickered constantly….about everything! Bills, jobs around the house, even the television. Any visits to my parents' house were made by me alone! I still led Mum and Dad to believe all was well and made excuses for Anthony's absence through jokey comments about his busy social life.

Work was causing yet another problem for me, due to my forgetfulness and a total lack of concentration. It was the girls, my friends who were the first to start making comments,

'Hello? Are you with us, Helen?', 'What planet are you on today, honey?' and 'Is anyone at home in there?' I also became aware that most of the staff watched me from time to time out of the corners of their eyes. I seldom saw smiles in my dealings with any of them – those had been replaced with subtle concerned scrutiny. The comments *and* the looks got me worrying even more. I knew that if I didn't get myself in check soon, there would be awkward questions coming my way. Awkward questions with even more awkward and deceptive answers to them. I needed to be more alert – self-aware.

When the new working week started I was full of determination. I dug into my depths and walked into the office with a refreshed, more cheery persona, it could almost have given the impression that I'd just recovered from a nasty virus…or pre-menstrual tension. I kept up the happy person act for most of the week, whilst also being conscious of *every* move I made.

As the week went by the results of my self-observations were greatly disturbing me. I was struggling to eat my lunch - it was as if I couldn't swallow. I was lining pens up in neat rows, stacking files neatly at the very corner with the files perfectly square with the edges of the desk, and my blotting pad also had to be lined up square. My doodling on the blotter also had to be symmetrical. And I was back to washing my hands and arms a dozen times a day. I was out of control - my obsessive behaviour was visiting me during my working hours.

I felt totally out of my depth. I tried in vain to come up with a solution. I needed another outlet instead of letting it interfere with my working life. I was a threat to my own professionalism! I couldn't be obsessive at home. Anthony would notice. He'd start calling me a 'fucking weirdo' – there would be even more rows. He might also resort to telling my father. Dad would want to know what was causing it. No! I couldn't bear the thought that if Mum and Dad were to find out they would be pushing me towards seeing Mr Gillespie again. He would press for the cognitive behavioural therapy this time. I felt as if millions of grains of sand were raining down, their very weight threatening to totally engulf me – I couldn't see a means of escape.

I knew I had to take some action, and immediately. I made an appointment with a different GP at our surgery for 5.45pm that Friday night. I couldn't face seeing Dr Jack again, after Dad's insistence to him last time that he didn't want me on any tablets.

This time, I walked out of Dr Bell's office clutching a prescription for Fluoxetine, an anti-depressant frequently used in the treatment of O.C.D.

CHAPTER 20

I'd been taking my prescription drugs for over three weeks. My patience was non-existent as I waited each day for a sign. I had been expecting to see at least *some* indication that they were going to calm me, get my O.C.D. in order and…make me feel normal again. After all this time taking them, and with no apparent improvement, I was beginning to despair – feeling that normal, for me, would never return. Throwing the three month supply of anti-depressants into the bin was looking like the most sensible option.

It wasn't, however, the gradual improvement I'd been anticipating. It happened overnight. I woke up feeling like the old me again, totally calm and without the overwhelming compulsion to disinfect the whole house or poison Anthony. I'd lost the obsessive desire to scrub everything with bleach….my hands and arms included. I felt more positive that I could get back on track at work. I chose a book off the shelf in my bedroom and read it in one sitting – I hadn't read a book for months! I even found everyday things to smile about – a programme on the television, the politeness and genuine smile from a check-out operator at the supermarket. It was a nice feeling, to be back in control.

It was a pleasure to go to work and come away each night, achieving the finalising and signing off of accounts that had been waiting for my attention. I was rapidly getting through one of the obsessively neat piles of folders stacked on my desk. I noticed the acknowledgement in the face of, not just Ted, but each of my friends and colleagues, that I was back.

Janet brought some letters for me to sign just before Friday lunchtime and as she waited for me to go through them she asked hesitantly,

"Helen…we're all going out tonight, we haven't done it for ages. Not the city centre though - we thought maybe Ascot Village? Are you up for it? It'll do you good. You haven't been too well lately, have you?"

I looked up at her and smiled, touched by her concern. It sounded just the thing - it would get me back into socialising with the girls whose company I adored. I didn't need to think too long before giving her my answer.

"Janet, I would love too! Thank you for asking me. It will be the ideal opportunity to…celebrate the fact that I'm feeling better."

She was happy. She gave me a gentle thump on the arm before uttering,

"You'll love it, girl!" She scooped up the signed letters and left.

A night out! I'd almost forgotten what it was like to enjoy myself. It was an exciting thought that I would soon be finding that enjoyment once more. The butterflies of nervousness swooped up and down in my stomach as I started thinking what I would wear. We gathered in the staff canteen at lunchtime and made our final arrangements.

Not too many hours later we were in Jigz Club in Ascot - chosen because it offered everything that we wanted - food, a nightclub and a choice of bars. There were six of us, Janet, Nina, Gillian, Gemma, myself and a recent addition to the trainees, Leanne. We'd already dined and had a couple of drinks in one of the bars. It was packed with people and the atmosphere was lively. Although the bar that we were in had no music playing, the incessant buzz of different conversations all around us was deafening. We could barely hear each other speak to indulge in our own chitchat. Leanne, being the youngest, and the liveliest of us all, was eager to have a dance and she kept pointing to the door, miming the famous moves of Travolta in Saturday Night Fever. We all giggled at her like schoolgirls (she was crazy) but we followed her obediently as she led the way.

If we'd thought it noisy in the bar, it was nothing to the volume that was pumping out of the colossal speakers. Conversation was impossible. There were groups of people stood all around the packed dance floor, all at different degrees of intoxication. With talking being completely out of the equation, the only thing to do was to dance, whether the music was to our liking or not. Nina and I couldn't keep pace with the others and every four or five dances we got off the dance floor for ten or fifteen minutes to catch our breath.

It was during one of our dancing sessions I became aware of a guy standing at the edge of the dance floor staring hard at me. He appeared to be with three or four other men, obviously friends of his. I was straining my eyes to get a look at him, but it was hard work with the strobe lighting pulsing away to the music. I lost sight of him for a few minutes and then almost jumped out of my skin to find he was suddenly leaning in close to me. I jerked my head away from him quickly but seconds later a flash of light passed across his face – it was Alex Baker- Thompson!

Alex grabbed my hand and led me off the dance floor. He cupped both his hands to my ear and bellowed something inaudible. The only words I managed to make out were "….somewhere….quiet…talk.." I nodded my acquiescence. I managed to grab the attention of Nina and Leanne, pointed at Alex and the door and covered my ears, and I hoped they would get the gist of what I was trying to say. He grabbed my hand to guide me through the throng. Once clear of what had to be the noisiest experience of my life he asked,

"Fresh air or one of the quiet bars?" I considered for a second whilst he swept his hand across his hair, and his wedding ring glinted under the corridor lighting.

"Fresh air, please – the heat in there is nauseating." He smiled, his shoulders sagging a little releasing some of the tension,

"I'm so glad you said that, Helen. I must be getting old, I can't cope with the noise these days. To think that I used to love it all." His arm around my shoulder, he guided me again, through the crowds waiting around for cabs.

We sauntered along for five minutes, me grasping onto his left arm for support, my too high heels threatening to unbalance me should I place a foot in some unseen bump in the pavement. It was fresh and peaceful outside in the half light. Cars drove past us but any sound from them was insignificant. I wondered what we were doing – what had happened to the talk? I tried to think of something to say and he beat me to it.

152

"You're married then, Helen? I've noticed the ring." I didn't see any reason to lie.

"Yes. I'm married...estranged! I wear the ring because...appearances...there are people who don't need to know right now. Long story...! You wear a wedding ring too. Where's your wife, Alex?" I turned to look at his face as we continued our leisurely stroll but he didn't face me. He was deep in thought, eyes staring ahead.

"She's...um...with her mother. She cheated on me, I kicked her out."

I was astonished. So it didn't just happen to me then? I couldn't think of anything to say to him.

I wasn't sure how far we'd wondered in silence but we took a left turn into a road with less traffic. In quite a clumsy move, he suddenly swung around to face me.

"Helen, I'm really sorry! I am! We parted on bad terms last time and I didn't want that." He was waiting for me to say something and I couldn't find the appropriate words. Such a long time had passed and I'd just heard an apology I had never expected. I tried to remember how long ago...and he'd just dragged me out here to say sorry!

"Wh..." I started to comment but he cut me off quickly.

"Helen, I made you feel cheap. I tried to poke into your pants...I.." Those words were like a trigger - a starting gun to me. Poke...into my pants...my head was about to explode, sharp tingling in my tunnel. I needed, urgently, to be fucked and I felt myself losing control in that need.

153

I grabbed his hand roughly, shoving it straight up my skirt and into my pants. "Do…you…mean…poke like…like this, Alex?" and I pushed his fingers towards my fanny. I moaned out loud and released his hand, his fingers finding their own way. His lips were suddenly hard on my own, his tongue forcing its way in, but I wanted it urgently and needed his warmth in my mouth. I parted my lips for him. My hand fumbled desperately with the zip of his denims. As my breathing grew heavy and my need increased, I abandoned that attempt and reached down the top of them, into his underwear, and felt his stiffness expanding as I fondled it.

As our wildness became more urgent, we edged our way along the road, not noticing our steps. I groaned in frustration as he pulled his fingers out of my hole, my inner muscles throbbing in wait as, struggling with the zip that held his pulsing cock in place, he finally succeeding in freeing it for me. I pulled away from his probing tongue and as I bent over with the intention of going down on him, he grabbed my arm and hurried me another twenty yards down the road, and through a gap in a hedge into a small park.

His lips were on mine again, one eye watching as he steered me backwards, his fingers up me once more. I felt the back of my knees make contact with something and his fingers had gone yet again. He eased me into a sitting position and I took his cock into my mouth. He wasn't big lengthwise, but his girth was thick. As I sucked and enjoyed his thrusts into my mouth, I let my mind roam. I imagined how it would feel to have

154

that thickness inside my hole, hammering at me and filling me with his spunk. I still had my panties on, they were getting wet.

It all came pouring out of me – months of sexual frustration. My eagerness to be fucked was turning me into a madwoman, wild, as a tigress! I couldn't wait a second longer. I was insatiate. My hole needed filling, and fucking...wildly! I pulled my mouth away from his cock.

"What are you bloody waiting for?" then half screaming at him, *"Fuck me, Alex!"* I sensed he was feeling a similar wildness. I stood and pushed my panties down my thighs. In his own urgency to give it to me, he bent down and pulled my panties off one leg only. He lifted me off the ground with both arms and as I clasped my arms around his neck, and my legs around his waist, he lowered me towards his cock. With me holding on tight, he released my waist. One hand supporting my bottom - his other hand guiding his upstanding pole into my pussy! He staggered ten or twelve feet, his cock hard up inside me, to a tree trunk and pushed my back firmly into it. Breathless, he stammered,

"Helen....ca...can't..believe! You!"

He was almost on his toes with every upward thrust into me. His very girth was grazing me, each nerve alight, pubic bone rubbing fiercely at my clit. Within two minutes I came, my juices free flowing over his length, my mouth wide open with the shock of an experience long forgotten. I was greedy, I wanted more.

"Alex!" I urged "Don't move, leave it all the way in and don't move now, please!" The frustration was evident on his face, he wanted to carry on fucking, but I'd halted him. I was breathless, way too hyped, but it would only take me a minute. As he stood still, all my weight bearing down on his dick, tight inside me, I could feel every nerve of it as he throbbed within, alighting every nerve in my tunnel, and I screamed out with the intensity as I came again. My eyes closed and I held my breath, savouring every glorious moment.

When he pulled out and backed away, I couldn't wait to get him back inside me. Dropping to my knees and hitching my skirt up to my waist, the anticipation was sending me into a new frenzy. What was taking him so damned long, I wondered?

"Alex, what the…..*hell* are you doing? Hurry up…shove it….back in, *now!*"

"It's… on it's…..way! Babe, you…you're so… *fucking* impatient!"

I felt his fingers slide down beneath the cheeks of my backside and at that same moment his knob touched my labia in its new search for my warmth. I tipped my head back, my eyes crossed and every bloody nerve throughout my *body* felt engulfed in flames. That mere *hint* of more action to come - his *knob* against my fleshy outer parts, sent me into paroxysms with a new release of cum. It was beyond…pure heaven!

He twisted my hair around his hand as he fucked me crazily. "You're…turning…me…into a…raving…fucking luna…lunatic…Helen" he blurted, a word with each rough thrust into me, a perfect rhythm. Riding me, on and on, my hair as the reigns in his grip as I was enjoying every stroke of being re-acquainted with sexual wantonness!

I could feel a new wetness developing, his pre-cum, as, with his free hand, he delved into my bra and squeezed tightly on my left nipple. I groaned at the new pain, and moaned at my ecstasy down below. I heard his throatiness close to my ear as his thrusts continued, a new fiery urgency in each,

"Same ...again...Helen? Shall I...stick it...deep...in you...and...hold...as my...as my...cock...spurts...my cum?"

"Yes! Please...now...give it...to...me!" I was almost screaming again as one final (his hardest) thrust hit deep into me, pulsing strongly against the walls of my pussy as he let go, his warm juices spurting deliciously as I excreted my own cream once more...

"You're...fucking...amazing...Helen!" he whispered as his breathing started to slow.

As we traced our steps back to Jigz, he placed his arm around my shoulders. I was deep in thought about how I was going to pass this one off with my friends, who must all be wondering where the hell I'd disappeared too. We approached the door and Alex suddenly stopped and faced me, his lips seeking mine. I froze and stepped backwards.

"Helen, can't we...?" I cut him off sharply, sensing what was coming.

"No, Alex! I don't feel anything for you!

My head held high, I turned and walked into the club, straight to the ladies room.

I spotted the girls quickly enough. They were taking a breather at the edge of the dance floor, during a brief pause from the music system.

"Where the hell did you go? Who was that guy?" blurted Leanne, not in quite the discreet manner that the other girls would have used should they have had their chance to enquire first. She also winked in an all-too-knowing expression as her questions came out. It was nice to communicate without shouting for the first time that night.

"Oh, him? We went to school together, that's all! We've just had a catch up outside – so we could hear one another." They all looked toward the door,

"Jeeeez! What did you do to him, Helen? He's looking pretty pissed off!" I turned to look. Alex's eyes searched the room for his friends.

"Oh! He made a move on me, so I left him out there." And as I said it, I saw the reality of what had really happened. He'd just had the fuck of his life…and any further chances had been snatched away from him in an instant!

I relived some of those wild moments with Alex as I laid waiting for sleep to come. I had been a slut. On the very day I got my test results back; found out I hadn't contracted HIV, I have a one-night-stand for the first time in my life. I hadn't cared for him. I'd simply given in to my wildest needs. The self-respect I'd once had for my body had gone.

Heavenly, wild dirty sex – without the complications of even liking the guy who'd fucked me. Thank you, Anthony! And I spoke out

158

loud as I said my next words "It's all....your bloody fault!"

CHAPTER 21

Work was great fun on the Monday that followed our visit to Jigz. It was Ted's 60th birthday. We'd organised everything the previous Friday. Helium balloons were delivered to the office. One of the girls had seen some classy desk gadget and we had all chipped in to cover the cost. Hilary, his wife, came along to the office mid morning with freshly cooked bacon baps from a café further down the street and there were cream cakes to follow! She'd also brought a couple of bottles of champagne along and at dinner time in the staff kitchen, we toasted his health.....and behaved like juveniles in our champagne bubble induced silliness.

I was still on a high from my recent visit into the depths of sluttish behaviour and the intense pleasures I had experienced - my sexual re-awakening! My good mood prompted me to make sufficient food for Anthony to partake of. Again, something I hadn't done for quite some time. I was singing! Knife in my hand, chopping onions and mushrooms, and singing along to a Madonna song, "Like a Prayer." I knew I would have to be careful, when I told him that he could eat with me - I didn't want him reading between the lines. I shuddered at the thought, paused in mid lyrics, and felt my happiness wane a little.As he walked into the kitchen some time later I was plating up my meal and I gave him a cheery grin and offered,

"There's plenty left if you want some - spag bol," Seeing his eyebrows lifting in surprise, I quickly added "I did far too much just for me, it's a shame to waste it." I saw his mouth almost watering as he looked at my plate longingly. I nodded towards the wall unit "Get yourself a plate!"

"Thanks, Helen, I will. It looks good enough to eat" and as he laughed at his own little joke, it struck me as sad, that we used to be happy together, laughing so much and enjoying life. This was far removed from those times. Looking at me curiously as he piled up spaghetti on his plate and followed it with a generous serving of the bolognaise, he said "You're in a good mood tonight!"

"Yeah, it's been a great day at work. It was Ted's 60th today. We had champagne and precious little work got done."

After I cleared the dishes away, Anthony switched on the television and started watching a history documentary. Our pleasantries for the day were done with. I loaded the dishwasher, wiped the worktops down and went back through to the lounge. I picked up the new book I'd started reading just the previous night and settled on the settee to indulge myself. The volume of the programme he was watching was very loud at times; WW2 bombs raining down on London, it kept distracting me. I grabbed my MP3 player from down the side of the cushion, pushed the buds into my ears, pressed play and my reading was melodically accompanied by Beethoven instead of blackouts and bombs.

The music was soothing as I read. The suspense of the story was building and I was enthralled but my eyelids were feeling heavy. I jumped in such a panic as Anthony gently shook my shoulder.

"Helen, there's somebody knocking at the door! Are you expecting anybody?" My eyes darted up to the clock on the mantle – it was nine forty seven. Pulling my ear buds out, rubbing my eyes, and wishing I'd gone to bed to read instead of dropping off downstairs, I managed to say, with a groan,

"No!...Not!" I heard the loud banging, was it for the second or third time? A thought quickly entered my head and I was alert in an instant, I wondered if it was one of his...contacts! He stood and looked at me - too long, and I wondered if that same thought had occurred to him. Trying hard to shake off the remains of my tiredness I snapped him out of his thoughts. "Anthony! Go and bloody see who it is! Now! It sounds urgent! "He reluctantly left his programme to answer the continuous knocks.

I was struggling to hear what was being said. Anthony had closed the lounge door after him when he'd gone into the front hall to answer the knock. I could hear a very deep male voice, then a different one, not quite so deep. The front door closed and Anthony came back in through the lounge door, walking purposely towards me, his face unreadable, followed by two police officers. I stood up, tense.

"Helen...I..." stammered Anthony.

Oh shit, they'd come for him! I was holding my breath, waiting for him to tell me. My thoughts drifted, I wondered what my father would do, or say, when he finally found out what

Anthony, his dependable surrogate son had been up to. I cringed at my own cynicism.

"We'll take over from here, Sir!" the deeper-voiced one of the two said to Anthony, then he turned his head towards me,

"Are you Mrs Helen Pawson?" What the hell question was that? I was petrified. What would he want me for? I started shaking, coldness striking through me, my knees suddenly feeling weak. I nodded my affirmation.

"You may want to sit down, Helen. We have some news for you – bad news!"

My parents had been involved in a fatal accident. My father, who had been driving, had suffered a major heart attack at the wheel - he was dead. The car had veered into the path of an oncoming lorry. I listened to his words and I thought he must be lying to me. My mother was critical and on life support. I couldn't take it in. All the while he was speaking it was surreal. It wasn't really happening. It was happening elsewhere. The voices were speaking to someone else and not me. In slow motion. I was numb. I felt somebody put a coat around my shoulders, Anthony, and, was it really him, saying,

"I'll take you, Helen – to the hospital."

We were too late! By the time we arrived at the hospital, my mother's life support machine had been switched off. Anthony was taken away to make a formal identification of them both. It galled me that I had to leave everything to him, but I needed him. I didn't have anyone else to rely on. He called relations on both Mum's and Dad's sides of the family to break the news, he organised the joint funeral, organised the flowers.

For once, I was glad he was there. I was good for nothing. They had been my life and they had been taken. My heart had been savaged, torn apart. And I felt such devastation. I wanted to die too….to finally be free from the hurt...

DAVID

I stared in disbelief at the name on the caller display of my mobile phone as it bleeped in my hand. The call that I had hoped wouldn't happen. I looked around the room then back at the display, half hoping that I'd been hallucinating, but his name continued to flash up at me in time with the bleeping. Unable to do anything but stare, the bleeping finally ceased, his name gone! I exhaled at last, unaware that I'd been holding my breath for goodness knows how long. My heart was racing and as I stared at the phone in my trembling hand, I instantly regretted that I hadn't pressed 'answer'. Annoyed at him for ringing me, and with myself for not answering the call, I flung the phone onto the settee in disgust as I yelled out loud at him, absent though he was! "What the hell have you done this for? You're getting to me! Go the fuck away and leave me alone, can't you? I don't need this!"

Banging and clattering around the kitchen as I tidied up, my anger was at myself this time…for being so ridiculous. I had no wish to see David ever again, so why was I so upset that I hadn't responded to the call? I could have answered and told him…what? That I was too busy? Some excuse like, I was perhaps no longer a call girl? Or be truthful by telling him, I can't see you again David – it would be too risky for me to do so? I'd put coffee ready in the cup and switched the kettle on but when it eventually came to the boil I ignored it. Instead, I grabbed a bottle of Zinfandel from the fridge and poured myself a very generous measure. Anthony was due in from work within the next half hour and I seriously needed to get my emotions in check before then.

Just as I was about to sit down in the lounge, glass of wine still in my hand, I noticed the phone lit up again. I snatched it up quickly expecting it to start bleeping again. I was stunned to see that it showed two further missed calls from David. Too busy in the kitchen, I hadn't even heard it and I cursed at myself again.

I gulped greedily at my wine, barely pausing for breath. I fought the temptation to call him back - a battle royal going on inside my head. As I poured myself a second glass, I was thinking I had better make a decision and be quick about it. I wouldn't dare take David's call if he happened to ring me again once Anthony had arrived home. Having taken too long thinking about what to do, and coping with my inner confusion, I looked at the clock and realised I had five minutes left before Anthony would be here. Ring him…or switch off my mobile? It had to be a split second decision – I decided to switch it off! It wouldn't do for Anthony to walk in whilst I was in the middle of explaining to David that I wouldn't be available for a business transaction, *or* telling him that for me to see him again would be foolhardy to say the least.

I picked up the phone ready to press the off button and it rang again in my hand. I almost dropped it in surprise. It was him again. I inhaled deeply two or three times, heart racing again and pressed 'answer'. I couldn't get any words out. I listened in silence and I was shivering. It wasn't a good sign, I knew that. I felt exactly like I had done when I'd had a crush on one of the teachers in school. There had been no girls to giggle with then, just as there was no friend to giggle with now.

"Hello. Is that, Helen?" His voice was just as I remembered. How could I ever forget? I felt sure my heart skipped a beat and I could feel the heat rising up my face. I turned to look in the mirror. I *was* beetroot-coloured. 'You know you want to speak to him' I told my mirror image, 'just do it.' I still couldn't answer.

"Hello? Hello? Helen?" I knew I couldn't wait any longer, I didn't have long.

"Hello." It came out only slightly louder than a whisper.

"Helen, thank goodness. It's David – David Barnard."

My stomach felt as if it was doing back-flips. My emotions and body language would not be acting the way they were if it *wasn't* him. I took the plunge and I didn't know where the current would be taking me as I finally dived in.

"Hi, David. It's nice to hear from you again. What can I do for you?"

I ranted at myself 'what on earth made you ask that,' 'just tell him no to whatever it is he's wanting.'

"I was wondering if you were free for...um...tomorrow night, for the whole night if that's possible? I'm in London, so it's easier for you. I assume it will be the same...?" I didn't hear the rest of his words after that last bit, mortified as Anthony's car pulled into the drive. Shit! I knew I had to hurry so I focused my attention back to the call.

"Okay, David. Where in London and what time? I have to hurry now. A friend's car has just pulled up." I dashed over to the landline phone, where we always kept a notepad and pen. I listened carefully and wrote down the address in St John's Wood for which he gave me the directions from the tube station. I was to arrive for 7pm the next night, and he would be preparing dinner for us both. As he ended the call, I ripped the little piece of paper off the pad and stuffed it down my bra, just as the back door opened. I walked straight up the stairs to splash cold water on my face, but I flushed the toilet as well so that Anthony would think what I wanted him to think.

He'd asked me to stay overnight with him and when I'd said yes, I hadn't given it much thought, forgetting that I was meant to be working a shift at the hotel the very morning that I would now be waking up next to David. I phoned Mrs Flintoff the next morning, feigned starting with the flu and asked her if there was anyone who I could swap a couple of shifts with. She phoned me back almost immediately and had said it was fine – she'd managed to get my shift covered.

It had been six weeks since our first date, assignation, rendezvous – I didn't really know the correct terminology for a hooker's appointment with a client. I really didn't understand what had happened to my decision not to see him. I think it was the voice, so hot and friendly and caring. I had closed my eyes on hearing it - imagined hearing him speaking in the same room as me, close to me. My mind had pulled his image from the very depths of my memories. I knew I shouldn't have gone ahead with the transaction, but I had been powerless to stop myself.

I left a note for Anthony saying that I was out all night with the girls from work. (He still thought I worked at the Hopkins Partnership and as he hadn't ever bothered to get to know any of my friends from there it would be highly likely that he would never find out.) Rather than struggle to park my car near the address, I decided I would take the tube.

It was ten minutes to seven when I knocked on the door of one of the most beautiful mews cottages I had ever seen. I could feel the nerves kicking in as I stood waiting. I didn't know if I was going to be able to eat; my insides were taking tumbles and making rumbles. It felt like my heart was galloping and for a few seconds I considered *doing* just that. I heard a key turning in the lock and the door opened. There he stood, smiling and gesturing for me to enter with a sweep of his arm and lowering his head. I felt like I was floating on a cloud, lost in limbo between Heaven and Earth. Then quickly coming back down to reality – this guy posed a danger to me and my sanity. I didn't want or need to be feeling the very emotion that I was trying to escape from. I should be running.

Armani denims and T-shirt – an entirely different look to the one I was expecting to greet me, it was not his usual suit and tie. He looked sensational and his eyes were positively sparkling. He took my hand in his and as he leaned in to kiss me on the cheek, he said in a very intimate way, "Helen. How lovely to see you again. You're looking even more stunning than I remembered."

Those compliments again. Why did this *one* man actually make me believe him when he said nice things? I flushed, more in pleasure than embarrassment and tried to put the thoughts out of my head and make a response.

"It's lovely to see you again" I said as I took in the beauty of my surroundings for the first time; cream plush carpets and two leather sofas, one coffee table, no armchairs - very minimalist. I had always loved *my* house, but this…was something else. The décor was tastefully done and the furnishings and carpets – clearly no expense had been spared. I quickly added, "Wow! What a gorgeous cottage, David. Are you renting it for the week?" My eyes scanned every inch of the room in amazement.

"I'm fairly pleased with it myself. I bought it two years ago. I needed a base in London. My two daughters helped me with the design and furniture."

Had I heard him correctly? He'd just said the word 'daughters!' I slowly turned to face him. I'd just discovered something about him I hadn't wished to know, and yet already I wanted to know the rest of it. He would probably volunteer the information if I didn't ask, but I raised my eyebrows anyway "Daughters? So where are they, David – with your wife?" I detected too much of a hint of sarcasm in my own words.

"Yes, daughters. And I expect they will be with their mother, Heidi, at the moment, but she's not my wife anymore, Helen. She hasn't been my wife for over eight years."

I was speechless and was wondering if I could manage to come up with something to say but he added,

"I've been married again since then. She was called, Joanna. We divorced four years ago."

This was indeed a revelation. I was finding out things I didn't want to know. I intended that this business transaction should be only that. Knowing personal things about my clients' lives just made it seem…like...as if I was involved. I'm telling myself all these things, trying to come to terms with the fact that I have this knowledge and my mouth acted of it's own accord as I blurted out,

"So what went wrong then? An affair? Did you have affairs and they…" He chuckled at that and I instantly felt sorry for my outburst, after all, it was none of my business. I'm his whore. I had no right to be giving him the third degree.

"It's my work, Helen. I travel around the world on business three parts of the year. It was a lonely life for them both, we grew apart. No affairs though!"

Crap! I wondered if I'd offended him and I wished I could eat the bloody words that had just spewed out of my mouth. It was making me feel a little uncomfortable. I had hoped for a better start to the evening.

"And no, you haven't offended me in the slightest, Helen, so don't worry. Now, are you ever going to sit down and make yourself at home and let me finish up in the kitchen…or should I just take you upstairs right now and tie you to the bed?"

I picked up on it immediately - how the hell had he known that I was worrying? I hadn't realised that I was so transparent. Or were we just in tune to each other? Yet again, I started feeling uneasy. I was not supposed to be thinking any of this. I felt a great urge to tell him that he *should* take me upstairs to bed but he was going to finish preparing a meal for us – a meal I was convincing myself would remain on my plate - untouched.

He took my hand and led me to the settee. He waited and watched, smiling at me all the while, whilst I parked my bottom. He grabbed a couple of magazines from the coffee table, placed them in my lap and departed for the kitchen without another word. I was supposed to be here on business, carrying out a duty that I was going to be paid for. And, just like the first time we had met, he was wining and dining me. Most of my clients want to leap on my bones the minute I walk through their door, fuck me in any manner they see fit, thrust the payment into my hands and get me back out of the door. I couldn't understand David at all. He was far too warm and caring to be a client, and why the hell would he even need a tart with his good looks and his bank balance?

I was totally lost in thought due to an argument that was going on between the two halves of my brain. Summing up, one half was saying 'run like hell, fast as you can,' the other half responding with 'enjoy, you like him, don't you?' Forgetting where I was for a minute, such was my dilemma I was jolted from my thoughts by David shouting at me from the kitchen.

"Take a seat at the dining table your ladyship - first course will be served in two minutes."

David's cooking was excellent. He served up avocado with raspberries as a starter. The main course was beef wellington, new potatoes and vegetables, which had been cooked to perfection. For dessert he had done dark chocolate soufflés and once they were on our plates he quickly made a hole in the top of each and poured in some white chocolate sauce. It was heavenly. Each course was complimented with a fresh glass of wine, and all the while we talked about our favourite foods and our restaurant experiences. After he'd cleared away the last course he joined me at the dining table again. The reservations I'd had earlier about whether I would be able to eat had been unfounded. I was comfortable, relaxed and feeling prematurely inebriated.

Elbows on the table, chin resting on his fists, he smiled across the table at me, and I could feel every beat of my heart as his eyes didn't leave mine. I felt tipsy, nervous and excited all at once – a bad mix. Could I trust myself to even speak? I doubted it.

"So, Helen? You know a little bit more about me tonight. My turn now. Start talking – I'm listening."

I smiled back at him following his lead, placing my elbows on the table and returning his gaze, playing a game with him. I tried hard to assume an air of mystery but I amused myself with a silly thought that 'pissed' was more appropriate than 'air of mystery'. I giggled, still deciding on what personal details I should reveal to him.

He laughed, "You're relaxed – the wine has seen to that. Time to reveal all! I'll get you started, Helen…Do you have a husband…boyfriend…maybe?"

Why did he have to ask *that* of all questions? It was a topic I hadn't wanted to discuss, but due to my earlier outburst it was inevitable that he would want to know.

"He's an ex, but we still live under the same roof." He looked concerned, the smile had disappeared and a question was forming on his lips,

"He's not a pimp, David. He doesn't even know what I do for a living these days. He's not a nice person."

"Then why…?

I'd already said far more than I'd wanted but I didn't need him worrying about me or asking any more awkward questions.

"Why are you still living with him? Is that what you meant? He was abusive to me some time ago and…it's a long story." His body tensed and he got up from his chair and walked around the table towards me, "Helen? You p…"

"Don't worry. He's not abusive any more. The reason I'm still there is…is to see his downfall, and it will be coming soon. I know it will. Can we drop the subject please, David, it's depressing me?"

He pulled out the dining chair that was nearest to me and sat down again. "Of course we can. So what are your reasons for doing this…as a job, I mean?"

He stared into my eyes again, and I wished he wouldn't do it. That all too familiar feeling of unease returned quickly, scaring me even more so I answered him.

"Sex! I can enjoy sex without the need to fall in love again. If I don't fall in love, I can't get hurt."

Even as the words came out I wondered how much of those statements would prove to be true. Needing to break the intense eye contact between us, I leaned over the dining table for the empty wine bottle and waved it in front of his nose.

"Do you have any more wine in the fridge, David?"

He seemed a little distant as he replied, "What? Oh...yes…plenty, take your pick."

As I walked through to the kitchen, his eyes hadn't followed my moves as usual. He was staring at the wall straight ahead of him, deep in thought.

On my return from the kitchen with our third bottle of wine, he had snapped out of his reverie. As I was about to sit down at the dining table he got up, hooked up both our empty glasses in his hand by their stems and led me over to one of the big leather sofas. I handed the bottle of wine to David to pour whilst I removed my shoes. I wanted to recline with my feet up without causing any damage with my heels. He waited until I was propped up on one elbow at one end of the sofa before handing me my wine. He then made himself comfortable in a similar position at the opposite end, before picking his own glass of wine up off the floor.

We laid in silence for a while, downing our wine at a steady pace. I felt so relaxed in his company and it was a comfortable silence. It was nice to just gaze at him and take time to appreciate his sexy good looks, and enjoy those moments without conversation interrupting my thoughts. I smiled at him and he bowled me over when he reciprocated, and moved his legs to intertwine with mine.

It dawned on me what was happening between us, the sexual tension was building. To be so still, our legs touching with no more than a hint of movement from either of us, was the very foundation from which our sexual chemistry would emerge.

I pulled myself upright to lean over David and reach out for the bottle of wine which was on the floor at his side of the sofa. As I reached over him, my breast brushed against his hand. He never made any deliberate movement to touch or fondle, it was just a chance contact…that sent shock waves throughout my body. That closeness without any sexual action was…electric! I poured his wine (whilst still reaching over him), topped up my own glass and reclined once more. He gazed across at me and I saw it in his eyes too…the longing, sparked by our hint of contact. He opened his mouth as if ready to speak and I placed a finger to my lips to silence him. I wanted to enjoy the tension, the anticipation – and feel every formula, every element of the chemistry and wait for the conclusion of the experiments that were playing out in my thoughts.

I wanted us to take our time. I could also feel the wine starting to take effect, rapidly. I felt giddy and my thoughts started drifting away from David fucking me to…waiting, we must wait, waiting would make it better, no rushing, the sooner it started the sooner it would be over and I didn't want it to be over. Such illogical thoughts. Drink induced. I started giggling. David reached out to touch both my hands, he held them, and giggled with me.

"Helen?" It was David's voice. I opened my eyes and his face was almost touching mine. I felt as if I had been asleep for a long time, but glancing towards the wall clock, it indicated I had only closed my eyes momentarily. As I brought my eyes back to meet his, his lips touched mine and he kissed me, tentatively. I was so shocked I couldn't respond immediately, but his warmth and tenderness seemed to meld with my lips. I felt the passion and intensity radiate throughout my entire body and fill me with need. Before I realised it was happening, I was kissing him back, softly at first, and then, as his tongue parted my lips, I knew I wanted him. My self-imposed rules about kissing were broken. The wine was my downfall. Self-control had deserted me.

Kissing each other with a sudden urgency, we rolled off the sofa and onto the carpet. David was fighting with the buttons of my shirt as I pulled his T-shirt over his head. I had to pull away from the kiss. I feasted my eyes on his chest and his biceps. I ran my fingers through his chest hair, stroked his biceps, then held his cheeks in my hands and I found it hard not to stare at him in amazement. He was perfection. He finally

177

managed to undo all my buttons and I raised my arms and pulled them free of the white cotton.

I rolled him over onto his back and started removing his denims and boxers, but only managed to get them to below his hips, too distracted by his cock. It was rigid and the temptation too great.

He moaned as I took his knob into my mouth for an instant. I loved hearing him moan out loud. I shuddered with delight to know that I was pleasuring him. I wanted to hear him groan and shout out in pure bliss. I was deliberately tormenting him, wanting to send him over the edge. I licked slowly around his ridge. My thoughts drifted, my own excitement bringing me wave after wave of longing.

"Oooh, yes! Helen…you're…" he stammered.

"Shush, David. Enjoy!" I let my tongue wander lazily up and down every inch of his shaft, but I had to stop, I had to remove his denims there and then, freeing his lower body to allow me better access. Once I'd pulled his lower clothing from his feet, I removed my skirt, panties and bra and lay down between his legs, focusing all my attention on his inner thighs, his cock and his scrotum. It was getting damp between my legs. Tantalising his sac with my tongue, I gradually looked up towards his face, not even missing one inch…his cock…his stomach abs…chest…so masculine. His neck, so kissable and biteable…his face…so handsome. My heart was like a drum beat, loud within me, pounding, beating out a sound of passion and need. My stomach had an

178

empty feel, it was waiting to be filled, from down below. I needed that fulfilment to come from…

"Helen…swing your body round…bring your legs…over my head!

I want to kiss you…your pussy…your clit. I want you to come. Lovely juices, babe!"

He was tempting me to come by his words alone. A sixty-niner! My favourite position! Perspiration was forming on my forehead. I was getting turned on by words, the promise of things to come. I wanted to cum, but I also wanted it to last, for both of us. I couldn't wait though. As I tried hard not to break contact with his wonderful length of stiffness, I swivelled my body around until I was kneeling, almost sitting on his face and as he thrust his hardness into my mouth, his tongue attacked my clitoris, goading me into being a vixen. Putting gentle pressure on each ball in turn, I traced my fingers between his scrotum and his thighs. I suddenly found it hard to concentrate as his tongue stopped tweaking my clit and entered my pussy, tasting and exploring as far as it could possibly reach. His fingers were caressing my clit as the same time. It was pure heaven. With hardly any warning, I felt a fire inside of me, exciting flames, threatening to engulf me and I shuddered in ecstasy. I cried out in delight through every second of my orgasm. Before my breathing steadied, I once again gave my full attention to his cock and scrotum. I wanted him to feel the same beautiful intensity. My hand moved up and down his shaft, faster and faster as I sucked on the head of it. He groaned louder with each passing minute. He was poking fingers inside me, working on my clit again and I never wanted it to end.

"Helen…don't…suck…so…hard! Don't! I don't…want…to come…in…your mouth! I was surprised. I thought that was every man's dream. I was prepared to let him squirt into my mouth, taste his juices. I had never done it before, but I was prepared to do it for David.

"Why…not…David? I'm…I…want…to do…that…for you."

He pulled out of my mouth and shuffled away from underneath me. "On your side, Helen, quick! I feel it, coming!"

I couldn't answer, I just did it, I wanted his cum. I got into position. He cuddled up behind me like spoons and rammed it in my pussy from behind. He gripped around me, holding my hips tight in place as he gave three or four quick thrusts and I could feel his spurts of come as they were released. His fingers were rubbing hard against my swollen clit, and my juices seeped into his as I climaxed yet again. I felt like I was soaring through the universe with my eyes closed. I was aware of nothing except for the two of us, the passion and excitement of what we had just done. Nobody else existed. As David's breathing gradually slowed, he kissed my neck and continued to hold his perfect body tight to mine. After ten minutes he pulled me around to face him and he kissed me passionately on the lips. I responded. During that kiss I suddenly remembered our lips meeting earlier, how much I had enjoyed it. It had been full of fire…and not something I had intended to do. The wine had weakened my resolve!

His lips gently broke contact with mine and I felt them touch my ear as he whispered "Oh shit! Helen, I've got something to tell you!"

I was suddenly tense, not knowing what to expect. Was it something I wanted to hear or didn't want to hear. I wasn't even clear in my head what words I would like to hear. I wondered if it was at all possible to…No! I told myself I couldn't think like that, not if I was to get through life without complications. I was feeling nauseous again, dreading what he might say.

"Yes? Go on then…tell!" I closed my eyes and held my breath.

"We have been down here, naked, and fucking!"

"Yes? Your point being, David?"

"Look at the window, Helen."

I lifted my head off the floor. It took all of ten seconds for me to realise what David had brought to my attention. It was dark outside. The wall-lights were on in his lounge. The blinds were not closed. We had been indulging in gloriously naughty oral sex in full view of anybody who chose to nosily look through his window.

We looked at each other in mock horror, and started laughing uncontrollably. We went to bed half an hour later.

I was aware of David's hard-on tapping on my back about six thirty in the morning. Within five minutes we were at it, shagging like a couple of dogs. When each of us were fully satiated some thirty minutes later, he turned on his side and tried to kiss me, but I tilted my head, his kisses falling on my cheek instead. I couldn't forget that we had kissed the previous night, and it

181

had troubled me before I drifted off to sleep. I didn't want to be involved with him on that level. I had to make a concerted effort not to fall into that again. I put it down to the wine and the lack of control on my part, due to intoxication. I knew I had to be in control in future –*not too much to drink in the future when with clients!*

David needed to be at a business meeting in the city for eleven. After he'd served breakfast, I showered and dressed and was in the lounge preparing to leave. He sat at the dining table sorting through his briefcase whilst I was fastening my sandals. I wasn't looking forward to going home. I had a kind of empty feeling in the pit of my stomach. David would be flying out to Geneva later in the evening. He had already told me that he wouldn't be back in the country for two or three months, and the thought had left me feeling lonely. I couldn't understand why. He was not my partner or husband, I wasn't used to being with him all the time, and yet the thought of not seeing him for so long filled me with dread. I would miss the mind-blowing sex - that was it.

He came to the door with me as I was leaving and he moved towards me once more to try and kiss me. I would have loved to be able to kiss him back, lovingly or urgently, but I knew I mustn't do that. He held me by my shoulders, and as I moved my lips away, he asked, "What are you scared of, Helen?"

I wanted to tell him. I really wanted to tell him that it was him I was scared of. Scared of what he was doing to me. I was frightened to kiss him, frightened of what I might feel. I looked him straight in the eye. "What do you mean, David? Scared?"

"You know exactly what I mean. You won't let me kiss you, Helen."

I had to get away from him. I couldn't get in too deep with this conversation. I couldn't let him know any more.

"David, you're my client. I must go now. Take care." I leaned forward and gave him a quick peck on the lips, not giving him enough time to respond. I turned and walked down the street, not daring to look back at him. I could feel his eyes watching me all the way, until I turned the corner into the next street.

PART 2
Sex....

CHAPTER 22

I spent the first week after my parents' death in either total disbelief or total devastation, alternating between the two. When Anthony took me back home from the funeral, I crawled into a corner and howled the place down. A box of tissues constantly by my side; I took to pouring brandy down my neck all day, every day. It didn't go down very well with the tablets. It didn't do anything to numb the pain for me. I reached a stage where the tears ceased completely. There were no more tears to cry. Anthony didn't go into the office. I think he must have been worried about me. He made sure I tried to eat something and stood over me at times to make sure that I did. The rocking stage came next. I sat cross-legged, arms around my knees, and rocked constantly. Anthony called our doctor who came out two nights in a row and gave me a sedative to help me sleep. He also left a new prescription - an increased dosage of my anti-depressants.

Three weeks after the funeral I went into the office –but not to work. I hadn't been in touch with anyone since my parents had died. I realised I was not being fair to Ted, I had behaved badly but I couldn't face seeing people or even speaking to them. I had relied on Anthony far too much to protect me from people. I knew that it had to stop sometime, and this was the time. I needed to see Mr Hopkins. I knocked on his door, popped my head around and said "Can I come in please, Ted?"

"Helen, please do." He gestured towards the chair opposite him

"I didn't expect to see you back yet. Surely…you need a little more time. Take all you need, it's not a problem."

I felt guilty. I had been inconsiderate and I didn't want him to be nice to me. I couldn't even look him in the eye, I would start crying again.

"Ted, the reason I've come in is…" I hesitated, "I can't return, I just can't, it wouldn't be fair to you, or to any of the staff. I've not been pulling my weight lately. You know that, so does everyone else. My parents…I'm devastated. I have serious problems in my marriage. I have other issues too, which you can't fail to have noticed, I know some of the girls have noticed. I can't concentrate, I can't work. I'm no good to anyone, so it's only fair that I should leave. It will give you the chance to employ somebody, or take another partner on, someone who can give one hundred percent. I'm not even capable of giving ten percent at the moment and I can't see that improving in the near future. It is going to take me a long time to get over this…Mum and Dad…my marriage. I don't know how long…"

"Helen, could you not even think this through for…who knows…however long it takes? Three or possibly four months even? We could get by – just. You're jumping the gun, it's still early days."

He was such a lovely man, so compassionate and so patient, I hated doing this to him. The trouble was it could be too detrimental to the business if I stayed and couldn't give one hundred percent, I couldn't do that to him.

"But it's not just the grieving, Ted, it's all the other issues - my marriage, I can't keep my O.C.D. in check. I *am* leaving, Ted, I *have* to."

His eyes showed his disappointment although he smiled kindly at me.

"Well, you're still a partner here. You can have your percentage of the profits. I can't say fairer than this – I'll get an agency worker. Take what you need, one year or maybe two, but come back please."

I couldn't give him my promise so I didn't say anything. He came with me to my office, and I cleared my personal bits and pieces from my desk. There wasn't much, a few of my favourite pens and a picture of Anthony (which I intended slinging into the nearest bin once I left the office). My laptop was already at home so there wasn't much else. I tried to give Ted an update on the files that I had been working on to bring him up to speed, although with everything that had happened to me, my recollections were vague. I stepped towards him and put the pile of files in his arms. Ted being the way he is, immediately put them back down onto my desk and held his arms out to give me a hug.

"I am so sorry, Helen. Please stay in touch. I really hadn't expected this bombshell today, but I want you to know, I do understand your reasons, I really do. If there's anything I can ever do to help..."

"Thank you, Ted. Can I just ask one more thing of you please?"

"Certainly, what can I do?"

"Would you please mind telling the staff after I've gone? I love them all dearly but I can't face them, the way I'm feeling…Tell them I will be in touch - when I'm ready."

"Consider it done, my dear."

"Thank you again, Ted."

I walked out of the door relieved that I had one less thing preying on my mind. Remembering the picture of Anthony in my handbag, I tossed it in a waste bin at the end of the street, and I took little pleasure from doing so. I didn't know where I was going, or what I was going to do. Just over the road from the waste bin, I spotted the tube station and crossed over. I got on the first train that stopped and I had no idea which direction it was going, or where I was going to get off.

I don't know how long I had been travelling when I woke up from my daydreams, but the train had just stopped at Oxford Circus tube station. I must have been staring at the man who was sat opposite me (not intentionally), because he was glaring back at me as if I was some alien from another planet. He made me feel uncomfortable, so I quickly snatched up my handbag and left the train.   Once out of the station into the open again, I walked. Half of the time I didn't know where I was but I just kept on going, changing direction without realising and totally unaware of the length of time I had been walking.

It suddenly dawned on me that people were looking at me, and I couldn't understand why. I started to taste the tears that rolled into my lips. I was then aware that I couldn't make out the faces of the people that stared, they were blurred. Feeling embarrassed, I turned to what I thought was a shop window on the pretext that I was window shopping. Only it wasn't a dress shop, or any other shop for that matter. I was looking straight at the job vacancies in a recruitment office. "Chambermaids wanted, apply within." I quickly dabbed at my eyes and went in.

One hour later, I was emerging from a top London hotel, with a bag containing two chambermaid uniforms with instructions on who to report to the next Monday morning. When I arrived home (it seemed a stupid thought, but that's how I still referred to the marital house I shared with Anthony), I ignored the mess in the house, I ignored the mail sat on the doormat near the front door and went up to my room. Opening the bag I took out the uniforms, and wondered what the hell had gotten into me. I was a qualified accountant for heaven's sake. What on earth had possessed me to apply for a job as a cleaner in a hotel? I started an argument with myself there and then. *Yes girl, but you are an accountant who can't even do her job anymore. Too much going on in your life, you can't concentrate, you can't even do anything right any more. So you've found yourself a job that you can actually do, haven't you? You can clean. You can make a good job of this - you've got O.C.D. for heaven's sake. Just turn up there on Monday morning. Do it. Get out of the house, away from him. Nobody need know what you are doing. But Mum and Dad would have gone crazy if they knew about this. They will do. They'll be watching over you Helen. That's what they always did. Watch over me.* The argument within, carried on for over two hours, covering the same ground, asking the same questions, answering the same answers. My mind was made up. I would turn up for that job on Monday morning. Anthony needn't know. I was not going to make him any the wiser, and there was nobody else to tell him.

CHAPTER 23

I turned up at the hotel with ten minutes to spare on my first day. I checked in with head housekeeper, Mrs Fenwick, first and filled in some of my personal details on the form she handed me. She handed over my name badge and showed me to the locker room where I had to change into one of the little black dresses and crisp white maid's aprons that had been provided. One of the girls, Sandra, took me to the floor that I would be working on and introduced me to Jodie, the girl who would spend the day with me to show me the ropes.

Jodie was a nice kid, more mature than I would have expected for an eighteen year old and unusually conscientious for someone of her years. As we chatted our way through the morning, I happened to mention to her that I detected more than a hint of iciness in Mrs Fenwick's manner. She laughed her agreement as she told me that all the staff referred to the head housekeeper as 'Frigid Flo.' I enjoyed Jodie's constant chattering and at least if she was doing all the talking, I didn't have to say much. I preferred to keep it that way - it would keep things simple. I made up my mind that I wouldn't reveal any details about my recent devastating news or my disastrous private life.

I was relying on my O.C.D. to help get me through each working day and it struck me as ironic that my mental health issue actually had a use! I cleaned, scrubbed and took a genuine pride in my work, or so Jodie thought, but she was unaware of the inner demons I was attempting to rid myself of. There were more than a few occasions when I caught her glancing at me suspiciously, and it didn't shake me in the slightest when she posed the question,

"Have you done this type of work before, Helen? Because you're making a great job of these rooms. It surprises me because you don't actually look the type. You look kind of…educated, if you don't mind my saying so."

I returned her smile as I quickly scoured my head for what to say. I sensed that if I didn't volunteer something about my private life she would keep pushing.

"Thank you, Jodie. You're right! I did have a good education."

Her eyes were agog. She plonked herself on the bed we had just made, laid on her side, propped up on one elbow. Getting comfortable for a heart to heart, she wanted more and looked at me expectantly. I reluctantly obliged.

"I *was* married but he…he cheated. I've still got the bills to pay so I do anything I can to earn money. It's very hard, living alone, but it's what I have to do to keep my house and pay the bills. I work from home as well, doing business on the internet, which I can do on a night and weekends. I work as many hours in a day as I can."

She seemed to accept quite happily what I'd just told her and we got on with the rest of the day's work on our floor. I wasn't happy with myself but I couldn't tell her that I had worked in accountancy or that I suffered with O.C.D. I liked the girl a lot and her chitchat kept me amused for the most part. At other times, I tried to switch off

192

from her. I also kept attempting to visualise my parents, but it was hard. I hoped they wouldn't think bad of me or be disappointed – think that I was weak for giving into my grief and throwing away my career.

Mrs Fenwick came out of her office to see me the next morning. She had apparently heard excellent reports about my work from Jodie *and* the shift supervisor, and from that morning onwards I would be working alone. She handed me the details of the rooms I would be working on that day. The solitude was lovely. I cleaned and scrubbed, only focusing on what was in front of my eyes. I didn't have to think, or concentrate. I disinfected, I cleaned out my mind. Cleared it of hurtful thoughts! Thoughts of Gavin, Anthony, rape and my grief over the death of my parents! But the hurt returned with a vengeance each time I left the hotel. It didn't feel like I would ever be over it. And for the first time ever, I wished I had a brother or sister – a sibling, someone who would be able to understand my grief and be my shoulder to cry on.

I wondered if I could have better coped with my grief if I didn't have so many other issues - if I had a loving husband at home to talk to and care for me. It further grieved me that I didn't even have *that*!

Anthony was absolutely clueless where I was going or what I was doing each day; I left home in my car every morning, parked up in a car park near the tube station and caught the train into the city centre. It wasn't likely that he would ever find out. He'd never phoned me at work *before* we became estranged and I doubted he would do that now.

CHAPTER 24

I carried on going to work each day from Monday to Friday. I had specifically requested not to be given weekend shifts, mainly for the reason that I didn't want Anthony to realise what I was doing. Our indifference towards each other was as much a routine for us as our working hours. We shared a bottle of wine at times, but conversation between us was still almost non-existent.

After I'd been working at the hotel for no more than a few weeks, Mrs Fenwick told me I was being promoted to the top floor where all the penthouse suites were situated.

"They are much bigger than those you have been used to. The standard of cleaning must be exceptional, Helen. There's more to do, but you don't have so many of them." She continued to tell me, "I'm bringing down one of the other girls, she's been missing a few things lately and we've received complaints. I can't afford to let that happen where special guests are concerned. Don't let me down on this, Helen. You've worked hard and you are now my best chambermaid, so I'm giving you this opportunity – I'm putting my trust in you."

It was ironic. My O.C.D. had done well for me. Was I expected to be pleased? I tried to find some emotion from within but I came up with…indifference. My good manners however came to the fore.

"Thank you, Mrs Fenwick, I'll try not to let you down."

I had been told by the other staff that she very rarely made an appearance on the top floor to check the suites, so I would have to check my own work. I knew my pride would be hurt if she ever received any complaints. Every shift from then on I made my way up in the lift to the top floor; Garden, Kensington, Thames and Tower.

She hadn't been wrong about the extra work. The bathrooms were large, the bedrooms bigger, and a decent sized lounge with dining areas to each. I tried not to think of the job as cleaning for an employer. I rather fancied that each of these little apartments was my own personal flat and I was keeping it immaculate for my own satisfaction. There were times I met some of the V.I.P. occupants and whilst there was one or two who talked down to me, the majority were fairly respectful and chatted to me as I worked. The male clientele were especially attentive, or at least they were when they didn't have wives or lovers with them, and I could always feel their eyes burning into me as they drank in every detail of my long legs and bottom.

About ten days after I'd started working on the upper floor, I knocked on the door of one of the suites and waited for a response. It was a male guest who opened the door to me.

"Come in, young lady, and put the latch on the door behind you. I don't want to be disturbed by anybody else. I'm busy doing some work. Start in the bathroom and bedroom please, and I shall make myself scarce when you want to do the living area."

"Yes Sir, I will."

I latched the door as he'd instructed and quietly made my way into the bedroom. The door was ajar, and whilst I was working I could see that he had his laptop plugged in over on the desk, although he was actually sat on the settee with a pile of buff folders next to him. He was busy reading the contents of the folders. I busied myself with the dusting and polishing and changing the linen on the bed. I decided I would do the vacuuming when he eventually disappeared as he had said he would. I was out of the bedroom after about thirty minutes and I went to work on the bathroom. I disinfected the toilet, washed the tiles around the toilet area, and moved the used towels onto the floor so that I could clean the bath.

I was bent over the bath reaching to the furthest edge, and without any warning at all, I felt my skirt suddenly being raised up my back, and my tights pulled down to my knees. A couple of fingers slid into my pussy as my knickers were pulled to one side. I didn't move away but stopped dead in my tracks.

"Sir, what do you think you are doing?" I asked him politely.

He was breathing heavily. "I've been watching you working - from the bedroom. You didn't hear me, did you? You've got a very hot body and I would love you to show me how hot it can get."

He continued groping around inside me and I still didn't move. I hadn't had anything inside me for about two or three months and I had almost forgotten how good it felt, the excitement coursing through my whole body.

"I…I'm supposed…to be…working. I don't do things like that, Sir. T…Take your fingers out…I can do my job...and you can do yours." Whilst I listened to my own words, I realised that he wasn't convinced. Hell, I was struggling to convince myself. "That's…what we're…both here for. If my boss…knocked at the door…I wouldn't have a job anymore."

I was shocked. I had a big problem. This was sexual harassment in the workplace – by one of the special guests. My trouble was that I wanted it to continue. I actually *wanted* him to keep poking me…fingers…his dick. I was on fire and the flames had to die out naturally. I didn't want them extinguished.
Beautiful…feeling…beautiful flames. I turned my face to look into his eyes. Did he realise he was playing with fire? That if I lodged a complaint…but he was *not* playing games. His eyes showed how much he wanted me…and his determination to get what he wanted.

"Come on…! You know you want to. You would have moved away by now if you didn't."

That much was true. I finally moved to my left and his fingers slid back out of me as I moved. I tried to convince myself that I didn't feel horny.

"Wouldn't you rather be fucked than finish the cleaning? I won't tell anyone. I want to fuck you. Come on, how much would it cost me? Name your price."

I didn't quite know what to think. He was suggesting I prostitute myself. I turned my back on him, pulled my tights up and straightened my skirt.

"Okay, if you won't name a price, I'll suggest one. Come on, honey, play the game. I want to fuck you real bad."

I wanted to be fucked real bad too. He wasn't particularly attractive, maybe fiftyish, but there was something…or was it just my need to have a shag after weeks without? His first offer was one thousand pounds – I shook my head without saying a word. It wasn't about the money. If only he'd rip my clothes off instead of talking money, he would be able to fuck me for nothing…my body was awakened and I was gagging for it.

"I'm just going to get on with my work. Please forget it, Sir. I'm not a prostitute."

He kept raising his price and I just continued shaking my head and repeating "No! I'm not doing this."

Undeterred, he kept upping the offer. I stopped shaking my head so often, pausing in thought for a few seconds between his bids. When he reached the figure where my interest took a sudden lurch, I turned and looked at him.

"Do you actually have that much money on you? I'm nobody's fool. It's got to be cash or it doesn't happen - your choice."

He had broken into a sweat and his hands were shaking, his eyes were undressing the goods and he started stuttering.

"I'll…I'll…go to my…my bank later and…br…bring the cash back for you."

"No. You'd better get the cash now…or I'll just do my job and get out of here."

Five minutes later he was out of the door with his briefcase. I asked myself what the hell I thought I was doing and I couldn't come up with an answer. My work had come to a standstill, I was unable to concentrate because my mind was now focused on one thing only – getting laid. Somehow I didn't expect him to return. Once he was out on the street with me out of his sight, he would come to his senses and realise he couldn't cheat on his wife or partner.

Half an hour later, my heart leapt as I heard the click as his card bleeped in the lock. He replaced the security chain once he'd closed the door. Beckoning me over to the dining table, he opened his briefcase and showed me the cash. I stood gaping…but not at the cash. What had caught my attention, and gave me my second big shock of the day – the guy was a barrister. The curly white wig was laid at the side of some A4 Oyez legal forms. Backing away, I was intending to return to my duties, suddenly very wary of him.

"You could make yourself a fortune with your body and your looks - a nice side-line for you; get you away from all this." He gestured towards the housekeeping trolley.

I looked directly into his eyes, thinking that he was quite attractive after all, and throwing caution to the wind, I asked "What do you want?"

He smiled, his brown eyes showing his desire and he came up close and almost whispered in my ear.

"I want to play with you, taste you and fuck you. I want you to make it really nice and welcoming for me. You can treat me like all men want to be treated. Do it right and you get all that cash that's in the briefcase! You've seen it - now let's see if you want to earn it. Nobody will ever get to know, trust me."

I don't know whether it was because the guy was vaguely handsome, or whether it was the thought of the amount of cash, but I was feeling hot and clammy, my panties still damp from his earlier exploration. It would be another escape from my current existence and depression. He started peeling off his clothes down to his tight trunks as he walked towards the bed. He was slightly overweight with a hint of a paunch, but not too unattractive. I was quite naïve as to how prostitutes behaved with their clients and for want of something better to say I put on my best seductive voice and asked "Would Sir like to unwrap his very expensive present or have it unwrapped for him?"

"First of all, Sir, would like you to call him Simon," quick glance at my name tag, "and, Helen, I love opening surprises myself." He patted the bed, and I think I maybe overdid it with the provocative walk. "Please don't act like a pro, Helen. Be yourself," he scolded.

I lay down on the bed next to him and my thoughts turned from sex to being found in bed with a hotel guest and I couldn't relax as tension started to creep through my body.

"What if someone knocks on the door, Sir…Simon?" He considered.

"I shout and tell them to bugger off. On this floor nobody argues with us…shall we say, very important guests!"

I was slightly pacified to hear it, but it still didn't feel quite right.

"Let's continue where we left off in the bathroom, shall we?" He moved in to kiss me and I turned my head away,

"No, don't do that please. We are not lovers, Sir..Simon, it wouldn't seem right."

He shrugged and looked down at my body. The bathroom scene unfolded once again as he drew up my skirt and pushed my tights and panties down. Although the scenario was totally alien to me, I was excited in a way I had never been excited – yet tense at the same time. The tension was a mixture of wanting…and fear. I hadn't had sex in weeks and could hardly wait for his fingers to once again edge their way teasingly into my warmth and wetness. The underlying fear was intensifying the pleasure. I was feeling tarty, and shameless. I placed my hands under my bra and fondled my breasts…a new experience. He watched me and I got the impression it was something he'd never seen before, his mouth gaped in excitement. I jumped, but pleasurably so, when he unexpectedly twiddled with my clit for a short time before moving his attention to my fanny. His right hand was awkwardly groping about with the top half of my clothes so I helped him.

"You are eager, Helen. I see that. You want fucking as much as I want to fuck you, don't you? You take your clothes off while I attend to this beautiful pussy."

I pulled my blouse off quickly, but I was struggling to hold back, the anticipation edging ahead in the battle. His fingers were in my hole again, probing and shoving. Every damn nerve in my tunnel was alert, waiting and already tingling,

202

ready to surrender. As he bent his finger towards my G spot I couldn't hold back any longer. My body arched backwards as I moaned out loud and my upper thighs gripped his arm, keeping his fingers firmly in place. I could feel my juices flowing and I wanted more. I was truly on fire. I let the first wave of orgasm subside. I unfastened my bra, threw it to the floor, and my skirt followed in one movement, up and over my head. I was panting in pleasure…and fascinated by my own behaviour.

"Wow. I can feel your love syrup all over my fingers. I wanted that love syrup over my cock. Let's see if you've got some more to give."

"Oh, I've definitely got more to give," I said throatily. "I can see the bulge in your undies. I want that bulge inside me, fucking me. First you are going to feel my mouth pleasuring your cock."

I knelt on the bed and pushed his boxers down his legs. They only reached his ankles at the full stretch of my arm so he kicked them off with one of his feet. I was pleasantly surprised when the bulge sprang out of his tight trunks, its hardness twanging as it slapped back against his stomach, thick and superbly erect. I wanted it inside me, there and then, but I couldn't be selfish. My aim was to please the man and earn the cash. I barely recognised myself and wondered what the hell I was doing as I leaned over and wrapped my fuchsia lips around his knob. I teased around the rim of the head and tickled its tiny orifice with my tongue – that orifice which would soon be spewing out his sex juices when he ejaculated.

He moaned almost silently as I stroked the length of his cock with my tongue. I changed position until I was leaning over the bed, my head between his legs. Taking one of his balls into my mouth, I grasped at his cock with my right hand and rubbed it up and down his length, slowly at first and then steadily increasing the speed. He was groaning again, as I flicked his ball back and forth in my mouth with my tongue. I eased the first one out of my mouth and taunted the other for a minute before also encasing that one in my mouth. My hand was moving rapidly up and down his tool, and he steadied it,

"Slower, ease off. I'm getting too hot and eager…eager to spill my spunk."

He lifted his back off the bed, and grabbing under my arms, hauled me up his body, my probing tongue licking his body throughout the movement, from his pubic bone through his navel and up to his chest. He pulled me upwards until my pussy was at the tip of his cock and then eased me back down and onto it in one deft move. We both groaned at the same time. It felt awesome and every nerve was throbbing within my hole. My need was making me light headed.

"Your fanny is deliciously wet and exciting and it feels so tight and hot around my cock. Fuck it now, let that sweet syrup flow." I pushed my pubic bone downwards and the feel of his muscle inside me was amazing – tight, stinging and throbbing. I moved with ease, ever the accomplished rider, I sat on his stiffness, and feeling the pleasure of every inch as my vagina rubbed at it abrasively, my clit being massaged against his pubic bone. He bit hard into my neck, and then my shoulder as I rode him roughly, giving everything I had, putting it all into getting my reward and it was there, ready to explode, his bites making me gasp in pleasure and in pain.

I came, more explosively this time, so much wetness. He reached down to where his cock entered me and felt around its hardness with his finger. It was so sensitised down there, just the touch of his finger on the lips of my labia sent me soaring to new heights. I was breathing heavily and could feel that my body was aglow with warmth and wetness.

"Is that good, Helen - me fucking you? You have so much syrup in such a short time. When were you last fucked?" I was totally incapable of answering - breathless and still shaking from my orgasm.

"It doesn't really matter. You're enjoying yourself. I'm coated in your syrup." He rolled me over onto my back and as he did so, I lost contact with his throbbing cock. It was his turn to go down on me and he thrust his tongue into my newly acquired wetness and tasted.

"So sweet, baby! So sweet, as I knew you would be. I knew you would taste good and you didn't disappoint."

His tongue was moving wonderfully inside me and I didn't know when this orgasm was going to cease, it was so intense. Then the tongue was gone, and he eased himself up my body, and his cock found its target again. The stinging tightness - that feeling of being fucked by something so hard and thick! I gripped my fanny around his muscle and squeezed each time he thrust into me, and it felt so good. It was hot and…I had almost forgotten what it felt like to be fucked…I loved it. He was getting faster, thrusting harder and he was biting at my neck again, then my shoulder. The nibbling and the hard thrusting was driving me into a new frenzy, my body tensed, so taut I was being driven crazy, I could feel myself going cross-eyed and I didn't know what to do with myself. My nails were digging into his back as I exploded again. He pulled out quickly and said urgently,

"Quick, - onto your knees!" I squeezed my fanny tight around his tool as he rammed it in from behind and it tipped him over the edge. He threw his head back, gritted his teeth, and shouted out in his ultimate pleasure. It took his breathing ten minutes to calm.

When he finally lifted his weight from my body, I felt his wetness rush out and spill between my thighs. I was still shaking uncontrollably, but I jumped off the bed in a hurry when the reality hit me.

I showered in such a rush, desperate to get back to work should somebody be looking for me. He sat and watched me towel myself dry and put my slightly crumpled uniform back on.

"You could do well for yourself, Helen. You love to be fucked, and you certainly know how to pleasure a man. I know some men, wealthy men who…well, would pay lots of money to fuck you and be fucked back as good as you do. Men who need total discretion. I would pay you again. Don't let this be a one-off. Give me your number - I'll get you some clients. Are you interested in being rich, Helen?"

I was staggered by what he was suggesting – enjoy being fucked and get paid for it. I was also trying to come to terms with what I'd just done – prostituted myself whilst I was at work. I could feel my face flushing with guilt.

"I…I'm not sure, Simon. I shouldn't have done that – it was out of character…I…there are freaks out there. I don't want to be in any danger. I shouldn't, can't."

"I can almost swear to you that any person I give your number to will not be a freak. They will pay you well, no question of it, and you will not be in any danger. Give me your mobile number, Helen - I'll get you the work and I'll tell them you're called…Kat, Cougar, Puma or something equally ridiculous." He laughed at his little joke and paused in his laughter a second, waiting for my reaction.

More at ease now that I was dressed and ready for work, I smiled vaguely and jotted down my mobile number as he passed me the cash. I stuffed it safely down the front of my tights and we said our goodbyes.

I don't know how I managed to get through the rest of my duties. Every time I caught sight of myself in a mirror my face looked crimson. I imagined that everybody was staring at me, wondering what crime I had just committed. One thing I did realise – if I went ahead with this ridiculous suggestion of Simon's, I would be able to have a sex life when I wanted, earn fantastic money and I didn't need to fall in love. But the biggest bonus for me, I wouldn't have my heart broken ever again – no more hurt. It was that

handsome bonus that persuaded me it was the
right thing to do.

CHAPTER 25

I cried every day, but my initial disbelief had progressed towards acceptance and the anti-depressants were doing their job. I still hadn't been able to face going over to my parents' house to sort anything. I had asked Anthony to go and fetch a list of the things I wanted – mainly some of their personal effects and the family photograph albums. That was all I wanted. The estate agent I called had the house on the market and was confident of a quick sale. Hopefully, I would soon be able to arrange for the furniture to go to auction. Mum's car had already been sold by a local garage.

On the Saturday morning, a few days after Simon had brought about my initiation into the world of prostitution, I was having a well earned lie-in for once. (Work, along with its big surprise, had been hectic all week). I'd been downstairs, made myself a pot of coffee and toast and was back in bed having a quiet read, amongst plenty of tears for my parents, and mixed feelings about dipping my toes into the sordid sex trade. Whilst I was partly disgusted with myself at my last two rampant sex sessions with Alex and Simon, I had found both experiences very dirty, but exhilarating. I felt twinges and dampness just thinking about them again.

I heard Anthony's bedroom door open and close and was surprised to hear him tapping on my bedroom door,

"Helen, are you awake?"

My peace and thoughts disturbed, I sighed,

"Yes, I'm awake."

There were a few moments of hesitation from him, maybe pondering what he was going to say.

"Can you come downstairs soon, please? There's…there's…some things I need to…to…tell you. Things you need to know that can't wait any longer." He sounded on edge, tired.

I started panicking, wondering what the hell was going on now. I sensed from his voice that it would be things I didn't want to hear.

I felt a sinking feeling in my stomach. Did I really want to know?

"Helen…?"

"Okay. Yes. I'll be down in five minutes."

He was still in his dressing gown sat in his favourite armchair, a fresh pot of coffee on the table and an empty cup, so I poured one for myself and sat at the edge of the settee, feeling tense.

"Well?"

He took a few sips of his coffee, then gazed down into his cup, avoiding my eye, and mumbled,

"I haven't been sleeping well lately, and last night, not at all."

This news didn't move me in the slightest and feeling rather smart- arsed, I remarked "Well, unfortunately I'm not your G.P. but it could be down to the many things on your conscience."

He scowled at me, evidently affronted.

"Don't you *ever* let things drop, Helen?"

I felt like bloody slapping him. He was riling me before I even knew what else was coming in my direction. Did he really expect to be off the hook? He obviously had things he wanted to say, he had such a frustrated look on his face, so I decided to keep quiet and let him speak.

"Go ahead then. You want to explain why you're not sleeping I presume?"

His face was red, he'd put down his coffee cup and was fiddling with and picking at his finger nails.

"I've wanted to tell you before now, Helen. I didn't think you could cope with it on top of your grief. You've had more than enough to deal with."

I couldn't disagree with that, but he'd been the cause of everything except the death of my parents.

He took a minute or two to compose himself and finally looked directly at me.

"The business is finished, Helen. The bank has called the official receiver in."

I stood up, started pacing the room. I felt as if I'd been hit with a sledge-hammer. It must be wrong, my father wouldn't let...

"My dad's business? Finished? You...He..."

I couldn't take it in. Then it hit me even more quickly, like a wrecking ball. I could feel my anger building and I unleashed it at him in an instant.

"My father's business, ruined! HE'S ONLY BEEN DEAD THREE FUCKING MONTHS AND YOU'VE MANAGED TO FUCK IT ALL UP IN THAT SHORT SPACE OF

211

TIME? EVERYTHING HE FUCKING WORKED FOR! GET…"

"Helen…NO! It's been…" But I was relentless in my fury.

"WHAT WOULD MY DAD SAY IF HE KNEW? HE FUCKING TRUSTED YOU! YOU BASTARD!"

I was shaking with rage. Of all the things he'd done, even to me, this was by far the worst - destroying Dad's business. Something that I had hoped would live on forever…something Dad had started from scratch and built up over the years, and now that had died with him! Such an overwhelming sadness just crept up on me and rendered me speechless as I let that thought sink in.

Taking advantage of my silence, Anthony, who was still sat down, leaned forward and held his hands up as if he could calm me.

"Helen! Helen! Ken knew about it. It hasn't just happened overnight, or without his knowledge! He knew! It's been going on for months now."

I glared at him angrily. Was this something else he thought he could talk his way out of? If he was hoping to pacify me, he'd have to do better than that!

"Helen, sit down! Let me explain! You're an accountant, Helen, for fuck's sake! You should know that businesses don't just fail overnight!"

I started pacing again, refusing to do as he'd told me by sitting down. I was feeling violent towards him. He was my father's finance director, in a position of trust, how could he have let this happen?

"COME ON THEN, ANTHONY, EXPLAIN IT TO ME! HOW THE FUCK DID YOU LET IT HAPPEN?" I bellowed. I was losing control.

Throughout the next half hour, I heard the whole story. I'd finally calmed down enough to hear him out. Ten or eleven months ago, Anthony had found out through some business contact, that two smaller advertising companies were about to go into administration. Keen to help build up my father's business even further, Anthony had seen the opportunity to gain more clients as one not to be missed. He convinced my father to look into the matter further and they had gone together to meetings with the receivers for both businesses. Persuaded by Anthony's cashflow forecasts for the next five years, Dad had agreed to purchase both companies for a pittance, along with their liabilities.

They had taken a big risk and it had failed. The trade creditors had unanimously agreed to bear with them, receiving an agreed figure per month, pleased to be getting more than the expected nine pence in the pound the receiver would have paid. However, by the time the PAYE and VAT liabilities had been settled for both failed businesses, which had far exceeded Anthony's predictions, the company bank had started putting pressure on Dad. The expected new portfolio of clients had never materialised. Those clients, obviously suspecting that taking on all the liabilities of two failed companies would cripple Dad's business, had taken their business elsewhere.

"Ken was desperate to save the business, Helen. We've both been worried for months. On the day of the accident, he had made an appointment for us to see the bank. He was going to ask them to increase the overdraft or if they would accept their house as security for a loan."

My head was going round in circles, trying to fathom who had been to blame in all this. Anthony; for telling my father about the two businesses. Or subsequently; his worthless cash-flow forecasts. Or Dad and his stupidity - stupidity for placing his trust in Anthony and his judgements. I couldn't think straight in my fury and as if to add insult to injury, he added,

"That's why I've been behaving like an arsehole these last few months, Helen. The worry, I couldn't take it anymore!"

He finally tipped me over the edge with his words. I picked up the nearest thing to me, a heavy glass paperweight, and flung it at him with as much force as I could muster. He ducked and it went smashing through the lounge window.

CHAPTER 26

Within ten minutes of dodging my missile, Anthony was dressed and gone. I didn't trust myself to do or say anything else. I was livid. I'd shot off upstairs with a bottle of wine before he'd left, determined to drink myself into oblivion.

I lay on the bed trying to get a grip, but it wasn't easy. I tried to work things out in my mind. I couldn't understand how Dad had been so taken in by Anthony, so much so that he'd even pushed me towards him, thinking he was perfect husband material. I started blaming myself. If only I have told Dad months ago – about the rent boy, the rape, the gang bang and the cocaine. It could have prevented all this…and probably my parents' deaths. All the worry had caused Dad's heart attack, I knew that. But hadn't Anthony just said it was the worry that had made him behave badly? So that must mean the businesses were taken over before Anthony's scandalous behaviour. Why hadn't Dad asked me, a qualified accountant, to produce cash-flow figures for him? Anthony had a degree in design. That's why he'd started working for my father. He had very little knowledge of accounts other than what he'd picked up from Dad. What the hell had my father been thinking of, making him Finance Director? I went over everything – every conversation I could recall over the last nine to ten months, sifting through to ask myself if there was anything, any words that I should have picked up on that would have given some indication.

I came up with nothing.

I woke up at ten minutes to four, my mobile was ringing. My eyes searched for the bottle of wine first – it was still more than half full. I remembered finishing the first glass and there was still half a glassful remaining of the second one I'd poured. Not quite the oblivion I'd been hoping for. I sighed and answered the call.

"Hello? Helen Pawson."

"Helen? Hello, it's Simon speaking. You remember?"

I sat bolt upright, suddenly alert. How could I forget? I'd never be able to forget.

"Yes, I remember, Simon!"

"Have you thought any more about my suggestion?"

I trembled, knowing where this conversation was heading, but not quite sure yet what my final decision would be.

"Yes, I have thought about it, but I've had quite a few other things to think about as well. What answers do you want from me?"

"As I said, Helen, I can get you some clients, good ones that I can vouch for. I have a gentleman who wants to meet you in the next few days, you can do it at the hotel, nobody will know. Can I give him your number?"

It was going way too fast for my liking. The thought of uncomplicated sex was very attractive to me but there were some little matters that needed to be discussed before I would even consider it.

"Have you considered my safety? These people could be…"

He interrupted sharply,

"He's hardly going to murder you in a hotel room, Helen. Come on!"

He was starting to piss me off, being too presumptuous.

"I work there, Simon, it's not a brothel. I won't be able to meet people there indefinitely."

"Well then, you call me before each and every meeting - let me know where and when. That should put your mind at rest."

He seemed to have all the answers ready. I wondered why he was so eager for me to do this, but then I had another thought.

"So what's in it for you then? Have you always cherished some weird ambition to be a pimp?"

He didn't really strike me as that type, but there had to be something – some reason he wanted me to be a hooker. I held my breath as I waited for his reply.

"As if! Helen, I don't want your money, I promise."

I swirled my remaining wine around in its glass, listening dubiously at his attempts to sound convincing.

"Then why, Simon? You're being too pushy."

He hesitated as if thinking of a valid excuse.

"Well, for one thing, I'd quite like to see some of my clients *and* acquaintances stay out of the divorce courts and keep their names out of the nationals. It will end up that way for some of them if you don't go ahead with this…"

He stopped at that point and he had my attention, fully, but something else was coming. He needed a little more prompting though,

"So why, Simon? What *is* in it for you? There has to be!"

Finally! It dawned on me the split second before his reply.

"I get to have you for free, three or four times a year – think of it as my commission."

I didn't need to give my answer too much thought. I had *my* own needs to think about. My mouth was already watering; I needed it so much,

"Okay, that's a fair request. So, yes! Give this…erm…gentleman my number then, Simon."

Hell, I was feeling horny all of a sudden – wonderful, dirty sex to look forward to, my heart rate was speeding away.

"Just a minute, Helen! One more thing you need to be made aware of! If ever you should decide to talk about what you did with your clients, and their names – a word of warning, you're the one that will come out of it all looking bad, not my clients!"

Within twenty minutes my first client had called me. He had booked to stay at the hotel and would be checking in on the following Wednesday afternoon. He gave me his name, told me what he expected from me, and gave firm instructions as to what I was to wear. I would have to go shopping.

CHAPTER 27

Rushing down Piccadilly from Green Park tube station on my way to my 'business meeting', I stopped and carried out another quick rummage in my bag, wanting to be certain that I had everything I needed. It had been rather a rush getting away, as our neighbour had caught me putting the rubbish out. I think he came out deliberately to ask what all the shouting and swearing had been about on the Saturday morning, he'd also heard the glass from our front window smashing. He didn't even ask if I was okay. He didn't give two hoots about me or anybody else for that matter. There was a not so subtle undertone, when he had brought the subject up, that was implying 'I hope this is a one-off because I don't want to hear it again, it's not what we expect in this neighbourhood.' I quickly put him out of my mind.

Satisfied that I had all the essentials for my evening's work, I stepped up the pace and quickly rounded the corner into the little side street that would take me to the rear entrance of my place of work – one of London's top, five star hotels – *the business*. Rather than arrange this appointment for the Thursday morning and take the big risk of being caught, I had thought it best to sneak in at night and take the chance that I wouldn't be noticed prowling around the corridors.

As I was going up in the service lift I began to have doubts about what I was doing. Not about the sex, it was what I needed after all. It was the creeping around like a burglar that I didn't like. I was bound to get caught, and that thought worried me. Emerging from the lift, my eyes scanned the corridors, but there was nobody around. Once I was stood in front of Tower Suite,' I knocked gently,

"Room service, Sir" I uttered, in what was no more than a whisper, knowing that there was a certain VIP in the suite.

"Yes, come in!"

As I walked into the suite and engaged the chain on the door, his dressing-gowned back disappeared rapidly into the bedroom. I had ten minutes to get myself ready (in the bathroom as I'd already been told), and as I passed through the bedroom, he was getting undressed. I quickly checked my make-up, not that it mattered much on this occasion, and started to remove my clothes, hanging them carefully on the hooks behind the door. I took the special clothes from my satchel that he had asked me to purchase. I squeezed my way into the tight-fitting, full body suit. It was made in a luxurious, velvety-feel, black fabric, two cut out holes to expose my breasts and an open crotch that would expose the area from my pussy to my anus. Two minutes to spare - so I fiddled about to get my other accessories in place - my beautiful cat mask, complete with whiskers and two pointy ears, and the belt that dropped low onto my hips that let the pussy-cat tail fall over the crack in my bottom.

Dropping down onto my hands and knees, I quickly crawled over to the saucer of milk that had been left for me by the shower cubicle door, and started lapping. Faultless timing on my part, I was aware of the bathroom door opening and peered between my front and back legs. The dog was padding slowly towards me across the room. Seconds later, I could feel his cold, hard nose and I could hear him sniffing around my anus and pussy. His tongue started slowly teasing and tormenting around the outside of each orifice, taking care to keep me waiting, to keep himself waiting, prolonging this sex game of his for as long as he determined, his anticipation and excitement held in check, whilst awaiting his ultimate pleasure. Sensing my eagerness, he rubbed his tongue over my clit and it was *my* heaven – the clit flicking, again with his tongue. Pushing me backwards towards the tongue minutes later, I got my reward as it started thrusting gently into my pussy, oh so slowly …and mind-blowing. Violently quivering all over as I came, he continued thrusting, stopping every few seconds as he took greedy licks at my freely flowing juice, savouring the taste briefly, before thrusting again to induce the second explosion, which came faster this time, but not quite so intense. As my shakes subsided, I started to feel the weight of him on my back, and I could also feel his rock hard and very *human* cock swaying, desperately seeking the pussy it desired, now deliciously wet and accommodating. The cock found its entrance and the dog was thrusting hard and fast, pushing and pushing and I could feel its thickness pulsating inside my hole as it was painfully tight.

My arms started tiring as he grunted away. I could feel my top end slowly starting to sink and seconds later, my arms had numbed and given way, my face was in the saucer of milk. To save myself from drowning (I wondered how he would explain that one) I quickly turned my head on a side, so that my ear was in the milk, rather than my nose (and whiskers). Such pain followed as he roughly grabbed me by my nipples and starting gripping so hard, as if to give himself greater purchase for each of his thrusts. We were moving around the bathroom with his thrusts, the saucer scraping its way across the tiled floor, slopping some of its contents onto the floor in the process. Its journey came to an end as the top of my head reached the tiled wall. I could go no further, my skull felt as if it would cave in with the pressure as the increasing crescendo reached its finale and the fucking came to an end with the cock's explosion of semen, both inside me and on the floor. To make the act more credible, for ten minutes we tried to separate, me attempting to pull forwards and away, him still thrusting into me, but seemingly trying to pull away (like the dogs I watched shagging once when I was a kid, and I had been fascinated until Mum had caught me watching). For fuck's sake, get that thing out of me, I was thinking, when finally he did pull out, and I felt the wetness starting to trickle down my inner thighs. With that, he was gone, back to his bedroom.

I ran some water into the bath, and I soaked and washed out my nether regions, ridding myself of his deposits, and preparing for the next onslaught.

I was amazed that the remainder of the evening was quite straight forward. He had discarded his dog costume and he wanted me to play with his cock, rubbing and fondling it, until he'd summoned up sufficient energy to start fucking me again, in an assortment of positions of his choosing. His cock never once lost its stiffness, in fact it seemed…unnaturally stiff. I suspected he'd been taking Viagra. He fucked me for over three hours, with the exception of a few short breaks to catch his breath, but there were no further orgasms to be had for either of us.

Once dressed, I grabbed the things off the bathroom floor and stuffed them back in my satchel. There was just one thing left for me to collect. Walking through the suite, I grabbed the envelope that had been left on the dining room table for me. He had disappeared back into the bedroom. No doubt he would be showering, rinsing away all traces of me, and our sordid business transaction. It was quarter past one in the morning when I left through the back door of the hotel.

Not one word had been exchanged between us throughout the night. Other than use me as his sex toy, what subject could he possibly find to converse with me about? He was a Sir – a member of the House of Lords, and former cabinet minister…and I was just…a hooker!

CHAPTER 28

Since Anthony's revelations about my father's business a few weeks ago, we had barely exchanged more than a few words in passing, other than one night when I had far too much wine. I'd started screaming and shouting at him, blaming his ineptitude for the failure of the business, which in return had caused the death of my parents. I was totally relentless. It all came pouring out, everything! His parents' attitude towards me, his rent boy, rape, the orgy and the cocaine they'd been snorting – nothing escaped my vicious attack – with the exception of the envelope. My knowledge of that was unknown to him and I intended keeping it that way – at least until I'd gleaned some more information.

Towards the end of my drunken outburst, he'd turned his back on me and gone out, probably fearing an action replay with something a bit larger than a paper-weight – and with a better placed shot.

He didn't return that night, leaving me to cry in frustration and sleep off the drink on the settee.

I didn't see him again until I got home from work the next day. He had thrown his jacket and tie onto the armchair. He was sprawled on the settee, already looking bleary eyed, with one empty wine bottle kicked over on the floor. His half empty glass in one hand and a second bottle in the other, he acknowledged my presence by raising the glass as I walked into the lounge. He was struggling to keep the glass upright in his hand but managed to slur a toast to himself,

"To me! Unemployed as from today! Receiver closed the doors on Daddy's business at lunchtime today." I glared at him in disgust, and went upstairs to throw a few things into a bag. It was my turn to stay out all night. I was eager to avoid another confrontation.

CHAPTER 29

I received a call from my fourth client, right out of the blue and with no warning call from Simon, who seemed to be confidently giving out my number without checking with me first.

I chatted to the gentleman for five minutes, breaking the ice a little. He told me his name and that he was a majority share-holder in one of the UK's better mobile phone businesses. He wanted me to visit him in one of London's finest hotels (fortunately, not my place of employment), at eight o'clock. During our call, it had slipped my mind to ask if he wanted me to bring anything special along, so as usual I filled my satchel with a small selection of outfits and sex toys. After dressing in one of my classiest outfits (a look very apt for the hotel in question), I made my usual quick call to Simon, selected Yves Saint Laurent sunglasses, Chanel No. 5 perfume, and caught a cab.

I didn't quite know what to expect as I knocked on the door of Room 905. His nice sexy telephone voice had me guessing that he was fortyish, but I didn't always trust my judgement on the matter. For once my guess had been spot on – tall, good looking, dark hair with some hints of grey around the temples and sideburns. Once I was inside the room he indicated the sofa, so I parked my bottom and sat my bag on the floor at the side of me.

"Fresh coffee?" he asked, but I noticed he never awaited my reply and proceeded to pour one for me to accompany the one he'd just poured for himself.

"Thank you," I indicated for him to stop, so there was room for the milk "that's fine."

He gestured to an envelope that was on the coffee table,

"It's all there. Would you like to count it?"

I laughed and shook my head, surprised at him for wanting to get the matter of money out of the way first.

"I can do that later, when…you know."

"Right – yes." He looked a little embarrassed, but smiled before sitting down opposite me.

I poured the milk in my coffee and added sugar. As I stirred the coffee, I could sense that he was watching me, so I watched his expression carefully. I'd seen that curious look on the faces of previous clients already.

"You are one beautiful girl, looks like yours, your figure - you could be anything you wanted to be - model, actress. Why this? What makes you do this? I'm told by Simon that you are very intelligent and that you come from a decent background. You don't need the money."

He looked at me quizzically. Yes, the same old questions. The same old questions that yet again I would not be answering.

I focused on a picture hanging on the wall behind him, instead of maintaining the eye contact.

"It's kind of…a long story. One that I think both you and my other clients would find hard to understand, so I am not even going to try. I'm not sure even *I* fully understand my reasons, so if I can't understand it myself, how could I possibly begin to explain it to you?"

He digested this for a few seconds as he continued to look at me, but the curious look disappeared - he'd accepted my answer it seemed.

We talked, drank our coffee and, feeling calmer, I carefully watched his body language and his face as we talked. He didn't seem nervous in any way so I assumed he'd done this before. I wasn't interested in knowing, so I certainly wasn't going to ask him. Whilst watching his hands I noticed his wedding ring. I hoped he wouldn't talk about his personal life. He was rather attractive and the only thing on my mind was getting laid.

Once he'd cleared the cups and coffee pot, I showed him the couple of outfits and sex toys in my satchel, and did he have a preference?

"It's your day job, isn't it? Let's have you in the maid's outfit" he enthused "with the stockings and suspender belt. And wear the thong as well."

I grabbed my satchel and went to the bathroom to change. Well, I was a little shocked already, I hadn't envisaged him wanting me to wear any clothes – I had been thinking along the lines of lots of cuddles, sex in the missionary position, make him feel like somebody cared. It takes all kinds. The next shock followed when I walked out of the bathroom, he was sat on the sofa, still fully clothed, playing with what must have been a few thousand pounds worth of Nikon D4 SLR camera.

"Just go about your business, Helen – I'll be with you shortly."

"That's what I'm here for – business. I can't really do it...alone."

"Clean, darling. You're a maid, yes?"

What the hell? Was he for real? He wanted me to clean his hotel suite for the wad of cash I was to receive? Now I had heard it all. I was more than a bit confused. I wondered if the camera was the type that also took videos and if he was intending filming himself fucking me. My insides tingled at the very idea.

"In case you haven't noticed, I don't carry cleaning items around with me, in *this* line of business." I offered gently.

"Erm...No. I don't suppose you do. Use...the face-cloth. Start in the bathroom, pretend a bit."

Obeying his orders, I did as I was told and went to the bathroom. Picking up the face-cloth, as I had been instructed, I bent over the bath *pretending* to clean it. I was finding this little scenario rather amusing – pretending to be a chambermaid and getting paid the rates of a top-class whore. I wondered what the bullies from school would have said if they could have seen me. I was smiling to myself at that thought when I heard the bathroom door open.

"Lose the skirt, darling."

It sounded promising. We were getting down to business at last. I unfastened the skirt, letting it drop to my ankles, flicked it up with my foot, caught it deftly with my right hand and hung it behind the bathroom door.

"Carry on. Sort of...pretend to clean the bath. Bend over, but stand with your legs apart."

229

I expected him stuffing me from behind as I bent over; my anticipation was making me moist down below. I felt some movement between the tops of my thighs, but it wasn't his hands or his dick. I heard him whispering to me,

"Your other client, that is, my friend, has told me that you have the most beautiful pussy he has ever seen. I'm going to be seeing if that's true - very shortly."

It was his camera lens I could feel moving between my legs and I heard the whirring, clicking noises as he took multiple shots with the lens almost touching the crotch of my thong.

"Now, just stay where you are, put one leg up on the side of the bath, then pull the thong to one side so we can get a better shot," he ordered.

The camera did its work again, we moved through to the lounge and I continued to do all that was asked of me – bent over the sofa, legs apart, then one leg on a dining chair, I bent over the bed, I got down on my hands and knees, (sometimes with my thong pulled to one side, sometimes not), and patiently waited for the next instructions whilst his camera lens moved ever closer to my fanny.

"Remove the thong now, please. We will start in the bathroom again, all the same poses, please."

What the hell was all this about? What pleasure was he getting from almost sticking a camera lens up my hole? The suspense was killing me - as was my need. Perhaps he would start feeling horny when he had all the shots he wanted?

Thong off, I posed yet again for all the same shots, I was getting quite turned on by the suggestion of penetration that the camera lens was giving, wondering how long it would be before he wanted to fuck me. How long until I could climax. I needed that. We repeated every last shot and finally he said,

"Go and lie on the bed, Helen. On your back, and open your legs, please."

He still had the camera in his hands, and he still had his clothes on. I would be here overnight at this rate. I was getting desperate for it and frustrated that things were moving too slowly.

"Oh wow! That really *is* the prettiest fanny I ever saw. He was right, your client…so right."

Get any closer and that lens is going to be up it, I was thinking. (In fact I might grab the lens and shove it up myself if he didn't get on with it soon.)

"What I want you to do now sweetheart, is really show me just how pretty that fanny is. Pull the labia aside, let me see the vagina, and your clit as well, let me photograph their beauty."

I opened up for him. The camera responded to his push of the button, more shots taken, every imaginable angle that he could.

"Right, I've got it. Now stick your fingers in there baby, right up, all the way up. Yes! What a shot!"

More snaps, plenty more, and I'd had enough. How undignified. I was on a bed, in a posh hotel suite, my own fingers delving into the depths of my privates.

"Hey! Is there a remote chance that you are going to start fucking me at some point in the near future? I'm getting quite bored now with you poking me with nothing but that bloody camera lens," I urged.

"I'm through, sweetheart. You can get dressed now."

"What is this? No fucking? I'm kind of ready to be fucked if you know what I mean. I *need* to be fucked right now."

"Sweetheart, you got me all wrong. I don't fuck with anyone but my wife – I don't need to. See this…?" He grabbed his genitalia in his trousers to show me - the softness of it all in his hands.

"Does this dick look excited to you, honey? I love my wife, and I make love *only* with my wife."

"Then why? What are you paying me for, if you don't want to fuck me?" I could hear the tone of my voice – a little high-pitched with irritation.

"I collect pictures of beauty - *we* appreciate beauty. *You* are being paid to provide some of that beauty. I didn't realise that you were in this business for anything other than the money. I never imagined that you would actually *want* to be fucked."

Ten minutes later I was paid, dressed and out of there. In the lift, going down, I was still breathing heavily; flushed and angry. It was the proverbial itch that I couldn't scratch. It didn't happen very often, thank goodness.I had never been too good at getting off by myself. I couldn't seem to get it right - it would be a waste of my

232

time even to try. The more I tried to concentrate on coming, the further away it seemed. I usually gave it up as a bad job. When I arrived home that night, I had a long, cold shower before I climbed into bed.

CHAPTER 30

I couldn't understand what Anthony was up to. I'd been puzzling for a couple of weeks. He'd said he was officially unemployed when the receivers closed the doors on my father's business, and yet he was still going out every morning before me. Sometimes he was dressed smartly in a suit, at other times he was smart casual – expensive jeans and a sweatshirt.

He was also arriving home after me each evening, as he usually had done. He never volunteered any information and I didn't want to ask him. I couldn't ask, in case it gave him the impression that I was interested. The truth was, I didn't really care what he was doing. The only thing that concerned me was that it looked like it would be down to me to pay the mortgage and bills until he was earning. I knew he would be expecting some statutory redundancy pay, but that wouldn't go far.

I had expected him to be depressed, but unless he was an extremely good actor, which I sincerely doubted, he didn't appear to be down in any way. We still didn't communicate, unless it was to snap at one another, but he seemed cheerful; whistling and even singing at times. It crossed my mind that he was maybe spending his days at his parents' house. I couldn't come up with an answer for the suit and tie though, unless interviews were on his agenda.

I sat at the kitchen counter drinking my coffee, lost in my thoughts about Anthony and his new found unemployed status when something came flooding back into my mind. The envelope in the greenhouse! With everything that had happened recently, the funeral, grief, my O.C.D., my job at the hotel, *and* my new sideline, it had not occurred to me to keep checking the greenhouse. I knew that he had probably only used the greenhouse as a last resort emergency hiding place when I arrived home early, but would *he* think it to be less likely that his goods would be discovered in there than in the house? He didn't know that I'd found them…so maybe.

I got up and rifled through one of the kitchen drawers where I recalled seeing an old notebook. I went out to the patio and checked the pots in the greenhouse – nothing! I had made a note of the dates the first envelope had arrived and disappeared, as they were firmly imprinted on my brain. I added today's entry and I would keep checking *every* day and log my findings. I felt positive that, whatever Anthony's involvement was with the envelope, it wouldn't be a one-off. I even started to wonder if drugs were maybe his new career move. I hated being suspicious in case I was totally wrong…..but his behaviour didn't inspire much confidence.

A call from the estate agent affected my mood later in the day. It was pleasing in a way, to hear that my parents' home had been attracting a lot of interest, with more than sixty viewings, but an incredible sadness caught me in its grasp the minute I ended the call. The home where I'd spent my childhood, my parents' dream home, would sometime in the near future be occupied by strangers. They would change things for sure, as anybody would want to. I could understand that, but the very thought of it sickened me. I was toying with the idea of forcing myself to make one last visit, but I was worried about the effect that it would have on me.

CHAPTER 31

My mobile phone rang at six o'clock one Sunday evening. Anthony was at home, getting pissed and nodding off to sleep every few minutes during a 'Top Gear Special,' and getting on my nerves as always. I walked out into the garden to take my call. It was a new client, my sixth, and I had been expecting his call around eleven that morning. Simon had called me the previous day to ask my permission this time, the guy was a television presenter. I'd seen him fairly regularly on a particular programme and had never much cared for him but…business is business. Simon had called him 'a good man,' so…

After I'd answered the call, he greeted me politely and introduced himself, but in a manner that seemed a little offhand, or perhaps I was being judgmental because of my limited knowledge of him. I noted he was well-spoken, but I had already discovered in my short time as a call girl, that that didn't mean a thing.

"I'm booked into the Kensington Suite at your place of employment and would like to use your…um…services tomorrow morning if at all possible."

I wasn't particularly happy about doing the session during my working hours at the hotel, but he insisted that he already had a very busy schedule for his time in London. I explained that I couldn't guarantee a time, as we had certain routines at the hotel that must be adhered to. Our appointment would depend on how much work was involved in the first three suites and

Kensington would be the last suite. He sounded a little disgruntled.

"I will wait until two o'clock and no later. I have somewhere to be by four." It sounded like he thought *he* was doing *me* a favour, not the other way around. Irritated, but keeping my voice steady and polite I asked,

"Would you like me to bring anything special along, Sir?"

There was silence at the end of the phone as he considered his answer. I cast a glance towards the house and noticed Anthony watching me from the kitchen window. I hoped he would stay where he was whilst I was on the phone.

At the other end of the phone he finally snapped his answer at me, "Like what for instance? Just your presence will do!"

Still polite, but getting rattled by Anthony's presence at the kitchen window, I asked, "Do you have details of the cost of the transaction, and you know that the payment should be in cash?"

"I have everything that you require, young lady, just be sure that what I need is there no later than two, please."

His manner had completely riled me and I was beginning to wish I'd said I couldn't do it. I assumed he would want sex, so what would he do for his fuck if I failed to turn up before two o'clock? Go to the street corner where he may end up with more than just getting his leg over? Go back home to his frigid or frumpy wife to try to get what she doesn't normally give him? That's exactly why these guys want a hooker, isn't it? Because their wives don't want sex, or perverted sex at least! Sixty percent of the time the sex wasn't the least bit perverted, some guys just needed company, or so I'd been led to believe. These thoughts rumbled around in my mind and I felt half inclined to ring him back and cancel.

I was more than a little nervous the next morning as I made my way into work. I'd decided when I woke up that I would go ahead, but I'm always wary with new clients, you just never know what ideas they've come up with - what they could inflict on their whore. Another reason for my apprehension was the dangerous game I was playing, again – being a whore to some of the hotel's very important clientele *and* during my working hours. It was the very presence of this type of prominent client that made staff very reluctant to cause more intrusion than was absolutely necessary. It was very unlikely that even my superiors would come to check up on me.

My first two suites that morning were easy. In 'Garden' there was nothing to do. The bed had not even been slept in. Clothes had been deposited in the wardrobe by its occupant – female, who loved her designer clothes. I took a peak into the bedside cabinet drawer and half concealed under 'The Holy Bible' was a gigantic (9 inch) black cock vibrator with quite a sizeable girth. Hell! My eyes started watering and I was just *looking* at the bloody thing. There was quite a little stash of other interesting sex toys, some of a type that previous clients had used on me a couple of times. Carefully shutting the drawer lest I disturb anything, I started tiptoeing towards the bathroom. Tiptoeing? Guilt! I had just invaded the privacy of this faceless person – someone who liked big dicks. I sniggered to myself and went about my business as usual without the tiptoeing. The bathroom had clearly not been used, clean towels still neatly folded on the rack provided. Perhaps this female had got lucky the previous night. I felt quite horny. I'd stared at the black cock and other paraphernalia for a few seconds too long. It had been a long fortnight.

I caught the very distinguished looking gentleman in 'Thames' just as he was about to place the 'Do not disturb' on his door knob. He was wearing an expensive silk dressing gown, and had a twinkle in his eye. He didn't look the type who was about to take part in extra-marital sex. He pressed £20 into my hand and winked,

"We don't need cleaning today, pet. I'm sure you have other things to do."

I smiled at him, touched by his gesture.

"Sir, I don't want your £20, enjoy your...morning. I still have plenty to keep me occupied," I said, pushing the £20 note back into his hand.

He gave me a final wink, closed the door and (I assumed) disappeared back to his wife.

I filled the rest of my time by cleaning and re-cleaning 'Tower' quite a few times, which helped feed my O.C.D. needs for the day.

My client in 'Kensington' was already naked. He had stepped aside as he opened the door, out of view of the main corridor. I wheeled the trolley in ahead of me and his hand came around the door to pass me the 'Do not disturb' sign to hang on the door knob. He must have seen my eyes bulge out when I noticed the size of his cock! I hardly noticed anything else about him. The black dick vibrator I'd spotted earlier must have been an omen. This guy's cock almost matched it, both in length and girth. I could hear my own gulp and a sudden constriction in my throat.

I felt an overwhelming desire to run - utter panic at the thought that this cock would never get inside me. Not a black cock this time, but a purple veined variety. It was already at full stretch - the credits still rolling on a 'Pay per View' movie. He'd obviously been preparing for me. I'd hardly had chance to close the door when he leapt on me and planted his lips firmly over mine. I quickly turned my head to the side, already on edge,

"Don't kiss me!" I gave more than a hint of warning.

He bit hard on my neck instead, and shoved his hand straight in my panties. Three fingers shot into my pussy. I winced, he was hurting me. After five minutes of his finger nails stabbing at my vagina he tried to shove his dick in the side of my knickers and stuff me, stood right up against the door. Being much taller than him there was no way it was going to work. Grunting to himself he stuck his fingers back in my hole even more roughly than before, and with his other hand, was rapidly trying to tug my panties down at one side.

In his desperation to get at me, he didn't seem to comprehend that it was his poking hand that was preventing the undies coming off. I pulled his hand away from my crotch and rolled them down for him.

241

"Shouldn't I get undressed before you go any further?" I suggested.

He shrugged impatiently. "Just the knickers and skirt, leave the rest."

"No bra? Don't you want to see my breasts?" I offered.

"I want to fuck this" he said, grabbing at my fanny again, "not look at two useless pieces of muscle – tits don't do anything for me."

I felt a sense of foreboding, beads of moisture forming on my forehead. With all my lower clothing removed, he grabbed my arm and lowered me to the floor, just behind the door. I wasn't even two metres into the room. Just as I had feared, he struggled to get his cock into my pussy. The pain was excruciating, even with his lubrication. I had felt its slime on my inner thighs before he tried to ram it in, his seminal fluid having already dribbled steadily. Minute by minute he made more progress, inching his way further in until that was it, he wasn't going to get it in any further. I was already sore, stinging. My natural lubrication had dried up completely.

Once it dawned on him that he couldn't get anymore in, he started thrusting violently at me, but it wasn't going in and out at all. With every bit of force he put into his thrust he was just moving me further along the carpet, and I felt the burn on my back, just another thing to strengthen the regrets I already felt.

After fifteen minutes of me feeling nothing but pain, and him pushing me round the floor with his dick, I put my arms around his shoulders and rolled him onto his back, determined to get something from this other than pain and money. I lowered my body over his and rode him, stimulating my clit expectantly, the first bit of pleasure I'd felt since stepping through his door. I was finally producing some lubrication - his dick was moving freely inside me and…I was tingling and ready to come. A sharp stinging slap to my left cheek took me by surprise.

"Stop trying to finish me off, you bitch. I'll come when I'm fucking ready to come!" he snapped.

I was furious, my eyes filled with tears, I lashed out back at him with my tongue,

"Who's trying to make *you* come? I'm trying to make myself come, which you seem incapable of doing!"

The second blow came, the other cheek this time, but I'd turned my head slightly before contact was made, the stinging not quite so severe.

"I'm not paying you colossal amounts of fucking money so *you* can come – I get the fuck, you get the fucking money, got it?"

With that he rolled me onto my back again and resumed fucking me around the suite ….I lost track of time, but after what seemed like forever he pulled out and rolled me face down. His finger edging into my anus, I snarled at him,

"DON'T EVEN CONSIDER IT!" and he must have thought better of it. After pushing his dribbling tool back into my hole, he reached both arms around my hips and rubbed at my clitoris with his fingertips whilst he rammed into me like a man possessed. I came just in time before his dick twitched and he grunted like a pig as his seed exploded into me.

He brought a cup of coffee and some of the complimentary chocolates to me as I washed my private parts in his bathroom. He actually held some ice to my cheeks and apologised for his exuberance, both with his dick, and his slaps. Sitting on the edge of the bath, he watched as I tried to cover the redness on my face with some products from my satchel. As he handed me an envelope containing the cash he muttered,

"Could I…call you again please, Helen? I'll be in London again in a couple of months."

I couldn't resist a dig and the words came readily to me.

"Wife neglecting you these days?" He rammed his hands into his pockets and gave me such an icy look, so I quickly added,

"Sorry. That was out of order. Yes, by all means ring me, but I can't use the hotel again. You will have to meet me elsewhere."

I checked my appearance carefully before leaving his suite. I'd made a decent job with the make-up. I couldn't resist calling Simon later that day and telling him I didn't think much to his idea of 'a good man.'

CHAPTER 32

It was late June and a very hot Saturday evening. As I drove up the street after pulling out of the drive, I breathed in the familiar smell of barbecues. Earlier that day, the supermarket had been crammed with shoppers, the shorts and T-shirts out in force, and the women had been filling their trolleys with sausages, burgers, bread buns, and a variety of salad items. As for the husbands…they were the usual fright; beer-bellied, T-shirts riding up, proudly carrying 2 or 3 multi-packs of 'on offer' beer or lager (instead of putting them in the trolley). They were making a statement. What the image portrayed was…look at me, I've got my beer, I'm tough, nobody messes with me. It was a sight I detested – no class. I don't usually have a snobby side…if only they would put their packs of beer in the trolley…

I was heading into the countryside, away from the suburban areas, and hopefully it would be quiet. The young and the not so young singles would be heading out to the pubs and clubs. A large number of families would be having their friendly gatherings serving up their charcoal-tinged offerings, cheap vodka and beer, and bouncy castles and paddling pools for the kids.

I arrived at Hollow Hill Wood at six thirty, pulled off the main road onto a narrow dirt track and drove slowly for five or ten minutes until I found a small clearing where my car would not be seen from the main road. To the best of my knowledge, it should be safe for a couple of hours whilst I went for a walk.

After locking my car door I set off into the wood. I noticed how the lower temperature in the cover of the trees was far more pleasant, much less humid than it had been in the scorching sun. I had grabbed my light weight cardigan in case the temperature suddenly took a sharp dip. There was a stillness and beauty about the woods that I loved and had done since my childhood. My parents had regularly taken me on Sunday outings to local beauty spots – woods, waterfalls, and parklands and I was thankful I had grown up with their appreciation for nature. Woodland flowers grew and various needles and leaves crunched under foot as I sauntered along. Birds chattered to each other, and I was enjoying the solitude of my rambling, gazing at all of nature's delights, as each came into my vision. I picked my way carefully through the trees for the next fifteen minutes, trying to keep to tracks others had used before me, and taking care not to wander too deep into the darkness. I looked behind me on two or three occasions, thinking I heard the crackling of undergrowth snapping - noises that hadn't been caused by *my* footsteps. There was nothing, nobody to be seen – perhaps a wild animal, a rabbit hopping along or a young deer, trying to remain elusive. I stopped and listened again when I heard yet another noise, and as I turned around, somebody launched himself at me from my left, and I screamed. A hand quickly covered my mouth and nose, and I started panicking, unable to breath. A voice whispered into my ear,

"Quit the fucking screaming or you'll get hurt, understand?"

I nodded at him, my eyes wide with fear as his other hand was struggling with the button on my denims, and then the zip.

"Push your shorts down your legs."

The hand over my mouth eased its pressure and I instantly tried to bite on his fingers, determined not to give in to his intentions without a fight. I wasn't going to push my own shorts down for him. It was obvious he was going to rape me and he'd have to do the work himself.

"Stop the fucking biting, you bitch," he snarled, as he forced me to lower my body.

Once I was on the ground, he threw his body across mine to prevent my escape, one hand still over my mouth and the other fighting to push the shorts down my legs. I pushed at him and kicked out with my legs, but I struggled to make contact as he dodged my kicks. One of my arms was firmly trapped between my body and his, but with my free arm I lashed out at his head. I was trying to scream again… the sound that escaped between his fingers sounded like a strangled yawn. He moved his hand from over my mouth and slid it down to my throat, gripping it tightly. I could feel his cock on the top of my thigh. Struggle though it was for him with one hand, I could now feel my shorts around my knees, and the reality dawned on me at last, there was no escaping him.

I was about to be abused - fucked against my will. Painful memories of being raped by Anthony came flooding back to me and I was about to relive them. The tears came easily. Unable to push my shorts further down my legs, and without releasing his firm grasp of my throat, he used his foot. I felt the rubber sole of his shoe scrape down the side of my shin as he kicked down at the shorts until they were free. His bodyweight shifted. After a battle with his own attire for a few moments, I felt his cock again. It was shoved into me with such tremendous force and the pain racked through my body. He started fucking me violently and I sobbed, partly due to the pain down below, but most of it I could attribute to what was happening in my head – reliving that horrible night nearly one year ago.

The pressure on my throat was soon hurting more, as with each powerful thrust his grip seemed to tighten. I kicked out again with my feet, and I tried to dig my nails into any bare flesh I could see or feel. But with his free hand he fought and succeeded in getting both my wrists together and held them way back over my head. I continued to sob quietly as his brutal and frenzied shagging went on. After what seemed like forever he pulled out, quickly forced my arms down by my sides, and positioned his knees so that they were holding my arms firmly in place, and he was almost sat on my chest. He lifted my head off the ground and forced his cock into my mouth. He placed his hands at either side of my head and pushed it back and forth so that his cock was going in and out. I gagged and tried to move my head away.

"Close your mouth! Make it tight around my cock or you'll gag all the more!" he ordered.

If I obeyed, perhaps there would be a chance we could get it over with quicker, and I could go home. I hoped and prayed that he wasn't going to kill me. There was no sign of a knife or a gun… he was very muscular and would soon be able to overpower me, but I wouldn't give up. He fucked at my mouth for what seemed an eternity, and I gagged all the while, feeling like I was ready to vomit. I tried to think happy thoughts, sing songs in my head, anything I could think of to keep me calm, as I knew it was the panic that was making me choke. I think he was on the verge of spurting spunk into my mouth and as his cock entered for another thrust I made sure to close my mouth a bit tighter, grazing his tool as he forced it in.

"You bitch, you've nicked my cock on your teeth!" and he roughly slapped the side of my head as he pulled out of my mouth. I opened my eyes and noticed that his hard on had softened somewhat in that last minute – a result!

In one swift movement he was off me, rolled me so I was face down and was on top again, trying to shove his softened dick into my anus. Laughing inwardly, I felt confident that it couldn't happen… his dick was almost flaccid, but almost instantly I felt sick with worry – he poked with his finger alongside his dick and I felt it getting hard again.

Once his excitement was aroused to new heights by the buggery about to take place, and once his cock had made initial contact with my arse, its length and stiffness were soon regained. My attempts to fight were feeble and all I was physically able to do was kick at his backside with my legs. My fingers were nipping or gripping any area I could reach, fingernails digging in, but the bruising that I was inflicting on him would be nothing. Nothing compared to the broken nose, the head injuries or the blows reigned down on him in the boxing ring.

He fucked my backside for ten minutes and the pain seemed infinite. I felt as if he was going to split me internally and I couldn't wait for it all to end…for that final explosion into my depths. That moment came at last and as he climaxed he bit into the back of my neck. His strength sapped with his last bit of exertion and he flopped, my body taking his full weight for five minutes whilst his breathing returned to normal. Then I was free at last as he stood up. Even without the weight that had held me down for so long, I stayed put, head on one side, watching as he zipped himself up, looking down at me with a smirk on his face.

He nodded at me once and was gone. Two minutes later I was dressed but bedraggled, re-tracing my steps back through the woodlands and back to my car. I could see the brake lights of his Porsche 911 some distance away through the trees as he negotiated the twisting dirt track. An envelope was tucked under one of my car's wiper blades.

I'd been paid to act like a rape victim, my second time. Although no rape had actually taken place this time I knew it was not in good taste. This guy had hinted during our phone conversation that he would be contacting me again, probably in three months time. The client was turned on by the fight, the screaming and kicking and nipping…the knowledge that his victim didn't want him…and the power of being able to force himself on a woman, and take what didn't belong to him. Whilst acting out this grossly indecent charade, I took some consolation from the knowledge that I had probably saved an innocent woman from being violated. I had saved some female from having to re-live that nightmare every day of their life, and probably being unable, *ever*, to have a normal sexual relationship. No female should ever have to endure what Anthony had put me through. He was to blame for the lack of regard that I had for my own body.

CHAPTER 33

I was staring into space, in the greenhouse. I couldn't help but wonder where things were heading for Anthony. I had been checking the greenhouse each day for the last ten days and had found nothing. But today, Friday…there was another envelope, with the same squishy powdery contents. It had been hidden here by Anthony at some point whilst I had been at work. I lifted the top plant pots off again, as if my eyes had been deceiving me the first time – it was still there, I hadn't been hallucinating.

He'd been dressed in his suit when he'd left home before me that morning. I laughed at myself as I was digging deep into my mind to recall what he'd been wearing - I felt like a private investigator, the only trouble was I was not usually around between Monday and Friday. I wanted to see if somebody would call to collect the envelope or whether Anthony would retrieve it and deliver it somewhere. It was bugging me, but I didn't think there was anything I could do about it. I doubted he would make any arrangements to move the envelope on a weekend when I would be at home most of the time.

I went back inside and made myself something to eat, but all the while I couldn't get the envelope or its contents off my mind. Having no desire to be in the lounge once Anthony came home, I was pouring a glass of wine to take upstairs with me, when he walked in the back door. I hadn't heard his car pull in the drive so it took me by surprise.

"Would you mind pouring one for me?" he asked before he'd even closed the door, "I've had a hell of a day!"

"Yeah, sure!"

I smiled to myself, thinking he couldn't have given me a better opportunity if he'd tried. I was quite excited at the thought that maybe I could find some useful information.

As I grabbed another glass, I casually commented, "I thought you were unemployed. How come you've had a hell of a day?"

I didn't really want to ask him direct questions if I could avoid it. I was hoping he would volunteer what I wanted to know.

"I'm not unemployed. I got a job almost straight away. In advertising!"

He knelt down on the pretext of re-fastening his shoe-lace – shoes he would take off when he went into the lounge. I knew it was done deliberately to avoid eye contact with me.

"That's good then. At least I'm not left paying the mortgage and the bills," and as a little afterthought I added,

"I thought the suits were maybe for interviews."

He grunted something I couldn't quite make out. He'd not bothered answering my question about his day, so I asked again,

"So…your day? Hell, you said!"

I turned my attention to clearing my plate away, eagerly awaiting his reply.

"Oh that! I've been in Brighton all day – new client, maybe. The meeting didn't go so well."

A little later, as I lay in the bath sipping at my wine and thinking he'd lied to me about Brighton, a point I hadn't considered before suddenly came in to the equation. Anthony wasn't necessarily the person who'd put the envelope in the greenhouse. Anybody could have walked up our drive and round to the back of the house – somebody who had been told exactly where to leave it.

CHAPTER 34

I'd received a call from a new client, another of Simon's acquaintances, who had introduced himself as Thomas. All he told me was that he was involved in football in a big way, although he was not, and never had been a footballer. I guessed that he was maybe a club chairman or perhaps something to do with the F.A., but it wasn't really important to me, whatever he did. He'd asked me to spend the whole Friday night with him, so at least I was warned.

It was seven o'clock when I knocked on the door of his suite in a superb Knightsbridge hotel. As is usual with a first-timer, I didn't know what to expect, but when he opened the door to me, and I saw his welcoming smile, I liked him. He was shorter than me, with grey hair that still had tinges of red. He wore a smart pair of trousers, and an expensive jumper over his shirt, but no tie. He reminded me of a lovely maths teacher at my school. He had the kindest eyes and such a lovely manner. I held out my hand and he took it between his hands and kissed it.

"Come in, my dear. What a pleasure to meet you."

He nodded his approval and smiled at me, his eyes lighting up.

"Thank you, Sir. It's lovely to meet you too. How are you?"

He didn't answer my question, but politely gestured towards the couch.

"Please, won't you sit down? And it's Thomas to you. Can I get you a glass of wine?"

He didn't wait for me to answer. I think his nervousness was prompting him to keep talking.

"Which do you prefer, red? Or, perhaps a dry white? If I don't have a bottle that you would like I could order room service."

He paused for breath and looked at me expectantly.

"I would prefer gin and tonic if you have some gin?"

"Oh excellent, I do have gin, I'm rather partial to a few G & T's myself."

I watched his hand as he poured us both a large gin, he was shaking. Somehow his nerves were managing to make me feel relaxed and confident.

"Are you nervous? I don't bite, Thomas. Most of my clients survive our dates." I laughed to put him at ease, and he laughed with me.

"Well this is the first time - the first time I have, you know, had a…a date with a…ever."

"You can say the word; Thomas…hooker. I know what I am, it doesn't offend me these days."

"No. Not that, I was going to say, lady friend. You are my first ever lady friend, besides my wife. I have never…I haven't asked you here for sex, my dear. I just want to talk with you, that is all."

His revelation didn't surprise me in the least. The guy was certainly not the type who visited hookers, and most likely had never cheated on his wife, or even looked at another woman. I admired his loyalty and regretted the fact that the men I'd had in my life had not been more like Thomas.

"Thomas, you have my full attention for (I looked at my watch,) let's say, hmm, I will leave at 8am, it's 7.15pm now, that's twelve and three quarter hours, so talk to me. I am almost as good at listening as I am at…providing sexual services."

I took the G & T that he'd offered and settled down to listen, hoping that my demeanour would have a calming effect on him.

He was a little slow to get started, I don't think he really knew where to start, but with a little coaxing from me, his words were soon in full flow.

He told me about his privileged background, very much like my own. The private education, private music lessons, horse-riding lessons - money was literally thrown at him. There was, however, one major difference between Thomas' childhood and mine. I was very fortunate to have had loving parents –parents who had loved each other almost as much as they loved me. His parents' marriage had been one of deceit, selfishness, lies, adultery and more selfishness. The only people to have shown Thomas any love and affection had been his full-time nanny and the hired help at his (family?) home.

There had been the gardener who had played his beloved football with him on their beautiful lawns whilst his parents were away on their many business trips. A handyman who had built him a tree house in the orchard, and a cook who made him gingerbread men and let him lick out the bowl.

His 'Nanny Jane' had nursed him through the various childhood illnesses, the falls and scrapes, and the upset that went hand in hand with parents who didn't kiss, cuddle or tell their only son that they loved him. For the first time in my life, my maternal instincts surfaced from within. I felt a sudden urge to hug him; I really did feel for him. I tried to imagine how my childhood would have been without the love from my parents. That thought, this soon into my personal grieving process was enough to traumatise me, so I quickly cast it from my mind.

His love of football had come from watching the game on television.

"Football was not played at my school, it was always rugby. I was always the one who came off the field with ripped ears, missing teeth and a broken nose, I hated it. Mr Tyerman, our gardener at home, would always let me sit in his shed and watch football matches on his portable television. Once I was past eleven years old, and Nanny Jane's supervision wasn't quite as strict, I stayed awake late on Saturday nights just so that I could watch 'Match of the Day.' I knew that I would never be good enough to play football, but I was determined to go against everything my parents wanted for me, and seek a career in anything to do with football."

I watched his eyes as he spoke, and I could see the passion in them. Football had been, and probably always would be, his greatest love.

I listened intently as he talked me through his qualifications, his university days and his career to date, and the disapproval he had met from his parents at his choice of studies and his career moves. They had never communicated with Thomas from the day he had left university, although he had remained in touch with Nanny Jane and Mr Tyerman for many years.

We were rapidly getting down the bottle of gin, and whilst waiting for room service, Thomas encouraged me to talk,

"Your turn now, my dear, before we start on the relationships."

My worst fear rose to the surface and my stomach lurched. I had made it a rule never to reveal my private life to my clients. I stalled for a minute or two.

"Oh dear, do I have to? You don't want to hear about my life, Thomas. I think you would find it pretty mundane, after everything you have revealed about yourself." I groaned inwardly and quickly considered what would be safe for me to discuss.

I briefly told him about being bullied at school, and then I very sneakily flipped over the subject matter by talking about my favourite films, books, art and music, and started drawing him into a conversation of my choosing. He raised his eyes to the ceiling and then back at me.

"You are being very evasive I think…so intelligent…but so transparent. What are you trying to hide? Is your past painful to talk about?" he asked.

I laughed at that.

"No, it's not that at all. I'm asked so often that I get sick of telling the same old stories to my clients, can you understand that?"

He nodded unconvincingly, and I was left wondering if I was completely off the hook.

"Thomas, tell me about your marriage please?" I was really curious. I had been trying to read between the lines all evening, wondering why he was paying me.

"Which one?"

It was my turn to raise my eyebrows.

"Sorry, I didn't realise."

"You couldn't possibly have known, dear, don't apologise."

It took him half an hour to tell me about how he had met his first wife. They would have loved to have started a family together, but it just never happened and after seven years of happiness (well, he said he was happy), she had left him for one of England's soccer legends. I could still see some of the old hurt surfacing as he barely whispered,

"She was pregnant by him within the year, I thought perhaps if it had happened for us…"

He swiftly moved onto the subject of his current marriage.

"Jenna. My beautiful, Jenna! She married me for my money. I'm no fool - I realised that fourteen years ago. We haven't had sex for…it must be five years now. Since a year or two after we married, we only ever had sex when she was drunk, or she wanted a few thousand pounds to go shopping. We have a son. I think he's mine. His birth certificate says he's mine. He's twelve years old. I love him so much, he reminds me of me. I send him to a private school, one where they play football as well as rugby. Jenna is indifferent. Oh, she's not horrible to him or anything like that, but I think it's an inconvenience to her when he is around. She doesn't show a great deal of interest in his education, but if he makes something of himself, if he became famous or rich, she would then be so proud of him and manage to find some love for him from somewhere. She is a very cold-hearted woman, so selfish. She does not know how to love - she doesn't love me."

Due to her snobbishness, dinner parties were frequent at home, and she would spend the evening trying to belittle Thomas in front of their guests. I found myself disliking her intensely after what he had revealed to me, and I didn't even know her. He deserved so much better, this true gentleman with his impeccable manners, I found him an absolute delight, but I was also puzzled.

"Thomas, why don't you leave her? Divorce her. You need some happiness in your life."

"I'm afraid I can't do that. Jenna is a prize bitch, she has affairs, she treats me badly, she is not a suitable mother, but as long as she returns to our home, I have hope. I love her, I will always love her."

We went to bed around midnight, I kissed him goodnight on the cheek and I wondered if my nakedness might arouse what had lain dormant for five years. He faced me for a while as we talked some more, and his eyes at times glanced fleetingly at my breasts and the rest of my body. I could sense a discomfort about him, he wanted me, but he didn't want me, and he turned his back to me and muttered goodnight yet again.

"Thomas, I don't want you to feel uncomfortable about this, but I am going to put my arms around you, cuddle you and hold you. No ulterior motive on my part. I want you to feel loved and that someone cares about you, because no-one has held you for so long. You want to be true to Jenna, I understand that. Just enjoy the feeling of being loved and held, pretend its Jenna. Go to sleep happy for once, with arms holding you tight."

I left the hotel during the night while Thomas was sound asleep.

I didn't want his money. Nobody should ever have to pay just to have someone listen to them; someone who showed some compassion. We were very similar in many ways, I had a very lonely and sad existence like him, but our night together had made me realise that I had so much more than him. I struggled to fight back my tears as I made my way along the road, tears for Thomas – for his childhood in particular. At least I had memories of loving parents and for that I would always be grateful. My client had actually helped *me*. I hadn't told Thomas that I was grieving for the loss of my parents, but just hearing about the cold, cold people who happened to be his parents, I felt was a turning point for me. I would have no more selfish thoughts about how I couldn't cope without them.

I wasn't the least bit surprised when Thomas called me on the Saturday afternoon, asking why I had left the hotel without allowing him to pay me. When I had explained to him about my decision to leave in the early hours of the morning, I also felt compelled to tell him how he had helped me come to terms with my grief. He expressed his deepest sympathy and concern for me and he wished I had told him of my loss face to face. We chatted for half an hour, and before we ended the call, he insisted that I keep in touch. I had made a friend.

CHAPTER 35

"'Allo, Mees. Fo... give me, my...'ow you say...friend (I gasped in shock when I heard his friend's name, one of Simon's clients) say to give you...a reeng! 'Ee say 'ow you may ...elp...wiz...ze...my...porbelm, oui?"

"Prob-lem, you mean? I offered,

"Oui...erm...yes...prob...lem!" I smiled as I was listening to his broken English, totally bemused.

"Is it a problem of a sexual nature?"

"Erm...yes...je...I 'ave a certain...'ow you say...needs...'eez zis...er ...cor rect?"

"Yes, that is correct Monsieur. You want to organise a date?"

"Oui, Mademoiselle! Je compren...non...I...er...understan...wot cost eez in uros (he pronounced it ooros), yes?"

I took the advantage whilst we were discussing money, to tell him how much it would cost him in pounds sterling.

"Certainement.'Eez 'zis...er ...prob lem...for you...my..'otel...(he told me its name)...Eathrow...Aeroport...sep...er...nine..tee n...hundred... heures, tomorrow?"

Well, this promised to be fun. He didn't bother telling me his room number, he said it was hard to find and it would just be easier to meet me in the foyer. He would be wearing a purple shirt, and talking into his mobile phone, near the reception desk. I was not to approach him, or talk to him - just follow him, at a discreet distance. I'd told him what I would be wearing and also that I would use a purple clip in my hair.

I caught a train to Heathrow, and opted for a short cab ride, instead of taking the fifteen to twenty minute walk to the hotel. Being a little too early, I approached the bar, ordered a G & T and sat down on one of the big squashy sofas. I positioned myself so that I was able to see most of the reception desk and beyond, took a book out of my satchel, and made a show of being engrossed. For the next twenty minutes, my eyes felt like they were doing a dance, glancing first at the book, up towards reception, then to my wristwatch. I've always had a habit of checking my watch every thirty seconds or so when I'm nervously waiting to meet someone for the first time. Each time I check I find myself hoping that the pointers have miraculously jumped forward in time – so eager to get the initial awkwardness over and done with.

I checked my mobile next for something different to do, feigning writing and sending text messages. My eyes darted back to my watch again, it was five past seven and I started wondering if the call had been a hoax. I was on the verge of wanting a second G & T, and as I stood up to go to the bar again, my client had just appeared near reception, taking his mobile phone out of his shirt pocket.

He was stood with his back to me, glancing towards the main entrance door. What the hell would I do if he didn't change his position, and continued to monitor the revolving door? *He* was late after all, so surely he would expect me to be here on time and waiting somewhere nearby. As I left the carpeted lounge area, the noise of my heels on the tiled reception hall caused him to turn, he'd noticed me. I quickly glanced down on the pretext of searching my satchel for something.

He walked away around a corner and away from the reception desk. I sauntered some twenty or thirty metres behind him, still pretending to show more interest in my handbag than in my surroundings. I looked up as he arrived at the lift, and when he indicated that I was to hurry, I assumed that no-one was behind me, to witness the handsome, dark-haired, French international footballer and a mystery brunette entering a hotel lift together.

We exchanged greetings as the lift began its ascent, his steely grey eyes quickly scanning the goods on sale and his head nodded slowly in approval. I did a quick appraisal of him. I had heard his name many times, but never having had an interest in football, I had never even seen the guy before, not even his picture in the sports pages of the national dailies. He was not my idea of handsome. Acceptable, maybe! There was a slight bump on the bridge of his nose and he had a sort of effeminate look about him. I didn't feel any immediate attraction and I was curious as to how this was going to pan out.

When the doors opened at the ninth floor, he stepped into the corridor, checked the coast was clear and indicated to me to leave the lift. All was quiet and as he used his key card to unlock his door, I increased my pace and hurried into his room. He quickly closed the door before putting the security chain in place.

He didn't waste a second. I barely had a moment to catch my breath before he'd removed all my clothes. He gestured, since that would be the easiest way; that I was to do the same to him. I unfastened his shirt, left it open and moved on to his denims. I unbuttoned his flies, my intention being to pull his denims and boxers down in the same move. As I was lowering myself with the movement, his swollen dick sprang out of the boxers in front of my mouth. Nice. I reached a hand out, but he took hold of it himself with both of his hands and placed it on my lips.

"Sucer…s'il vous plait…pleez…suck."

I was only too happy to oblige, realising that my first impressions had been wrong.

"It will…make things…much easier…if we don't..have to…talk…no worries...about…translation."

I managed to get out, between my licks at his cock…a very *handsome* cock, and its size – perfect! I carried on sucking and admiring, and he watched my every move with approval, clearly enjoying the feel of my lips moving all over his length. I took one of his balls in my mouth, sucking hard whilst I fondled the other. I changed over within a minute, letting both testicles get their turn at individual ecstasy. I let my fingers play in his pubic hair, teasing him. I enjoyed listening to his moans and feeling his hands stroking and running through my hair as he stood. Feeling the need to taunt him more, I changed course with my fingers towards that sensitive area between scrotum and anus. He was on fire, and I felt that fire myself. I could hear him panting with delight as he pushed his hair from his eyes, the better to keep watching me as I continued sucking on him. His eyes closed and his groaning got louder by the minute.

"Oui…oh…oui."

I thought he was about to come, but it was his eagerness showing, and he started thrusting way to the back of my mouth. I was no longer in control of his cock and I started to gag. He quickly got the message and tugged me quickly across to the bed. Somehow he managed to tell me to lie on my back. He knelt between my legs first, wiggling just one finger about on my clit, through my pubic hair and then into my pussy.

He repeated the process again five minutes later, this time he used two fingers, and he watched all the time, fascinated, reminiscent of two kids playing doctors and nurses. The attraction of the thrusting fingers waned, and still kneeling, he pulled my legs over his shoulders, and with his hand guiding his beautiful tool, he wiggled it through my fanny hair, rubbed the end of it on my clit, it felt beautiful. I gazed at the ceiling, eagerly anticipating the feeling, waiting for that cock to stuff me good. His cock was out of my sight though. He was fucking me with his tongue. He stopped what he was doing and licked all over my vulva, concentrating on my clit again, and I was enjoying every minute, it was breathtaking. His fingers had disappeared; how could he tongue fuck me without his fingers on my pussy. He didn't realise what I wanted him to do with his fingers. I was on the verge of coming, but I wanted more, and he wasn't getting the message, so I showed him – I shoved my fingers up my pussy, and I groaned as he carried on sucking my clit.

"Ah…je…I…do…zat," he said, moving my fingers out of the way, and he did it slower that I had done, it was so sensual. I came in no time, not a fast burst but a beautifully slow release. The intensity was….*very* intense. It lasted a while, not a multiple orgasm, but one long, and slow, and *beautiful.*

"You…er…amour…love…fucking…yes ?"

I wonder how he had guessed. I was hot, sticky, wet, and wanting so much more.

"Yes, I love to be fucked, and fucked again. Keep fucking me, please, use your cock now."

So he fucked me, right there, the missionary position, and he grunted hard with each thrust, and I moaned, loudly. I was aware of giggling outside in the corridor, as footsteps passing the room slowed in their progress. People were listening to the loud and vocal fucking that was taking place, which was increasing in volume as he neared his climax. Then with a few violent thrusts, he shouted out, before biting hard on my breast, with his final squirt of come.

Rolling onto his back, with his cock still inside me, he said,

"Seet…on…my...face…pleez, oui?"

He just came inside me, and he wanted to stick his tongue up there. You're been paid, Helen, just do what the client wants. I sat on his face and he licked his semen from out of my hole, relishing the experience. I stayed in that position, waiting for him to finish his meal, but I certainly didn't expect the next instructions.

"Leeft...your...'ow you say...bot...tom, pleez." I did so.

"Now...you...pees...dans..er...in...my ...mous, pleez."

I couldn't believe it, what I was hearing.

"Wh...what...the...the hell?" I stammered, "I don't think I...let me get this right! You want me to piss in your mouth?"

"Oui...er yes."

The humour of the words was not entirely lost, but I was too incensed to be amused.

"Listen. You pay to fuck me. I do dirty, yes. I do dirty in a sexual manner. I do *not* do dirty as in a toilet nature. You will have to pay someone else to do that - sorry."

This was a totally new experience for me. I had thought I was well past the stage of feeling such shock, but I found the suggestion more than repulsive.

"I pay for, I get," he was indignant. I climbed off him, my earlier enjoyment almost forgotten. He watched until I was almost dressed, before he came out with my next shock,

"I get disc...er ..discount? Yes? For...er...non...pisser. You...er ...get...five hun red...less."

I wondered if it was a thing with the French. Who actually did things like that? The sex had been fantastic until that point, but I'd been totally turned off.

"Fine! Just let me get out of here. Maybe some street girl will be happy if you pay her five hundred pounds to piss in your mouth. There may be plenty of *them* around." He shrugged his shoulders dismissively, as if it had been nothing!

"We…er…fuck…again…one day…oui?" Amazingly, I got the impression he hadn't been too offended by the refusal.

"I don't know! Perhaps, but no…er…non pisser. Not ever! Okay?"

"Okay."

I giggled myself to sleep that night, two words running around my head, oui and piss! I figured I was over the worst of the shock if I could laugh about the incident, but I'd learned about an act that I didn't really want to know about. I made a mental note to mention the matter to Simon, the next time he called me.

CHAPTER 36

I was deliriously happy, singing out loud as I searched my wardrobe for something to wear. Janet, my friend from the Hopkins Partnership, had just called and asked me to join her on a night out with all the girls. I couldn't remember the last time I had been out, other than my…little business trips! I had plenty of time left to get ready for the evening, but I just wanted to find the right clothes early enough. I didn't want to be searching wildly at the last minute, then changing my mind every few seconds.

The taxi would be picking me up at seven thirty and the timing could not have been better. Anthony had left (leaving yet another envelope hidden in the greenhouse) on a business trip the day before, or so he said. At least I didn't have to worry about coming home drunk and him…I didn't dwell on *that* matter too long. I didn't want anything to spoil the rest of the day. Janet had wanted to keep everything from me – where we were going, what the plans were for the night. I was just thrilled to have been asked, and I knew that whatever we ended up doing, I would at least be in the company of my wonderful friends.

I was feeling very emotional as the cab pulled up. I couldn't believe it when they all climbed out to greet me with big hugs as I walked down the drive towards them.

"Helen! You're looking great!"

"We've missed you so much at the office!"

"How are you feeling?"

272

"How are you keeping yourself busy all day, Helen?"

The look on the face of the cab driver was priceless – a typically male reaction to women being over giddy and demonstrative - raised eyebrows and a shrug of the shoulders. Not to mention the impatient glances at his watch. They all shouted and chattered over the top of each other and I cried, touched by their concern and evident excitement to have me back in their midst for a few hours. I realised just how much I had missed them all. I couldn't wait to ask,

"So, tell me where you're taking me – I'm dying to know!"

They looked at each other sheepishly, and Gillian finally asked the others,

"Should we or not, girls?"

"Pleeeease tell me, pleeeease!" I begged like an excited teenager and we all laughed. Despite the laughter, they still didn't feel inclined to let me in on the secret.

All eyes turned towards me as we approached the last two or three hundred yards of the journey, eagerly awaiting my reaction. The instant I recognized the road and our intended destination, I could feel my face start to drop as I stared, open-mouthed, out of the cab window as we approached Jigz Club. My stomach felt so queasy and I couldn't imagine why this had been their choice for our get-together.

"Helen? Helen, what's matter?"

I tried to snap out of it. The girls were doing their best to give me a good night out and I must have looked so ungrateful. I smiled, trying to look happier and said,

273

"Oh, nothing! I just got..."

"Helen, if this is to do with that guy from your school, Alec Barker-whatshisface…?" Leanne piped up. I was pleased she'd interrupted me because I hadn't had a clue what words would have come out next, had she let me carry on speaking.

"No! It's not that…I'm fine! Really!" And before the subject of Alex cropped up again, I asked, "Are we eating first then?"

I felt such a relief! Everyone's attention was now on food as we settled up with the cab driver and made our way to the restaurant. All through our meal, I listened carefully as the girls chatted about work - their work. Whilst they tried hard to include me in the conversation, telling me any news on the other staff, or the clients for that matter, I didn't really feel a part of it anymore. They may as well have been talking about aliens. About to change the subject to more common ground I was suddenly curious about Leanne and her earlier comment about 'that guy from your school.'

"Leanne, what was it that you were saying early about Alex Baker-Thompson, that's his real name by the way – you know, 'if it's about that guy from your school'…?"

"Oh, that! Well…what I was going to say was, if it was about him…you know…why you weren't keen on coming here, well, I don't think you have any cause for concern!"

I couldn't understand what she was getting at. I hadn't told them what had really happened that night, but I couldn't wait to hear what she had to say.

"No, it wasn't to do with him. What made you think that?" I pushed my food around the plate wondering what she would come out with, and I didn't understand why I felt so nervous. I even noticed goose bumps forming on my arms.

"You said that he'd tried it on with you. I thought maybe that was the reason, because if it was, you have no need to worry."

I chuckled at what she'd just said and tried to make light of the conversation.

"So why have I got no reason to worry? I wasn't worried about him anyway."

"We've…um…been back here three times since…since…you know, your parents' accident. He was here the first time we came, with his friends. He stared all night, looking over at us all the time, probably wondering where you were." The other girls nodded at this, confirming that what Leanne said had been true.

"But he hasn't been back since – not when we've been here, anyway!"

Gillian added, "He must have really liked you, Helen…to come back looking for you!"

I looked at each of them in turn and they all looked guilty, as if they'd done something wrong - Leanne was tearing her napkin into shreds, Gemma was busy wiping her own lipstick off her glass.

"Girls, look! I realise that Ted must have told you all that my marriage is over, but you didn't bring me here in the hopes that Alex was here did you? Please tell me you didn't!"

I looked at their faces, trying to read their thoughts, to understand what their true intentions had been. Suddenly, feeling tired of the whole conversation, I stood up,

"Enough! Come on, we came here to enjoy ourselves, let's do that!"

We headed to the night club, to the loud music and dancing. The noise was a blessing to me. Conversation was impossible and I was grateful for that. During our meal I had begun to realise that I was alone – no longer a part of their world. Conversations about accounts, boyfriends, husbands and holidays are just a part of my past. I didn't fit in – and if the girls, my friends, ever found out about the new me, they would disown me. It was a depressing thought.

When the cab dropped me at home around half past one, the girls hugged and kissed me again. They had been delighted that I had gone out with them and told me they were longing for my return to work at some stage. I didn't have the heart to tell them that I wouldn't be returning, ever. I couldn't.

I poured myself a large glass of wine and sat in the armchair all night, mulling things over. I had learned a lot from my night out with the girls. They led normal lives, with loving husbands or boyfriends, nights out together, nine to five jobs. Then there was me – no loving relationship, a menial job that satisfied my mental health problems and a secret life as a call girl. Sordid visits to hotel rooms, taking money for sex, sometimes perverted sex, being paid in addition to achieving my own sexual gratification. I didn't know myself anymore; I used to be a different person, leading a very different life.

Sometime just before daylight, and succumbing to sleep, I recognised a few similarities between myself and Anthony.

CHAPTER 37

My mobile rang about ten minutes before I was due to finish work for the day.

"Hi, Helen! It's me. Sorry about the disruption to plans – our flight from New York was delayed nearly twenty four hours because of the weather in the States. I cancelled last night's hotel booking when I realised."

(I hadn't been happy that previous night, sneaking about in the service lift and hotel corridors to find that his usual suite was unoccupied. I was taking a big enough risk as it was, conducting my illicit business in the place where I was employed). He went on to ask if I was free in the evening. Being as I had nothing else planned I told him it wouldn't be a problem. After he'd told me when and where, a lodge, part of an estate, and a fellow actor's residence, I hung up. I sent a quick email to Simon once I was ready and I set off walking. After I'd turned the corner and out of sight of Anthony, I hailed a black cab.

Twenty five minutes later I arrived at my destination and knocked on the door. The guy who answered the door took my coat and showed me into a tastefully decorated sitting room where a beautiful log fire was burning, and where my client waited. He jumped up and smiled as I walked across towards him. I couldn't help but notice the blonde highlights in his sandy coloured hair. He looked much hotter than I remembered, but not quite as hot as the sex that I was looking forward to. I could feel my tingling starting down below, memories of our last steamy session re-surfacing quickly.

"How are you, Helen?" he asked as he kissed my cheek "How long is it since…?"

"Two mon…" but before I could finish he cut in rather rudely,

"Helen, there's somebody I would like you to meet tonight." And as if that had been her cue, she walked in from what must have been the door to the kitchen - about five foot six, with a body so painfully thin. Her hair was blonde and cut in a shaggy style – she was very pretty with cheekbones many girls would die for. It dawned on me that I had seen her before – she had been in a film where my client had been the leading male, but her total exposure throughout the whole film had been five minutes, tops. I didn't need any warning bells here though, it smacked me in the face instantly – he wanted a threesome.

"Phebes, this is, Helen. Helen, this is…"

Still feeling irritated by his interruption seconds before, and the fact that I was not particularly happy about this little twistm I couldn't resist snapping back,

"Phebes? Yes, you just said!"

She never approached me to shake hands and whilst it occurred to me to do so, I was too bloody annoyed. This had just been sprung on me at the last minute and my head was in complete turmoil. I had never been touched by a woman sexually, neither had I ever been involved in a threesome. I felt repulsed. My stomach was lurching, and I felt half inclined to leave.

Remembering that I was getting paid to give what the client asked of me, I nodded when he asked if I wanted white wine. I didn't trust myself to speak, I was so shaken, but I knew the wine would relax me – it usually did the trick. Phebes poured herself a whisky and sat down next to me. I felt only slightly more at ease after I'd had a couple of glasses. We indulged in some idle gossip and although I still had nagging doubts I did my best to contribute to the conversation. Over and over in my mind I kept telling myself you are still here, you could have gone home thirty minutes ago.

Phebes eventually moved onto the rug in front of the fire and she immediately started to remove her clothing. I felt nervous. My skin was hot and clammy, but it also felt as if a giant icicle was living within me, and I wondered if it was about to thaw. Glancing over at my client for some indication of what I was expected to do, I shrugged my shoulders at him. Sensing my apprehension and naivety, he tried to put me at ease. Leaning towards me, he almost whispered in my ear,

"Why don't you go and sit with Phebes on the rug – get to know her better?"

My insides were cringing, but after taking a little longer than normal to finish off the dregs in my glass, I did as he'd suggested. I stiffly plonked myself down about two feet away from her, following her lead by unbuttoning my top. Coming closer towards me she put her hand on mine and held it still. I winced at her touch and she looked directly into my eyes.

"Don't, Helen. *I* will do that – it will be *my* pleasure," she said eagerly. She moved in to kiss me, but realising from my grimace that kissing was not on offer, she kissed around my throat and neck instead. A little unsure how I felt about having a woman's lips kiss me, I was tense…but…it wasn't entirely unpleasant. Her hands slowly unbuttoned my top and unfastened the clasp on my bra. Looking into my eyes for a reaction all the while, she slid my denims down my legs and flung them into a chair. She moved her hands teasingly up my thighs and let her fingers edge their way into my thong. My head was telling me that it didn't feel right but my body was surprisingly experiencing the early ripples of an excitement I couldn't begin to explain.

I looked across at my client, expecting him to join us. He nodded back at me - a nod that told me just to get on with it. He had started to unzip his trousers though. I gave a sigh of relief – *this* was not my normal sort of business. It seemed as if Phebes had no inhibitions at all. She behaved as if this was something she was more than familiar with. She was running her fingers through my pussy hair whilst with her other hand she fondled my breasts, biting occasionally on my nipples, and I squealed in pain each time. Suddenly, she yanked on my thong and it snapped.

She pushed my fingers quickly towards her own bush and, alarmed by the move, I sat upright. I had no desire to touch her in that way.

"Don't think for one minute, that *I* am going to fuck *you,* Phebes!" I snapped, "I don't *do* the fucking – I *get* fucked!"

"And I am *happy* to fuck you, honey. I just wanted you to feel that woman part of me, my cunt, before we get down to it – relax, you don't have to touch me if you don't want to."

281

I wondered why he wasn't joining us just yet. I needed some normality to ease my panic. I tried to put thoughts of Phebes to the back of my mind by concentrating on another client, a special someone, special sex. I laid down again, more relaxed but…not quite resigned.

"Lay on your stomach, Helen."

As I rolled over I caught sight of him again - completely naked on the settee, his hand slowly massaging his piece of muscle, with its wrinkled skin. She passed me three cushions off the settee.

"Put these under your tummy - raise your bottom into the air,." bossed Phebes.

I was hardly in position before I could feel her tongue licking all around my buttocks, her hands around the front of my thighs, yet again stroking my pubes. She teased, she tormented, brushed her fingers gently, but swiftly, over my clit and away again. Her tongue barely touched my anus, and was moved quickly away. I closed my eyes. I didn't have to, but I couldn't see her anyway, so I imagined the tongue and fingers to be those of a man, a special man. I had always been good at pretending when I had to, and it was essential for me in this new situation. It was feeling good, I was enjoying every second of the anticipation…the waiting…waiting for the tongue to lick my pussy, waiting for the fingers to slide into it, then for the tongue to lick my clit.

This had to be a man pleasuring me, preparing me to be well and truly fucked. I didn't have to wait too long. His tongue, I was almost believing it *was* him, started gently stabbing into my anus, gentle thrusts that started making me shudder with delight. His finger, a lovely male finger, replaced the tongue which had moved to my sensitive area between anus and pussy. He was rubbing it, moving more rapidly. He slid his tongue quickly in my hole and out again. Such torment! He shoved his fingers hard in me, in and out, in and out. They entered my hole again and again as his tongue worked over my clit with such deliberation. I moaned with delight, savouring every second as I felt my juice flow, coming and coming again, and I wanted the feeling to go on forever. I placed my hands on the floor and raised my upper body throwing my head back in intense pleasure, before lowering myself down just a few seconds later.

Whilst I lay there still shaking from the multiple orgasm that had rocked my body, I was aware that contact between us had broken. I was aware only of some movement, somebody passing something over me, it all happened in a flash. Then he was inside me properly, not his tongue or his fingers but his cock, inside me, fucking me like crazy, and his cock felt strange - different, knobbly even. But I loved it. The knobbles were massaging every glorious nerve ending contained within my vagina. I held on as long as I could, which wasn't long. I had no choice but to let go as one *giant* orgasm sent me soaring into outer space and back. It was delicious and I cried out with the over sensitivity as his cock continued fucking me hard and fast, thrusting furiously.

"Stop…please!" I was spent; my body sagged into the cushions. He stopped and rolled me on to my back to face him and I realised with horror that it was *her* that was looking down on

283

me. *She* had made me come. *She* had fucked me with *her* cock – a knobbly, strap-on cock. As I lay there, reeling with shock, she got onto her hands and knees, bent over me and kissed my throat, and with one hand she guided her cock in and started fucking me again. My client, fully hard at last, came over and bent over her. He shagged her, very roughly, up the backside, holding on to her tight as he thrust into her, thrusting into me. His powerful thrusts into her gave more momentum to her thrusting into me.

I was on fire; the dirty fucking was taking me places I had never been before. I was euphoric when I came again, producing fresher spurts of wetness caused as much by the *thought* of crudity as the physical feelings inside me. I lost all sense of control at that moment. I raised my head and sucked hard on her breasts, reaching down with my hand I fingered her clit before sliding them inside her. It didn't take her long. She climaxed quickly and moved out of the way still moaning. After removing the strap-on cock she sat on the edge of the settee, shoved it up herself, and proceeded to pleasure herself with it. As I was already on my back he didn't waste his time moving me. He quickly forced my legs in the air over his shoulders and rammed his cock hard inside me, thrusting as if his life depended on it. I could feel his balls smacking hard against my backside and it was me who got his juices ten minutes later as he climaxed, yelling out loud.

His excitement at watching us had clearly induced his pleasure to dizzying heights. Phebes was on her hands and knees again and grasped my hand, and with her in control of my fingers over her clit, she came violently, and with screams of ecstasy.

She wanted to share a bath afterwards and I suspected that she was maybe seeking something extra, but I was totally wrong. She was in fact trying to act like she was my new best friend – though I've never had a best friend who wanted to share a bath with me. I played along in an amiable manner - discussing fashion, our favourite designer labels and our favourite stores to shop in London.

After drying myself off, I dressed and went back into the lounge to collect my payment. He offered me a glass of wine or something a little stronger. I quickly checked my watch – I had fifteen minutes until my cab was due to return for me – so I accepted. He handed me the wine and my payment and we indulged in small talk until Phebes joined us in a beautifully made, silk kimono. Feeling unusually out-spoken, I asked about the relationship between the pair, to be told that they didn't regard what they did together to be an affair. They considered it a business arrangement that takes place once or twice a year. It sounded as if she would also be getting paid for her services. She was even spending the whole night with him – I wondered how much that extra service was costing him.

Hearing a car approaching the lodge which would more than likely be my cab, I picked up my satchel and said goodbye to them both. Sitting in the back of the cab, I gazed out of the window throughout my journey home, lost in my thoughts…and shocked at what I had just done, but not denying how much I had enjoyed the experience. I climbed into bed forty five minutes later, fit to drop.

CHAPTER 38

Just as I had expected, the last envelope that I had found in the greenhouse stayed there all weekend. I made the effort to get up early on both the Saturday and the Sunday morning. Whether it was because I was either working or reading in the kitchen, I don't know, but Anthony went out both days without retrieving the envelope. I had checked the greenhouse again just on the off chance that he stayed awake during the night to get the envelope whilst I was sleeping.

It was sometime whilst I was at work on Tuesday that the envelope disappeared - another date for my secret log.

CHAPTER 39

Simon called me on the Wednesday night. He had passed my name and number to another client of his. The man was in one of the F1 Constructors teams, involved in the design of the cars. When he called me, he had first asked if I would be willing to collect him and take him to my house for our business transaction. With having the rather large problem of Anthony living under the same roof and not knowing where *he* was planning to be, I told the client that my house was out of the question. The next option he offered was for me to travel to his lodge. He was renting a country lodge near Silverstone. It would be a fair drive for me, but as it was well out of reach to anyone who knew me, I thought it shouldn't pose too much of a problem. Simon, as usual, had vouched for him.

"He's a great guy, you'll like him, Helen." I was satisfied at that, but as always, I would make my own judgement after our first meeting.

I arrived at 11am the following Saturday morning as instructed. Even though I had planned to arrive ten minutes sooner, my sat nav had its limitations and I ended up first of all at a farm that was one mile beyond the programmed destination. I quickly turned around in the farmyard and drove away, before someone came out to enquire if I was lost.

My new client wasn't exactly what you would call rude to me, but he was not particularly friendly or welcoming either. He pointed to where I could go to get ready and suggested we get started as soon as possible. He had somewhere else ne needed to be at 4pm and a car was coming to collect him at 3pm. I had asked him if there was anything specific he wanted me to bring and he had told me that he was into 'uniforms of some description,' but he wasn't too bothered what I chose. Other than kinky underwear, school uniform, a maid outfit (from work) and a nurse's attire, I didn't own much else. I had decided to visit a fancy dress shop the previous day and I purchased, especially for this date, a policewoman's uniform.

In the tiny little bedroom he had taken me to, so that I could change, I stripped off and dressed in a black suspender belt, black seamed stockings and black bra. I purposely took my panties off. The uniform completed the image. I dashed into the bathroom to check my make-up and then went in search of the guy, not knowing where he wanted me, but thinking it would be the master bedroom or the lounge. I found him in the kitchen. He was standing at the sink swallowing some tablets. He spun around when I entered the room and for some reason, I thought I saw a look of anger flash across his face…which just as quickly disappeared again.

He moved one of the chairs away from the kitchen table and pushed me backwards until I was sort of sitting on the edge of it. He pulled at my white shirt, ripping the buttonholes as he shoved my bra up over my breasts. Not wasting any time at all, his teeth bit into my left nipple as he roughly pushed the skirt up my thighs, feeling first for the suspender belt, then my fanny hair. Just as quickly the hand left my fanny and I heard the telltale sound of him unzipping his jeans. Then it was his dick that he was guiding with his hand. I was feeling hot and I wanted to be vulgar. It had been over a week and I wanted fucking real bad - dirty fucking, fucking that would satisfy me…and hurt. He poked his knob between the suspender elastic and my thigh, rubbed it through my fanny hair and roughly shoved it up my hole.

"Fuck it then. Let me see if you can fuck me good. I so need it." I was feeling so horny. It turned me on, talking to him like that…telling him to fuck me good, and I held my breath with anticipation.

"Suspenders and stockings – nice choice, Helen! They make me feel like indulging in pure filth," he snarled in my ear,

"And I *am* going to indulge in filth, I'm going to fuck you. And I'm going to hurt you as much as you've hurt me."

I enjoyed my first orgasm as he rubbed his cock over my clit; I shuddered in pleasure, as much from his dirty talk as well as the friction on my clit.

My mind drifted from my vulgar thoughts for a few seconds to wonder who had hurt him…who he wanted to punish…after all, it wasn't me who had hurt him. I was jolted back to reality again as he pushed me back over onto the table. He fucked me rough and hard for twenty minutes, grinding his pubic area hard into mine, the edge of the table cutting into my buttocks. I was soon wet down below from my second orgasm and I wanted more. His fingers were nipping hard at my thighs and then my tits, especially the nipples. He was thrusting his cock so hard into me, up as far as he could go (it felt like he was trying to get his testicles in as well) my stomach was beginning to hurt – in fact, I was hurting all over. I cried out in pain, and he punched me in the eye. His hands went to my throat and he squeezed in a threatening manner as he growled,

"Is it hurting to be fucked like this? I hope so, because I want to hear you cry out - I *want* to hurt you, you filth. I want to hurt your fucking cunt, and I'm going to hurt more than your cunt, you're going to experience what pain is all about."

He carried on squeezing my throat with one hand, whilst with his free hand he slapped me across the face half a dozen times. I felt frightened. I didn't want to come anymore, the sexual excitement had passed and all I wanted to do was go home. He bit my bottom lip and the fleshy part of my boob, and I prayed that this was going to be the extent of the pain. This guy could fuck. But his hurt was even better. After more than half an hour of him shagging my pussy hard, he was nowhere near coming and I was sore, very sore. My excitement had long passed and I was finding his behaviour intimidating.

Without a word of warning, he pulled his cock out and rolled me over so that I was bent over the table face down. He pushed my head down towards the table, his cock found it's way into my back passage, and just as he'd promised he would – he hurt me like hell. I cried out in my desperation – quite a few times – which made him thrust even harder. He was yanking at my hair at the same time, pulling it hard and hurting my scalp. After what seemed like forever, he pulled his throbbing cock from my anus, and flung me onto the tiled floor,

"Hands and knees, filth!"

I quickly obeyed lest I should get a fist in my other eye. I expected he was going to stuff his cock up my arse again, but surprisingly, he started fucking my fanny again, and already sore from his previous battering of it, it felt like it was on fire, as he fucked harder, and harder still, and I finally felt that dead give away, the throbbing of a cock about to explode. He pulled out rapidly, turned me onto my back, and cock in hand, ejaculated all over me – my hair, my face, my breasts, stomach, and fanny hair. It was over. I held my breath in disbelief, but scared he had more to inflict on me.

"You asked for that, so don't start fucking complaining," he said as he watched me standing at the kitchen sink, dabbing at my face and eye, with cold water,

"and you're getting well paid for it." I was mortified. I couldn't understand what it was he was implying. "I don't recall asking for anything. How did I ask for it?" I challenged him, acting more confrontational than I felt,

"You are the one who asked me to come here!"

"You're the one who chose to dress as a fucking policewoman! I never told you to do that!"

I felt totally bewildered, near to tears and hurting everywhere. Somehow I'd messed up, but I carried on fighting my corner, and started to be alarmed at my own cockiness, but I couldn't stop

292

myself, I was angry at the way the meeting had turned out.

"You said any uniform, you weren't too bothered! I wasn't to know …what that would make you do to me!" I indicated my face and the eye that I was softly patting with the towel.

"Well, the bitch caught me drink driving. She lost me my fucking licence for two years! I need my licence for work – she made it difficult for me! The shower is through there…" he dismissed me, pointing to the bathroom door, "…and your money's there." He indicated a white envelope on the kitchen worktop, "Next time don't come as a cop, and you won't get hurt."

I couldn't go in to work the next week. The skin around my eye was black, the white was no longer white, my cheeks, breasts and thighs were badly bruised. I was also bleeding down below and my back was hurting from being thrown onto the hard tiled floor. I had taken a beating or two prior to this one, but this guy won hands down, the prize for causing me the most pain. I called Simon and told him exactly what the guy had put me through and that I didn't want to meet with him again. He promised me faithfully that he would deal with it. I received a call from Frigid Flo at the hotel, telling me to be back at work the following Monday, or I would be receiving a P45.

CHAPTER 40

As I walked down the street from the tube station, I carefully checked in my mirror to see if my make-up looked perfect before announcing my arrival to David with a text message.

There was no need for me to knock on the door. He was already there with the door open wide. As I stepped over the threshold he gave me a hug and a kiss on each cheek. He looked as amazing as ever and was wearing some gorgeous, 'come and fuck me' fragrance. His tanned face and arms had been acquired during his recent business trip to Indonesia.

"You're looking breathtakingly hot, darling," he greeted me. I quivered with excitement at his compliment. He was like a drug to me - his every word a turn-on.

"Compliment back at you, David – love the tan."

His eyes sparkled as he held me by the shoulders. He was taking in every inch of me. My mind raced ahead. I couldn't wait to take every inch of him into me. I knew I shouldn't be feeling things for him, but I was struggling to control it. I had been battling with the feelings for quite a few months, and I feared how things would end. He was a client.

"I've got champagne chilling. Sit down, Helen!"

I made myself at home, sandals off, legs curled up, whilst he poured our first glass of the evening, a Bollinger Rosé.

"How are things? Are you still putting up with that abusive boyfriend of yours?"

I cringed, I had forgotten that David had assumed that Anthony was my partner and I hadn't corrected him at the time. I didn't like being deceitful, particularly with David.

"David, don't worry about me, I can handle myself! He will be getting what's coming to him – sometime over the next six months, I think, maybe sooner! He's going to wonder what's hit him, by the time I've finished!" I assured him.

"I don't know what you're planning, but I'm sure he deserves it. Just keep safe, Helen – from what you've told me, he can be dangerous, and I worry for you." He looked genuinely concerned. My heart melted at his warmth, I felt a rush of affection and I wanted to hug him and never let go.

"True – he can be nasty, but he can also be very naïve. He is totally in the dark, trust me. Shall I put some music on?"

He seemed to be deep in thought but managed to nod his assent.

"Bizet do?"

"What? Oh…yes, Bizet."

I inserted the CD and pressed play, wondering what he was thinking, wondering if he could read my mind. We lazed around listening to beautiful music for the rest of the evening and flirted silently with each other. It was all part of the game we played during our sessions, the anticipation being almost as enjoyable as the sex. We finished the bottle of Bollinger and started a second one.

It was late when we went up to bed. For some reason, David asked me to get ready for bed in the only other bedroom in the cottage with an en suite. I wondered what on earth he was up to – whatever the surprise he was planning, I was excited about the sex that would be following. Feeling the pleasant naughty tingling starting within me, I dressed in my new underwear - a pair of white, high leg, lacy panties and white hold-up stockings. I picked up the matching bra and decided not to bother. David loved my pert little breasts, so they would grab his attention immediately. I carried out a quick check of my make-up once again, before crossing the landing to the master bedroom, already feeling moist down below.

He was ready for me, totally naked, his bottom on a towel, and some equipment laid by his side – scissors, shaving foam and a battery razor. My face must have been a picture, and he laid there smirking at me. I laughed out loud, totally bemused,

"David? What…the…hell…are…you…doing?" I could hardly get the words out for my laughter, "Is…this…your…new…perverted…idea…of…fo replay?" He snorted with laughter at me and said,

"I wanted to make it more pleasant for you tonight, Helen. I recall you almost choked last time on one of my…you called it a…wait a minute….yes….you called it an…obscenely coarse pube!" he carried on snorting, "Get rid of them for me. I can't have you choking on me, Helen. How would that look in an autopsy?"

296

I had to wait until our laughter calmed down before I dared to start work on his wonderful nether regions, both my hands and his body were shaking with our raucous laughter. I started with the scissors, carefully trimming back his wiry pubic hairs around the base of his cock and his pubic region. Trusting me implicitly, he relaxed enjoying my touch, his stomach muscles tightening as I worked my way down. I noticed his cock expanding, but I didn't want to think about; the temptation to climb on top of him and ride him would be too great. I kept on trimming until all his pubic hair was short enough. After squirting the shaving foam into my hand, I gently lathered the whole area and started with the razor until the whole area was clean shaven. I was amazed with the results – his cock appeared to be longer. It looked fantastic – *so* rock hard and eager. David and I both enjoyed oral but we had to exercise some restraint for a little while longer as there were a few stray hairs to deal with.

I filled the bath for the pair of us to share, to wash away all traces of pubes and shaving foam. I found some tea-lights and candles in the bathroom cupboard, lit them and placed them all around the edge of the bath. We took a glass of champagne each and sat in the bath indulging in some dirty and wildly erotic foreplay. I took hold of his stiffness and massaged it slowly. I fondled his scrotum. He squeezed my breasts, bit on my nipples and poked first his fingers then the cock-shaped soap inside me. Twenty minutes of wonderful fun passed and we both shivered, the water had lost its warmth. We quickly headed for the bedroom, far too excited to bother about

297

drying thoroughly. The anticipation had been wonderful but I felt taunted and tantalised enough – I wanted it for real.

Once he was lying down on the bed, I immediately sat astride his face and took his cock into my mouth, my favourite sixty-niner. I let my tongue slide up and down every inch of his tool and he moaned longingly for more. I squeezed his balls, not for one second giving thought to anything other than pleasuring his cock in any way that I could. All the while, his tongue was inside my pussy, twisting in all directions, his nose rubbing my clit as he strived to push his tongue further in and it felt like heaven. My mind was on David only, I was his for the night and I wanted to give him all my attention, sexual and otherwise. I felt so hot, I wanted more and yet I didn't want it to end. He pulled his tongue out every minute or so and poked my pussy with his fingers while he captured some air before diving in again and each time he thrust his tongue in, it was more pleasurable than the last. I wasn't ready for it to finish too soon, so when I felt in danger of coming I quickly changed position, moving my body down the bed with my pussy well away from his face until I was bent over the bottom of the bed licking his testicles and he was groaning in delight. Wanting him to groan some more, my attention and my tongue diverted to his backside. I quickly flicked my tongue over it time and again and he moaned louder in his pleasure. Sensing his impatience for things to move on I sucked on his dick, giving sharp little licks around the ridge of the knob. He was totally rigid – the perfect stiffness.

"Come back up here, baby – I want to tongue fuck you," he whispered.

I was ready for it. I shuffled my backside around the side of the bed without my mouth losing contact with his cock. He raised my leg up in the air and over him, lifting his head eagerly to get his tongue in my pussy, before I lowered myself onto his face. It felt so good, and I shuddered in delight, my enthusiasm for sucking his cock matched that of his exploration with his tongue. I wanked him with my hand whilst my lips were tight around his knob, moving up and down its length rapidly. If his nose wasn't rubbing my clit, his hand was – it was all so intense! I could feel the onset of my wonderful tingling. I wanted his cock in my tunnel, I needed it badly - I was damp with perspiration and my love juice.

It seemed to me as if he was determined to make me wait for his shaft. He stuck three fingers in my hole and then his tongue flicked around my labia and clit. His bottom started thrusting upwards, forcing his cock to the back of my throat. I sucked harder and harder until I could feel his muscles twitching - his wonderful cum spurting into my mouth, salty and warm, my juices being released at the same time – it felt as if I was going to shudder forever as he continued licking at my vagina. A little of his semen still dribbled down my chin and onto his stomach as we moved apart after ten minutes – both satiated for the moment.

We snuggled up like two spoons, and I enjoyed, for once, being able to lie next to a man and feel his arms around me. It was a terrifying thought to me, something I never intended to do again. Just once in a while, it was nice to feel somebody's body warmth close to me. Before I fell away into the grasp of sleep, I wondered if David was in a relationship with anybody. He had never volunteered the information and I had never dared to ask. I was scared of what his answer would be. The thought made me feel insanely jealous, and the memories of our oral sex and my orgasms faded away as sleep overcame me.

I woke up not knowing what time it was, but I guessed I had been asleep maybe two hours. Glancing at the digital clock, I noticed it was around three o'clock. David's hand was squeezing my left boob, and I could feel his stiffness, between my thighs – I was instantly aroused. He pulled me over onto my back, kissed and licked my tits for five minutes and then he was into my pussy, his cock needing no guidance, thrusting away hard and fast. He lifted my legs over his shoulders, thrusting even harder, and his cock felt beautiful, fucking me hard, reaching my wonderful G-spot. His pubic bone rubbing really close to my clit, making me come, again and again, and when he shot his load this time, He stopped thrusting, his dick as far up my fanny as it could go, and the feeling inside me, when I felt each squirt with the pounding of every muscle in his cock was magnificent.

I laid there smiling to myself, long after David started snoring, trying to recall every fucking session we'd had - how he made me feel. I loved being fucked by him, in so many different ways, from our first encounter. He made me feel…and I couldn't explain where the thought suddenly popped up from, he made me feel like I should run. I didn't want my head and my heart to feel like this – like they were constantly battling.

Just before seven o'clock, we were both awake again, enjoying a coffee and cuddles in bed. I was first to the bathroom for a shower and to brush my teeth. After I emerged from the bathroom, David went in, slapping my bottom playfully as we passed each other. Oral session number two commenced after that. An action replay of the previous evening's antics was well under way, our tongues and fingers, poking and probing each and every orifice, such excitement for us both, but this time as I felt my shudders and tingling I begged him urgently.

"Come inside me please, David –come inside my pussy, *please.*"

"Yes, baby. Quickly then, hands and knees, it's coming – quick!"

A quick scrambling about by both of us and we were just in time, he was ejaculating as his cock entered my fanny, spurting his semen, which met my own juices, and we both cried out loudly. For fifteen minutes we stayed in that same position, our heartbeats taking time to slow down, panting, sweating, and for five crazy minutes, I started thinking that I never wanted to leave that room; I wanted to stay, locked in there, with David – forever. I tried telling myself that I didn't love him, not really, it was only because our fucking, oral or otherwise, gets better and better, the orgasms, *more* beautiful, and even more – *violent.* I truly loved being fucked by this man. It was the fucking, not him that I was in love with, it had to be!

After we had both finished in the bathroom, I got dressed and was almost ready to leave. David had been lounging around downstairs in his bathrobe as I was upstairs putting the finishing touches to my make-up.

"Come down here, babe, I have something for you." Before I was even half way down the stairs he held a little gift bag up in the air to show me. I was astounded! I had never once received a gift from a client. I never expected to - they paid me, cash!

"What's that? What are you buying me a gift for? You don't need to do that, David," I scolded.

"I know I don't, but you are one very special lady, and I couldn't resist – open it!"

My hands shook as I removed a gift-wrapped box from the bag, wondering what the hell he was up to. He didn't need to be giving me a gift of any kind. As I removed the paper and the ribbon, from what was obviously an item of jewellery, the thought also crept into my mind, that *I* should perhaps pay David for the pleasure he gave to me, instead of the other way around. Opening the box, I was almost blinded by the dazzle of the rather large, diamond pendant sat on the black velvety lining. It was exquisite. I sat open-mouthed, not knowing what to say next.

"Do you like it, babes? What's the matter – you're not saying anything?" I didn't know what to say. I couldn't voice my thoughts to him. Thoughts I didn't want or need. Suddenly, I couldn't stop myself.

"David, can I ask you something, please? No…that's stupid…I'm being…a bit presumptuous…you're not…you're not in love with me by any chance, are you? No! Of course you're not…how silly of me…to suggest such a thing. Please, tell me you're not!"

He chuckled, but I recognised the sound of a nervous swallowing on his part.

"Sweetheart, I couldn't possibly let myself fall for you. I couldn't. I know what you do…go with…other men. It's just a gift…for a beautiful lady, and you are very special to me, special moments. I care for you, Helen…but I'm not in love with you."

I felt an icy hand…of disappointment snatch at my heart, but I let it pass. It was on the tip of my tongue – to say that if I did love him and if he loved me…I would give it all up for him. But I didn't! I didn't really love him. We just had, like he had said, special moments together – *don't go confusing this with love, you idiot*. And his denial sounded convincing enough. He handed me the envelope with my payment, but I waved it away,

"I can't do it, David – I can't take money off you. You've bought me a beautiful gift, and I've had some excellent fun – let's leave it at that. I can't take money off you again."

"Accept the gift for what it is, babe - just a treat for a special lady. I haven't got anyone else to spend my money on, apart from my two girls. I can afford it. Take the money as well – it was a business transaction, after all. You deserve it all. Now go! It's not up for discussion. I will be back again in a couple of months, I'll ring you - and I'll look forward to it."

I quickly gathered up my belongings, we had a hug, pecked each other on the cheek, and I was out of there. And missing him already!

CHAPTER 41

I was in the changing rooms at work, my Monday shift was just ending and my mobile phone started ringing. I recognised the phone number – the estate agents. I was half expecting it. They had spoken to me two days previously, on the Friday, telling me that they had received an offer on my parents' house at last. The offer was quite a few thousand below the asking price but they had advised me to wait a little longer. Apparently, there was another couple very interested, who needed to speak with their mortgage company before making their first offer.

I felt cold. Since the call of two days ago, my O.C.D. had been quite bad. On Saturday I had emptied the kitchen cupboards, cleaned them all out and put everything back. Two hours later, I had repeated the whole process. Anthony had not gone out that day, nor had he spoken to me, but every time he'd come into the kitchen, I could feel his eyes burning into my back, I could almost visualise the expressions he would have had on his face. He thought I was losing it.

Telling him that I was going out with the girls from the Hopkins Partnership, I'd left the house at six thirty and returned around midnight. In truth, I had visited a client in his Belgravia apartment. It hadn't been a particularly pleasant experience, and it niggled me even more when I arrived home to find that Anthony was not only at home, but he hadn't gone to bed. I couldn't help being nasty to him, telling him it wouldn't be long before I would be gone from the house for good. I didn't hang around downstairs too long. I thought it would be more sensible to go to bed instead of causing yet another fracas.

The estate agent's words kept coming back to me before I finally dozed off, and I was saddened again at the thought of my parents' house being occupied by strangers. A crazy idea suddenly occurred to me – I would go and live in my parents' house - it was mine now anyway, and Anthony could keep our house. That way, I would sign our house over to Anthony. I would make sure he had no claim on what had been my parents' house.

When I had woken up on the Sunday morning, I realised that my plan would be impossible. I knew I couldn't return to my mum and dad's house. I had been coping better with my grief since getting to know Thomas and to return to what had once been my home, would have a detrimental effect on me and my ever present, O.C.D.

I finally answered the call to be told that the first people had upped their offer to the asking price, a cash buyer – they wanted the sale to go through as quickly as possible. I told the agent to accept the offer and instruct my solicitor.

I kept it from Anthony. I didn't see the need to tell him. He didn't even know about the villa in Marbella, or the Paris apartment that Dad had purchased in my name whilst I was in my teens. It was only after my father's death that their solicitor had informed me that I was already owner of the title deeds for both the villa and apartment. I had been puzzled at the time as to why, Anthony, who had been trusted by my father, had never been made privy to that little snippet of information.

CHAPTER 42

I'd been chained to his bed for four hours seventeen minutes, and I'd been feeling extremely pissed off since the first hour. He always paid me extra for the hours involved, but I sometimes question whether it's worth it. I detest this bondage thing. I find it very restricting and I hate lying on my back unless I am being fucked. Without freedom of movement, I am never able to achieve a decent orgasm. Plus there's the boredom of all his messing about to contend with. The sexual action during the past few hours I'd been chained up had been roughly ten minutes every half hour. That was barely much more than seventy or eighty minutes in the time I'd been there. He left me chained to the bed all the time, returning to his office on the ground floor to do some work - at least that is what he claimed. I suspected he was searching the house for anything he could find to shove inside me - phallic symbols.

During the last four hours he'd used a candle, a banana, a vibrator, and the last idea he'd just put to use, with its rough knob on the end - one of his microphones.

"I'll still be able to smell your fanny on it when I'm singing at my next gig." he announced as he removed it and proceeded to sniff every inch in delight, purely for effect. I couldn't help but wonder about his upbringing. I glowered at him but I knew there was more to come. I closed my eyes and let my mind drift for a short time – to pleasant memories of my other encounters – with David.

This guy also had an obsession. Except for my panties, which he'd ripped off me and thrown across the room, I was still fully clothed. Grey socks that came over my knees, grey school skirt and cardigan, white blouse and school tie. I was attired like a certain young pop star in one of her finest videos, and that famous track had been playing on repeat in the background since I'd arrived.

I heard his footsteps on the stairs again. I wondered what the hell he was going to poke me with this time. Surprisingly enough, as he walked though the door I could see that he didn't have any objects in his hands. He was minus his T-shirt now and his flies were undone – he looked quite attractive, his jet black hair with plum coloured highlights slightly mussed.

"Okay, I'm going to undo your shackles - you had better be good. I want you to oil my body first, all over, every last inch of it, and I want you to do it sensually, not like the masseuse at the parlour I was at yesterday, rough as fuck she was."

Irritated by his challenging remark, I was quick to defend myself.

"You know I do a great job. That's why you've called me a second time."

He shrugged his shoulders and pulled a face,

"Well you'll have to show me again, won't you? I've forgotten. You will have to be good. I don't like naughty girls." I felt relief at least, he was making positive moves. I'd been in one position too long and I felt totally numb.

Once he'd unfastened all my ties, he thrust the bottle of baby oil in my hand, turned his back on me and peeled off his denims. From sitting on the edge of the bed, he quickly flipped into a face down position without me catching even a glimpse of his cock. I chuckled to myself and wondered if he'd turned shy all of a sudden.

I started on his shoulders and gently massaged the oil in, careful not to use too much. As I concentrated on smoothing out a few small knots of muscle, he moaned out loud,

"That feels good. Keep at it."

Rubbing every inch of his back, slowly and in a sensual manner, I worked my way down towards his firm and nicely rounded bottom. I teasingly rubbed one finger down his crack and his body tensed as I taunted him with my finger dancing so near to his anus.

"Tease it, baby, tease it!" he urged. My client was bad, yet my whole body was aching to be touched by him. I started shaking with my need and my head was telling me to be brave, speed things up.

"Would you like me to remove my clothes or should I remain the naughty schoolgirl?" I asked, in my throatiest of voices. I was feeling hot, wanting him that very moment, but I still had work to do. I wondered what his fans would give to be in the room with him right at that moment.

"Okay, as a treat. Just leave the socks on, I fucking love the socks."

Moving down his thighs, I continued my torment of his body with one hand, as I struggled to remove the rest of my clothes. As the last item, my bra, landed on the floor, I quickly got both hands to work again, still intent on mocking his thighs and edging my fingers in between them towards his scrotum. When I reached the backs of his knees I was amazed at how he squirmed beneath me. It was evidently a very sensitive area for him and I caressed each, though only briefly. I was getting impatient, I hadn't had sex for a week and I was ready for it, hungry for it. My every nerve was tingling as I oiled his bulging calves, his ankles – and then I grabbed his waist and rolled him onto his back…

My eyes were drawn straight to his cock and what surrounded it. I felt my eyes bulge out in surprise. I'd found out why he kept his back to me when he got on the bed. The backdrop behind his amazing shaft was fire, a very recent and painful looking tattoo of fire - cavorting flames of fire, not a pubic hair in sight. Hell fire!

"You, silly little girl, I wasn't ready to show you just yet!" he yelled, and sat bolt upright, "Now bend over…no, over my thighs, you deserve a good slap for seeing your present before I was ready to show it!"

I moved into position, obeying his order and he spanked my backside…softly to start with. Every twenty or so slaps he stopped and poked his fingers in and out of my fanny for a few seconds. I didn't want him to stop the poking, it had been nice, my first hint of better things to come. I wanted him to keep shoving them in. I was on fire like his wild crazy flames, I wanted to be shagged. I wanted to let go of my juices, get my reward.

The slaps on my arse kept coming and every session of slapping was getting harder and stinging more, the fingers delved further inside me each time, rougher than before, his nails seeking and finding my G spot. It was hurting, I was on fire, and…I was almost salivating. As fast as the slapping started, it ceased without warning when he rolled me off him and he was laid on his back again, his solid rock of muscle almost tapping on my lips. I chewed gently at the edge of his knob and tantalised his foreskin with my tongue, careful to avoid catching his ring piercing with my teeth. He whimpered as I fondled his scrotum at the same time.

Reaching out with both hands he stretched towards me to cup my breasts and nip hard on each of my buds. I squealed out in pain …and delight. I took the whole of his knob in my mouth and sucked, tracing my tongue all around the edge, slowly working my hand up and down that beautiful rod; the rod of steel that nearly reached his navel. Faster and faster with my hands and I took almost the full extent of him into my mouth and I could feel his throbbing through my gums, my tongue and my teeth. I could taste his release of pre-cum, hear the guttural noises trying to escape his lips, and he reluctantly lifted my head away from his cock.

"Quick, sit on top of him. You want his full length don't you?" he asked.

I could hardly answer, my breathing felt so heavy, and every inch of me wanting his shaft to fuck me. I moved to straddle him and before I was in position I could feel the gold ring rub against my labia and I lowered myself heavily and felt his hardness push its way into my depths, thick, throbbing and probing. Clenching my inner muscles around it I held it tight - the tighter I clenched, the more I felt his throbbing piece of machinery. My excitement was ready to peak.

I gripped tightly and for a few seconds it almost felt as if he was going to come, but I knew him better than that, he had excellent control. I waited and the impending release subsided. I started to ride him, pushing my clit down onto his pubic bone and rubbing it against his artwork. He squeezed a hand between our lower bellies and fingered my clit, flicking, nipping until I could feel my own climax start. With his free arm around my waist he pulled me along, joining in with my rhythm.

"It's time, baby, let your creamy juices come onto my flames now. Rub your clit, baby, feel it, fuck my cock and cum."

I tightened my muscles around his shaft once more and held it tight whilst I rode on, imagining my fanny to be squeezing his juices out of him, and that thought brought about my explosion. I shuddered as my wetness seeped around his cock. I collapsed onto his chest and he eased me over onto my back and parted my legs. I expected him to start fucking me, but he lowered himself down the bed and put a pillow under my bottom. His put his tongue to work this time, my clit still hard, the spasms of my orgasm not yet silenced. He worked quickly, thrusting his tongue into my crevice greedily, his hand firmly pressing circles over my clit, one finger occasionally poking into me, vying with his tongue.

"Your fanny juices taste delicious…so sweet…so sweet, baby."

He put his hands under my cheeks and raised my bottom in the air and I felt his tongue around my anus, licking, teasing...I arched my back in anticipation. He carefully lowered my bottom onto his little finger, and he rammed two fingers of his other hand into my hole and sucked at my clitoris, and I pushed down onto all his fingers and my body was racked with the throes of my second orgasm. Damp with perspiration, sore, and shaking, I felt drunk with ecstasy.

"I'm going to fuck you from behind now. I'm going to hurt you. You like being hurt, don't you? You deserve to be hurt, don't you? Too many treats for one day, don't you think?"

I was breathless.

"Answer me!"

"Yes. Too many treats...I deserve to be hurt," I whispered, as I turned over and he stuffed the pillow beneath me to raise my bottom into the air.

Not prepared for the force with which he entered me, I screamed out as the top of my head was shoved up hard against the headboard. His cock felt like it was trying to break through my cervix. Each time he shoved harder than before and my stomach was wracked with pain at each ramming, his gold ring scratching its way to the top of my burning depths. He pounded and pounded, his balls slapping against me and after ten minutes, the telltale twitching of orgasm. He gripped me tight, stopped pounding, pushed his cock harder inside me, and ceased all movement, and I felt the intensity of every last spurt of his spunk pumping as he climaxed with loud groans of satisfaction.

Ninety minutes later I was back at home. Anthony eyed me suspiciously as I walked through the lounge and straight upstairs to bed, but I wasn't in the mood to converse with him. I needed to climb into my bed and sleep…after I'd relived the latter part of today's business meeting in my mind.

CHAPTER 43

The phone call from David came as a big surprise. It had only been three weeks since our last date, so I certainly wasn't expecting to hear from him for at least another five weeks. He wasn't in a rush to get off the phone, so we chatted for twenty minutes or so. It was lovely to hear his voice, I tried to picture him. But in my mind he wasn't in his car, or at his desk, he was reclining on his bed in his mews cottage in St John's Wood. I enjoyed that thought and let my heart race. If only.

He was overjoyed. His daughter, Catherine, had just been accepted at the University she had wanted – she had excelled with her 'A' Levels and had achieved much better grades than had been required. She hoped to become a Forensic scientist and I could hear the pride in his voice as he spoke of her. The pride quickly changed to concern – his ex wife had recently caught their other daughter, fifteen year old Ruby, in bed with a young man, also fifteen and in the same school year. She was, apparently, going through a very rebellious stage and it sounded as if David's ex-wife was finding her quite a handful. He was upset – concerned about the risks she was taking, S.T.D.s, unwanted pregnancy and his biggest concern – drugs. I did my best to bolster his mood for the remainder of our call, but I couldn't help but think that despite managing to elicit a few laughs from him, he sounded so down.

Maybe after his jetlag had worn off and he'd been to visit his girls he would be feeling much better about things before our next date at the weekend. Even though I had been listening carefully, hanging onto his every word, I managed to control my excitement.

Before we had started chatting about our news he had asked me for my company. It was a real bonus this time. We were actually going to spend almost the whole weekend together – a special weekend he had said. From Saturday morning at ten o'clock until late Sunday night, at his cottage – it would feel like two full days. It would be my pleasure. The very thought was juice inducing - positively orgasmic!

A mini spending spree was called for. I wanted to look stunning for my favourite client. I needed something sophisticated, so I could dress for dinner, which was going to be delivered by caterers. I wanted new undies, shoes, a silk robe, and I needed to find a gift for him. I considered getting a new perfume, but I remembered how he always loved still smelling my perfume on his clothes for a few days after our dates, so I decided to stick with what David liked.

I took three days holiday from the hotel and I went shopping in Knightsbridge. I made the search for a gift for him my number one priority. I had plenty of clothes to choose from at home if I couldn't find exactly what I had in mind. From my little knowledge of him, he seemed to have everything he wanted. I didn't have a clue what I could buy for him. At least, I hadn't...until I stopped to look at men's watches in a jeweller's shop window. My eyes were drawn to a watch with a beautiful face, and for some reason, I found I couldn't take my eyes off that watch face – I was seeing David's face, and his beauty. After staring for sometime I snapped out of my reverie, entered the shop, and asked if the watch could be engraved with a few words on the back. I was assured it wouldn't be a problem and I would be able to collect it the next day, Friday, so I paid and went off to get the rest of my things. I was thrilled about the watch and I hoped that David would be as delighted to receive it, as I was to give it. I expected, of course, to be severely reprimanded.

The clothes somehow didn't seem important anymore, after I'd bought the watch. I had lots of gorgeous clothes anyway and many that David had not seen before. I did buy some gorgeous new undies though and a sexy, but classy, silk robe, as opposed to sexy and tarty. I booked an appointment for a manicure and French polish, and at the same salon I decided on a facial. When I arrived home, I had lots to do, and my first task was to select my clothes carefully. I wanted smart clothes to arrive in and clothes to wear to leave in. I hadn't even got there yet, and already I was choosing an outfit for when I would be leaving. I was so organised, but I had to put the thought about leaving him out of my mind – I didn't want to dwell on that!

Armani blue jeans, a pair of diamante mules on a wedge I'd found in Harrods, and an expensive, plain white cotton shirt, worn open over an equally expensive vest top. I tried on my choices and, reasonably happy, decided that this was the arrival outfit – simple, stunning, classy. The little black dress collection was next and I um-ed and ah-ed for ten minutes, before opting for a little jade number, not too low-cut, or too short, just on the knee and with a pair of jade sandals. I had already settled on wearing David's diamond pendant as my jewellery, my 'special lady' gift. Three or four different searches that night and my wardrobes did not have anything to offer, in the way of a leaving outfit. I had always considered myself very fortunate, to have such a selection of beautiful clothes, so why then, could I not see anything appropriate? The answer came to me in an instant. I couldn't face choosing a leaving outfit, simply because I didn't want to think about the leaving part.

The ringing of my mobile woke me at seven o'clock on the Friday morning. It was a regular client of mine, calling to see if I was available that same night. I knew it was totally out of the question. I didn't want to have sex with anyone the evening before my weekend with David. I told him that I was spending the whole weekend with another client. I got the impression that he was not too happy about it - he was due to fly out to Frankfurt again first thing Monday morning, so there would be no further opportunities for sex with me on this visit.

"If you can call me two days in advance next time you are in the country," I told him "I will make sure your needs are my priority." It seemed as if I'd managed to pacify him, although I imagined he would seek some female company on his travels rather than wait until a next appointment with me.

"Okay. You can't offer fairer than that, thanks." Before he ended the call, he gave a much friendlier, "Goodbye, my dear."

David's watch was ready on time as promised by the jeweller. The engraving of my little message was exceptional and I was confident that he would be touched by my gesture. Cross with me, yes, but secretly very pleased. I had one more appointment before returning home - a quick visit to my dentist for a scale and polish, two months ahead of time. Everything had to be perfect. I soaked for over an hour in the bath, painted my toe nails, and then I carefully moisturised every square inch of my body with a product that contained a very light tanning agent. Since my morning coffee, I had been on detox the rest of the day – I wanted to feel good as much as I wanted to look good. The last part of the day's feel good treatments was to apply my night creams; one for the eyes, and one for the rest of my face. Early night after that – I needed my beauty sleep.

By nine o'clock the next morning I was ready. I had quickly laid my hands on a leaving outfit that would fit the bill, but I was still unwilling to dwell on that part. My make-up had been applied with the utmost attention to detail, the natural look – no eye shadow, just the right amount of mascara, a hint of foundation in a moisturiser, and subtle lipstick and blusher. I was happy with the result – natural looking, instead of being too painted. I called for a cab as I didn't want to risk travelling the underground system with the contents of my handbag and travel case being valuable. My bedroom door was locked so that Anthony wouldn't be able to go nosing about. He was at home when the cab arrived for me, but I didn't feel the need to offer any information.

PART 3

...and hurt!

CHAPTER 44

What a welcome I received when he opened the door. He looked me up and down, stunned into silence for a few seconds. Then he took me in his arms for the biggest of hugs, and we both kissed the air beside each other's cheeks. He pushed my hair behind my right ear and whispered,

"I need you, Helen. Now!"

I was relieved to hear this as I wanted him badly. I had been thinking about sex with him from the minute I opened my eyes, but I was a little surprised it would be happening so soon.

"What? No champagne chilling, David? You're sacked – I need my champers to put me in the mood." I laughed

He grabbed my hand and led me upstairs to the bedroom, before replying,

"No you don't, stop fibbing, Helen. It's not quite chilled enough yet and I hadn't planned on wanting you this soon, you just look so…ravishing. We don't need the champers anyway."

Once in the bedroom, he sat me on the edge of the bed and, not letting go of my hand, he sat down with me, looking into my eyes as he did so. Returning his gaze, I wondered why he looked so serious. I also noticed how tired he looked around his eyes.

"You look *exhausted*, David. Are you sleeping properly?"

He was fast to fob me off.

"A bit of jetlag, babe, too much flying in too few days – I'll be okay."

We sat there for ages. For somebody who'd wanted me badly he was wasting valuable time. He rubbed my hand between both of his and kept looking into my eyes, maybe trying to read me. The air was full of tension, I could see a question coming, but he was being pretty hesitant about it. I leaned my head on his shoulder, hoping to give him the prompt – and it worked.

"Babe, I want to ask, if you will do something different for me this weekend. I'm praying it won't be a problem for you – it's something I really want."

I was shocked. He'd never seemed like a client with perverted needs, so I was suddenly wary, not wanting to commit myself, before hearing what it was he wanted. Maybe *that's* why he'd given me the diamond necklace first, payment up front for something a bit different?

"Tell." I ordered.

"Babe, what I want you to do is…please will you let me kiss you? I understand if you..."

I cut him off mid-sentence as I planted my lips firmly on his, kissing him tenderly, his eyes wide open then, his turn to be shocked for a few seconds, then he was kissing me back. Our bodies were both shaking, a little nervous with each other, finding ourselves outside the confines of our normal comfort zone.

We took it slowly and gently, enjoying a new and beautiful experience, (stone cold sober this time), teasing each other every now and again, our tongues doing nothing more than tasting each other's lips. Eventually, we leaned back over onto the bed and I felt his hands unfastening, first my denims, then he slipped my shirt off my shoulders. My hands wandered to his denims and I unzipped him. I put my hands up his t-shirt, stroking his chest, and we carried on, slowly undressing each other while we continued to kiss. I stroked his hair, his cheeks, I nibbled his ear lobes and it was so beautiful, to be touching him, and him touching me in return. We explored each other, slowly and lovingly, every square inch. We were excited with what we were discovering, our ticklish parts, our sensitive parts, and for the first time the sensitive parts were *not* our sexual organs - not my breasts or vagina, not his penis, not bottoms! The sensitive parts were behind the knees, the backs of arms, our feet, and our necks – anywhere. This was sensual, loving foreplay – not sexual, animal needs.

As was inevitable, our explorations became urgent. Our hands started to wander to the tops of thighs, edging closer, each minute, towards ultimate excitement. Our mouths were parting, tongues probing, as our needs become apparent. Each move was still gentle but we could sense each other's wanting – wanting more, wanting that fusion, when two become one, when we couldn't possibly get any closer than we already were.

That moment arrived at last, and as he entered me, we both moaned in ecstasy, he kissed me, gazed into my eyes and for the first time I saw love in his eyes. I wished and hoped that he could read me - see through my eyes and into my mind, and instantly know that I loved him. His thrusting was gentle and I pushed myself upwards to meet the thrusting, to show him my eagerness, my willingness to take part, to get ever closer to him. I felt so emotional, taken aback at the direction our relationship had taken - and suddenly I felt as if it was all a dream, I was frightened to believe in him. We continued our movements, my hands on his buttocks, stroking and then pulling his bottom towards me, helping each gentle thrust, until that thrusting became faster, and deeper, and he asked,

"Are you ready for me, babe?"

I knew in that instant that I would always be ready for him, my heart ached for him.

"Always!"

We climaxed together a few minutes later and we both cried out in ecstasy at the intensity. An intensity that was not born of just sexual gratification, it was a deep emotional intensity from a coupling that, for the first time, had been about passion…and making love. I was unwilling to move afterwards, to break that connection, I lay there in his arms and I let the tears fall. I cried. My head was on his chest, and he was stroking my hair, his breathing finally starting to slow down.

"Babe, why is my chest wet?" he laughed, as he lifted my head to look into my eyes and I was surprised to see that his cheeks were also wet with tears. I also started to laugh, and before long the bed was shaking as we were laughing together. For me it was a reaction of happiness, a relief – that we both knew our relationship had changed - into something more deep and meaningful. But words of love had not been uttered from either of us, just yet.

It was two in the afternoon when we finally made our move from the bedroom. We showered together in the wet room, embracing and kissing as we washed each other's bodies. No ulterior motive, no sexual innuendo - just a mutual desire to do things together, enjoy each other's company. We dried each other with the fluffy towels, then donned our bathrobes and made sandwiches and coffee together in the kitchen. We took our snack through to the coffee table in the lounge. We indulged in some surprisingly normal conversation at last, maybe trying to bring things back down to earth, and skirting around the subject of what had just taken place.

"Tell me what you've been up to since I saw you last." I wanted to know "Where have you been on business? How are things with your daughters?"

He pulled a face, shrugging off my questions.

"No. I don't want to talk about me and my life. It's been business as usual. What have you been up to?"

I pulled a face, I didn't want to talk about my husband, or my cleaning work, or…anything.

"I have been busy preparing myself for you, David. Beauty treatments, shopping for the right clothes for this weekend, I hope you like them, by the way. And…I've been shopping. I bought…a present for you. But I will be giving it to you tomorrow, before I go home."

"You didn't…you shouldn't have…I…"

"Neither should you." I cut in, "My present is for a very special man – you. Tit for tat, getting even, doing something similar in return, you do it, I do it…."

"Okay, okay, I get the message. Shut up. Now!" and to make sure I did, he kissed me hard on the lips for a minute, "But you didn't need to, babe."

"You shut up." and I kissed him back, to shut *him* up. We started laughing again, raucous laughter, and picked up cushions and started a very juvenile cushion fight, jumping over the back of the settees and chairs, chasing each other around the room, laughing uncontrollably. It had been a very long time since I'd had this much fun and I loved every minute of it. I could tell that David was enjoying himself as well. We ended up flopping down on the settee together, out of breath, our laughter dying down, but for the odd giggle here and there.

"I'll put the T.V. on and find us a film to watch. *If* I can find one at this time on a Saturday afternoon, that is."

"Sure, sounds great to me."

He flicked back and forth through the channels with the remote, settled on one film, an old war movie, for a few minutes. Without me saying one word he realised he should look for something that was more light-hearted so he flicked through again until he found an old *rom-com*. I grabbed the bottle of champagne that David had put to chill much earlier, poured us a glass each, and then we snuggled up together, and watched the film. Every now and again, he would turn towards me and plant a kiss on my cheek or forehead, or my lips, and it struck me that things seemed so normal – a couple thing – and normal felt good to me.

Towards the last half hour of the film, I heard David's breathing get much deeper and a little nasal – familiar sounds of someone who has just started to doze off. I didn't bother to disturb him, I could see that his jet-lag was starting to kick in, and he looked peaceful, so I watched the remainder of the film by myself. I hadn't watched a film in ages and I thoroughly enjoyed it. For once I felt everything was looking positive.

When the film finished I carefully tried to extract myself from David's arms without waking him. He stirred for a minute or so, shifted his position slightly and within minutes was snoring softly again. I busied myself in his kitchen for a while, washing the few plates and knives from our sandwich making. When I went back to the lounge I poured myself another glass of champagne and sat down in one of the armchairs to gaze in wonder at my lovely man as he slept.

I reminded myself that I didn't know if he actually was *my* man.

I watched him sleeping until after six o'clock, when it suddenly occurred to me that dinner was being delivered at some point this evening, courtesy of a local firm of caterers, but I couldn't recall David mentioning a time. I knelt down on the floor next to the sofa and pressed gently on his arm,

"David?"

Oh hell. He was so sound asleep, I hated having to do this but I was reluctant to let a meal go to waste, and we both needed to eat, so I shook his arm this time,

"David? Wake up, sweetheart," I whispered.

His eyes opened and he was a little disorientated, surprised to see me there. I stroked his arm gently and kissed the top of his nose.

"Oh. What…?"

"What time is the meal being delivered, David?"

"What? Meal? Oh...seven thirty…I think."

"Okay. I'm going to go and get ready then. I'm dressing for dinner – formal. Take your time."

I made a pot of coffee and left it on the coffee table for him as he was struggling to get his eyes fully opened. I went to the bathroom for a freshen-up. Fifteen minutes later I had nearly finished applying my make-up when I heard him coming up the stairs. I shouted to ask if he would mind getting ready in one of the other bedrooms.

"Yes no problem, babe," he answered "I take it you want to surprise me then? Good – I love surprises."

"Go downstairs when you are ready and I will make my grand entrance, I hope you like it," I shouted back.

"One hundred percent guaranteed."

I felt like I had done when I was a teenager, going out on my first ever date and I could hardly contain my excitement. I smiled to myself. Looking in the mirror, I was thrilled with my reflection as it smiled back at me. The dress looked stunning, the diamond pendant sparkled and I had a glow about me that was nothing at all to do with my blusher. I heard David going downstairs just a few minutes before I finished, so it was time to go. I started feeling rather nervous again as I made my way down the stairs, where he waited at the bottom, his back to me, and his hands held over his eyes.

"Can I look yet?"

When I reached the bottom step, I paused, took a deep breath and said yes. He turned around, took my hand, and in that superb old-fashioned manner of yesteryear, kissed the back of it.

"Your ladyship, forgive me, but you are looking extremely stunning this evening. The dress brings out the colour in your eyes and the overall result is breathtakingly beautiful."

My heart was racing at his compliments once again, and it felt like no-one else existed in the world but the two of us.

"Thank you for the compliment, kind Sir." I acknowledged "And if I may return the compliment, Sir is looking very handsome and distinguished." We giggled as he led me through to the lounge.

"Would your Ladyship care to partake of a small libation, perhaps a nice glass of jolly old Bollinger?" he carried on in his mock, poshest of posh voice.

"Yes, she bloody would." I laughed.

He sat down opposite me.

"Because I want to sit and stare at you," he explained.

I didn't mind sitting and staring at him either - he looked truly handsome. He was wearing one of his business suits, charcoal grey, very well-tailored, and an expensive shirt. He even had a black evening tie. I hadn't seen him dressed in this way before. He was usually attired in smart casual, a bathrobe, or completely naked, when we had our dates.

The caterers were prompt, knocking on the door at precisely 7.30pm. I was impressed with the service, they laid the table, served up the starters, and they went on to serve each course in turn, and clear everything away when we finished dining. Whilst we ate each exquisite course, they discreetly stayed out of the way in the kitchen.

Before we tucked into our starter, I was surprised at his next question,

"Babe, will you stay with me until Monday morning?" He explained that his flight would be leaving Heathrow at five past three in the afternoon and that an appointment he originally had for nine o'clock had been cancelled leaving him free for the morning.

"Of course, I would love to. There's my shift at the hotel, but I'll call in sick. I've never done that before but it won't matter, it's not as if I have a bad attendance record."

The presentation of all three courses was excellent. For a small, local, catering company, the chef was excellent, and the food was better than some meals I have been served up in a few top class restaurants over the years. I didn't know what each dish was called, but there was very little left on my plate. David's appetite was not as good as mine, but again, I think this was all down to his body clock being out of sync. After the caterers had gone we still sat at the dining table, working our way down the second bottle of wine.

"Can I still give you your present tomorrow, David, or does that have to wait until Monday now?"

"No, babe. It has to be Monday. I have another present for you as well…but don't start protesting, please," he added, just as I opened my mouth to do so.

We sat in silence for a few moments longer before he took my hand, led me from the dining table, switching off the dining room light and the stereo en route, and up the stairs.

We made love for the second time since my arrival. I noticed the difference with our oral sex this time. It was all part of our love-making session, carried out with passion, tenderness, exploration, and pure joy. There was no urgency for climax, at least, not at the start, though our actions were leaving us breathless. When I sensed that he was ready to enter me, I urged him to sit on the floor, with his back resting against the bed. I sat astride him, and he was inside me, already moaning with need. He was tired so I told him to him to leave it to me. I rode him, my inner muscles gripping around his penis, gently at first, then more tightly, and faster, as I was ready to take his love juice and feel that passion exploding from me too.

I slept well, other than waking briefly in the early hours and glancing across towards David who was laid on his back. I just managed to make out, by his silhouette, that his eyes were open, and he was looking up towards the ceiling. I hoped he would soon get back into his normal sleep pattern. I hated seeing him looking so exhausted. I asked him to turn over and I cuddled up close to him. I didn't turn away from him until he was fast asleep.

He made us breakfast on the Sunday morning and brought it upstairs to bed. He had been busy – he'd even popped out and bought Sunday newspapers. It was a real novelty for me. I wasn't really a breakfast person, but to have it brought up to bed, along with the papers, yes I could cope with that - with David by my side at least. He'd removed his clothing before getting back into bed with me. Thankfully, it was a light breakfast - fruit juice, some cereal, croissants, some toast with a variety of conserves and freshly ground coffee. We ate and drank our coffee in silence as we scanned the main news articles in the papers, then we shifted these off the bed and cuddled up together,

"What would you like to do today, sweetie?" I asked him.

"I'll leave it up to you, Helen. I'm not too bothered. I just want to enjoy every precious second with you."

I couldn't believe I was hearing those words from a client. Words I loved hearing, but words that filled me with such fear. I started thinking about Monday morning, about saying goodbye, and I had to turn my face away from him as my eyes glazed with tears. We never left the house throughout the day, making love once in the morning and again in the afternoon, lots of kissing, and talking. We listened to music all day, played two games of chess and talked.

David decided on a ride into the country that evening to find a quiet country pub where nobody would be likely to recognise us. We were quite hungry, not having eaten since our breakfast in bed. Fortunately, there were only one or two

333

locals in the pub we found. We ordered two chicken salads and within an hour and a half, we were full and heading back. I didn't feel like talking on the journey back and he kept asking if I was okay. I wanted to open up to him and tell him I didn't want to leave him the next day, but he didn't seem to have a lot to say either, so I thought it best not to mention it. He still looked very tired. I hoped he would get a good night's sleep before his week's agenda.

"Early night for us, sweetie. Let's make love first and then you must get plenty of sleep," I told him.

"That suits me."

Not bothering with the usual wine or champers we headed straight upstairs to bed. We laid there doing nothing except kiss for half an hour until we both started exploring with our hands. I couldn't wait to make love one more time, but for some reason, no matter how much I fondled, and tried to coax his penis along, it did not want to play. He said he wanted me badly, but after ten minutes or so it was clear to us both that a hard-on was just not going to happen. He started getting angry with himself and his dick,

"Babe, I want you so much and this fucking thing is not bloody having it. I'm sorry."

"It's not a problem, David – you are far too tired. We'll leave it until morning."

Neither of us slept well. I was fretting about our parting the next morning, not knowing when I would see him again. I lay there staring into space, facing the window, all night. David was very restless and tossed and turned constantly. I think I finally gave in to sleep around four o'clock and when I woke again it was ten past six. David was asleep, but as I didn't know how long it had been since he'd dropped off, I carefully climbed out of bed so as not to wake him.

I got things ready for breakfast, putting David's present next to his plate. I was looking forward to seeing his face when he saw the watch and when he heard what I had to say to him. I sat in the lounge in silence, going over time and again what I had already rehearsed in my head. I heard footsteps, first across the bedroom floor and then on the stairs.

"Helen. Where did you go? What are you doing down here? I missed you."

"Come and sit down, let's go in the dining room, breakfast can be ready in five minutes - I want to give you your present." I was getting excited.

"I need to talk to you, Helen."

"I need to talk to you, too." I grabbed his hand and dragged him through to the dining room, plonked him on the chair in front of the present and urged him,

"Go on, open it."

"Babe..."

"Just open it, David."

I watched, as his hands shook, he started to peel off the wrapping paper.

"I...oh, hell, babe. You...shouldn't..." His eyes registered the shock as he stared at the watch and he handled it so carefully.

"Turn it over. See the engraving on the back."

"Oh, my god! It's truly…beautiful. Thank you, Helen."

There were tears beginning to form in his eyes, as he read the tiny words. ♥♥ Came together! All my love, Helen xx

"Two hearts - came together. I like the sexual innuendo that you cleverly worked in," he chuckled. "It's beautiful, Helen. I won't ask how much..."

I was puzzled, he'd chuckled, smiled and been emotional when he had seen the engraving, but he looked serious. I felt an uneasiness I couldn't explain.

"No. Don't."

"I will go and get my present to you. Then we must talk." He made his way to the sideboard in the lounge.

He came back with an identical gift bag to the one he had handed me those few weeks back. I opened it slowly, savouring each second of excitement. He watched me with eyes that were glazed over, doing his best to hold back his tears. I began to realize what a caring and emotional man he was. This time his gift was a diamond bracelet that matched the pendant I already had - eight diamonds, smaller than that on the pendant, but no less beautiful. I was stunned.

"Here, let me," and his hands fiddled shakily with the clasp for a moment or two until my right wrist displayed the new bracelet. Without a word of warning he dropped his bombshell.

"Babe…Helen…this is the last time we can see each other. I can't…"

The very words I had dreaded. I felt sick, devastated.

"What? But I thought…?"

"That…I loved you? Yes. I do. Believe me, I do."

"Then why? I love you. I…is this because of what I do?"

"Yes. No, I mean…"

I butted in, alarm bells ringing in my head, dreading what he was going to say if I didn't cut him off.

"Because I would give it all up for you - my clients, everything!"

I felt such desperation to plead to him, beg him not to do this, I had to try.

"Helen, I know you would give it all up. I hope you will one day. I'm doing this to protect you…because I love you."

"Protect me from what exactly, David? You don't have to protect me from anything, if we're together. I just want…"

"…to be with me? I know. But you can't be. Helen. It's my job, we wouldn't get the time together. You'd end up being hurt by me, like my two ex-wives…and my daughters. The distance…and the time apart, it has *killed* my relationships in the past, not just wives, there have been girlfriends too that have fallen by the wayside. I can't be in a relationship, Helen – people get hurt. That's what I'm trying to protect you from, the hurt. The loneliness - it's not what I want for you."

"But I'm used to the loneliness. I am actually *married*; you assumed he's my boyfriend. I have been *very* alone every day during that

337

marriage. I could cope. I could even come with you - everywhere."

"It's not a holiday, babe. It would mean you being alone all the time, in a hotel room, whilst I'm in business meetings and some go on until late at night. Or you would be wandering around a city alone. It's not the same. It's not the life I want for you."

"Please, David…?"

"No, Helen. This is my final word. This is hurting me like hell to do this to you - to hurt you, but I have to, for both our sakes. Please try to understand."

He had let his tears start to flow and in understanding that he meant it, that he was not to be talked out of it, this was actually his final word - I cried too. He came and held me and we stood for an age, holding each other, weeping with our mutual sadness until I broke away and demanded,

"Make love to me, David…one last time…please. Because you love me…?"

"I can't, Helen. That's why I couldn't do it last night…because of all this. I can't do it again. It would hurt me all the more. And it would hurt you even more afterwards, I know it would."

He was right. I was hurting already. I felt as if the bottom had fallen out of my world. I wanted to crawl into a corner and never emerge. I couldn't even bear to look at him.

"I've got to get out of here, now. The longer I stay, the worse it will be. I won't be able to leave you."

I showered as fast as I could then, but I skipped putting on any make-up for once. There didn't seem to be any point. As I threw my belongings in my overnighter he was sat on the bed watching me, his tears had almost stopped, but he was powerless - unable to comfort me, trying hard as he was, to deal with his own hurt. As I zipped up my bag I cast him a quick glance and made for the bedroom door and downstairs. I just wanted to be gone, away from him.

He ran down the stairs after me and clutching at straws, I turned around, hoping he'd had a last minute change of heart.

"Here's your money, babe," he said, holding out an envelope.

"I'm not taking it from you. I don't want it," I snapped "What are you paying me for, David? For…for…loving you?"

This was the first time I had ever snapped at him and he reeled with shock, almost staggering backwards. The hurt in his eyes was genuine and I softened towards him.

"I'm so sorry, David. I shouldn't have said it in that manner. I *do* love you."

"I'm sorry too. Please, don't let's part on bad terms, Helen. Come here."

We shared a final embrace and a final passionate kiss, and I let go of him. I didn't dare look back, as I walked away down the street.

I put a call in to work when I got home. I said I was really ill and would be visiting my G.P. later that day. My doctor signed me off for an interim period of two weeks. I had used my O.C.D. as an excuse. I used my time alone to try to get over him. I convinced myself that I hadn't really been in love with him. He had been the first person to show me affection and warmth since me parents had died and I think I had somehow latched onto that and believed I was in love with him.

I didn't receive any client calls whilst I was off work and I was at least relieved about that. I returned to the hotel two weeks later, feeling better. I started taking client calls again the same week.

CHAPTER 45

I let myself in the front door with the key that I had been given, and told to keep, not so many months ago. He was one of my regulars and I was visiting him at his home. He worked in London's Stock Exchange. He was fifty eight and he had been divorced for eleven years, his wife preferring the company of a twenty two year old toy boy with a much bigger cock, as she had so hurtfully put it to my client. The poor guy had so many hang ups after that, it had taken him over nine years without sex, before he had heard through Simon about my services and had plucked up the courage to call me a month after he got my number.

Our first appointment had been over very quickly. He was still dressed when I had arrived at his home and he explained how shy he was and the reasons behind it. His ex wife had destroyed his confidence, persistently taunting him about the size of his dick. I decided to play it very cautiously and try to help him rebuild some confidence. We had talked for hours. I eventually put my hand on his knee and asked if he would like to remove some of my clothing. He'd stuttered and stammered, his face turning into a rich shade of beetroot, that he would prefer me to take my own clothes off down to bra and pants.

Once I had removed my denims and top, I had looked him in the eye as I did so, giving him the come on – I wanted him to feel like he was the most important man in the world - it was him that I wanted. He'd eyed me up and down and I sat down very close to him. I leaned over him, my lips almost making contact with his, but I let them linger on his cheek as I grabbed his hand, and with mine guiding it, we pushed up my bra together.

"Feel my nipple, honey, feel how erect it is," I encouraged. After tweaking it for a few seconds I guided his hand downwards over my tummy and down into my pants,

"Stick a couple of fingers up my pussy, feel how nice it is. After so long without one, enjoy…do you like that word? Pussy? What turns you on best, what word do you want me to use for the hole that you are going to fuck?"

He was sweating profusely, and his hand was shaking in my pubic hair, he looked terrified. I was longing to be fucked, but I wasn't feeling too confident with the guy, his shyness. I knew where it was going to end.

"You are going to fuck again. I will call it what you want, honey, whatever turns you on - pussy, fanny, hole …or cunt?"

His enthusiasm had moved up a gear on hearing the 'c' word, his fingers hadn't needed any further guidance and he'd shoved them up and down inside. My new role as sex teacher/trainer was exciting me and I had started to feel a bit damp down below. I heard the inevitable noises as his fingers had waggled about inside my hole. I let go of his hand and unzipped his trousers, pushing my hand into his boxer shorts to pull out his cock. What a shock. His evil bitch of an ex-wife! His cock was average sized and nothing at all to be ashamed of. But that is all it took - one move for me to pull out his cock. He had closed his eyes then, partly in ecstasy, but with a disappointed groan because he'd been so ashamed – his cum was all over my hand, his boxers and denims.

"Sorry, love. It's been…" he apologised.

I'd been right. I was disappointed myself. Even to have had his cock penetrate my hole for a couple of minutes would have done it for me…

"Hey, don't worry about it. The length of time you've gone without, I wouldn't have been surprised if you'd unloaded when I got undressed – it sometimes happens."

I was willing to accept a reduction in my payment since he never got to fuck me, but he insisted I take it all. As I put my clothes back on, I needed to make his day,

"Your ex-wife is one evil cow. There is nothing small about your dick. It is average sized - most men have average sized dicks. Never be ashamed of it, ever."

He had such a look of disbelief on his face, I couldn't help but smile that I'd been able to say something encouraging.

"Really? You're not kidding me?"

"Crikey, have you never stood next to other men at the urinals?"

"Yes. But…I've never looked. It doesn't feel right."

I laughed. I don't make suggestions to my clients when they are ones who have to pay, but he was the one who suddenly made the suggestion that we should have a few liaisons close together, to get him used to having sex again, and hopefully, this would help him control his premature ejaculation. I also hinted that maybe the odd porn DVD or magazines may help.

The second session had taken place a week later, and that time he managed to hold back on his orgasm until he'd got his cock inside of me. Things were slightly improved again a week later, when he managed to fuck me for at least ten minutes. I had told him to pull out as soon as he felt too excited, which would hopefully delay his ejaculation, but without any warning I suddenly felt the twitching of his cock and it was too late, he shot his lot, and groaned with disappointment,

"I didn't get any warning and then it was there," he'd grumbled.

"You did well." I encouraged, "Ten minutes is better than quite a few of my clients can manage, honestly."

Determined to make him go the distance, a few days later, I had packed my faithful suspender belt and stockings, a vibrator and some 'delay spray' into my satchel. The emphasis had been on plenty of oral, and getting him to use the vibrator on me. I also used the vibrator, rubbing it up and down his cock, making him familiar with the sensation and learning how to control his urges when the feelings became too intense. It worked - he performed well throughout the foreplay and during copulation we used the delay spray just twice. We bonked for forty four minutes and it was tiredness getting the better of him, that prompted him to come, rather than lack of self-control. He lay there afterwards with a beaming smile on his face, and he was so full of gratitude for my help.

"You'll be able to get yourself another wife now," I was amused by his restored pride in himself, "but this time find somebody who won't destroy your confidence and belittle you at every opportunity. You won't have any need for me, when you do."

He'd found a girlfriend - a career woman, a newspaper reporter who jetted off for months at a time leaving his sexual needs unattended to yet again. So the calls had continued. I didn't mind, I just took my money at the end of each date. I just didn't care for the first half hour or so of our dates now. Every time it was the same routine, and it was getting rather tedious.

I was in the bathroom and almost in my uniform, which included suspenders and stocking tops just showing beneath the hem of my dress, when his voice called out,

"Bedpan please, nurse – now."

"On its way!"

I rolled my eyes up to the ceiling and played along. He had developed a thing for nurses, so we had to role play every time for the first half hour. Every time I had to take his temperature, his blood pressure and go through the horrendous bedpan bit before commencing the bed bath.

As I soaped and rinsed his entire body, his hands grabbed at my breasts, his fingers poked into my knickers. It was done in a feeble manner at first, the manner of a patient who was tired and not feeling at all well. As he started feeling a bit better, and after I had given him a spoonful of his magic potion, his fingers were rammed up my vagina. He sat up and lifted the dress over my head, one-handed. The dress cast aside, I stepped out of my thong and shifted position for him, so he could poke around my backside with his finger.

I leaned over the bed and performed fellatio for a few minutes whilst his fingers and hands continued to grope and probe at my whole body. My breathing was getting heavy and my fanny was feeling hot and moist, ready to welcome his swollen stick of muscle. He gave me permission, after ten minutes, to climb aboard and fuck him until I came. He enthusiastically encouraged and cheered me on as I closed my eyes, my clit rubbed against him and my early throes of orgasm became evident.

"Go on baby…fuck it good…let those juices soak my cock…is that nice baby…squeeze my cock with those fanny muscles. Mmm…that's feeling good now, cum for me baby…yes…that's so nice…yes, you're there, baby. You're wetting my dick nicely."

I shook with the waves of my coming as he finished urging me. He quickly rolled me off him and all traces of his fake illness completely gone, leapt off the bed with a fitness more apt for a ten-year-old, and said urgently,

"Get over the edge, you need fucking, I need to fuck you. Sweat it out of me!"

I knew the whole routine well and was in position for him in a flash. He shagged me doggy style for what seemed like forever, poking me up the rectum with his finger. After my earlier orgasm, I wasn't expecting to cum again but suddenly I felt the throbs of his cock followed by his explosion of semen and his tool seemed to be stiffening even more inside me. My vagina had never felt so full and I came again. My new wetness flowed together with his and trickled down my thighs. He collapsed onto me, totally

346

spent, and it was five minutes before he rolled off my back and with the biggest smirk ever, announced "Over an hour – my record."

Despite the bed bath and bonking boredom, I was glad I had been able to help the guy.

CHAPTER 46

It was half past eleven on Saturday morning and it was late for me to be getting up at that time. But I had been awake since eight thirty. I'd been downstairs early and taken a coffee back up to bed with me. On the Friday night I had had a late night meeting with Simon (at the home of one of his friends who was out of the country on business). It had been his freebie, my payment to him for the number of clients he had sent my way over the last year. He was a true gentleman and someone I trusted. His sexual needs could be quite vulgar, but he had never failed to excite me and fuck me senseless, and he loved that I did exactly the same to him. He always liked me to tell him 'fuck me roughly, Simon'; or 'put your cock up my cunt' and 'let me feel you cum.' He was always nice to me, so I indulged him. It was his big turn on to hear the crude expletives from me – a well-educated, well-spoken, fairly posh and attractive…whore.

I had intentionally stayed upstairs out of the way until after I'd heard Anthony leave the house. Anthony had been slamming doors, searching the things he needed to pack for his business trip to Brussels. He hadn't actually told me about it. I'd seen the tickets for his flights on the coffee table along with his passport. I'd checked the dates on the tickets and he would be away for a full week. I was ecstatic. (I had already been considering telling one of my clients that he could have his session at my house for a change. But, as he was another prominent figure in politics, the idea might not be so attractive to him). As soon as I'd heard Anthony's car racing off to the end of the street, running late as always, I showered and went down to the kitchen for my second caffeine fix of the day. Feeling more relaxed than I had in a long time, and in the knowledge that he was out of my way for a week, I nibbled on a croissant whilst the coffee was filtering. Once it was ready, I carried a cup through to the lounge, where I could sit in total peace for once. I couldn't help but grin…some me time. I gazed around the room in wonder…all my space…a whole week! Then…I spotted it…sat on the coffee table. A newspaper…with a quarter of the front page taken up by his picture…and my grin quickly faded as I snatched it into my hands.

BRITISH MULTI-MILLIONAIRE BUSINESSMAN, DAVID BARNARD 43, DIES AT HIS SWISS HOME

"David Barnard aged 43, died on Thursday morning, a Company Spokesman announced last night. Mr Barnard had been diagnosed with terminal pancreatic cancer, some thirteen weeks ago. His daughters, Catherine, aged 18, and Ruby, aged 15, were at his bedside when he died, being comforted by the presence of their mother, Heidi, 42, first wife to Mr Barnard. It is understood that Mr Barnard had remained single, since being divorced from his second wife, Joanna, 38, four years ago. His daughters had flown out to Switzerland with their mother ten days ago, when they were informed by their father that he was in the final stages of the disease. Mr Barnard, born in 1965, graduated from Kings College, Cambridge with an Honours degree in Civil Engineering……"

The report droned on, giving details of his academic achievements, his upbringing, and of course, his successful businessman story, but I couldn't bring myself to read any further. I read those first few lines over and over again until the reality of it started to hit home.

I looked at the date of the newspaper - it was Friday's, left on the coffee table by Anthony yesterday, and I hadn't noticed it. The story would also have made the National News, but I rarely watch T.V. Suddenly, it was extremely important to me to remember what I had been doing on Thursday, and since David's body had been laid in a Chapel of Rest somewhere, spent and cold. I had been working at the hotel on Thursday…and yesterday. With a jolt I remembered Friday Night's antics, and me, being shagged by the barrister who had put David in touch with me in the first place. I was mortified. I had been doing that whilst David had been gone from this world and me, forever. My body was racked by violent shaking, as my sobs of guilt, grief, and sadness all came pouring out. I howled the place down. I felt broken, like somebody had just wrenched out my heart. I loved David so much, and until reading that newspaper report, I had been totally convinced that it wasn't the end for us. I had genuinely thought that I would definitely be seeing him again in the not too distant future – and it had all just been snatched away from me - that hope. Hope that was now laid to rest - along with the man I loved.

When I woke up in bed in total darkness, I glanced at my alarm clock to see that it was quarter past nine. I couldn't even remember climbing the stairs. At some point during my outpouring of grief, I had obviously gone upstairs, where I had continued my crying, and, exhaustion taking over, cried myself to sleep. I hadn't touched any alcohol but my head felt painful and my eyes were stinging. I got up to go and wash my face, and switching on my bedside lamp, I noticed the newspaper on the floor at the side of my bed. A distressing thought occurred to me – I didn't even possess one solitary snapshot of him. All I had to look at to remind me of him was the bloody picture on the front page of a newspaper that announced his death. But it was better than nothing. I lovingly picked up the newspaper, as if by doing so, I was being gentle with him. Not wanting him to suffer any more pain or hurt.

I sat all night in the lounge, in total silence, my mind running through our few special memories, time and again. I thought back to every conversation we ever had. I tried to recall every delicious moment of passion and excitement; of when we had sex, and more recently, our love-making, and I relived those times in my mind. The laughter we had shared, our meals together. I was digging deep for every precious moment. I tried to console myself with those memories – they were all I had left, but at least they would always be with me. My mind and body were exhausted and I couldn't muster enough energy. I gave in when my eyes had started closing. I woke on the settee sometime around daylight. I can recall hearing the morning chorus and thinking how sad it made me feel that morning. That awakening of life, at a time when my sadness for the end of David's life was all consuming, caused my sadness to sink to new levels, and it hurt so much.

I made coffee and sat around, not knowing what to do. What could I possibly do – I felt so helpless. Other emotions started to surface. I felt a terrific thirst to glean more information about David, anything about him that I didn't

351

already know. I scoured that newspaper report again and again, greedily clinging to every new little snippet it revealed about him, no matter how trivial. I felt angry at David – for cutting me out of his life when he needed me the most. I was livid with the mother of his daughters – for being at his bedside when he died, when it should have been me. I was seething at the fucking cancer that had taken him from me. Most of all, I felt furious at the fact that I was probably the last to hear about his illness and death. The thing that was the most devastating was that he had *known* - that last weekend we had spent together, he *knew* he had cancer and didn't tell me. I got to hear about the cancer, and his death, from a fucking newspaper. There would be his funeral to come, a private family gathering, the newspaper had said, and *I* just couldn't turn up unannounced as a chief mourner, taking my rightful place as the woman he loved. That wouldn't be the done thing. His daughters wouldn't even know I existed. How could I do that to them at the height of their own personal grief? I couldn't pay my respects.

Throughout the morning my emotions swiftly changed with every passing minute and I eventually snapped out of the anger. An idea had crossed my mind. I *could* pay my respects to David. I would do it in private. Focussing on nothing else but David, I ran upstairs, had a shower, then searched my wardrobe for a favourite black dress of his. It was a dress I had worn during one of our private dinner parties, when we had decided to dress formally. I applied a little make-up without any mascara, picked up David's gifts of jewellery and lovingly caressed each piece before putting them on. Before I dressed, I searched for four beautiful candles. I didn't know why, but I knew in my mind that it had to be four, and I placed them on top of the fireplace, two on each side of David's newspaper photo, which I had carefully removed from the rest of the newspaper. I placed a CD in the player in readiness, his favourite Beethoven music and, once dressed, I lit the candles and pressed the play button on the CD player. His music played in the background, the candles burned, and I sat gazing at David's picture, my memories in replay, silently crying.

Mid-afternoon, my mobile phone rang – a client was trying to contact me. I ignored his call and turned off my phone.

On Monday, the doubts started kicking in. Questions I had no answers to, but I asked them of myself time and again. *Had David really loved me? He said he did. But if he did, surely he would have wanted to spend his last few weeks with me. Why did he really buy me the jewellery? I can't have been as special to him as he had made out. He was very rich and money no object, so did he just buy the jewellery because he had nobody closer to him than I was at the time? Had he perhaps bought the jewellery for a previous lover, and the relationship had broken up before he had chance to give the gifts, so he gave them to me? Had he perhaps just thought that he loved me, and confused our sexual compatibility and our rapport for love? Had he really liked my present to him? Or was he just being polite as it was our last weekend together? Why had he lied to me about why our relationship couldn't*

353

continue? Did he really end it because of his
cancer? How was that going to protect me from
the hurt, when he knew I would be hurt to hear
about his death in the way that I just had been?
Was it really because he couldn't have a
permanent relationship with me; because of how I
had been earning money? Had he thought that I
was a gold-digger? That wasn't true. His money
was not important to me. I would give all his
money back, all my clients' money back, give all
my parents' money to charity if it would only
bring David back to me. Why had he asked me to
stay that extra night? Was he just lonely and had
needed my company after he had been diagnosed?
These questions and doubts, contradictions, and
let's not forget, *the hurt*, just kept coming at me,
relentlessly trying to knock me down.

CHAPTER 47

On Thursday, that same week – the week I was mourning David, the week Anthony was away on business, I was in the kitchen, when I heard the postman dropping some letters through the box. I wasn't in any rush to go and pick them up, assuming it would be more bills for Anthony, garage bills, (there was always one of his three cars getting some expensive part or other), subscription reminders, credit card statements, or even a package in plain brown jiffy-bags (usually his dodgy porn DVD's). There was very rarely any personal mail for me.

I carried on with what I was doing and forgot about the mail until later. I was on my way through the hall to go upstairs to the bathroom. There were about eight envelopes in all and I gave them a quick shuffle - one for me and the remainder, just as I had expected, were all for Anthony. I left his mail on the bureau that stood in the hallway. Climbing the stairs, I didn't give much thought to the white A5 envelope that I was peeling open. I sat on the edge of the bed and pulled out the contents – a solicitor's letter and another standard size envelope, which was addressed to me and marked 'Private and Confidential,' – in David's handwriting! My heart skipped a beat, my hands were shaking and my head refused to take in what I was seeing. I turned the envelope over in my hands a few times, barely able to take my eyes off his writing, as if by doing so, the contents would be magically revealed. I hesitated, not sure whether I wanted to open it - certain that I wouldn't want to read the contents. I picked up the accompanying letter and started to read,

[xxxxxxxxxxxxxxx]
xxxxxxxxxxxxxxx
LONDON
14th November 2008
Client Ref: BA546/D131108

Mrs H Pawson

xxxxxxxxxxxx

xxxxxxxxxxxx

Dear Mrs Pawson

RE: MR DAVID BARNARD DECEASED –
CLIENT REF BA546/D131108

It is with deep regret that I write to inform you of the death of our client, Mr David Barnard on Thursday 13th November 2008. Due to the inevitable media coverage of Mr Barnard's death, I feel sure that you may already be aware of this sad news.

During my last meeting with my client, some two weeks prior to his death, I received various instructions, mainly with regard to his estate, but one further instruction I received, was that after his death, I was to forward to you the enclosed letter which he had already penned, the night before our meeting. I understand that you had a very close relationship with my client and I sincerely hope that the contents of his letter to you can offer some comfort and peace of mind at this very sad time.

If I can be of any further assistance to you, please do not hesitate to contact me on the above number, quoting the client reference.

Please accept my condolences for your very sad loss.

Yours sincerely

William J Douglas LLB

The waterworks were in full flow by the time I was halfway through the letter, leaving one or two telltale splashes on the page. I needed to quickly compose myself, so I grabbed a handful of tissues off the bedside cabinet. I needed to see clearly to read David's one and only letter to me, but I also needed a stiff drink to give me the courage to open that second envelope. I wasn't sure if I was ready to read it. I was fearful of what it might contain; things I didn't want to hear. Somehow, I found the courage.

My darling Helen,

Where to start? We were both hurting so much when we said our goodbyes all those weeks ago. By the time you read this letter my suffering will be over, Babe, but the hurt for you, will continue for some time to come.

I am so deeply sorry for all the hurt I caused you by ending our relationship, and for the excuses that I used to do so. You now know just what I was protecting you from, and I will always be happy that I made the right decision, I did that for you and you alone.

I watched my father die from cancer eight years ago and I was with him when he passed away. Helen, I have never been able to rid myself of that vision of him in his final hours, his body wasted away, his loss of dignity, his pain and discomfort, and his fear. These last eight years I have tried hard to focus, picture him when he was happy and healthy, and I do, for seconds only, then it all just melts away into that horrible vision, and it haunts me constantly.

What I am going to tell you next will cause more hurt for you I know, but I hope that, in a strange way, it will also make you happy. Can you remember the weekend when I gave you the pendant, Babe? You asked me if I was in love with you and I said that I couldn't let myself fall for you because of what you do – and that I bought you the gift 'for a very special lady'. I lied to you again, Helen. I have known for some time now that I love you, special lady. When you left me after that weekend I was determined that on our next date (do you recall that I said it would be a couple of months?) I would tell you how much I love you, and if you loved me also I would ask you if we could try to make some sort of life together. It was devastating for me when I was given the diagnosis, but the most devastating thought was not that I have terminal cancer, but that I have been cheated – cheated for not being able to spend my life with you, Helen. I knew that I had to see you again very soon, (hence the three weeks) and that I had to take some more special memories from our last weekend together Those special memories are with me now, my darling, and they will be with me until I take my last breath, and beyond.

It seems my letter is a fully signed confession. I have already confessed to lying to you and there is more to come. I knew that I would need to know your address, so that this letter would find you – along with the accompanying letter from my solicitor. I stayed awake all night waiting for you to go to sleep so that I could go through your handbag to hopefully find something which would provide me with your details – your credit card only confirmed your name, but I found your driving licence and took the address from that. So once again my darling, I apologise for sneaking about and nosing through your handbag – I know I have invaded your privacy by doing so.

I have enjoyed every precious moment we have spent together since our very first date. You are intelligent, funny, caring, and very beautiful, and you have put a sparkle back into my life, a sparkle that any diamond would be jealous of. Please remember these words and try to smile about them each time you wear my diamonds, special lady.

I have organised my own funeral and I will tell you this, Helen – my treasured watch will be coming with me, reminding me that, 'two hearts came together.'

Over these last few days I have told Catherine and Ruby about you! Not everything. I have told them about your career…in accountancy! They know that you are very special to me and they know how much I love you. They always wanted me to find happiness and someone to love since the day their mother found happiness. It is my dearest wish that they get to know you and that you get to know them, so that they can see what it is about you that I love. I think they will be in touch with you when all the fuss has died down. Please do this small thing for me, Helen – I want them to know you, it means a lot.

You told me that you would give up your work for me. I know you don't have a life with me to look forward to anymore but would you please consider giving up your work now? I worry for you, Helen. I want you to be safe and happy. Make this decision only when you are ready though.

It hurts me a lot, that I can't see you for one last time, but it would hurt me much more to see you. The knowledge that I can't make love to you again, hold you in my arms and tell you how much I love you is just an added burden for me to bear.

I know how much you love me, my darling, and I also know how much you will be hurting when you finish reading this letter. I sincerely hope the day will come soon, when you can cry no more tears and that you can be happy - happy that we found love with each other, and that we shared very special moments together, and happy now that you have the knowledge. The knowledge that I love you so much and that I really wanted to share my life with you, had things been so different. You have no reason to doubt anymore, Helen.

Stay safe, Helen. I hope one day we will be together again, in a better, kinder world, and where love is infinite. In the meantime, I truly hope with all my heart, than you do find happiness in this life with someone else to care for you the way I do – nobody deserves that more than you!

All my love, special lady
From YOUR David
Xxx

I can't begin to describe every emotion that I felt as I read David's dying words to me. I had a letter that would be treasured. I knew in my heart that I would read, and re-read it, many times over. It was so irrational, but suddenly I couldn't help being terrified by the thought that my tears might somehow obliterate his words to me.

The following few weeks were surreal. Once Anthony had returned from his business trip, I tried to be out of the house as much as I could. I wandered around the parks, and shops, not shopping, just walking. I went everywhere - but not seeing anything. I only returned home at times when I knew Anthony would be out. I didn't need any confrontation – I didn't need any distractions from my thoughts and memories of David - I needed to grieve. And I did grieve.

CHAPTER 48

After the first couple of weeks of grieving for David, it crossed my mind, late one night that I hadn't checked up on the greenhouse situation during that time. It was a welcome distraction from my tears and gazing longingly at his picture. It would give me something else to focus on the next day. It was the first thing I planned to do the following morning, when David had gone out.

Yet again my hands were shaking as I lifted the top section of plant pots, wondering if there would be an envelope there or not. I didn't really know how I should be feeling when I found yet another envelope hidden there. I told myself that feeling pleased was not appropriate. How could it be appropriate to be pleased about the fact that Anthony was drug dealing? Yet, I couldn't help smiling. The reason I felt like smiling was because I fully intended that Anthony was finally going to get his come-uppance, and soon.

When I returned to the kitchen, I made a fresh pot of coffee and sat at the kitchen table. I needed to get myself fully awake and do some serious thinking. Just a few weeks back, it had occurred to me that if David had actually been at work, somebody must have either come to the greenhouse to deliver and/or collect the envelopes. Over the last few months my car had mostly been left in the drive as I had been taking the tube to work. Maybe Anthony had told whoever it had been who called, that I go out to work on the tube so they needn't worry about the Mazda in the drive. Also, over the last few weeks, even though I hadn't been at work, I had been going out most days, indulging in my walks of grief around the city and its numerous parks.

I couldn't take my eyes off the record I had been keeping of the envelope deliveries and collections. I was almost willing it to speak to me and point out to me exactly what I was missing. I twiddled a pen around between my fingers and doodled a border around the edges of the paper. I was transfixed, but nothing jumped out at me. I asked myself what I knew. I knew the envelopes came and I knew the envelopes went. That was all – only those two things! Somebody had to be coming sometime soon for the envelope that was sat in the greenhouse. Oh, crap!

I shot up from the kitchen table, made sure the back door was locked and tore through the lounge and up the stairs like a lunatic.

I had suddenly realised just how vulnerable I was sitting at the kitchen table, and without net curtains or blinds to hide my presence from any visitor to our greenhouse. With the conifer hedges between our house and our neighbours' houses we'd never thought it necessary. Still shaking, I sat on the bed for a while wondering what I could do. Whilst I showered and dressed the only answer that I could come up with was that it was down to me. I had to stay holed up in my bedroom, a very slight gap in the vertical blinds and wait for whoever…for however long. The thought filled me with dread.

CHAPTER 49

Two months after reading of David's death, and the letter he had written just days before he died, I picked up my mail to find another envelope, which I recognised instantly to be from his solicitor's office. I quickly tore into the letter hoping to find yet another letter from David - something else he had written in his final days. But I was disappointed to find there was no letter marked 'Private and Confidential' within the envelope this time.

No more words of love penned by my man – there was nothing inside that I could add to my treasures. I gave a loud sigh of disappointment and started reading the correspondence from Bill Douglas asking me to make an appointment to see him, as I was one of David's beneficiaries. He had apparently left me something in his will.

I started wondering about his daughters. I felt sure they would have inherited everything. I imagined that David, having been a shrewd businessman but also a sensible father, would have been certain to make sure they never wanted for anything. Even in the short time we had spent together I could almost guarantee that there would be trust funds - they wouldn't have access to vast amounts of money until they reached thirty years old. I know he wanted them both to have a career - to understand what it meant to work for a living. He didn't want them to be two rich bitches doing nothing but shop, take expensive holidays, attend wild parties and take drugs. Nor did he want them to become alcoholics, who perhaps once a year, would need to check in to The Priory for a drying out session. I felt cold and I grabbed my dressing gown and put it around my shoulders, though the house was warm. The time that David and I had spent together could be measured in hours, I had provided a service to begin with and we fell in love. It felt to me as if, whatever I inherited would be an increase in my hourly rate. I felt cheap. I didn't want David's money, I wanted David.

Although I felt very strongly about not wanting David's money, I badly wanted to meet Bill Douglas. I was curious to know exactly what David had shared with him. I called his office and made an appointment before going along to meet Bill. He turned out to be a lovely and charming gentleman who, at almost seventy, still working full-time in the practice. He shook my hand and then held it gently between both of his whilst expressing his sadness at David's death. He subsequently enquired as to how I was coping. I found it difficult to find the words to answer him and although I hadn't cried over the last three weeks, the tears were threatening.

Once our pleasantries were out of the way the subject turned to David's will. Bill informed me that there would be a pro rata distribution from the current funds available. David had left me a substantial amount and I was to receive an interim payment of £500,000 for the time being, which Bill handed to me as we spoke. I was struggling for words, and my hand was quivering as I stared at the cheque.

"I…"

Bill looked at me kindly and interrupted,

"David was clearly, very much in love with you, Helen. We had many conversations in his final weeks and he expressed to me his own personal grief for having to make the decision to break off your relationship. I can see that you are still hurting - it shows in your eyes, as it did with David. I do understand though - his reasons for ending it. He told me how he wanted to spend his life with you, and you with him. His cancer would have made those final weeks even more hell had you been together – for both of you."

I realised I had started crying again only because Bill thrust a box of tissues at me that had been sat on his desk. I felt that I was so used to crying that I wasn't always aware of my tears, until I found it difficult to see with the blurred vision.

"David's girls…" I started, but he cut me off again,

"…are extremely well provided for. This is David's wish, Helen – that you have this money now, the balance will be paid out at some future date, which can not be determined at this moment in time. There are assets to be sold, mainly properties and shares. The shares of course, will be sold when the bank's financial expert deems the FTSE prices more favourable."

I didn't wish to hear about the money I didn't want. My selfish grief demanded to know more about David.

"Did you read his, er…David's letter to me, Mr…Bill?" I asked.

"I did, Helen. David had always valued my opinion on…certain matters. He asked me to read the letter, from the point of view of you…erm, the recipient, and he wanted me to ascertain if his correspondence would leave you in no doubt as to his true feelings for you – I assured him that the message was conveyed loud and clear."

So David had spoken openly to his solicitor about our relationship. I was at peace about his love for me, and I had to make Bill aware of my feelings.

"Then please understand this, Bill. I am now in no doubt whatsoever of David's feelings for me - how could I possibly be, after his letter? I loved David with all my heart, therefore, I can not accept this cheque. Give it to charity or something. What good is this money to me, without him?"

"He knew you well, Helen. David predicted that you would be, in his words, troublesome, about accepting the bequest. That is the reason behind my request for an appointment with you. His instructions were clear – 'do not let her out of your office without the cheque, Bill. Do not let me down.' I can not let you leave the office unless you agree to take the cheque, Helen, or I shall have failed to carry out my client's last instruction. Please take it."

I looked at him and wondered how often he had to plead for someone to accept a cheque. I knew David had always held him in very high regard, and deservedly so. I couldn't fail to notice Bill's continued loyalty to his deceased client and his genuine desire to fulfil, down to the last minute detail, everything that had been asked of him. I folded up the cheque and placed it in my handbag.

"Thank you for your loyalty to David and your kindness, Bill. You've given me the cheque.

You have carried out David's instructions to the letter, so I will also thank you on behalf of him. He regarded you as a personal friend."

I was very close to crying again. I had only met Bill for the first time today. A guy much admired and respected by David, and this had been the first time I had discussed our relationship with anyone. It had felt right to do so.

"There's just one more thing to mention, Helen. Catherine, David's eldest daughter has told me that she would like to get in touch with you, and hopefully meet you at some point in the future - when she feels more able to talk about things. She asked if it would be acceptable to write to you, if you don't mind me giving her your address, that is."

My first thoughts were, what if Anthony were to find her letter? I mumbled some excuse that I would possibly be moving house.

"Can I give you my mobile number to give her please, Bill? If she is a little apprehensive about calling me herself, you could always call and we can make arrangements through you. David wanted me to get to know his daughters and I will. I am sure of it."

Before I left his office Bill shook my hand and said he would look forward to meeting me again in the future. I smirked as I stepped out of the main entrance door and into the street. I had a cheque in my handbag; but no intentions of ever paying it into my bank.

CHAPTER 50

The envelope had been picked up just three days after I had discovered it, but I had been wrong in thinking Anthony would be delivering it somewhere.

An Audi A5 convertible had pulled into the drive behind my car. I'd heard the car door open, but because the car had pulled too close to the house, it was a bad angle for me to get a decent look at the guy who had climbed out of it. Whilst he had gone around to the back garden, I opened the blinds a little and took a picture of the car with my mobile phone. (This was the only use my phone had had in months – it was turned off most of the time, which allowed me to avoid the never ending calls from my past clients, and Simon).

It had been impossible to capture the registration number whilst the car had been parked in the drive, but I had taken another shot once it had reversed out of the drive; the driver facing forwards ready to cruise up the road. I felt chilled, but also buoyed by the feeling that I was doing something positive.

I uploaded the image from my mobile phone to my laptop, printed an image of the car and locked it in my briefcase. I kept checking the greenhouse each day and carried on with my log of the envelope activity. It had reached the stage where it was becoming a very regular occurrence, with up to two envelopes appearing and disappearing within the same week. I was growing increasingly worried though, something wasn't stacking up. I photographed each car as it drove away, then ten minutes later, I ventured down to the greenhouse to find each envelope gone. No longer, did I find any envelopes *appearing* after the presence of the strangers' cars in our drive. The thought made me very uneasy but it had to be true – somebody was depositing the envelopes during the night while we were asleep. But then where was Anthony's involvement in it all? Finally I had my answer – *he* was putting the envelopes in the greenhouse while I was sleeping.

I tried staying awake at night, but the medication I was taking persisted in making me far too drowsy to listen out for Anthony's nocturnal activities.

A week passed by with no greenhouse activity whatsoever, so I stopped hiding away in the bedroom, although I still preferred to stay away from the kitchen during daylight hours. In the middle of watching a chick flick one Thursday morning, I jumped as a car door slammed in our drive. The vertical blinds were closed, so, not having a good vantage point, I stayed away from the window. I had already made sure the door was shut between the kitchen and the lounge, so I felt fairly safe in the knowledge that nobody could see me. I turned the volume of the TV to mute…and heard the tell-tale sound of our garage door opening…and closing two minutes later. As I heard the vehicle reverse out of the drive, I chanced a look out of the blinds - the Audi convertible again.

I felt as if I was a complete wreck, I dashed through to the kitchen and poured myself a large gin (with only the tiniest drop of tonic). I paced around the kitchen, puzzling over the use of the garage. I had yet another question to ask myself, when did any money change hands? It was at least thirty minutes before I decided to take a look in the garage. I'd rarely set foot in the place since Anthony and I had bought the house, but I scoured every inch of the place for the next twenty minutes.

It was the last place I looked, one of those large, rigid, folding tool-boxes. I felt like vomiting as I opened it. I should have realised much sooner and wondered why it was even there. Why would Anthony own a tool-box, he wouldn't have known what to do with any tools! In a plain brown box under the bottom section there must have been about twenty of the envelopes, of the soft squishy powdery substances! I had him!

CHAPTER 51

For five months, I opened my purse each morning before work and looked at the cheque that Bill Douglas had handed to me. Five seconds was all it took each time. I would return it to the secret zip compartment after its brief airing. I couldn't bring myself to do anything with the damn cheque, yet it made me incredibly sad to look at it every day. But I couldn't get out of the habit. (It had become yet another of my obsessive routines.) I didn't want to bank it, but I didn't want to tear it up and put it in the garbage.

I had a new cleaning job now at a different hotel, having been fired for the considerable length of time I had taken off after David had died. I didn't need to work from a financial point of view. My job was merely a way of escaping from the house, and I needed to clean somewhere, anywhere. My obsessions were at their worst. Anthony hadn't failed to notice how many times I had cleaned throughout the house in the previous weeks, and I had felt sickened by his vicious remarks,

"You seriously need help, Helen, you are mentally unstable." And then,

"Get a life. Get a job."

"I had a life, and a job, until you fucked it all up for me, Anthony!" I bit back.

I felt I was unable to return to my career in accountancy. My ability to concentrate on business, figures, or simple matters like reading a novel or watching a movie was at an all time low – non-existent in fact. I knew it was only a matter of time before I would need professional help for my mental problems. I could not have carried on like that indefinitely. I didn't need to be told why this was happening to me again. I knew the cause, but I wasn't able to control the obsessions.

I had told Anthony I had a new job. He'd assumed it was accountancy. I didn't lie to him - just failed to correct his assumption.

My mobile rang at ten o'clock one morning, and looking at the screen I saw that it was Bill Douglas calling me.

"Good morning, Bill, what a pleasant surprise. How are you?"

"Hello, Helen. I am very well, thank you, my dear. And yourself? I hope I haven't caught you at an inconvenient time?" Considerate as ever. I laughed.

"It's always convenient to speak to you, Bill. I'm keeping busy, it's the best way to deal with things, and I am managing to cope. What can I do for you?"

"The reason for my call, Helen, is that Catherine…um…David's daughter has finally been in touch. She would like to meet up with you - fairly soon if you can manage that. She…um...mentioned tomorrow – if that is not too short notice for you? She understands if it won't be possible."

My hand was shaking as I took in what he was saying. I knew I wasn't really ready for meeting David's girls at that point.

"That is fine, Bill, I can meet them at any time she wants and Catherine can choose where she would like us to meet up. Would you mind asking her and getting back to me with the details please?" then as an afterthought,

"Bill…would you mind telling…asking Catherine…that I don't have a nice picture of David, if she could oblige please…all I have is the picture from the newspaper."

"Certainly, Helen. I will call you back as soon as I have made contact with Catherine again."

We both hung up. Thirty minutes later he called me back to tell me to meet Catherine and Ruby at St James' Park, near 'Inn the Park' at eleven. Bill had failed to ask how I might recognise them, so I asked if he would contact them again, to say that I would wear denims, a black jacket, a cream chiffon scarf with orange butterflies, one of David's favourites, and I would be carrying a black Radley shoulder bag.

I was so nervous the next morning, wondering what his girls would think about me, whether they would even like me; and I also wondered how much of David I would be able to see in *them*. Would it be David's eyes that I saw, when we finally came face to face?

I wanted to be early for our meeting. I planned to stand somewhere out of sight so that I could catch a glimpse of the girls (if I could recognise them) before they saw me. I didn't know if it was a good idea or not. I thought I might be tempted to run, should I see a hint of hostility in their faces. They had no reason to be hostile towards me but I couldn't help feeling like the other woman. I was also feeling guilty that David had left me money that rightfully belonged to their inheritance. I didn't feel right about the meeting at all, but I was doing it for David – he had wanted it.

373

It was ten to eleven when I arrived at St. James Park. I kept a little distance from 'Inn the Park' for a few minutes, but eagerly looked in that direction to see if I could manage to pick out the girls before I made my approach. But for the fact that I was looking out for *two* young ladies, I might have spotted Catherine sooner than I did. She was obviously looking around for somebody she had agreed to meet, so I took this as my cue to start walking towards her. I could see that she was tall, about 5ft 10" and dark haired, and, when I was just ten yards away from her I knew I was looking at Catherine, David's eldest daughter. Her eyes were those of her father, in fact all her facial features were unmistakably his. I saw her quick glance at my attire and finally she made eye contact with me. She walked tentatively towards me and offered her hand, which I took in both of mine,

"You are Catherine, am I right?"

"Yes. Catherine. And you are, Helen?" she enquired.

We gave each other a nervous hug, and I could feel the tension in her shoulders, a tension mirrored by my own.

"Sh…shall we walk for a little while? Or would you rather go inside and have coffee, or tea?" I asked.

"Yes, to the walk. I am sorry my sister can't be here, she is, being rather troublesome at this moment in time. I thought it best to come alone. I hope you don't mind, Helen? She can come along next time, if she's in the right frame of mind."

So there was going to be a next time. She didn't even yet know me. I was touched by her confidence.

"That's not a problem, Catherine. If she wants to, I will look forward to meeting her next time in that case."

We walked along the path for a few seconds, and her next words stunned me,

"You loved my father?"

"Very much! He was so special, we would have been together now, if it wasn't for..." I couldn't bring myself to say the word and she looked at me sympathetically, and immediately understood,

"I know. I hate the word too."

She turned to face me as we continued to stroll.

"Dad told us about you, Helen - how much he loved you. You were very special to him too. You must be hurting? That he ended it with you…to protect you? *And* that you found out about his death through the media. If only we had thought to look for his mobile phone. We found it three weeks later, your number is on there…I could have called you. I'm so sorry. It must have been awful for you."

Her eyes had glazed over, but her grief was plain to see.

"No more so, than the way it must have been for you and Ruby. I want you to know that David was everything to me. I never understood why he ended our relationship. He told me that it was his work, the amount of time he spent travelling; he said it caused the break-up between him and your mum - that was the reason he gave me. He said he was ending it to protect me from all that. Somehow I didn't really believe it to be true. I know now though, don't I? I've forgiven him for keeping the truth from me…even though it still hurts."

"How did you meet?" she asked me after a brief silence.

How was I to answer that one? I didn't want to lie, but she didn't need to know the truth.

"I met David through business, a mutual acquaintance introduced us. It snowballed from there really."

We walked on for fifteen minutes in silence, she linked her arm into mine, and I was touched by the show of warmth from someone who had been a stranger to me just half an hour before. I liked this girl, she was genuine; she wanted the cold, hard facts about my relationship with her father, but she showed compassion for my loss, whilst still dealing with her own.

"Would you like to go for a coffee, or perhaps something to eat, Helen? Or are you in a rush to return to work? I have no wish to hold you up, if so."

"I've booked a days' leave. We can do whatever *you* would like. I'm quite hungry too. First eating place we come to okay with you, or did you have somewhere in mind?"

"I like Pizza Express, there's one in Victoria Street."

"Pizza Express it is then."

We ordered food and found a quiet corner where we could sit and talk without the distractions of the comings and goings of other customers and staff. I loved hearing her talk about

David. What type of father he had been, the practical jokes he had played on them all throughout his marriage to Heidi, his hobbies, anything at all – and she obliged. She talked about University and her dream to become a forensic scientist. Another topic that caused her plenty of distress was Ruby and the havoc she had caused before David's death and ever since.

Our food arrived, so there was a lull in the conversation for a few minutes as we ate. We ordered a second bottle of wine between us. I was certainly not expecting the next question she threw at me and my stomach sank.

"Why haven't you paid in the cheque that Bill gave to you? You've had it for five months now."

She looked straight into my eyes, waiting for the answer that I was struggling with,

"I…I...never wanted David's money. It was David that I wanted, still *do* want. I can't take it. I don't need it, Catherine. I have more than enough to keep me comfortable. It belongs to you and Ruby, it doesn't belong to me."

"It is not *our* money, Helen. Our father wanted you to have it, *and* the balance when the estate is finally sorted. Ruby and I are very wealthy. We have far more than we will ever get through. This is rightfully yours. Dad wanted you to have it, so do it for him, for *your* David – pay it into your bank…tomorrow."

My emotions got the better of me, I couldn't look into her eyes at that point, I didn't want her to see the tears that rolled down my cheeks; and she knew. She quickly moved around to join me on my side of the table, put her arm

around me, and she laid her head on my shoulder.
I turned towards her and enfolded her in my arms.
We sobbed silently on each other's shoulder for a
few minutes, then giggled together like
schoolgirls when we realised that we had a small
audience. She moved back to her side of the table.
I told her again,

"I loved him so much, Catherine, he was
everything to me."

"I know that, I can tell how much you
loved him. I would not be sat here with you
otherwise."

After I had settled the bill, to much
protest from Catherine, we left the restaurant and
wandered aimlessly around London for most of
the afternoon. Sometimes Catherine's arm was
linked in mine, and when it wasn't, my arm was
linked in hers. We called into a bar or two - a gin
and tonic for me, a pint of Fosters for Catherine,
(it was good to tell she was at Uni); the odd shop
here and there…if and when something in the
windows caught our attention. I was not looking
forward to saying our goodbyes. I felt as if I
needed to be near her. I felt closer to David than
ever when I was in her company, and I liked to
think that he was looking down, giving an
approving nod at our new friendship.

That moment of parting did come around
all too soon, and at seven o'clock we exchanged
mobile numbers, promising to stay in touch.
Catherine promised me that she would try her best
to get Ruby to come along to meet me next time.
After we embraced for the final time that day, her
hand rummaged in her handbag and she passed
me a white envelope,

"A couple of photos of Dad – I remembered. The one of him by himself was taken just a few weeks before he was diagnosed."

"Thank you, Catherine. I won't look just yet, I will save them for when I'm alone - I know I'll get upset. I've enjoyed today very much, thank you," and I quickly added, "I will pay the cheque into the bank, if that is what you want me to do."

"It is. Bye, Helen, we'll speak soon, yes?"

"Count on it."

I watched as she walked away from me. I felt such a rush of affection for her. She was certainly a credit to David…and Heidi. So mature…and so like David. It crossed my mind that maybe that was the reason behind my feelings towards her.

CHAPTER 52

After my pleasant afternoon with Catherine, I went home (fortunately, Anthony was out), poured myself a large glass of wine and went upstairs to the privacy of my bedroom. Once I had taken a few sips, I carefully opened the envelope that Catherine had given to me. Both the pictures were mounted and had been facing each other in the envelope before I had taken them out. The first one that I turned over was a picture of David with his girls. It was dated May 2007 and had been taken in Sicily on the top of Mount Etna. I remember David telling me about that particular holiday during our pillow talk all those months ago. The skies were incredibly blue, there was plenty of snow on the ground, and all three of them were huddled together shivering with their fleeces on. I recognized Catherine easily now, but have to say that Ruby's looks were neither like David nor Catherine, so I assumed that she took after her mother. She was certainly an attractive young lady. David had told me how hot it had been on the beach in Taormina, and yet, just an hour's drive away, at a height of 3350 metres above sea level, the temperatures had been -12C with the wind cutting through them like knives. The second photograph was of my David, and he smiled up at me as I gazed lovingly at him and stroked his cheek. He was almost as handsome on paper, as he had been in life. I smiled back at him and watery-eyed, asked him in a whisper,

"Why did you have to go and leave me, David? I'm missing you so much, and it hurts."

My sadness engulfed me and I sought an answer in those beautiful eyes but they couldn't give any response. His lips, whilst smiling, could not produce any words to console me. I propped the photograph up against my bedside lamp, sipped at my wine and my eyes scanned every corner of the room, hoping for, and trying to catch a glimpse of his hazy image watching over me. I took some comfort from that possibility.

The following Monday when I finished work at the hotel, (and after a full weekend of giving the matter some careful consideration), I went to my bank and paid in the cheque. Had it not been for Catherine questioning me as to why I hadn't done so, I think I might have just added it to my collection of keepsakes. Once the cheque cleared, I would be transferring the money to my offshore bank account. It was time to bail out of the marital home, and furthermore, time that Anthony got the life that he deserved.

CHAPTER 53

I had a quite a few phone calls to make so I finally turned my mobile phone on, for the purpose of making and receiving calls, instead of taking pictures of drug dealers' cars. My phone beeped constantly for five minutes notifying me of almost fifty missed calls and even more incoming text messages from the past weeks.

Simon's voice sounded more than a little cross to hear my voice.

"Helen, where the fuck have you been? I've been ringing you, again and again. I've had your clients pestering me, wondering where the hell you've been. What's going on?"

It was nice to hear a friendly voice again, angry though he was. I felt a bit wary. He wouldn't like what I would be telling him over the next few minutes, but I had to do it, it was only fair.

"I've had a bereavement. It's taken a long time. It's been very difficult for me, Simon!"

He sighed down the phone, and I raised my eyes to the ceiling, I knew what was coming next.

"Well, yes, I'm sorry! But you already told me about your parents, Helen. You started having clients after that – it never stopped you before."

I took a deep breath,

"Simon, it…wasn't my parents this time. It was the man I loved, you knew him. David. David Barnard."

There was a long silence before he finally asked, incredulous,

"David Barnard? Helen...you fell in love with a client?"

It was out at last, and it took all of five seconds to tell him,

"Clients? I won't be having any more clients, Simon!" and I ended the call.

Over the course of the next two days I packed some suitcases with the clothes and personal items I would need and loaded them into my car. I also helped myself to one of the incriminating envelopes from the toolbox in the garage. I needed it to put the next part of my plan into action. After I had left Anthony a letter on the kitchen worktop, telling him that I would no longer be living in the house, or cramping his style, I checked into the 'Kensington' suite at the hotel. The classy hotel where I'd first been employed as a chambermaid, and the very suite where Simon had fucked me, and a little later, talked me into becoming a hooker.

Using my laptop I started composing a letter - a letter that would be sent without my signature or name at the bottom. Once it was completed, I placed it into a large 'jiffy' bag together with the envelope I'd stolen from Anthony along with the images of all the vehicles that I had managed to capture on my mobile phone.

My second letter was for Leanne, the young trainee at the Hopkins Partnership. I drove out to where she lived with her parents and, after parking my car in the drive, posted the envelope containing my car keys and registration document through the letterbox. She'd always loved my Mazda. I took the tube back into the city centre and returned to the hotel. Using the telephone in my suite, I hired a car for what would be my last twenty four hours in London.

CHAPTER 54

My late night timing was perfect. I dropped my envelope into the doorway of the Thames Valley Police station in Windsor and made a follow up call from a public payphone shortly afterwards to make sure they had received it. I already knew they had found it though. I had watched a young constable pick it up as he'd entered the station at ten o'clock, either just starting or finishing his shift I expect. From there I drove towards Anthony's house in my rental car, but parking a discreet distance away, under the shade of some trees. I sat waiting for what felt like hours; eighty four minutes to be exact, until three or four police vehicles turned into the road and parked at the front of the house. I watched as he opened the front door to them. Ten minutes later the police entered the garage. After one hour and fifty three minutes, Anthony was led out of the house and into the back of one of the police cars.

My luggage already in the back of the car, I drove straight to London Heathrow where I deposited the rental car. As I made my way to the check-in desk, all I felt was an incredible sadness, accompanied by an overwhelming relief. I had done the right thing – not as soon as I should have done, had I not had my grief to contend with, but I'd finally set the wheels in motion!

I took my window seat and, bemused as always, indulged in a little 'people watching.' Folks who were pulling their tiny cabin cases on wheels, too busy looking up at the seat numbers, and totally unaware that they were dragging their luggage over other passengers' toes, or grazing a few ankles in the process; people who messed about stowing their carry-ons in the overhead storage compartments and blocking the aisle, two hundred or so passengers at a total standstill; those who sat down in an aisle seat and immediately fastened their safety belts and then gave a vicious scowl because they had to unbuckle again when the window seat passenger finally turned up. It was a constant source of amusement.

As the wheels left the tarmac and the pilot subsequently started banking the plane, I looked down on the City and wondered what else life had in store for me. I felt elated to be leaving it all behind, but nervous at the same time. I didn't know what I was going to do. I wasn't sure whether to get a job in Paris; I wondered if I should seek some serious help for my O.C.D. and whether it would work if I did.

I didn't really know anybody who lived in the apartment block, or anyone else for that matter. The only people I expected to be seeing in the next few months were Catherine and Ruby, David's daughters. I've yet to meet Ruby but I'd promised Catherine they could come to stay with me for a week.

I seriously hoped that living in Paris would be the start of a new life for me, and a chance to recover, mentally, from all that had been wrong with my life. I had still been dealing with the tragic death of both my parents when I had heard the sad news about David. I was still feeling bitter that the three people I had loved, more than life itself, had been taken away from me – the most caring, loving people I had ever known. I didn't think I'd done anything wrong, but there were times I wondered if I was being punished for sins committed by me in a former life. Before David had come into my life, I had first loved Gavin, and he, and my one and only best friend, had broken my heart. My disastrous marriage to Anthony had followed, with the numerous stunts he had pulled that had broken my heart for the second time. No more falling in love for me.

On the approach to Paris CDG, I looked out at the terminal buildings as they quickly grew larger. My thoughts drifted again. I'd done it. I'd left London, and my problems well behind me. I was no longer a chambermaid, or a call girl, I had no friends in Paris who I could have a social life with, plus - there would be no more boyfriends or husbands!

As the wheels hit the runway with a loud thud, a sudden thought passed through my mind…

CHAPTER 55

…what would I do for sex?

COMING SOON – JUNE 2014

'Comings and Goings'

5908476R00228

Printed in Great Britain
by Amazon.co.uk, Ltd.,
Marston Gate.